Blindsighted

a novel by
Zan Hough

ISBN 979-8-9948667-0-2

First paperback edition. April 2026

*Dedicated to queer youth as a guide to recognizing and
cultivating healthy relationships and boundaries.*

*A special thank you to an incredible alpha and beta
team: A.J. Norris, Laurie Daniels, Jon Garcia, and so
many others for their contributions
to this work.*

*Thank you also to English teachers who inspired me
from a young age to write: Edie Parrott, and Gwen Lee.*

For my husband, Jon.

Happy 23rd Anniversary.

Prologue

*Infirmary, Doncaster, South Yorkshire, England,
United Kingdom*

Cade faded in and out of consciousness from the pain meds. He could hear the fuss outside the hospital room door, but he couldn't quite make out the words until a comforting voice standing closest to him inside the room whispered, *"This wasn't your fault."*

"Neil?"

The pencil sketch of Kyle wasn't a keepsake—it was a reminder of everything **Neil Erickson** had outgrown. He had drawn it months ago, but Kyle, ever the "*real artist*," couldn't resist correcting the proportions. Neil was ready to move on and make room for someone new.

"It's time," he said. With one toss, he let go of the guy, the critique, and the entire waste of memory, watching the jagged scrap of cardboard land where it belonged: in a rubbish bin in Edinburgh, where it would be disposed of nearly four thousand miles from Kyle and on a different continent.

He hadn't come to Edinburgh for castles or cathedrals—his only objective was to outrun his memories of Kyle and to lose himself in a crowd of classmates who didn't ask questions.

Through the most ancient part of the city, the Royal Mile stretched like a stone spine between Edinburgh Castle and Holyrood Palace, its cobbles echoing with the footsteps of centuries of boots, hooves, and tourists' sneakers.

And then there was **Cade Riley**, who wasn't thinking about history. He was thinking about how far his voice could carry and how many in his Nashville prep school travel group could hear him from the one o'clock gun in the courtyard of the castle.

"Guys!" he shouted, all puckish grin and zero volume control—enough to make a few German retirees glance over. "Castle-wall shouting starts now! Last one standing gets bragging rights; first one to bail buys breakfast. Including haggis. Especially haggis."

Laughter erupted from the Penderton Academy soccer boys orbiting him, their letterman jackets unbuttoned despite the cold. They were a wall of noise—snapping photos, daring each other to pronounce street names, tripping over cobblestones, and making inside jokes.

Cade thrived on it. Shoulders squared, grin sharp. He knew half of Edinburgh could hear them, and honestly? That was the point.

They bought cheap tartan scarves from a street vendor, posed with a kilted bagpiper blasting "Scotland the Brave," and dared each other to eat haggis from a steaming food stall. Cade egged them all on—pulling faces, yelling compliments to every stranger who made eye contact. To the Penderton boys, the Royal Mile wasn't a tourist strip; it was their personal parade route.

Meanwhile, a quieter procession moved the other way.

Neil Erickson walked with four classmates, each armed with a guidebook bristling with sticky notes. They moved at a pace calculated for maximum absorption—stop, read the plaque, murmur observations, and jot notes for later essays.

As they passed, Cade gave an exaggerated bow. He meant it as a playful attempt to get a smile out of Neil, but his friends took it as a mockery of the "smart kids" and burst out laughing. Neil and his group didn't flinch. They'd learned that ignoring the athlete's obnoxious noise was the quickest way through it.

"Technically, this street isn't one mile," said Mads Chandler, the group's resident fact-checker, pushing her glasses up her nose as Kip Wendell—their chaos, tea-fueled (truth-telling) engine in a vintage fitted mid sleeve tee and green corduroy jacket—clipped Mad's latest purchase to her backpack. It was a plush JellyCat penguin named Peanut, freshly adopted from a peachy-pink boutique called Squish on Victoria Street.

"Yeah," Neil said with a small smile. "It's closer to a Scots mile—longer than ours. That's why it stretches from the castle all the way down to Holyrood."

His tone was calm and unforced. When they passed the same piper Cade had heckled, Neil paused to listen with genuine interest, even clapping politely when the tune ended.

Where Cade saw props for a performance, Neil saw culture worth preserving.

Cade noticed.

"Hey, safety book boy!" Cade's teammate, Trevor, yelled. "You got a Band-Aid?"

Neil paused, looked up, and said nothing.

Trevor puffed out his chest and flexed like he was onstage at a bodybuilding expo.

"'Cause I'm **CUT!**"

One of the other boys whooped and lifted his shirt to show off an aggressively overconfident set of abs. Tourists actually glanced over.

Trevor kept going, thrilled with himself.

"Wait—don't leave! You got a needle and thread? 'Cause I'm **RIPPED!**"

The teammates in letterman jackets cackled, slapping each other's shoulders, the laughter echoing between the stone buildings like it deserved an award.

Neil blinked once. Just once, unamused.

Then, utterly calm, he said:

"Cool. What's it like being defined by two adjectives and a single-digit IQ?"

The laughter died so fast it left a trail of smoke.

Even the bagpiper seemed to falter for half a beat.

Trevor's face froze mid-flex.

Mads, three steps behind Neil, clapped a hand over her mouth to muffle a snort.

A group of German tourists paused, interested.

And Cade, he stared at Neil like he'd just watched a quiet librarian punt a football through the castle gates.

Neil snapped the guidebook shut with a polite little thwip.

"Shall we?" he said to his friends as they walked away.

Cade ducked into a narrow alley—one of Edinburgh's ancient closes—to regroup after the sting of rejection hit harder than it should've, his chance at catching Neil's eye ruined by his friends being complete dicks in the worst possible moment. He wanted to blame his teammates for laughing, but he took ownership of the miss.

Leaning against the damp stone wall, he exhaled and closed his eyes. In his head, the moment replayed the way it should have gone.

They'd be alone, just the two of them, the noise of the city fading behind. Neil would stand close—close enough that nothing could be misunderstood. Cade would look at him, steady this time, and ask, "Do you trust me?"

Neil would nod.

Together, they'd step into the dark interior of the

close, walking side by side into the unknown.

Snapped back into reality, footsteps whispered through the close. Cade looked up to find Neil approaching with Jenna beside him—his closest friend, whose calm stare suggested she'd already decided whether Cade was trouble, and in what quantity.

"I guess the Fleshmarket really was a meat market in its day," Neil said, grinning as he glanced at Cade.

"What?" Cade blinked.

Neil pointed to the brass plate above the entryway.

Cade stepped back from the wall and looked up. The sign read Fleshmarket Close. By the time he could think of something clever to say, Neil and Jenna were already halfway down the stairs.

"I did it—again!" Cade groaned, dragging his palms down his face until they covered his eyes. "Unbelievable." He tipped his head back against the stone with a muted thud.

Jenna turned, puzzled. "What in the world?"

Neil paused mid-step, watching Cade lightly kick the front of a stair.

"I hope he's okay," Neil said. "I'm his safety liaison—should I check?"

"You're not his liaison until tomorrow," Jenna said, tugging his sleeve. "Let him figure this one out."

Mads passed through on her way behind Neil and Jenna and saw Cade upset.

"Tissue?" she said to Cade.

That afternoon, both groups traded city streets for nature. They climbed Arthur's Seat—Penderton students divided into two noisy expeditions hollering at each other from rocky outcrops, their voices swept up by the wind and flung across the city.

Cade scrambled ahead, shouting, "King of the mountain! Ah-Rooooooo!" as if the jagged volcanic rock had been placed there just for him. His friends whooped and shoved each other, so loud that passing hikers gave them a wide berth.

Neil's group climbed too, but differently—pausing often to look back at the rooftops below, noting how the crags framed the skyline. Neil pulled out his notebook and sketched the slope of the hill, the habit he used to anchor new places in his memory.

At the summit, they stood quietly. The wind tugged at their jackets, and the city unfurled below in soft, smoky light. Where Cade filled the air with laughter, Neil filled it with silence. For him, quiet wasn't emptiness. It was reverence.

The next morning, the itinerary took both groups to Leith to tour the Royal Yacht Britannia.

Cade clattered down the gangway with his entourage, laughing too loudly when he spotted the Rolls-Royce displayed on board. "Boys! The Queen had a better ride than mine—look at this thing!" He pressed his face to the glass, leaving a smudge that a weary docent wiped away with a polite but pained smile.

Neil, in another tour group, lingered in the engine room, fascinated by the contrast of elegance and machinery. He traced the dials and brass fittings with his eyes, whispering to Mads about how the yacht embodied both grandeur and obsolescence—beautiful, but already a relic. When they reached the Queen's bedroom, he stood back, hands folded behind him, giving others space to see it.

That night, the two worlds brushed closer, once again.

Back at the hotel, Cade and two of his soccer buddies burst through the lobby doors, stumbling dramatically, cheeks flushed and grins too wide. They leaned into one another like stage drunks, slurring their words with Oscar-level exaggeration.

"Scotland loves us, man," Trevor declared, suggesting they had been on a pub crawl. They hadn't.

Another clutched his stomach, groaning, "I think I'm fluent in Scottish now."

"Scots speak English, idiot," said Sophie McCallister, whose quiet snark hit harder precisely because she never raised her voice. She was usually very quiet and rarely called attention to herself. Today was an exception.

Cade staggered toward the elevator, wagging a finger at the nearest chaperone. "Relax, Coach—we're fiiiiine. Must've been the altitude on Arthur's Seat, right, boys?"

The three athletes dissolved into cackles, tripping over backpacks. It was apparent the whole thing was an act, but they were milking the moment like they'd survived a full Highland pub crawl.

Across the lobby, Neil and his group stood in line for the elevators, their arms full of brochures and notebooks. Jenna wrinkled her nose and muttered, "Why do they have to be so gross and disrespectful?"

Neil didn't argue. He just tightened his grip on his guidebook. Cade Riley was loud enough that even from across the lobby, he seemed to take up all the oxygen.

Later, in his hotel room, Neil sat cross-legged on the bed, double-checking the roster for tomorrow's train departure. As safety liaison for his group, it was his job to account for every student before they boarded.

He scanned the neat list of names, lips moving faintly as he ticked them off in his head—until one name made him stop.

Cade Riley.

Neil stared a moment longer than necessary, pen hovering over the page. He thought of the fake stumble in the lobby, the shouted dares on Arthur's Seat, and the fingerprint Cade had left on the glass of the Rolls Royce on the Britannia—like even the Queen's yacht wasn't off-limits to him.

With a sigh, Neil shut the roster. "I'm not sure I'm the right person to keep someone like Cade Riley safe," he muttered.

Then another thought crept in, quieter but sharper. If Cade needed to feel important—needed the spotlight like air—maybe Neil could use that.

What if I ask him to help? He wondered. *Not rein him in, just... redirect him. Let him think he's the backup muscle, the hero of the group. If he feels needed, maybe he'll behave.*

It wasn't foolproof. But it was a plan.

Neil set the roster aside and stretched out on the bed, staring at the ceiling. From somewhere down the hall, Cade's laugh echoed—loud, bright, and unmistakable.

Neil had barely finished brushing his teeth when someone pounded on the hotel door.

"SAFETY BOOK BOY!" Trevor yelled. "OPEN UP!"

Kip froze. "Neil, I heard them say that they were

gonna 'initiate' you. I—"

A wet splat hit the door.

Another.

Kip's eyes widened. "Is that… spaghetti?"

Neil opened the door a crack.

Instant regret.

A fistful of cold noodles with tomato sauce slapped him in the chest and slid to the carpet.

Trevor and the other athletes stared, caught mid-throw.

Neil shut the door. Calmly.

Kip whispered, "Their weapon of choice is pasta?"

Neil snapped a picture of the mess and sent it to Coach Ramirez.

Then he opened the door again—this time fully, phone raised, camera pointed at the boys.

They froze.

Neil silently took a photo.

Trevor blanched. "Dude, no—no, delete that! Coach is literally on our floor!"

"He's actually doing room checks right now, and—" Neil said calmly.

Right on cue, a roar echoed up the stairwell:

"TREVOR? WHY IS THERE FOOD ON THE FOURTH-FLOOR CARPET?!"

All four athletes scattered, slipping in their own spaghetti as they sprinted down the hall, tracing a path of evidence.

Neil closed the door and brushed a noodle off his shirt.

Kip blinked at him, stunned. "Remind me never to cross you."

"Never disrespect pasta," Neil said.

Somewhere in the hallway, Trevor shrieked as Coach Ramirez found him.

Neil smiled.

Chapter One.

The train doors whispered open at Waverly Station, stopping with a popping noise, just as Cade Riley stepped onto platform five. And there he was—Neil Erickson—clipboard flashing like a badge, Penderton's star student and, apparently, captain of this European traveling circus.

Cade checked the lines twice—then a third time—to make sure he'd landed in Neil's. He had a few more students than Jenna's, but that was fine. Worth it. He adjusted his bag on his shoulder and wiped away a bead of sweat from his brow just as Neil turned to him.

"Hey, Cade," he said, scanning his clipboard: flyer,

smile, the whole package.

"Hey, Neil."

"Nice to see you." Neil's tone was brisk but warm, professional in a way that made it hard to tell if he was nervous or just efficient. "Okay, you're checked in. Here's your safety flyer. The dining car and facilities are toward the front." He hesitated, pen hovering. "Oh—and you're on the soccer team, right?"

Cade raised an eyebrow. Everyone knew that. Even the AP legends. "Yeah. Why?"

"In case I need backup muscle. Think I could count on you?"

"Anytime," Cade said. Then, grinning, "You look like you could handle most things, though."

Neil's grin matched his—quick, genuine, unexpected. "Thanks. Have a great trip, Cade. I'll try not to bug you."

Please. Bug me, Cade thought, biting back a smile. *If you only knew.*

Everyone at Penderton knew Neil. Not because he made announcements, but because he never hid who he was. If someone asked, he'd shrug—yeah, he dated guys. No drama, no banners, just out and honest.

Cade had never dated a guy—not officially—but he'd known for a while. In locker rooms, on late nights, alone with his thoughts—it wasn't just girls in his head. If he ever did date a guy, though, it would be a guy like Neil: sharp, funny, and smart enough to run a European trip with an electronic tablet. And Neil's style? Authentically at one hundred.

Cade caught himself smiling as Neil moved down the line, checking names like he was greeting guests at a five-star resort. What a guy. Of course, he'd have a boyfriend—solid, if Neil's Instagram was accurate and up to date.

Officially, the senior trip was billed as an *educational rail experience abroad.* Reality: thirty-two Penderton seniors crammed into school-logo fast fashion, one headmaster already regretting every life choice, and an itinerary so ambitious Netflix could've produced it.

Then, somewhere near York, chaos found Cade Riley.

It started as a dare and ended in disaster. The train car had been peaceful enough: AP kids buried in guidebooks, soccer players half-asleep with earbuds on, and teachers murmuring about tomorrow's schedule. Boredom hung thick throughout the train car.

Then Tyler Haskins decided the overhead luggage rack was fair game. Another teammate scrambled up beside him like it was a jungle gym, limbs flailing while the rest of the car egged him on.

"Chicken battle!" someone shouted.

"CHICKEN BATTLE!" roared a voice from the back.

That was the match.

The train car detonated into noise. Laughter boomed, sneakers stomped the floor, and half the soccer team pounded the seatbacks like they were in the student section at a home game. A notebook launched across the aisle, its pages fluttering like confetti. Someone's folder burst open, and a blizzard of math worksheets and essays filled the air.

Then the luggage went. One duffel slipped from the rack, clipped another, and the whole line gave way like dominoes. Backpacks, jackets, and one doomed souvenir bagpipe came crashing down—smack—squarely onto Cade Riley's face.

Silence.

Then chaos again—shrieks, gasps, a phone skittering under the seats, and a kid slipping on a stray worksheet and colliding with the snack cart. The ringleader bailed out of the luggage rack with a graceless thud, leaving Cade groaning on the floor, buried under the avalanche.

By the time the teachers stormed the aisle barking orders, the car looked like a disaster zone: papers plastered to windows, notebooks splayed like wounded birds, luggage dangling from the racks, and Cade Riley clutching his face—cursing loud enough to snap the chaperones straight into parent mode.

Neil unburied Cade, moving away all the bags on top of him. A fellow student helped him move the bagpipe.

"Are you okay?" Neil asked Cade. Then to another student, "Find Coach Ramirez."

"Something sucker punched me in the eyes," Cade said, sounding slightly embarrassed.

"You're really lucky the sharp mouthpiece missed you. Looks like the two small drones gave you what will be two black eyes," Neil said.

"Cade, can you look at me?" Coach Ramirez asked.

Cade nodded yes. "I'll be fine. It can't be that serious."

"We are required to get you checked out. We will get off at the next stop and have you evaluated," Coach Ramirez said.

It was chaos. The real twist? For once, Cade hadn't started it.

The hallway outside Cade's hospital room was chaos—muffled shouting, clipped syllables, and the unmistakable tone of adults trying very hard to blame each other without actually saying the words. Neil caught fragments through the cracked door:

"...liability—"

"...parents should have come—"

"It's the Rileys, for God's sake—"

"Legacy student or not—"

Neil attempted to tune it all out. He turned back into the dim room quietly, letting the door click shut behind him.

Cade lay motionless in the narrow hospital bed, bandages covering both eyes, the rise and fall of his chest steady and slow. The pain meds had knocked him out, finally giving him rest.

Neil pulled the chair closer, sat, and leaned forward. He didn't know why he needed to look at Cade carefully—like studying him would help make sense of the day—but he did.

Cade looked curiously peaceful. Innocent, even. Nothing like the loud, swagger-heavy version of himself he performed around the other athletes. Just... a boy breathing in a dark room.

Neil swallowed.

"This wasn't your fault," he whispered, mostly to fill the silence, mostly to reassure himself. Neil felt like it might even be his own fault.

"Neil?" Cade said softly.

Neil jumped up and back hard enough to bump the chair. "JESUS! I thought you were asleep." He barely escaped falling back on the chair.

"I was," Cade croaked, "until you said that." His voice was scratchy, but still unmistakably Cade. "Are you okay?"

"Yeah. Sorry," Neil huffed out a breath. "I meant it, though. Those jerks you hang out with that caused this are awful people."

Cade shifted, the bedsheets rustling. "What would you do, Neil? Revenge or nah?"

Neil scoffed. "I would never say another word to them. I'm sure it was... mostly an accident. But they go too far. All the time. They've done it to other people for years." He hesitated. "They just got one of their own this time."

A small smile tugged at Cade's mouth. "Yeah. I don't know if I'm as good a person as you are, Neil." A beat. "Where are we, anyway?"

"Doncaster." Neil leaned back in the chair. "I overheard them say you'll be fine, but your eyes might have to stay covered for a week. And yeah—seems like you're staying on the tour."

Cade sighed, trying for bravery but landing on resignation. "I didn't want to go home anyway."

Neil studied him. Something tugged at his chest.

"I have an idea," Neil said, pushing up from his chair. "I'll be right back."

Cade listened to the soft scuff of Neil's sneakers—familiar in a way he hadn't noticed before—carry across the room. The footsteps drifted toward the door, then faded into the muffled hallway. Without sight to anchor him, the sound was startlingly distinct; he could trace every step until Neil was gone.

Outside, Neil caught the doctor and two chaperones mid-conversation.

"...sensory deprivation is the biggest concern," the doctor was saying. "He'll need steady support."

Neil cleared his throat. "Would it help if I stayed with him? Until he's cleared? I mean—if someone needs to be with him constantly, I can do that."

The doctor looked up, surprised. "That might actually be a very good solution. It's a significant responsibility, though. Are you sure?"

"Neil is one of our most responsible students," Mr. Paulson said quickly. "If he's offering, we should take that seriously. We're stretched thin."

Neil kept his gaze steady. "I feel responsible for what happened. I want to help however I can."

"You're a generous young man," the doctor said.

"What's your name?"

"Neil Erickson, sir."

"Well, Neil," the doctor continued, folding his arms, "your friend will need careful guidance. With his vision temporarily offline, he may get dizzy or disoriented. Sleep might be difficult. Some patients experience vivid nightmares or even mild delusions as their brain compensates. And after the first day or so, his remaining senses will sharpen dramatically—sound, smell, touch, all of it. You'll need to make sure he eats and rests."

Neil nodded, absorbing each instruction. "What should I watch for with the medication? Side effects? Timing?"

He asked several follow-up questions—clear, focused, and far more adult than anyone expected from a high-schooler—until the doctor seemed fully satisfied.

Only then did Neil step back into the hospital room, slipping in before the chaperones followed, the soft squeak of his sneakers announcing his return.

Neil stepped close and rested a hand on Cade's forearm—gently, like asking permission.

"Cade," he said. "I talked to the chaperones. If you want, I can stay with you until the bandages come off. So you don't have to be dragged around by fifty-year-olds who smell like mothballs."

"You would do that?" Cade asked, voice suddenly small.

"Well... yeah." Neil shrugged, even though Cade couldn't see it. "Is that okay? They didn't want any of your friends guiding you, since—well, you know. And I didn't think you'd want that either."

Cade let out a breath that sounded like something unraveling. "As usual, you are the brightest in the pack, Erickson. I was having a dream about you earlier."

Neil blinked. "What? What does that even—"

The door swung open. Doctors entered, followed by two tired-looking chaperones.

"Okay, we are free to go," Mr. Paulson, an AP French teacher, announced. He looked from Cade to Neil. "Erickson is responsible for you for the next four days, Riley. Do not mistreat him. He's doing you a favor." Mr. Paulson continued, "You'll miss the sights between London and Paris, but you should be able to see all of Switzerland and Italy."

Cade turned his head toward Neil as if he hoped to see him through the bandages, his lips curving into something half grateful, half something he didn't have a name for yet, still adjusting to the strange weight of not being able to see.

And Neil felt it—a change in the air, a spark he tried

hard not to name.

A weight settling between them that wasn't there before Doncaster.

Four days.

Just the two of them.

Everything felt different suddenly, and Neil didn't yet know why.

Neil, Cade, and the chaperones returned an hour before the group was scheduled to board the next train, missing the entire London leg of the trip. Cade was given a quiet, private cabin. Neil hovered in the doorway, clipboard clutched like a shield.

"This must have been expensive," Neil said as he stepped inside, taking in the room.

"My parents arranged it," Cade replied. "Long story."

"I'm surprised they didn't come get you," Neil said. "My parents would've flipped out."

Cade let out a breath—half laugh, half frustration. "Yeah, well... they're currently sailing around the Mediterranean."

The words hung there.

Neil watched the flicker of hurt cross Cade's expression—quick, practiced, almost invisible if you weren't looking for it. Close enough to help, but distant enough not to intrude.

Neil nodded, said "Uh-huh" once, and let the silence settle.

He didn't ask more.

He didn't push.

Cade would talk about it when he was ready.

And Neil... Neil would be there when he did.

Cade sprawled across the seat, sun-bleached hair a mess, black patches taped over both eyes. Even sightless, he managed to look—of course—ridiculously good for someone physically hurt and maybe emotionally scarred from his parents being unresponsive.

"Thanks for volunteering to be my babysitter," Cade remarked.

"Well, Safety Liaison," Neil corrected, sliding into the opposite seat.

"Hot, but too formal. How about Safety Sidekick?" Cade grinned and reached into the void, palm open for a shake.

After a beat, Neil took it—warm, confident, lingering a second too long.

"Cool," Cade said. "Guess we're attached now. Just... don't let me get hit by any more luggage."

Neil smiled, though Cade couldn't see it. "That's the plan. I brought a menu. We can order in or—once it clears out—head to the dining car."

"Dining car. Definitely. I'm done marinating in here."

Neil's mouth twitched. "Good choice."

Later, as Neil guided Cade down the narrow corridor, Cade's hand rested lightly on his arm.

"Sorry," Cade said. "Don't want to face-check a wall."

"It's fine."

"You sound tense."

"I'm always a little tense," Neil admitted.

Cade laughed—warm, ridiculous, and loud enough to echo off the walls. It juddered through Neil's ribcage.

"Do me a favor," Cade said.

Neil glanced over, forgetting for a second that Cade couldn't see. "What kind of favor?"

"Paint me a picture. Tell me what I'm missing."

Neil froze. Cade could've asked the time, and it still would've felt like a test. "It's just a hallway. Beige walls, blue carpet. Smells like burnt oil."

"Cinematic," Cade teased. "I can smell the oil already. Try again."

Neil bit his lip. "Okay... there's a little girl up ahead with a stuffed rabbit—ears longer than her arms—staring at you like you're a superhero."

Cade chuckled. "Better. What else?"

"The dining-car windows are huge. Outside, it's just

green fields fading into the dark, stone walls in patchwork, clouds heavy... like they're waiting for something to happen."

"Foreshadowing. Love it." Cade tilted his head. "How about me? How do I look?"

Heat crept up Neil's neck. Cade couldn't see him, which meant Neil could look—really look—without getting caught. He could lie, or he could tell the truth.

"Honestly," Neil said quietly, "Pretty good for someone with a recent medical chart."

Cade's smile spread. "Bet. I'll take that over any trophy."

By the time they slid into the dining car, Neil realized Cade hadn't let go of his arm. He was surprised by how special it felt. A touch had never felt special before, even with a boyfriend.

The server appeared. "Coffee, gentlemen?"

"Espresso," Neil said. "Foam on the side, two sugar cubes."

"Make that two," Cade added.

"Right away."

When the waiter left, Cade asked, "Sugar cubes?"

"Yeah. More accurate that way. You'll see—Well, you know what I mean." Neil paused, realizing Cade couldn't actually see.

"Cure my vision coffee. Awesome," Cade said jokingly.

The cups arrived. Cade reached blindly, but Neil stopped him. "Wait—I have to do something first."

He pulled the cup closer, poured the foam, and traced a leaf shape on top.

"What are you doing?" Cade asked.

"My Nonna says coffee always tastes better when it looks nice."

"Even if you can't see it?" Cade asked.

"Especially if you can't see it," Neil slid the cup back toward him.

"At least take a picture of it," Cade said.

Neil did.

Cade sipped and smiled. "You were right. Best espresso ever. I'm going to remember this about you."

"I'm going to hold you to that."

What else can I hold to him, Cade thought.

"Okay—my turn to paint a picture," Cade said suddenly, trying to shake off the thought. "Dark brown hair. Green eyes. Sometimes glasses—Clark Kent vibes."

Neil blinked. "You can see through those patches?"

"No. But I've seen you."

"You've... seen me?"

"You're impossible to miss, Neil."

Neil scoffed lightly. "Your soccer bros might not agree."

"Well, I'm more than a soccer bro,—bro."

"How so?"

"Because I pay attention."

Neil smiled despite himself. "Bet."

"Neil Erickson," Cade continued, "Dean's List. Always at the top of the class. Probably valedictorian. Owns more notebooks than he has friends." He grinned. "No offense."

"None taken," Neil muttered, warmth creeping up his neck. "You should always have more notebooks than friends."

"Uh-huh." Cade tilted his head. "Then why do you sound flustered?"

"Do I sound flustered?"

Cade reached across, fingertips brushing Neil's chest. "Feeling a little hot?"

Neil's heart stuttered. He swatted Cade's hand away with mild annoyance, attempting to stand his ground. "Don't be rude. Are you on painkillers or something?"

"Just ibuprofen," Cade said, smirking. "Not that it matters. My hand—and your chest—tell me everything I need to know."

"That's really obnoxious, Cade. I could just go if you

want to be rude."

The train jolted, silverware rattling. Cade's hand slid to Neil's again, steadying himself. Their fingers didn't separate after that.

"Please don't go. I'm sorry," Cade asked.

Neil felt like there was more for Cade to say, but silence prevailed.

Outside, England blurred. Inside, everything went still—except the quiet, sure grip of Cade Riley's hand on Neil's.

Neil stayed.

Chapter Two.

On their last stop before Paris, Cade tugged at his bandages as Neil steered him down the street.

"Okay," Cade muttered, "I feel like a knockoff mummy. People are staring, right?"

"They're not—" Neil started, then caught a double-take from a passing couple mumbling to each other about the guy who looked like The Invisible Man. "Alright. Maybe a little."

"Do you have a second pair of sunglasses?"

Neil blinked. "Uh," he checked his pockets. "Yeah."

"Perfect. Put them on me. Please?"

Neil dug out his Ray-Ban aviators and slid them

gently over the bandages.

Somehow, Cade went from 'ER casualty' to 'Calvin Klein ad model with a dark backstory.'

"There," Cade said, chuckling. "Less medical drama, more mysterious international spy."

"You look ridiculously sus, but in a good way," Neil said, unsure why he was biting back a smile.

"Then you've got to match me. Sunglasses solidarity, seeing-eye boy."

"Okay."

So Neil pulled out his sunglasses, and together they walked like undercover agents with a very questionable disguise budget. For once, Neil didn't mind the stares.

They stopped at a café advertising gelato and ice cream. Neil ordered pistachio ice cream for both of them, then guided Cade to a bench.

"Careful," Neil said, pressing the cone into his hand. "It's already melting."

Cade licked once and sighed. "Okay, solid choice. Nutty. Sweet. Done."

"That's it? That's your review?"

Cade tilted his head. "We're eating the same thing, aren't we? You know what pistachio ice cream tastes like."

Neil shifted, wanting to stretch the moment. "I don't

know how it tastes to *you*." Neil went back to eating his cone.

Cade became still. Then he smiled—softer, almost shy.

"Well... it's cool on my tongue, but it kind of wakes everything up. Sweet at first, then toasted, like it lingers to remind you it was there. Makes me think of summer soccer games—when my mom would take me for ice cream, win or lose. Maybe I just wanted it because it was green."

"Ah."

"What?" Cade asked.

"Nothing. I just... wasn't expecting you to be nostalgic." Neil blinked, thrown. He'd expected sarcasm, maybe another joke. Not this—Cade Riley, talking like he carried memories in his back pocket.

"Hey, I can be nostalgic. I have feelings."

"I mean, maybe your friends know that, but outwardly most of us don't get to see it."

"Well, not everyone is Neil Erickson," Cade said playfully. "Psychoanalytical baby nerd."

Neil laughed.

"Privileged, right?" Neil said.

"And investigative." Cade felt Neil's eyes on him at that moment.

Neil stared down Cade, taking the opportunity to scan for body language. What was happening, anyway? For Cade to open up like this felt unusual.

That night, the hostel was a blur of squeaky bunk beds, damp socks, the smell of instant noodles, and an alarming number of seniors zoned out on their phones. Neil ended up on the bottom bunk across from Cade, who lay flat with the aviators still perched over his bandages like he couldn't give up the disguise.

"Hey, Neil?" Cade's voice cut through the din.

"Yeah?"

"Have you seen my teammates around?"

Neil frowned. "What do you mean?"

"I figured someone would've checked in with me. Usually, they're yelling my name across a room. But now it's like... they vanished."

Neil hesitated. He'd noticed it too—the way Cade's glittering circle thinned the second he wasn't the ringleader anymore. "Maybe they just don't know what to say. Or maybe... I don't know." He stopped. Maybe the silence said more than words.

Cade gave a short, humorless laugh. "Figures. Guess I'm not much fun blindfolded. Can you check my phone? Just see if anyone texted."

Neil crossed over and sat on the side of Cade's bunk, pulled the phone from his bag, and swiped through. "Uh... nope. Just the group chat debating kebabs tomorrow. Nothing personal."

"Okay, cool."

"They probably just figured you can't answer right now," Neil said gently. "I could set up VoiceOver—it'll read your messages out loud."

But Cade just shook his head. "Nah. If someone sends me something dumb, I'd rather not have Siri narrate it to the whole room." He turned his face toward Neil's voice. "Would you read them to me instead? Just... when they come in? That way it stays between us."

Neil was taken aback by Cade's trust. "Yeah. Of course. I don't mind."

Cade smiled—small, real, just for him. "Thanks. Guess I trust you more than Siri."

"Trusting me with your personal texts? Wow, Cade," Neil said, steadier than he had expected. He was a little proud of himself for poking at Cade.

"Hey, Kettle, it's Pot. You're black."

Neil laughed, still reading Cade's texts. "What?"

"We can't all be valedictorian, like you."

"I see you have mistaken me for our overachiever classmate, Larkin Collins," said Neil.

"Definitely not. She's scary."

"Bless her. She definitely wants the top spot more than I do."

Back on his bunk, Neil held Cade's phone in his lap, heart thudding. Cade Riley, who had a hundred friends and never needed anybody, had just chosen him to trust. That was cool.

"Are you still on my phone?"

"It's just sitting here. I'm on mine. Why?"

"Just wondering if you're rifling through my photos."

"I wouldn't do that, Cade."

"Okay," Cade said, a grin tugging at the corner of his mouth—lazy, knowing.

Neil looked down at Cade's phone, his thumb hovering. Maybe Cade wanted him to look. Perhaps this was some kind of test.

"Send me that cappuccino photo," Cade said.

"You mean espresso." Neil tried to sound casual, but Cade's grin didn't budge, and something in it made Neil's stomach turn over. He airdropped the picture, then said, "I'm just going to check if it saved, okay?"

"Yup."

Neil opened the Photos app. There it was—the espresso art. But the next image froze him: a photo of himself, gazing out of the train window, light painting his face gold. *Cade must have taken it moments before the accident,* he thought.

His breath hitched. For a second, the sounds of the other students in the building fell away.

He looked up. Cade turned toward him, no grin now—just quiet attention, like Neil was somehow in focus.

"Okay, it's in there," Neil said finally, voice low, steadying it against the flutter in his chest.

"Good," Cade murmured, his head still turned toward him, as if he were imagining looking at him.

Neil pretended to check another setting just to look away. He could feel the warmth of Cade beside him, their knees almost brushing.

Is there a world where we could actually... date? Or even crazier—fall in love? Neil thought.

Maybe Cade's easy charm isn't a mask at all. Maybe it's how he makes room for something real.

Chapter Three.

The hostel bathrooms weren't built for privacy. Rows of showerheads lined the powder-blue-tiled wall, like some Russian swim team locker room, the air thick with mildew, soap scum, and the sour tang of chlorine. Neil avoided them at peak hours—when Penderton boys belted Benson Boone at six-thirty sharp, competing like it was American Idol: Hostel Edition.

But today was different. Today, Cade needed backup.

"Look, I can handle the water part," Cade said, his voice ricocheting off the tiles as Neil steered him inside. "Just… make sure I don't run into a wall. Or worse—into Trevor. That guy whistles *Kill Bill* in the shower, and that is a war crime. Especially when you can't see."

"It's early," Neil said, shirtless, setting their towels on a bench and already removing his sleep shorts. "We're in the clear. The tiles are this dusty blue color from the 1980s. How much would you bet the girls' shower is dusty pink?"

"I'd bet both my eye patches on it," Cade smirked beneath the gauzy bandages. "So it's just you and me? In a steamy room? Stripping down? My mom would say that this sounds sus."

Neil gagged. "You know, no shade to your mom, but I wouldn't hate it if you stopped talking about her in the shower."

Cade's laugh echoed off the tiles as he tugged at his T-shirt, fumbling it over his head. Steam from the shower was already fogging the mirrors, curling around him like movie smoke. Neil's brain betrayed him instantly, tracking every detail: the lean lines of a soccer body, collarbones sharp enough to draw blood, and that easy confidence of someone completely unaware of how good he looked. Heart thudding, Neil twisted his own shower knob toward cold and forced his gaze away.

"You're not the first guy to see me shirtless," Cade teased, the smirk obvious in his voice.

"Is this what they call locker room talk?"

"Maybe."

They both laughed, the sound echoing as the whole room belonged to just the two of them.

"Awkward," Neil muttered, though his pulse was hammering.

Cade kicked off his shorts, toes brushing the cold tile as he stepped under the spray. He tilted his head back, water streaming over the bandages. "So if you're blushing right now, I don't even get to see it. What a waste."

"I'm not blushing."

"You so are. You sound like a chipmunk when you lie."

Neil shoved his face under the water, pretending it drowned him. "What an ego. You think everyone wants you?"

"And yet," Cade said, hand searching until it landed on Neil's shoulder, "you keep showing up."

"And for a job that pays in resume credit. Basic."

The touch was casual and steady—his fingers warm even through the spray—and Neil froze for half a second too long. Electricity ran the length of his arm. He was still reeling when Cade's foot slid on the slick tile.

"Cade—"

Too late.

Neil lunged, but momentum dragged them both down in a graceless heap. Skin against skin, slippery and shocking, steam rising like the heat between them.

Cade's laugh broke the silence. "Are you okay?" Neil asked, heart thudding like he'd sprinted.

"Totally fine," Cade said, sprawled and grinning like it was all part of the plan. "You?"

"Fine," Neil managed, heat crawling up his neck. "That could've gone way worse. Pretty sure I was zero help."

"No broken bones, no lawsuits. I'd call that a win."

Neil offered his hand. Cade clasped it, slick and solid, and Neil pulled him up. For one suspended second, they were chest to chest, their breath mingling, water streaking over both of them. Neither moved. The moment stretched, impossible and electric, before they broke apart in a flurry of awkward movements.

They were both fine. A little embarrassed. And if Neil admitted it, he was glad it happened. He was grateful in the moment that Cade couldn't see his... half-developed excitement. Then he noticed Cade was in a similar condition.

"You laughed," Neil accused, shoving wet hair out of his eyes. "Did you do that on purpose?"

"Doubt it. But hey—" Cade's grin widened.

"What?"

"You might need to get a pregnancy test."

"Shut up," Neil laughed, a little too loud.

"Let's find out if I have to marry you now."

"Not unless it's the nineteenth century, and you've seen my ankles first. We are not in England, you know? The French are very progressive."

"How *very* Victorian scandal," Cade said, in a warm English accent. "Flash me a sock, and I'll buy you dinner."

"You'd need working eyes for that."

Neil shoved a shampoo bottle into Cade's hand, a little rougher than necessary. Cade caught it easily, then went quiet, palms braced against the tiles.

Softer: "Hey. I know I joke a lot. Like a lot-a lot, but... thanks. You didn't sign up to babysit me through train stations and half-baked showers."

Neil blinked. "It's not a big deal. You're... entertaining, like an organ grinder's monkey."

"Now you want to talk about my organ?" Cade scoffed. "Otherwise, wow. Harsh review."

"I meant it, no joke," Neil said quickly, heat flooding his ears. "You've made this trip... better already."

Cade tilted his head. "Say more."

"Besides," Neil added, aiming for casual and missing, "I'm more excited about the Italy portion of the trip anyway."

"Oh yeah?" Cade asked. "The pasta? Gondolas? Shirtless Italian guys?"

Neil risked a glance at him through the steam. "...Maybe just the company. Three weeks post-breakup and still loading. If that hadn't crashed, I probably wouldn't even be here."

Cade froze. "I'm stunned, honestly." Cade fought back a smile. This was his window of opportunity.

"What do you mean?"

"You're a good-looking guy. Caring, obviously—you agreed to help me stumble around Europe. Feels like you'd dump someone before they dumped you."

"Thanks... I think."

"Geez, Neil. Take the compliment."

Neil sighed. "I just don't know what to make of you yet. I don't know you well, and the people you run with can't be trusted. They throw your secrets back in your face in the loudest way possible."

"You're not wrong," Cade said quietly. "But I swear, man. Total respect. You can say anything, and it won't go anywhere."

"...Thanks."

"What was his name?" Cade asked.

"Who?"

"The idiot who dumped you," Cade responded. "And yeah, I know it was a guy."

Neil was a little surprised that Cade immediately knew that.

"Kyle. You wouldn't know him. He goes to the public arts magnet school."

"MLK?"

"Yup."

"How long did you go out?"

"Maybe six months? We are just from different worlds. Still, I was hopeful."

"Was he hotter than me?"

"Cade—really, man," Neil responded, and they both laughed. Neil already knew that he was not going to answer. No one was hotter than Cade Riley, but he wasn't going to tell him that.

"You were going out with someone before that, though. Cade paused. "Josh, or something like that."

Neil looked at Cade, staring at him in wonder, knowing he couldn't look back at him.

"What?" Cade asked.

"You seem to know a lot about me. You couldn't have known Josh personally. He goes to a boarding school in Atlanta," Neil explained.

"Let's just say Insta is your autobiography. If you

don't want people to know things, don't post them. But what do I know?"

Why was Cade stalking my Instagram? Neil thought, but he didn't dare ask.

By breakfast, the cafeteria smelled like burnt toast and low morale. Neil grabbed two bowls of cornflakes and eggs that looked suspiciously powdered, then slid into Cade's banquette.

"Please tell me you didn't get the mystery sausages," Cade said. "I can smell them from here."

"Let's establish right now, I don't put crap like that in my body." Neil set the tray down.

"That's what she said," Cade quipped.

Neil didn't miss a beat. "Sometimes that's what he said, too."

Cade cackled. "Oh! Well played. See, this is why you're prime comedy track material. You just need a soundtrack and intro music."

"Anyway. Cornflakes. Safe. Unless the milk kills us."

Normally, Cade would've been at the center of everything—loud, magnetic, and impossible to ignore. Today, nobody sat with him. Eyes flicked over, then away. Cade's smile faltered.

"Guess I've been demoted from Homecoming King to

cafeteria cryptid," he muttered.

"Or maybe that's an upgrade."

"To what?"

"VIP status," Neil said. "Private table service. Elite banter. And let's be honest—you've known me a couple of days, and I'm already a better friend than the intellectual lightweights that you usually hang out with."

That cracked Cade up, shoulders loosening.

Across the cafeteria, a group whispered as they stared. Neil caught it, then turned back quickly.

Cade sensed the shift.

"What?" Cade asked.

"Nothing. Just... people noticing."

"Let them. Unless you mind."

"I don't."

And the strange part was—Neil really didn't.

The group spilled out of the hostel like cattle, duffels dragging, teachers shouting names like auctioneers. Disneyland Paris traffic blared at the curb.

"Status report, Safety Sidekick?" Cade asked, smirking as Neil guided him down the steps.

"Chaos," Neil reported. "Odds of survival: slim."

"Guess it's your job to keep me alive until Paris, when I can take these patches off."

"Trying," Neil muttered—then froze as Cade's hand slid down his arm and their fingers locked together, casual but certain.

"Easier this way," Cade said. "Besides... I like holding your hand."

"You're just saying that to be obnoxious."

"No, I'm not."

"Yes. Yes, you are." Neil still wasn't convinced that Cade was sincere because he had been such a clown for so many years.

Disneyland Paris opened wide and loud around them—buses belching smoke, taxis honking, crowds pressing like a living tide. Usually, Neil would've been at Cade's elbow, counting steps, guiding him up curbs, and translating the city into safe terrain. But not today.

"Erickson," Ms. Halstead said, intercepting him on the pavement. "Go with your friends. Enjoy the park. You've done enough. Mr. McCarthy's got Riley for the day."

Neil hesitated. Cade, bandaged and leaning lazily against a lamppost, smirked as if the whole arrangement was beneath him. Mr. McCarthy, already weary, positioned himself at Cade's side like a reluctant seeing-eye dog.

"Are you sure?" Neil asked.

"Go," she said firmly.

And so Neil went—with Jenna and two others—trailing toward fantasyland, which felt ironic to him since the possibilities with Cade seemed to be rolling around like marbles in his head.

In line for Big Thunder Mountain, Jenna tugged his sleeve. "So you're on Cade Riley safety duty again tomorrow, right?"

Neil exhaled. "Definitely. At least through Paris. Where is Kip?"

Sophie interrupted to say, "He's with some hot girl. Ugh. Long story."

Jenna's eyes narrowed. "Neil, even bandaged up, he's still a liability. I mean, you've seen him. He jokes through everything. He could probably manage to fall into a fake lake blindfolded."

Mads snorted. "He's like a clown. Only louder, but with nice abs," she said with an optimistic ending.

Neil didn't answer, staring instead at the red clay spires gleaming above them. But he couldn't deny the truth in their words.

"Seriously," Sophie pressed. "How do they expect you to keep him safe if he refuses to take anything seriously?"

Neil sighed. He thought about Cade in the shower—

how a casual hand on his shoulder had lit every nerve like electricity—and about breakfast, Cade cracking jokes like nothing could touch him. He was exhausting. He was chaos.

"Oh my God, you have a crush on him. Neil!" Jenna declared.

"Shut up," Neil responded with a nervous laugh. "Even if I did, it's kind of pointless. There's a chance he's baiting me, though."

"More information, please," said Mads.

"It's just that he says things, like he told me he likes holding my hand. He was really nostalgic over pistachio ice cream yesterday..." Neil trailed off.

"And?" Jenna asked. "Earth, Neil. Come back to us."

"He had this photo of me that he took right before the prank on the train. He knew about me dating Josh before Kyle." Neil paused. "I don't know, I feel like now I'm the one getting pranked. It was a really good photo of me. Also, the doctor said he might be a little delusional until he gets his vision back, so it could be simply that, right?"

"Wow," said Sophie. "Wait, how would he have known about Josh?"

"Apparently, he reads my Insta posts. Crazy, right?"

"Okay, fine, I'll ask it," Mads announced. "Didn't you

have to help him in the shower?"

"Oh, this should be good," Sophie chuckled.

Neil nodded with a shy yes.

Jenna and Sophie lightly squealed.

"Well, did you get a... rise out of him?" Mads asked.

Neil paused and looked at each of the girls, saying with urgency. "Okay, so he slipped, and he was already reaching for my arm at the time, and I reached out to help prevent his fall, and..."

"Oh my God, NEIL! You have me on the frickin' EDGE! Spit it out," Mads demanded.

"It's kind of dumb. We went down in a heap. One hundred percent locker room adult film quality disaster, and there was a comment from him that I should probably get a pregnancy test. It was funny once we established that neither of us was hurt."

Jenna's mouth gaped open. "It's a weird flirt, but really, really cute."

"Internally screaming here," Sophie said.

"That's it. I'm following you two around with a fully charged phone at all times," Mads declared. "And for the rest of your lives. We could all use the excitement."

"Kyle and I just broke up a few weeks ago. Don't you think I might be setting myself up for disaster with Cade? I don't want to be his next joke, or worse: his laugh track."

"Take off the black veil, Neil. It's time to come out of mourning. Also, for what? Kyle? He never seemed worth losing sleep over to me," Jenna continued. "Plus, if things go sideways, it's not like you're going to see him much longer. We graduate in ten months."

"Yeah, but what if things go well? What then?" Sophie asked optimistically.

"Plus, he has a lot of cute friends that none of us know." Mads paused.

Sophie cringed a little.

"Okay, Universe!" Mads said, putting everyone's hands together like she was casting a spell. "Make this happen for our friend, Neil. With the power of four, make Neil our whore."

"MADS!" the remaining three shouted.

"Geez, witchy lady," Sophie said lovingly to Mads. "Calm down."

That night, back at the hostel, Cade's laugh rang down the corridor, ricocheting off the walls as Mr. McCarthy trudged behind with the look of a man who'd herded a Labrador all day. Neil's friends shot him a pointed 'See?' look and smiled.

"Neil has a new project," Sophie said.

"And everyone knows how much Neil loves a project," Mads said.

Neil approached Mr. McCarthy. "Everything okay?"

"He's with another chaperone right now. I needed a break." Mr. McCarthy wiped his brow with a handkerchief. "I'm going to see if I can find you a relief person. I had no idea how exhausting Mr. Riley could be, Neil. He's a lot to manage."

"No, I'm fine. Somehow it hasn't been that bad for me."

"Neil, he somehow felt his way into the catering kitchen and turned over an entire tray of plates. I swear, if his parents weren't who they are..."

Neil wasn't surprised. He already knew Cade was chaotic when he was bored.

"Like a bull in there, I guess," Neil said.

"Maybe we can buy a cattle prod or something." McCarthy looked sheepish. "Let's just keep that between you and me?"

"I went AFK. What did you just say?" Neil said to assure Mr. McCarthy.

"Thank you. Okay, let me round him up for you."

Mr. McCarthy appeared with Cade, who looked like a sad, hurt pony. The chaperone scurried away. "All yours, Erickson."

"Neil?"

"I'm here. You look like you need mac and cheese with your chicken nuggets, little man."

"Little man? I'm your BIG man, babe."

"Alright, settle down, Romeo," Neil chuckled. "Sounds like you were a handful for poor Mr. McCarthy."

"Honestly," Cade leaned in. "It's nice to have you back. Mac-man is really far from being a Neil Erickson."

Neil silently swooned.

Chapter Four.

The rhythm of the train blurred time—steady, relentless—like the world had shrunk to a steel corridor and two facing seats. Cade leaned against the window, sunglasses perched over his bandages. Outside, France flickered past as the train moved south.

For once, the car was quiet. No classmates yelling over Uno, no teachers droning about "cultural etiquette." Just the sound of the engine and the rattle of the tracks prevailed.

Neil scrolled through Cade's phone, smirking. "So... apparently there's a group chat about who's going to 'accidentally' kiss you under the Eiffel Tower."

Cade barked a laugh. "Let me guess—half the girls already claimed dibs on me?"

"And three of the guys," Neil said. "Bold strategy."

"Amateurs," Cade said.

Neil rolled his eyes. "Maybe it's like *Sleeping Beauty*, and you'll fall in love with one of them after the magical kiss."

"Maybe not," Cade said. Then, lower: "But sometimes the real world is better."

"Meaning?"

Cade tapped the edge of his bandages. "I mean, I thought this trip was going to be selfies, baguette thievery, and seeing if I could convince Trevor Anderson that he was fluent in French by teaching him fake phrases. And now..." His grin softened. "It's just me and you, babe."

Neil tried for humor, his voice thinner than he had intended. "Downgrade?"

"Upgrade," Cade shot back instantly. "You're basically my seeing-eye boy. That's a hot commodity."

Neil coughed. "You make that sound like a dating app category."

"It could be," Cade said, leaning forward with a grin. "Swipe right for reliable guys who won't let you walk into fountains and make your cappuccino look amazing."

Neil groaned, covering a smile. "Espresso! Also, please say that first part louder so someone actually hears you and makes that a thing on the apps."

Cade opened his mouth and took a breath, but then Neil came across to his seat and covered Cade's mouth. "No... don't you dare," Neil said, and they laughed.

The train rattled on, silence stretching as it went over bridges.

Neil blurted, "So what were you like before all this?"

"Before all the bandages?"

"Yeah. Before sunglasses. Before I was your full-time tour guide."

Cade tilted his head, as though remembering himself. "Louder. Always in motion. I realize that I'm pretty much exhausting to be around, honestly. You probably already know that."

"Shocking, and I've seen some things, sure," Neil deadpanned.

"But..." Cade's grin went crooked, voice lowering, "Turns out sitting still with the right person is really nice. Who knew?"

Heat bloomed in Neil's face. "Okay, now you're just trying to sound profound."

"Maybe. Or maybe I'm just better at this flirting thing than you."

Neil scoffed, but his pulse jumped. "That was flirting? Don't flex for me, soccer lad."

"Oh, Neil," Cade said, slow and certain. "Everything's flirting if you do it right."

The words clung in the air. Neil's throat tightened. Cade tilted his head. "Hey—anyone nearby?"

Neil glanced. Classmates were six rows down, sharing Pringles. Their teacher was still snoring. "Nope. We're clear."

"Good," Cade smirked. "Because I didn't want to ruin my rep as the guy who only talks about soccer and bad music takes."

Neil frowned. "What are you talking about?"

"I like this," Cade said simply. "Hanging out with you. You're solid. Safe. And way funnier than people give you credit for."

Neil flushed. "That's... nice, and mildly hurtful."

"'Nice'? 'Hurtful'?" Cade groaned. "Seriously? Try again."

"I don't know—what do you want me to say?"

"That you've fallen desperately in love with me," Cade said without missing a beat.

Neil sputtered, heart lurching. "What?! You're unbelievable."

"Relax. I think you're *almost* there," Cade teased.

Neil scrunched his face, laughing despite himself. "You have such an ego, Cade. Have a seat. I'll let you know if I develop Lima syndrome."

"What's that?"

"Reverse Stockholm syndrome. Didn't you take psychology? You quoted the subject yesterday."

"And yet," Cade said smugly, "you're still here. Describing scenery like you're my personal audiobook. Admit it—I'm your favorite assignment."

Neil muttered into his hands, "So far, yes. Though honestly, it is a three-star audiobook. Great voice, questionable audience." He loudly flipped a page in his favorite book.

"See? That right there," Cade said softly. "That's what makes you interesting. You just called me out for questionable rizz. What are you reading?"

"*A Room with a View* by E.M. Forster. It's my go-to book. I'll probably read it twice on this trip."

The brakes hissed, the tunnels flickered, and the voices rose down the car.

The announcement came in French, smooth and lyrical.

"*Bienvenue à Paris.*"

Neil's heart jolted. "We're here? They said it would take longer to get to Paris."

Neil leaned toward the glass, words tumbling fast. "Okay—you've got to hear this." Neil made all of this up just to get a rise out of Cade. He couldn't see Paris from the train. "The skyline just opened up—rooftops everywhere, pale stone, chimneys stacked like dominoes. Sidewalk cafés. Balconies exploding with flowers. And— holy crap—the Eiffel Tower. It's right there... like the city's heartbeat."

Cade smiled faintly. "Sounds like you're falling in love."

Neil swallowed hard. "With the city," he said quickly.

"Sure," Cade said, smug. "Definitely just the city."

Cade couldn't quite gauge where he stood with Neil, and years of soccer had taught him one thing—when you're not sure, act like you are. His small comments weren't landing, his jokes skidding off harmlessly. So he took a breath, steadied his nerves, and decided it was time to take a bigger risk.

The train slowed, brakes still hissing. Classmates grabbed bags, teachers barked, and whistles shrilled. But the world had narrowed again—to the rattle of the tracks, the closeness of the seats, and the weight of Cade's words in Neil's chest.

Cade tilted his head, almost curious. "Hey. Come here for a second."

Neil blinked. "What—?"

"Just..." Cade gestured vaguely, lips tilting in a half-smile. "Closer."

Neil leaned across the narrow aisle, pulse roaring in his ears. He was close enough now to feel the warmth of Cade's skin, to smell the faint scent of soap and shampoo under the train's brake dust.

Cade's sunglasses caught a shard of light as his hand brushed Neil's wrist—barely there, but enough to ground him.

Did Cade need to whisper something to him in confidence?

"That's better," Cade murmured. His voice had dropped low, the kind of low that curled under Neil's ribs.

And then Cade tilted his head up, slow enough for Neil to stop it if he wanted.

He didn't.

Neil could feel Cade's breath.

Cade felt the heat of Neil's closeness.

Their lips met, and the kiss was careful at first—soft and exploratory.

Cade's lips were warm and uncertain against Neil's. The world went hushed.

Neil felt every detail: the give of Cade's mouth, the faint rasp of his breath, the saltiness of his lips, and the way the train seemed to sway in time with his pulse.

Cade smiled against him—an almost-laugh that broke the moment just enough to make it real. Neil's hand had found Cade's jaw without permission, thumb grazing the edge of the bandage, steadying them both.

When they pulled back, it was barely an inch, breaths tangled.

"Well," Cade said, voice ragged but playful. "Guess you beat the Eiffel Tower crowd."

Neil's lips tingled; his whole body lit up like someone had plunged him into cold water. He remained at least slightly fractured and mildly paralyzed.

Suddenly, Paris wasn't just a city waiting outside. It was this.

For the next few minutes, Neil internally wigged out over the freshness of his breath.

Always on silent, Neil's phone buzzed. A text from Jenna:

Jenna
How's it going over there with the man-baby?

Neil
It's going fine, I think?

Jenna
Wow, a glowing review. Should I start
planning the wedding or the rescue mission?

Neil
Statistically, things are trending
up—margin of error: my entire
emotional stability.

Jenna
Message from Mads and Sophie: "Stop
pretending you're fine and text details,
nerd." I'm just the messenger. But also, same.

Neil
Tell Mads I'm alive, tell Sophie to lower her
expectations, and I'll ask you to stop
being the group's press secretary. I have
updates, but I'll catch you up a bit later.

Chapter Five.

That night, the Penderton group gathered beneath the Eiffel Tower, necks craned, cameras flashing like fireworks. The iron lattice blazed against the dark sky, each spotlight slicing upward into forever.

While Yves Montand played in the background, Neil guided Cade through the throng, weaving past couples kissing and a billion kids taking endless selfies or live-streaming or eating Nutella crêpes bigger than their heads.

Jenna, Mads, Sophie, and Kip walked past them. Mads and Sophie stuck their tongues out, silently mimicking a terrible version of French kissing, and pointed at them as if to say, "That's what you guys look like."

Neil found a space off to the side, quieter, where

Cade tilted his bandaged face upward, as if he could feel the glow on his skin.

"Describe it," Cade said.

Neil swallowed, words catching. "It's... enormous. The whole tower is lit up, like it's made of fire. Against the sky, it looks impossible—like it shouldn't even stand, but it does. And everything around it feels smaller. Like the whole city is leaning in to watch."

Three flirty girls walked by, teasing Cade about having a kissing contest while his eyes were covered.

"Hot, but not quite the right moment," Cade said. The girls giggled and moved on.

Cade let out a breath. "Sounds incredible. You know, I always dreamed of kissing someone at the Eiffel Tower," he said to Neil.

Neil's heart lurched. He aimed for humor. "What, do you want me to kiss you? At least you know who I am." Neil also decided to be unassuming about what the kiss earlier meant.

He expected Cade's laugh—the teasing comeback. But Cade didn't laugh. He turned toward Neil, serious, voice low and steady.

"Yeah," he said with confidence, like he thought he had made that clear before on the train. "I'd like to kiss you again."

The words stole the ground from under Neil's feet. Around them, the crowd surged, but somehow no one was looking their way. They had a sliver of privacy under the floodlit steel.

Neil's pulse roared. "You... do?"

"Yeah," Cade whispered, a grin tugging faintly at his lips. "I *only* want it to be you."

Neil's doubts and defenses melted in the heat of the Tower's glow. The kiss on the train had been a surprise, an impulse, a preview. This—this was a choice. It wasn't that Neil thought of himself as less-than, unattractive, or having low self-esteem. It was more than Cade Riley being the total catch of Penderton Academy. It just didn't seem real that he would have any attraction to a guy, and then that guy would be Neil. That's what Neil was thinking anyway. Neil saw himself as the opposite of the golden boy, literally. He was very Italian in his comparative appearance, Mediterranean, with dark hair, green eyes, and light olive skin. Could this be what attracted Cade, perhaps? The opposite of his blond-ish hair and tan complexion?

So Neil leaned in before fear could stop him.

The world blurred around them. The crowd, the cameras, the murmur of voices in a dozen languages. There was only Cade, waiting, lips parted like he'd been ready forever. Their mouths met gently at first, careful, as if either of them might shatter. But Cade's hand slid to Neil's wrist, curling there, then climbing higher until his palm pressed against Neil's chest.

Neil's breath hitched; his whole body shuddered with it.

Cade kissed him back like he meant it, confident and hungry. He had never felt protected before, the way Neil watched out for him while he was blinded. It was new, and it was wonderful.

Neil gave in, his hand reaching to Cade's bicep, holding him close.

Above them, the structure erupted into a glittering display, the lights sparking to life on the hour. The crowd gasped and pointed skyward, phones lifting, giving Cade and Neil more cover.

Neil barely noticed. The whole city could be watching, and he still wouldn't have moved.

When they finally pulled apart, breathless, Cade's grin broke wide. "See?" he murmured. I've been wanting that since the eighth year."

Neil laughed, shaky and dizzy. "Uh," he whispered. "What?"

"*C'est trop chou,*"[1] a passing elderly woman said.

[1] *C'est trop chou*: That's so cute!

Neil was puzzled. "I think she said... something about too much cabbage?"

The woman responded in English. "It is a Parisian term. Means: 'it is so cute.'"

"*Merci,*" they both said as she walked away smiling.

"*C'est très gentil,*"[2] Neil said graciously.

They both giggled and began to walk back to the group.

"Cade?"

"Yeah?"

"What did you mean about eighth grade?"

"Oh, I'll tell you later. I want to be able to see you."

Neil spent a few minutes before bed sketching Cade under the Eiffel Tower, complete with eye patches and sunglasses at night.

[2] *C'est très gentil:* That is very kind.

Chapter Six.

Neil woke up staring at the ceiling of the hostel's room, heart hammering like he'd run a marathon in his sleep.

They'd kissed, for the second time now, once under the Eiffel Tower. The most cliché, cinematic kiss possible—and it had been with Cade Riley. Even an angelic old woman had commented like a scripted cast member.

Neil pressed the heel of his palm against his forehead, groaning. What did it mean? Was it just the Tower, the glow, the Paris air, or the kind of moment that tricks people into thinking they're in love? Or did Cade mean it? Really mean it? He couldn't see any of it, so it couldn't be the simple glow of the moment.

Across the narrow room, Cade stirred in his bunk, sunglasses still in place over the bandages. He stretched like a cat, yawned, and said, "Morning," as if he sensed Neil looking at him.

Neil swallowed. "Morning."

Cade tilted his head toward him, grinning even though he couldn't see. "You've been quiet. What's up?"

What's up? Neil thought. *What's up is that you kissed me, Cade Riley, and I liked it so much I might never recover.*

Instead, he muttered, "Didn't sleep much."

"Same," Cade admitted, voice softer now. "Too much Eiffel Tower magic, I guess."

Neil froze, blood roaring in his ears. Cade said it so casually, but the words hit like a jolt. Eiffel Tower magic. Not regret. Not 'oops, that was dumb.' *Magic.*

And that was somehow worse—because it made Neil want to believe in what was possible *with* Cade.

Cade was the kind of guy you couldn't help but notice, whether you wanted to or not. Loud, commanding personality in the hallways, always laughing too hard, always surrounded by people who thought being near him made them funnier, hotter, and/or cooler by osmosis. Neil honestly didn't want to be like those people or be seen as Cade's laugh track, as he'd told his friends back at Disneyland Paris.

From a distance, Neil pegged him as the classic golden boy—soccer captain, perfect hair, parents who probably sent him new sneakers every other week. Cade's world looked easy, the kind where teachers forgave late homework, and classmates forgave worse, because "that's just Cade."

He wasn't cruel, not exactly, but he didn't have to be. His friends did the work for him—overbearing, messy kids who made everything a competition: who could drink the most, sing the loudest, or make the sharpest joke at someone else's expense. Cade laughed along with them, and from where Neil sat—back row of the cafeteria, locker tucked in the quiet wing—it was hard to tell if Cade was in on the meanness or just so far above it he didn't notice. Neil also reflected that Cade had a mysterious sadness to him, something that no one could quite pinpoint. It made him more human than his friends, as if he clung to a secret that no one would ever learn about.

Neil figured it didn't matter. People like Cade Riley didn't see people like him. And if they did, it was only long enough to turn him into a punchline.

So Neil kept his distance, cataloguing Cade the way

you'd catalogue a constellation—bright, untouchable, and beautiful if you squinted, but useless up close. Or was he wrong? Time would tell.

The group was scattered across the hostel cafeteria, picking at croissants that flaked into a million pieces and cups of bitter coffee that no amount of sugar could fix. Neil sat across from Cade, watching him tilt his head toward the window, sunlight hitting the bandages in a way that almost looked like a halo.

Between bites, Cade said casually, like he was mentioning the weather:

"So, I can take the bandages off tomorrow."

Neil's stomach lurched. Tomorrow. He'd known it was coming, but hearing it out loud made his pulse spike.

Cade smiled faintly. "I'm looking forward to seeing you again."

"I'm looking forward to seeing your eyes," Neil said.

By late afternoon, the Penderton tour had become a blur of landmarks—Notre Dame, the Louvre, and Montmartre. Neil's voice was hoarse from narrating details Cade couldn't see, but Cade never stopped asking. *What do the gargoyles look like? How big is the glass pyramid? Are the painters at Montmartre any good?* None of the answers mattered because they didn't do any of that. Neil sat with Cade on a park bench or in a café during most of their visit to Paris because it was too stressful to put someone who couldn't see in all of the crowds. Neil created art on Cade's espresso at the cafe and enjoyed making sure he was safe. It felt very domestic and dreamy to him, and he wanted as much of it as Cade would give.

On their way back toward the bus, the streets were packed shoulder to shoulder. Souvenir stalls crowded the sidewalks, and teachers barked at the students to "stick together."

Cade slowed, then leaned closer. "Hey—mind if I...?" His hand slid down Neil's arm until it hooked at his forearm just below his elbow.

Neil looked over, startled. "Uh—sure. Need to steer through the crowd?"

"Yeah, that," Cade said with a grin. Then, quieter: "But also... not really. Truth is, I just wanted an excuse to hang closer to you."

Neil's heart thumped so loud he was sure Cade could hear it.

"I figure," Cade went on, his voice low, almost conspiratorial, "I've got one more day behind these bandages. Might as well get maximum benefit before they come off."

Neil nearly tripped on the uneven cobblestones. "Maximum benefit?"

"Yeah," Cade said easily, tightening his hold on Neil's arm. "Spending time with you like this. No distractions. No expectations. Just... us."

Neil opened his mouth, then shut it again. His pulse was still racing, but for once, he let himself lean into it— the weight of Cade's hand on his arm, the heat of the crowd blurring around them.

For everyone else, Paris was a collection of monuments and souvenirs. For Neil, it was Cade Riley walking beside him, choosing him, even in the middle of the busiest street in the world.

"So," Cade paused. "There was this one time... at an assembly last year."

Neil looked forward, scanning for anything that might be an obstruction for them, dangers lurking. "Okay," he said.

"There was a fight that broke out, and we all looked to see what the fuss was about."

Neil listened closely to Cade.

"You and a friend of yours broke it up and seemingly defused it. I thought that was really cool. That wasn't the first time I looked your way, but it was one of the best times," Cade said.

"Do you remember the first time?" Neil asked.

"Honestly, yes. I was going to wait until tomorrow to say this, but we spoke on our first day at Penderton."

"What? I would have remembered that," Neil said.

"Eighth grade. Mrs. Jordan's class. We had the same homeroom," Cade said.

"Oh my gosh. We did! Wow. I'm not trying to sound gooberish, but I honestly don't remember that. I wonder why."

"Well, I looked very different then. I'll pull up a picture on my phone tomorrow and show you."

"Okay," Neil decided to let that go and pick it back up when Cade could see his phone.

As the sun dipped low and the class shuffled back toward the bus, Neil guided Cade down the last stretch of cobblestones. The Eiffel Tower still glimmered faintly behind them, shrinking into the skyline.

"You know," Neil said, forcing a brightness into his tone he didn't feel, "tomorrow you'll get to take off the bandages just in time for the train ride out of Paris. Perfect timing. You'll actually get to see the city on your way out, probably."

Cade grinned under the sunglasses. "Yeah? Guess that's something else to look forward to."

But Neil's chest tightened as he added, softer, "After that, you won't really need me."

Cade stopped walking, tugging lightly on Neil's arm until he faced him. "What makes you say that?"

Neil tried to laugh it off. "I mean—you'll be able to see again. Navigate for yourself. I'll just be... a guy on the trip, and you can hang with your friends."

Cade's smile shifted into something gentler. "Neil. I don't want you around just because I need you. I want you around because I like you."

The words landed like a weight in Neil's soul, both terrifying and impossible to shake.

He nodded, swallowing hard, then turned them back toward the bus before Cade could say more. But all through the night, as the hostel settled into creaking silence, Neil couldn't stop hearing Cade's voice:

I want you around because I like you.

And with the morning looming, Neil didn't know if he was more afraid of Cade finally seeing him—or of Cade not wanting him anymore once he did.

Chapter Seven.

The hostel stirred awake in fits and starts—zippers rasping, shoes thumping, someone humming a song from *Wicked* down the hall. The air smelled of coffee from the kitchen below, sharp and a little burnt.

Neil sat on the edge of his bunk, lacing and unlacing his sneakers for the fifth time, his stomach tied in impossible knots.

Across the room, Cade sat upright, still in his sunglasses, bandages snug beneath. He stretched, raked a hand through his messy blond hair, and said lightly, almost too lightly:

"So... today's the day."

Neil swallowed. "Yeah. Today."

Cade turned toward his voice. "You nervous?"

Neil barked out a laugh that landed harsher than he meant. "Me? Why would I be nervous? You're the one about to—" He cut himself short, teetering too close to the truth. "You're the one getting out of vision jail."

Cade grinned. "Exactly. And the first thing I get to see is you."

Neil's heart slammed so hard it felt like everyone else in the hostel must've heard.

Cade reached up, fingers brushing the edge of the bandages. "I figure it's better to do it here—one clean moment instead of when we're rattling on a train with everyone watching."

Neil nodded quickly, then realized Cade couldn't see him. His throat worked. "Yeah. Let's do it before the sun gets too bright so that you can adjust. You're probably still gonna want the sunglasses while the sun is up, at least for the first few days."

For a beat, neither of them moved. Around them, classmates thumped duffels down the hall, teachers barked names like drill sergeants, and Paris called one last time through the open windows.

Then Cade's voice dipped, softer. "Neil?"

"Yeah?"

"Whatever happens when I take these off... don't disappear on me, okay?"

Neil froze. His chest went tight. "I—what? Why would I disappear?"

"Because sometimes," Cade said, fingers tightening around the frames of his sunglasses, "when the lights come on, people scatter. I don't want that with you."

Neil's throat closed, but somehow he managed: "You're describing a cockroach. Just don't smash me like one. I'm not going anywhere."

Cade smiled. "Good."

"*And* never say '6-7,' like you're one of your soccer lads," Neil said. "Then I'd have to take the L." Neil laughed, followed by Cade's snort.

"I'll save it for the locker room, then," Cade responded. "Okay, enough talking... let's get it on."

As if in slow motion, he lifted the glasses away and peeled the gauze pads loose, one trembling strip at a time.

Neil held his breath. His own palms were damp, gripping his knees. This was it.

Cade's lashes fluttered furiously as the light hit, eyes watering and red. He squinted against the brightness, blinking rapidly, as shapes swam into focus.

Neil shielded Cade from the sunlight streaming in

through the window with his hands.

And then—finally—Cade's gaze steadied on Neil.

A silence stretched, long enough that Neil's heart began to sink with every second Cade didn't speak. This was it, he thought. The moment of disappointment. The moment Cade would realize he'd wasted his trust.

But then Cade smiled. Slow. Certain.

"There you are," he said.

Neil's breath caught. "You're... not surprised? I mean, your vision—there are some broken vessels. Your eyes must be susceptible to light—"

Cade shook his head, eyes softening. "I told you. I remembered you. And yeah, I remembered you a little differently. Taller, maybe. But I like this version better." He paused, gaze steady now. "I like you better."

The tightness in Neil's chest released, like a dam breaking. "You... *like* me?"

"I kissed you under the Eiffel Tower, Neil." Cade's grin tilted wider. "Did you really think that was a rental moment?"

Neil let out a shaky laugh, air rushing back into his lungs. "I just didn't know if you'd still feel the same once you saw me. It makes everything so much more... real when you're looking at me."

Cade leaned forward until Neil could feel his warmth. His voice was low, meant only for him. "Trust me. Seeing you only makes it worse."

Neil laughed. "Worse?"

"In the best possible way," Cade scrambled. What he wanted to say and chickened out on was that it made his longing for Neil worse. "You know what I mean. Could I maybe get a hello kiss?" he suggested.

Neil kissed him.

"Well, hello," Neil said.

"Hi." Cade smiled, his mouth pressed to Neil's.

Cade got his hello kiss just as mayhem broke loose in the hallway.

Outside, someone shouted that the bus was loading. Backpacks thudded, doors slammed, and the world lurched forward. But inside the hostel room, Neil couldn't look anywhere else. For the first time, Cade Riley's eyes were looking right at him—blue, bright, and uncovered, with a busted vessel that made part of his left eye an evil red.

And it felt like the start of something bigger than either of them had planned for.

The train lurched forward, Paris slipping away in a

blur of rooftops and chimneys. Neil slid into a window seat, still dazed, his mind replaying every second of Cade's smile when the bandages came off.

"Here," Neil said, fumbling for words. "Wear my sunglasses. They're darker."

Cade dropped into the seat beside him, stretching his legs like he owned the whole row. His eyes—newly free, newly alive—kept flicking back to Neil, like he couldn't stop memorizing him.

They'd barely settled in when Cade's usual crew appeared in the aisle, loud and laughing, arms full of snacks and cards.

"Riley!" Savannah Holt called, grinning. "Come sit with us—we've got this giant can of Pringles, and we're going to play poker. Poker...chips. Get it?"

Neil's stomach sank. Of course. This was probably where Cade slipped back out of his orbit, back to the world where Neil didn't belong.

But Cade just leaned back, easy as anything, and waved them off. "I'll catch up later, alright? I'm good here."

Savannah blinked, then shrugged. "Okay." They drifted down the car, already laughing again with her friend, Ava.

Neil turned, startled. "You didn't have to—"

"Yeah, I did," Cade interrupted. His eyes held steady on Neil's. "I want to be here... with you."

Heat rushed up Neil's neck. He didn't fight it. He let himself smile—helpless, wide, deliriously happy. On a seemingly endless loop, Neil played it over and over in his head that Cade would rather spend time with him. He could have had all of them, but he chose just one, Neil Erickson, instead.

The train rattled on, countryside blurring past. Cade had tipped his head back against the seat, sunglasses hiding the worst of the glare, but every so often Neil caught him peeking over the rims—quick, certain looks like he was still memorizing him.

"Neil, here's that photo I was telling you about," Cade said as Neil sat closer to see Cade's phone.

"Aw, look at how cute little Cade was! Your hair was so dark, and you've definitely spent a lot of time in the gym since year eight," Neil said teasingly. "And you were so thin. Now you're jacked!"

"Cute in the past tense? Really, Neil. And yeah, I was fourteen and couldn't put on weight back then."

"I mean, now I wish I had known that guy a little better."

Cade smiled and looked at Neil, who was still smiling at his phone.

Neil's smile hadn't faded since Cade waved off his crew. He felt loose in his seat, lighter, like the whole train was carrying him somewhere he actually wanted to go.

But the feeling came with an ache too, sharp under the ribs. Because Paris was already behind them, and Nashville—school hallways, whispered jokes, cafeteria politics—was ahead.

He shifted, staring out of the window at the blur of fields. "Hey, Cade?"

"Yeah?"

Neil hesitated, words snagging. "What happens when we get back? To Nashville, I mean."

Cade turned his head toward him, expression unreadable behind the shades. "What do you mean?"

"I mean..." Neil swallowed. "This trip—it feels... safe. Like we're in this bubble. But once we're back? People aren't going to just... look the other way."

For a beat, Cade was quiet. Then he leaned his elbow on the armrest, angled toward Neil. "Honestly, I've been thinking about that, too." His grin softened. "Neil, I kissed you under the Eiffel Tower. I don't exactly do 'secret' very well. It's going to get out. Will you be okay with that?"

"I'm just not used to making a spectacle of myself," Neil muttered, heat creeping up his neck.

Cade reached out, fingers brushing Neil's wrist. "Seriously?" Gentle. Grounding. "Look, I can't promise it won't be messy. But I can promise I won't ditch you when the bubble pops. You kept me steady when I couldn't even see where I was going. I don't want you to think that I'm walking away now that I can."

Neil's breath snagged. Relief and fear tangled in his chest, fighting for space. He wanted to believe Cade. God, he did. But Nashville wasn't Paris. Nashville remembered every rumor, every mistake, every secret.

Still, with Cade's fingers warm against his wrist, Neil found himself nodding. "Okay," he whispered.

"Okay," Cade echoed, his grin breaking wider. "Now, quit stressing. You're ruining my dramatic French countryside vibe."

Neil huffed a laugh, the tension loosening—just a little.

But as the train carried them toward the next city, Neil couldn't shake the question pressing at the edges of his mind: What if Nashville wasn't ready for them?

And what if they weren't ready for Nashville?

Chapter Eight.

The promenade along Lake Geneva was obnoxiously picturesque—water glittering like someone spilled a bag of sequins, boats bobbing politely, and the French Alps doing their best impression of a desktop screensaver. Meanwhile, a flock of Gen Alpha tourists practiced TikTok dances dangerously close to the water.

At a wrought-iron bench overlooking the lake, four of the Fab Five gathered like a panel of judges ready to dock points from his life choices.

Jenna arrived first, striding down the promenade like she was late for a training montage. Her sunglasses were athletic, pink, and aerodynamic, and her braid swung like a weapon.

She dropped onto the bench just as Sophie dropped in. "We've been in Europe four days, and Neil has ditched us for... what... ninety percent of it?"

Sophie was in a flowy dress, a cardigan tied around her shoulders, giving off the vibe of a girl who constantly writes in a journal. "He's with Cade," she said, as if delivering a prophecy. "Again."

Jenna frowned. "Yes. We know. It's his default setting now."

Mads rolled up—because of course she'd found a way to longboard through Switzerland—hood up, sleeves pushed to the elbows, hair a little wind-destroyed. She kicked the board up with practiced flair.

"How was Neil on the boat ride?" asked Jenna.

"He skipped the boat ride," Mads announced, scandalized. "THE boat ride. Across Lake Geneva. Literally main-character behavior denied."

"He skipped gelato," Jenna added. "That's how I know Cade has fully infiltrated his brainstem."

Then came **Kip**, tottering toward them with his messenger bag slung crossbody and a lavender scarf fluttering behind him. He wore it with unshakeable confidence—and zero awareness that the entire aesthetic was aggressively not straight.

He sat delicately on the bench, knees together, smoothing his scarf like a couture runway model before clearing his throat.

"So," he said dramatically, "I'm not gossiping, because obviously I don't gossip—"

All three girls gave him a synchronized look.

"But," Kip continued, undeterred, "I feel like we should address the Neil situation."

Jenna groaned. "Ugh, so we are in solidarity."

Kip raised a finger, as if delivering a TED Talk titled "The Emotional Mismanagement of My Best Friend."

"I'm just saying," he continued, "Cade Riley is a force. He's like... like if a golden retriever became a Disney prince. Too charming. Too sparkly. Distracting."

He twirled his scarf meaningfully.

"Kip," Sophie said, "you are literally sparkling right now, kween."

"It's the Swiss humidity," Kip said primly. "And I'm straight, and a king."

"Sure, babe," Mads murmured, patting his knee. "So is spaghetti... until it cooks."

Kip sniffed. "Style has no sexuality."

Jenna pointed her smoothie straw at him. "Right. But you do realize you just said 'style has no sexuality' with jazz hands?"

Kip glared at his hands as if they'd betrayed him.

Sophie sighed dreamily, turning her attention back to the lake. "Personally, I think Cade is good for Neil. They look happy. Like... cheesy, postcard-of-Lake-Geneva happy."

Mads nodded. "I caught them sharing one pair of earbuds yesterday. One pair. That's basically swapping DNA."

Jenna made a strangled sound. "Okay, ew, and also yes."

Kip wrung his scarf as if it were wringing out emotional distress. "I just worry he's... replacing us."

Sophie softened. "Neil would never replace us."

"He doesn't even delete old notes on his phone," Mads added. "You think he can delete people?"

Jenna rolled her eyes but couldn't quite hide her smile. "Fine. Okay. I miss him. But I'm glad he's happy."

Kip exhaled dramatically, like a diva concluding a performance. "Well. As long as we're all in agreement."

They weren't.

But they were, in the way friend groups are—loud, chaotic, loyal, and entirely too invested in each other's relationships.

Fever Dream by mxmtoon played in the collective of the friend group as attention turned to the lakeshore, a distant shout echoed—Cade's voice.

The friends turned toward the sound.

There was Neil, jogging along the water, smiling so wide he looked like he might ascend.

Cade was trailing after him like the world's most enthusiastic golden retriever.

Kip gasped. "Oh, my God. Look at them. They're cute," he said with a hard stop.

Jenna groaned. "Ugh. They really are."

Mads smirked. "Aww. Let him cook, y'all."

Sophie clasped her hands to her chest. "I love love."

Kip adjusted his lavender scarf with a flourish. "I, *a straight man*, can appreciate aesthetics. And that? Is art."

Neil appeared out of breath as he jogged up the sand toward his friends. "Hey!"

THUD.

Cade tackled him in a full-body hug that sent both of them into a wobble.

"Oh! Okay, then," Sophie said, stepping neatly out of the splash zone. "Hi."

"Being friends with Neil isn't usually a contact sport," Mads added, sipping her drink like she was watching a nature documentary.

"Sorry," Neil wheezed. "Cade, you probably know everyone already. Jenna, Sophie, Mads... and Kip."

"Hi, Cade," Jenna said, eyebrow arching in appraisal.

"It is a pleasure to make your acquaintance," Kip announced, voice formal enough to belong at a royal coronation.

Cade blinked. "Yeah, you too. Hi, everyone." He paused with a look on his face of curiosity. "What's that sound?"

"What sound?" Jenna asked.

"It's like a click...more like a music box click."

"Oh!" Sophie said suddenly. She reached into her pocket and pulled out a mechanical pillbox timer. "It reminds me to take meds. How did you hear that? It is designed just to tap me and stay silent. It didn't even do that until after you mentioned it."

"I don't know. Just did." He pointed up the beach. "There's a bocce court up there—anyone play?"

"No," they all said in perfect, unimpressed unison.

Even the seagulls seemed to pause, offended on the bocce's behalf.

Sophie smiled really big, looked at Neil, and tilted her head. "Did anyone else witness that? Just me? Is Cade *actually* Superman?"

Chapter Nine.

Sophie McCallister

At age nine, the brown-wavy-haired and brown-eyed Saul Radford lived a simple, happy life in Tullahoma, Tennessee, an hour south of Nashville. He was a bright kid with a backyard full of cousins, a stay-at-home mom who adored him, and a father who worked long shifts at the factory but always made time for Friday-night barbecue. Nothing in their world seemed complicated.

Until the day everything quietly changed.

It was supposed to be a quick stop at the Tullahoma Mall. Marsha Radford had taken Saul to Belk's so he could look at new sneakers. She turned her back for ten seconds—maybe less—and when she looked again, he was gone. Panic hit first. She marched straight to the customer service desk, ready to have him paged over the intercom.

But before the clerk could even reach for the phone, Marsha spotted him.

Not in the boys' section.

Saul—still small, still soft-faced—stood in front of a mirror in girls' clothing. A training bra over his T-shirt. A flowy top. Skinny jeans rolled at the ankle. He was holding up a sparkly headband, swaying a little as he softly sang *Shake It Off* under his breath.

Something in Marsha went still.

Something in her finally made sense, too.

She didn't scold him. She didn't rush him away. She just stood there, heart breaking open in a way she didn't yet have words for.

A few weeks later, after a handful of quiet drives to a therapist in Nashville—appointments scheduled under vague excuses, tucked into the quiet hours of midafternoon—Saul sat beside her in the parked car, legs swinging, and said softly:

"I think I want to be Sophie."

Marsha nodded, breath catching. "Okay," she whispered. "Then Sophie it is."

They sat there awhile before she said, "Can we keep

this between us for a little while, baby? Just until we figure out how to keep you safe? The world can be… unkind. But I want you to always be happy and exactly who you are."

Sophie nodded. "Sure, Mom."

But secrets don't stay secrets long in small towns.

Dan Radford was the first to notice the changes. The clothes. The mannerisms. The brightness. And then the tension settled in their house like thick humidity—dense, choking, unavoidable. Marsha knew she had to act. Tullahoma wasn't safe. Not for Sophie. And not for a mother who dared to support her.

As fate—or maybe mercy—would have it, the inheritance Marsha's grandparents left her sat untouched in an account under her name only. It had been meant for Saul's college fund. But survival, she realized, mattered more urgently than the future.

With the help of Sophie's therapist and every resource she could gather, Marsha made a plan. A new start. A new name. A new city.

Nashville.

They left quietly. No one had to know about Saul. In Nashville, her daughter could simply be Sophie—no explanation, no argument, no shadow cast by who she had been before.

Dan didn't fight for custody in the divorce. He didn't fight for anything at all. When Marsha offered to waive child support if he let them leave freely, he agreed without question. By the time the papers were finalized, he had already begun fading into a distant memory.

Years later, Marsha met a dentist named Herby McCallister, a man with a warm laugh and gentler heart, who didn't just accept Sophie—he cherished her. He learned her story without flinching. He asked what she needed, rather than assuming. Eventually, he adopted her, and Sophie Radford became Sophie McCallister.

Their family was small, but the world inside it felt enormous: Marsha, Herby, and Sophie. A unit built on resilience, not secrecy.

Public school, however, was brutal in ways resilience couldn't always fix. Even with her quiet nature and her ability to pass without scrutiny, the hallways felt like a battlefield. When Sophie was fifteen, they found a solution in Penderton Academy—a private school that prized academics, offered structure, and kept athletes and scholars largely separated until senior year. It was the first place Sophie breathed easily in every corner of her life.

Penderton also gave her friendships that felt like anchors.

On day one, she met Madison Chandler—"Mads"—within minutes, who welcomed her with the chaotic warmth of a sister she didn't know she needed. Through Mads, she met Neil Erickson, who came out in his sophomore year and did so with more bravery than he believed he had. Through Neil came Jenna Frist, and then Kip Wendell, who hadn't quite settled on one label and didn't see why he needed to. They became Sophie's people. The group went from the Fab Four to the Fab Five with her as their newest member. Her safety net.

Now, nearly eighteen, Sophie found herself facing a new question—one she wasn't sure she dared to say aloud:

What does my future look like?

Her friends knew her story. They held it gently. They never pressed, never pried. And Sophie rarely brought it up because talking about it always felt like pulling open stitches she had spent years learning to close.

Passing wasn't just about appearance—it was a kind of invisibility she relied on. Sophie stayed quiet, observant, and careful. The fewer eyes on her, the safer she felt.

But senior year cracked that shell in ways she didn't expect.

There was a homecoming. And prom. And all the

rituals she had watched from a distance, yearning for something normal—something hers.

And then there was AJ.

AJ Collins, varsity soccer forward, golden-boy smile, the kind of effortless charisma that made people look twice, even when he wasn't trying. Sophie had convinced herself she had zero chance with someone like him. He wasn't even on her radar socially—athletes rarely were— but somehow AJ kept showing up: a held door, a shared joke in Chemistry, a smile that lingered longer than it should have.

Her friends had no idea. Not Mads. Not Neil. Not even Kip, who noticed everything. Sophie guarded the crush like something fragile and shimmering, afraid the world would crush it before it ever had a chance to breathe.

Senior year had brought her safety.

But it also brought possibility.

And possibility... was terrifying.

Chapter Ten.

Deeper into the alleys they wandered, until the noise of the crowds thinned into nothing but the sound of water licking stone. A single bridge arched over a narrow canal, lantern light flickering on its iron rail. Cade leaned against it, gazing out across the rippling dark.

Neil stood beside him, trying not to stare but failing. Now that Cade's eyes were uncovered, Neil found himself looking every chance he got. The blue irises were brighter than he remembered—clear and sharp, like they carried all the light Paris had spilled into them.

"You keep looking at me," Cade said suddenly, a teasing smile tugging at his mouth.

Neil flushed. "Sorry. I just..." He hesitated, tripping over his words. "I really like seeing your eyes. After all that time... I didn't realize how much I would like seeing them."

With his smile softening, Cade turned toward him. "Oh, really?"

"Yeah," Neil admitted, "it feels like it was longer than four days, like something was... unfinished." His voice dropped. "They suit you more than I imagined."

Cade blinked, the teasing gone. "You imagined me?"

Neil froze, then gave a shaky laugh. "You were kind of hard not to imagine."

For a moment, Cade just looked at him, the lantern light flickering across his face, eyes catching every bit of gold from the canal. Then, slowly, he reached over and brushed his fingers against Neil's hand on the rail.

"Well... you don't have to imagine anymore," Cade said quietly.

Neil's heart stuttered, Venice shimmering around them like a secret kept just for the two of them.

They stayed on the bridge longer than they probably should have, leaning side by side while the water shifted quietly beneath them. A gondola drifted past in the dark, its lantern glowing like a firefly, and the gondolier sang in a sentimental croon. Neil felt Cade's fingers still brushing against his, tentative but steady, like he was testing the idea of holding on. Finally, Neil reached for Cade's hand, his pulse jumping but not letting him pull away.

Cade smiled, eyes flicking down at their hands, then back up to Neil. "See? Even better when I can actually look at you."

Neil's laugh came out small and breathless. "You're going to make me self-conscious."

"Good," Cade said softly, leaning just a little closer. "Means you're paying attention."

They stood there in the hush of Venice, so close that Neil could feel Cade's warmth through the cool night air. His chest tightened with the weight of all the things he wanted to say but couldn't. How he'd dreaded this moment, terrified Cade wouldn't feel the same after he could see him. How, instead, Cade was looking at him like he'd been waiting for this all along.

Cade tilted his head, voice low. "Can I kiss you again? You know—without the Eiffel Tower stealing all the credit this time?"

Neil couldn't find his voice, so he just nodded.

The kiss was slower this time, deliberate, without the shield of spectacle or a glittering tower to distract them. Just lips meeting under the lantern glow, water rippling beneath their feet, the city holding its breath.

When they pulled back, Neil's heart was hammering, but Cade's hand was still tangled in his.

"Better," Cade whispered, smiling against the quiet.

Neil's throat tightened. "Yeah," he managed. "Better."

Neil realized he wasn't just seeing Venice. He was living it—here, with Cade, in a way no postcard or travel guide could've prepared him for.

The kiss lingered, slow and steady, until Neil forgot where he was—forgot the group, the trip, everything but the press of Cade's lips and the warmth of his hand.

Then, footsteps scuffed against the stone at the end of the bridge. A burst of laughter. Voices they recognized.

Neil and Cade broke apart fast, though their hands stayed tangled between them.

Two classmates rounded the corner, giggling, mid-story, then stopped short when they spotted the boys under the lantern light. "Ohhh," one of them drawled, grinning. "Well, well. Looks like Riley found his tour guide bonus package."

The other snickered. "Should we leave you two lovebirds alone?"

Cade didn't flinch. He just raised their joined hands slightly, smiling casually if anything. "Yeah, you probably should."

The classmates blinked, half expecting him to laugh it off, then shook their heads and wandered on, still giggling but losing interest.

Neil's pulse was still racing, his face hot, but Cade only looked at him, grinning. "See? Not even embarrassed."

Neil swallowed, heart thudding. "I am."

Cade squeezed his hand. "Well, I'm not."

The footsteps faded, leaving the canal quiet again. And though the spell had been broken, Neil couldn't stop smiling because Cade hadn't denied it. He hadn't laughed it off. He'd chosen him, even with an audience.

"I'm still figuring out what kind of man you are, Cade."

"Forget that. What kind of man do you need?"

Neil automatically swooned.

Chapter Eleven.

By the time Neil made it down to the hostel breakfast room, the smell of espresso and warm bread couldn't disguise the low whispers. Heads tilted. Eyes flicked his way. A couple of classmates at the far table snickered outright, one of them making a dramatic kissy face before dissolving into laughter.

Neil froze in the doorway, tray wobbling in his hands.

Cade, already halfway through a croissant, waved him over. "Hey, Erickson. Over here."

Neil slid into the chair across from him, trying to ignore the dozen pairs of eyes tracking their every move.

He leaned in with an ambivalent smirk. "They know."

Cade raised an eyebrow, calm as anything. "Of course, they know. We kissed on a bridge in Venice, not on Mars."

Neil groaned, dropping his face into his hands. "This is a nightmare."

"Nightmare?" Cade grinned, tearing off another bite of croissant. "Looks more like free breakfast entertainment."

Neil shot him a look, panicked. "You're not embarrassed?"

"Embarrassed?" Cade leaned back, stretching. "I finally got the guy I wanted to kiss. If they want to gossip, let them. Saves me the trouble of announcing it."

A hush fell over the room for half a second as his voice carried, and then the whispering started up again, louder this time, like bees stirred from a hive.

Neil's pulse skittered, but Cade just smirked, finishing his croissant like nothing was wrong.

"Relax," he said, his voice softer now, his eyes meeting Neil's across the table. "They'll find something else to gossip about by lunch. Trust me."

And the strangest part?

Neil almost believed him.

Neil was halfway through stirring sugar into his

coffee when a shadow fell across the table.

"Riley."

Neil looked up. One of Cade's closest soccer buddies, Tyler Haskins, stood there with arms crossed, the kind of stance that promised nothing good. Two more of Cade's crew lingered behind Tyler, watching with smirks that didn't quite reach their eyes.

Cade didn't even flinch. "Morning, Ty. Croissant?"

Tyler ignored the offer. His gaze flicked from Cade to Neil, sharp. "What's this?"

Cade tilted his head. "Breakfast?"

"You know what I mean." Tyler's voice was low, but not low enough. A couple of kids at the next table had already tuned in. "Four days in bandages, and suddenly you're glued to Erickson like he's your whole world? What is going on, man?"

Neil's throat went dry.

Cade sat back, calm but firm. "What happened is, you guys vanished when I needed you. Neil didn't. End of story."

"That's not fair," Tyler shot back. "We figured you needed space. And now you're—what? With him?" He jerked his chin toward Neil. "Since when?"

Neil wanted to sink through the floor. His ears burned, his pulse loud in his chest. He started to get up, but Cade stopped him.

Cade didn't look away. "Since Montreux," he said simply. "Maybe before that. Doesn't matter. What matters is, yeah—he's the one I want to be with. Don't worry about it."

A murmur rippled through the room. Neil nearly choked on his coffee.

Tyler blinked, like he'd been expecting a laugh, a denial, or some clever dodge. Instead, he got the truth, plain and unapologetic.

"Wow," Tyler finally said, shaking his head. "Guess you've changed, man."

"Guess I have," Cade said. "And I like it."

Tyler hesitated, then stalked off, his entourage trailing behind him.

The whispers around the room swelled again, but Neil barely heard them. He was still frozen in place, Cade's words ringing in his ears.

He's the one I want to be with.

The whispers still lingered in Neil's ears long after Tyler and his crew drifted off. Breakfast blurred into noise—chairs scraping, plates clattering, kids snickering at things he couldn't quite catch.

Cade finished his croissant as if nothing had

happened. Then he leaned across the table and said, "Do you want to get out of here?"

"Yeah, sure."

They slipped down a back hallway that opened onto the hostel's narrow courtyard. Potted geraniums lined the walls, and laundry hung overhead, swaying in the breeze. It was quiet, mercifully private.

Neil sank onto a stone bench, pressing his palms to his knees. "Why'd you do that?"

Cade leaned against the wall, folding his arms. "Do what?"

"Say all that. In front of everyone. Tyler practically announced it to the whole school."

Cade shrugged. "Because it's true."

Neil's chest tightened. "You made it sound so simple. Like it's nothing, Cade. They're all going to talk. They're already talking."

"Let them," Cade said evenly. He pushed off the wall and crossed the courtyard, stopping right in front of Neil. "You think I care what they say? After four days with bandages on, you really think I'm going to waste time worrying about people who didn't bother to check in on me? I mean—they caused that accident."

Neil blinked up at him, startled by the intensity in his voice.

Cade crouched down so they were at eye level. "I meant it. You're the one I want to be with. I don't care who knows."

Neil's breath hitched. "You can't just say things like that—"

"Why not?" Cade asked, softer now. "Because you don't believe me? Or because you're afraid you might feel that way too?"

Neil's throat worked, but no words came. Cade reached out, covering his hand where it rested on his knee. Warm. Steady.

"Neil," he said quietly, "I chose you. That's not changing. Gossip or no gossip."

Neil stared at him, heart pounding, and let himself believe it, knowing that the bullies weren't coming for Cade. They were coming for him.

Chapter Twelve.

By the time the train clattered south into Italy, the worst of the morning's gossip had fizzled into whispers. Most of their classmates were too busy swapping snacks and gossiping to keep the rumor mill spinning about Cade and Neil.

Neil, though, still felt the weight of eyes whenever he and Cade passed down the aisle.

So when Cade suggested they ditch the noise for the dining car, Neil didn't argue.

The dining car was dim and oddly elegant—white tablecloths, brass fixtures, and the faint smell of coffee and tomato sauce clinging to the air. The two of them slid into a booth.

A waiter approached, rattling off a greeting in rapid Italian. Without thinking, Neil answered him back in Italian just as quickly, his accent sharp and sure. He ordered water, pasta, and bread, two espressos with the usual request of two sugars each plus separate foam, then thanked him with a nod.

Cade blinked. "Okay, wait. What was that?"

Neil looked down at the menu, suddenly sheepish. "Uh. Italian."

"No kidding," Cade said, eyes wide. "Since when do you speak fluent food poetry?"

"I'm proficient, not fluent," Neil muttered, fiddling with his fork. "I just... took it for four years. I practice sometimes at home. My mom is Italian. Helps me feel like I'm somewhere else when I'm stuck in Nashville."

Neil drew leaf art on Cade's espresso foam for him before preparing his own.

"Thank you." Cade leaned forward, grinning. "Neil Erickson, secret Italian speaker. This trip keeps getting better."

"Don't make it a big deal. It's just... Italian mother meets Italian language classes since eighth grade."

"Too late." Cade shook his head, still smiling. "Seriously—hearing you speak it? It's... I don't know. Hot."

Neil nearly choked on his water. "Hot?"

"Yeah." Cade shrugged, unapologetic. "Guess I've got a thing for guys who can make spaghetti sound like a love song."

Neil pressed his lips together, trying not to laugh, but the warmth creeping up his neck gave him away.

And for a while, as the train carried them deeper into Italy, with pasta on the way and the countryside flashing through the windows, it felt like the gossip and the teachers and all the noise outside their booth had fallen away.

Just Neil. Just Cade. And a language that suddenly didn't feel like an escape anymore—just another way of being seen.

The train rolled into Florence just as the sky was sliding into evening. The students spilled out onto the platform in a noisy wave, but Neil barely heard them—his eyes were on the skyline.

The Duomo rose above the city like something out of a dream, its red-tiled dome glowing in the last light. Narrow streets fanned out in every direction, lined with shuttered windows, the smell of baking bread and roasted garlic drifting through the air.

The group made its way to a small hotel near the Arno

River, where the teachers herded everyone upstairs and issued warnings about curfews. By the time Neil and Cade slipped back out, the streets were strung with lights, the city alive with voices and music drifting from piazzas.

They wandered to the Ponte Vecchio, Cade leaned against the railing, gazing out. "Venice was unreal. Paris was magic. But this..." He trailed off, shaking his head. "This feels different. Like I've been here before in a dream."

Neil stood beside him, close enough to feel the warmth radiating from his arm. "I've wanted to see Florence my whole life," he admitted. "But I never thought I'd be standing here."

Cade turned, eyes catching the light, and for a moment, Neil released his breath in a forced way.

"What is your connection to this Florence?" Cade asked.

"It's," Neil paused. "Private. Personal, I guess."

"Sounds interesting—almost scandalous," Cade teased.

Neil stopped to look across the water where he recognized the Hotel degli Orafi. He did not turn to look at Cade. "It's not private because it's scandalous. It's private because it's mine," he said softly.

"Oh." Cade felt the boundary and respected it.

A violinist's notes drifted from somewhere down the street, soft and aching, performing Puccini: *O mio babbino caro.*

Cade's nervous fingers tapped the railing, restless. "Can I ask you something?"

Neil glanced at him. "Sure."

"What do you want—like, after this?" Cade's voice was quieter now, stripped of the usual teasing. "Not the trip. I mean, after graduation. Real life."

Neil blinked, caught off guard, and thought, *"I've seen the world so little—I felt so out of things in Italy. I have seen so little of life; one ought to come up to London more—not a cheap ticket like today, but to stop. I might even share a flat for a little with some other girl."*[1]

"Neil?"

"I... don't know. College, maybe. I've thought about studying languages. Or history. Something that gets me out of Nashville, anyway." He tried to laugh it off. "You?"

"Soccer, everyone assumes," Cade said, staring at the water. "But I don't know. Lately, I've been thinking maybe it's not about what I do, but who I'm with. Like, maybe that matters more."

[1] *A Room with a View,* E.M. Forster (Lucy Honeychurch)

Neil swooned internally. "That's... kind of big-picture for seventeen."

"Yeah, well," Cade said with a faint smile, "nearly losing your eyesight will do that to you."

Silence stretched, filled by the violin and by the murmur of voices on the far side of the bridge. Neil let his gaze drift to Cade's eyes again—clear, sharp, and alive. He thought of the days Cade had spent blindfolded, leaning on him, trusting him. And now, here in Florence, Cade was still looking at him like he was the only thing worth noticing.

Neil swallowed hard. "I've always wanted to see Florence, but it's better with you."

Cade turned, that same soft smile spreading. "Good. Because I don't want to imagine it without you."

The violin swelled, the lantern light flickered, and for a moment, the whole city seemed to hold its breath around them. Cade's hand brushed Neil's on the railing, but instead of taking it, he pulled back just enough to smile at Neil—a quiet promise.

"C'mon," he said. "Let's see what this city's hiding."

They slipped off the Ponte Vecchio and into the maze of streets, where the quiet canals gave way to noise and light. Piazza della Signoria burst open around them—cafés spilling out onto the cobblestones, voices echoing against centuries-old statues, the air rich with the scent of garlic and wine. Strings of lights hung overhead, and somewhere in the square, a band was playing something fast and bright that had people clapping in rhythm.

Their classmates were already there, scattered in clusters—some dancing, some snapping photos, some wolfing down local cuisine. A few noticed Cade and Neil entering together, eyes tracking them with the same curiosity that had followed since Venice.

But Cade didn't flinch. He steered them toward a trattoria at the edge of the square, pulling out a chair like he owned the place. "Sit. I'm starving. And you're going to order for us again, because of that Italian thing you did on the train? Still hot."

Neil groaned, face burning. "You're never letting that go, are you?"

"Nope," Cade said, grinning. "Not when I've got my own personal, incredibly cute translator."

The music swelled, laughter rose, and for a moment, Neil let himself sink into it—the lights, the noise, and the warm press of Florence at night.

With Cade across the table, watching him like he was part of the view, Neil realized it didn't matter what city they were in. As long as Cade kept looking at him like that, the rest of the world could spin however it wanted.

Chapter Thirteen.

Jenna Frist

University of Tennessee, Knoxville, on a Saturday
Last semester.

Jenna Frist had always been good at pretending she wasn't nervous—even when she absolutely was. She'd perfected the art over seventeen years: a deep inhale, a small toss of her hair, a tilt of her chin that said *I'm fine, obviously*. It worked on her parents, her friends, teachers, and even Neil, who usually saw through everyone.

But it did not work the moment she stepped onto the University of Tennessee campus for the Penderton–UT mentorship weekend and spotted Wyatt Cobey leaning against a folding table like he owned it.

He wasn't supposed to look like that.

Volunteers were supposed to be dorky overachievers. Wyatt... wasn't. Tall-ish, messy hair, sunburned nose, a smile that looked accidental and therefore lethal. He was wearing a faded UT T-shirt and a lanyard held together with duct tape.

When he handed her a pamphlet and a slice of free pizza, he said, "Hi. Welcome to the booth of Academic Chaos and Questionable Life Choices."

Jenna blinked. "I'm sorry—what?"

Wyatt shrugged like he didn't see the problem. "That's what this is. I'm just calling it what it is."

She tried not to laugh, but the corner of her mouth betrayed her. "Is that... official branding?"

"No, but I'm open to licensing deals."

She shouldn't have liked him already. But she did.

After the campus tours and the Q&A panel where someone's dad asked a fifteen-minute question about parking permits, Jenna drifted back to the volunteer booths. She told herself she wasn't looking for Wyatt—just taking a lap. Gathering information. Absorbing the vibe.

Wyatt spotted her first.

"You survived Parking Permit Guy," he said, handing her a cold bottle of water. "That's impressive. A lot of people don't come back from that."

She snorted before she could stop herself. "It was... educational."

"That's one word." Wyatt tossed his empty pizza plate into a recycling bin and then pointed at her name tag. "Jenna, right? Frist... from Nashville?"

"Brentwood," she corrected, then immediately regretted sounding like an admissions application.

"Oooh, fancy." He nodded, dead serious. "My roommate's from Brentwood. Guy ironed his bedsheets. I didn't know people did that."

"...Some people do," she said.

Wyatt grinned. "So, do you want the *not-boring* UT tour or what?"

She raised one eyebrow. "And what exactly makes your tour not boring?"

"I have a strong suspicion you might step in goose poop."

"Is that... supposed to be a selling point?"

"It's a character-building experience."

She laughed—actual, unfiltered laughing. The kind she didn't plan or square with an image.

"All right," she said. "Show me."

They walked across the lawns in the late-afternoon sun, his stride loose and unhurried, her steps a mixture of practiced confidence and the unfamiliar feeling of actually having fun. He pointed out buildings, professors, and shortcuts that were probably technically illegal.

At one point, he stopped at a patch of grass near the riverwalk. "This," he said dramatically, "is where my freshman roommate tried to grill chicken on a laptop."

Jenna blinked. "...Your—sorry, what?"

"Laptop. Grilled chicken. The fire department came."

She burst out laughing. "Oh, my God. Is he okay?"

"He's a business major. So... *unclear*."

They walked farther; they talked about everything and nothing. Tennis. Music. How she color-codes her planner. How he once tried to do laundry with dish soap and caused what he called "a small, festive avalanche, possibly a rave."

He didn't ask her what her GPA was, where else she was applying, or what her five-year plan looked like. He didn't treat her like one of the high-achieving kids he was supposed to impress.

He treated her like a person.

And Jenna, who spent so much of her life being the right version of herself, suddenly felt like she could just be herself.

As the sun dropped behind Ayres Hall, they lingered at the overlook, campus stretching below them in orange, gold, and the distant glow of Saturday-night football.

"So," Wyatt said, nudging her lightly, "would this place make your college spreadsheet?"

She smirked. "Maybe. Depends on whether laptop-grilled chicken is a common campus tradition."

"That was a one-time thing. Probably."

They stood side by side, quiet for a moment—comfortable in a way Jenna didn't often get to be.

She finally said, "Thanks for the tour. Really. It was... nice."

"'Nice'? Wow. Brutal review." He clutched his chest. "Crushed."

She rolled her eyes, fighting a smile. "Fine. It was good."

"Good? Devastating. You are a harsh critic."

She laughed, and then—because she was Jenna Frist and did not like being read too easily—she tried to retreat into sarcasm. But Wyatt looked at her right then, really looked, and something tightened in her chest.

"You know," he said quietly, "I'm glad you came back."

She swallowed. "Why?"

"Because you looked like someone who's always trying really hard not to look nervous." He shrugged. "I get that."

Jenna's breath hitched because nobody said things like that to her. Nobody noticed things like that about her.

Not unless they meant it and could back it up.

Wyatt glanced down at his phone, then back at her. "Here—if you ever want the sequel tour, text me." He handed his phone over. "I promise it involves less goose poop."

She took it before she could overthink, typed her number, and passed it back.

He looked at the screen, smiled, and slid it into his pocket. "Cool."

Cool. She almost hated how warm that word made her feel, at least when Wyatt said it.

That night, back on the Penderton bus, Jenna stared out the window as Knoxville's lights receded behind them. Neil and Sophie were arguing about who stole whose phone charger. Kip was reading something with the intensity of a NASA engineer. Mads was playing a game that involved a concerning amount of yelling at farm animals.

Jenna didn't hear any of it.

Her phone buzzed.

Wyatt
You made it out alive?

She typed back before stopping herself:

Jenna
Survived Parking Permit Guy and the
parking lot tour.

Three dots appeared.

Wyatt
So when's Part Two? I still need to show
you Cruze Family Ice Cream on South Gay Street

Her heart flipped.

Jenna Frist was used to planning everything. Mapping out her days, her years, her entire future. However, this boy with the sunburned nose and the easy laugh and the way he saw right through her—none of this was planned.

Jenna finally allowed herself to want something she didn't schedule, and his name might be Wyatt.

Chapter Fourteen.

Rome didn't arrive quietly—it exploded around them. The train deposited the Penderton seniors into a city of horns and scooters, with voices shouting from balconies, the air thick with heat and the smell of roasted chestnuts.

Neil's heart raced—not just from the sheer size of it, but because he'd been waiting for this moment. Rome. The city of emperors and ruins, of fountains and piazzas, the heart of everything he'd studied and daydreamed about.

"Okay," Cade said as they shuffled out into the plaza outside Termini station. "What's the plan, Safety Sidekick?"

Neil grinned despite himself. "The plan is... *when in Rome.*"

Cade looked at him, puzzled.

"Do as the Romans do. You've never heard that before?"

Neil proved it almost instantly. At a café stop, he chatted with the barista in easy Italian, ordering two cappuccinos and slipping into the language as if it were muscle memory. Cade watched, openly impressed.

"You just—switch," Cade said after the barista handed them their drinks. "Like a totally different Neil. It's... kind of wild."

Neil shrugged, embarrassed. "It's just practice."

"Uh, no," Cade corrected, leaning close. "It's amazing. Teach me something."

Neil blinked. "Like what?"

"Something useful. Something to make me sound less like a tourist who's about to get mugged."

Neil laughed, then relented. "Alright. Say: *Ciao, come stai?*"

"Chow... como... stay?" Cade tried, mangling it spectacularly.

Neil nearly spat out his cappuccino. "No, no—it's '*stai*,' like 'sty.' *Come stai?*"

"Styyyyy," Cade drawled, grinning. "Nailed it."

The waiter passing by chuckled at Cade's accent, muttering something in Italian that made Neil laugh harder.

"What'd he say?" Cade demanded.

"He said you sound like a lost opera singer."

Cade groaned, dropping his head into his hands. "Fantastic. Teach me another one. Something romantic this time. Impress me."

Neil hesitated, then leaned in. "*Sei bellissimo.*"

Cade raised an eyebrow. "What's that mean?"

"It means... you're handsome."

Cade's grin was immediate. "Now that's Italian I can use."

Neil's face burned as Cade repeated it back—bad accent and all—but the sincerity in his smile was undeniable through his beautiful Nashville accent.

And as Rome swirled around them—louder, hotter, and older than anything Neil had ever seen—he realized he didn't just want to see this city; he wanted to be a part of it and to share it with Cade.

They set off with the group, but it didn't take long for Cade and Neil to drift into their own orbit. Rome was a maze of alleys giving way to sudden piazzas, fountains bubbling like afterthoughts in courtyards far older than

America itself.

Neil couldn't help himself; he kept slipping into Italian whenever they stopped—asking for directions, buying bottled water, even haggling over postcards from a street vendor. Cade trailed behind him, watching as if he were seeing a whole new Neil come alive.

"Okay," Cade said as they reached the Colosseum, the stone arches looming massive against the sky. "Teach me how to say... uh... 'this place is insane.'"

Neil laughed. "*Questo posto è pazzesco.*" His eyes remained squarely on Cade's mouth.

"Questa pasta and pesto?" Cade tried.

Neil doubled over. "No! *Posto è pazzesco.*"

Cade grinned. "That's what I said."

"Not even close. You said something about noodles and basil in a jar of olive oil."

Later, they circled the Colosseum with the group, Neil tossing in bits of history—gladiators, emperors, the thousands of years under their feet. Cade pretended to listen, but mostly he was watching Neil's face, the way his eyes lit up as he talked.

By the Trevi Fountain, Cade demanded another phrase. "Something romantic. Something movie-worthy. You've seen this in a dozen films, right?"

Neil hesitated, then said softly, "*Vorrei baciarti.*"

Cade's smile turned wicked. "And that means...?"

Neil's ears burned. "It means... 'I'd like to kiss you.'"

Cade leaned in just enough to make Neil's pulse stutter. "Good to know."

At the Spanish Steps, Cade insisted on trying it out on a confused old woman selling roses, who laughed and corrected his pronunciation while Neil tried not to die of embarrassment. Cade just winked at him without an ounce of fear.

And as the sun slid low and painted Rome gold, Cade tugged Neil aside, away from the group, looking out over the rooftops. "You've got to stop teaching me this stuff," he said quietly. "Every time you do, I just want to use it on you."

Neil swallowed hard, the noise of the city fading under the weight of the moment until it felt like it was just the two of them standing above the city. Cade's full expression softened into something else—something quieter, heavier.

"You're doing that thing again," Neil murmured.

"What thing?"

"Looking at me like I'm... more than I am."

Cade tilted his head. "Maybe you are more than you think you are."

Before Neil could think of a reply, Cade closed the

space between them, his hand finding Neil's wrist, warm and steady. The kiss was softer than the one in Venice, less daring, and more certain—like Cade had been waiting for the right corner of the world to press his mouth to Neil's again.

The sounds of Rome spilled around them—voices echoing off stone, a Vespa rattling by, a singer in the distance belting out something dramatic in Italian—but Neil only felt Cade, only heard the rush of blood in his ears.

When they finally pulled back, Cade kept his eyes closed and his forehead against Neil's, whispering, *"Vorrei baciarti."*

Neil let out a shaky laugh. "You finally said it right."

"Good," Cade murmured, brushing his thumb against Neil's hand. "Maybe because I meant it."

Chapter Fifteen.

The train traveled south through the Italian countryside, morning light spilling over vineyards and olive groves. Most of their classmates were still dozing, but Neil sat rigid in his seat, staring at the blur of the window.

Rome had been dazzling. Overwhelming. But Naples—Napoli—was a new *different*.

Neil's family's city. His mother's family was from here.

He'd always carried Naples in his bones—but he'd never actually seen it, or at least not that he could remember. He was only a baby the last time he was here.

Beside him, Cade stretched, yawning like he hadn't a care in the world. "You're sitting like you're waiting for Santa Claus."

Neil laughed nervously. "It kind of feels like it. Just... personal."

Cade cocked his head. "Personal how?"

"My family's from there," Neil said, words tumbling out faster than he expected. "My great-grandparents grew up in Naples. They came over after the war, settled in New York, and then moved south. My dad says I got my stubborn streak straight from Naples." He smiled faintly. "Feels strange, going there for the first time as an almost-adult. Like meeting a part of myself I've only heard stories about."

Cade's teasing expression softened. "That's... huge, Neil. Like, way bigger than just sightseeing."

Neil nodded, throat tight. "Yeah. It is. Especially because I'm about to meet them for the first time since I was two years old."

"That's even bigger, Neil!"

Neil paused and then said, "You want to meet them?"

"Ugh, yeah!"

Neil smiled, "Yeah?"

"Guess I'll need my translator more than ever now. Lucky me."

Neil managed a smile, but his pulse raced. Rome had been magic. Venice had been dreamlike. But Naples—Naples was blood, history, and family.

Neil introduced Cade to his cousins, who had been given special permission from the school to pick him up for the day. He hesitated, then asked, "Do you want to come? I already cleared it with the chaperones. You can join us, and I packed some of your clothes."

"You're carrying my clothes in your bag?" Cade felt warm at the thought of Neil looking after him like that and smiled lovingly back at him.

"I mean, if you want to," Neil cautiously added.

The cousins overheard, clapping Cade on the shoulder like they'd already decided. "Of course! Family, family! You come!"

Cade laughed, letting himself get swept up.

They arrived at a bustling Casa de Giordano, filled with so many relatives that Neil couldn't keep track. The familiar kitchen aromas permeated through the entry, welcoming Neil home. Dinner was an eruption—platters of pasta, roasted fish, and bread still warm from the oven. Neil's cousins asked a million questions, slipping between Italian and broken English. At one point, an aunt leaned across the table, eyes sparkling as she pointed between Neil and Cade.

Neil blushed furiously, fumbling for words, but Cade just grinned.

"*Lui è il mio ragazzo, sì*", he repeated, glancing at Cade. "Yeah. He is."

"He is what?" Cade asked innocently while petting the family dog.

"They asked if you were my boyfriend. I hope it's okay that I said yes."

"*Sì, molto bene!* I am his boyfriend," Cade said excitedly to the dog.

The room erupted in cheers and laughter, and just like that, Cade was folded into the family. Most were impressed that Cade knew an Italian phrase, since it was the first he had spoken in the language since he had been there.

"What? I picked up a phrase or two," Cade said. "*Sì, cane?*" he said to the dog. Neil couldn't help but smile at Cade and then back at his aunt.

By the end of the night, Neil leaned back in his chair, pleasantly dizzy from pasta, wine, and the kind of affection he'd never quite learned how to brace for. Across the table, Cade was laughing with people he'd met only hours ago, already looking like he belonged to them—and they to him. Something warm and steady settled in Neil's chest.

The feast stretched late into the night, laughter spilling into the courtyard as coffee cups clinked and little glasses of limoncello made slow, joyful rounds. Neil felt full of food, of noise, of a kind of affection he hadn't expected to feel so quickly from people who had, in truth, only just met him.

At some point, Neil slipped out onto the narrow balcony to catch his breath. Naples spread out below, lights twinkling against the dark slope of Vesuvius in the distance. The night air was warm, thick with salt from the sea.

A moment later, Cade joined him, brushing past with a smile. "Your family is intense."

Neil laughed softly. "Yeah. That's the polite word for it."

"They adore you," Cade said, leaning against the railing beside him. "And... they are really nice to me. Like, I was worried I'd be the random American kid tagging along, but they treated me like..."

"Family," Neil finished.

"Yeah." Cade turned, eyes catching the glow of the street lamps. "That's been... really cool."

They stood in silence for a beat, listening to the city

sounds.

Neil swallowed, then said, "It means a lot, having you here. Sharing this with you. It feels almost like I've known you longer than a week."

Cade thought about reminding Neil of what he had so clearly forgotten years earlier, stumbling on what to say next, but then his hand found Neil's, warm and deliberate. "It means a lot that you wanted me here." He hesitated, then added, "I know we've only had a week, but—being with you? It feels like... home too."

As they explored the city, they passed Federico II University of Naples.

Oh Ma by Rocco Hunt played through one of Neil's earbuds.

"How cool would it be to go to university here?" Neil asked.

"I'd need better math scores," Cade said, but silently really enjoyed thinking about going to school in Italy if he could be with Neil and near his family.

"Maybe I can help you with that," Neil suggested.

"Yeah? I'd love that," Cade responded.

"I hope you are okay with attending a Catholic mass. We will be attending a small service in the morning before heading back to the cemetery. It won't be a long day, though."

Neil didn't feel particularly religious, but the rituals of his family's faith were all part of tradition, and he honestly wanted Cade to see it up close.

The basilica was alive with echoes.

Incense drifted upward in silver spirals, chandeliers glowed like distant stars, and the priest's Latin rolled against the marble walls like waves against a cliff. Neil slid into the pew beside Cade, cousins crowding the row around them. The wood was smooth from centuries of bodies kneeling and rising in practiced rhythm.

Neil crossed himself automatically, the sign clean and precise. His cousins followed suit, whispering the responses half a beat late. Cade, caught between them, shifted with uncertainty as a Protestant.

Neil leaned closer. "Just mirror me, if you want. There are no expectations," he murmured. "'I don't believe in this world-sorrow.'"[1]

The mass was in Latin. Cade's American boy features made it easy to forgive him for not knowing the rituals.

When the congregation rose, Neil stood fluidly, Cade copying a moment later. When they knelt, Neil guided him down, hands folding, head bowing. He whispered the responses softly, steady enough that Cade could

[1] *A Room with a View*, E.M. Forster (Lucy Honeychurch)

follow the cadence like a song he almost knew.

It felt strange, but good, to be the one leading. For once, Neil wasn't fumbling or apologizing—he belonged here, and he could carry Cade with him.

As the Mass built toward Communion, the cousins rose, shuffling into the aisle. His aunt shot Neil a look, as if to say, *"Are you staying?"*

Neil shook his head lightly, staying seated beside Cade.

"You're skipping?" Cade asked, low.

"It's etiquette," Neil said. "When you've got a guest who isn't Catholic, you stay with them. It's respectful."

Cade's brow furrowed, then softened. "That's... decent of you."

"It's a family tradition of respect."

Their cousins filed forward, heads bent, hands folded. Neil sat in the hush of the moment, shoulder brushing Cade's. The choir swelled, voices flooding the basilica in a wash of reverence.

The cousins returned, passing by Cade and Neil as they returned to the prayer benches, folding down from the pews ahead of them.

"You don't have to do this part, just lean forward so the people behind you aren't on your neck," Neil said as he knelt on the padded prayer bench with his family, clasping his hands and bowing his head in prayer. **"Dear God,** if you had anything to do with this, *thank you.*"

The candles flickered, casting a golden glow across Cade's profile as Neil glanced back, and for an instant, Neil felt something like peace—something holy, even. Meeting Cade was perhaps divine intervention.

When the cousins returned, one of them gave Neil a cute, quick eyebrow raise but let it drop. Sitting out wasn't shameful here—it was etiquette. It was a family signature.

Neil's chest loosened with relief. He had prayed not to be judged for it.

Cade leaned in, his voice barely audible under the music. "You make all of this Catholic choreography look easy."

Neil gave him a crooked half-smile. "The rituals? It's not. It hurts, and that's pretty much the point."

Cade looked at him, struck by the gravity of it—this boy he was falling for wasn't just Neil Erickson from Nashville. He carried whole centuries behind him, to be witnessed in his home country. Cade slipped his hand into Neil's, not caring who might see. "Guess I've got a lot to live up to, huh?"

Neil squeezed his hand back, steady and sure. "No. You just have to be you. That's enough."

Cade wanted the inner peace that he saw in Neil. He wanted to be part of it, but understood it wasn't religion that grounded him; it was his family and the rituals.

Neil hesitated, eyes glinting with something unspoken as he glanced at the names carved in stone. He found himself imagining not just his family's past but also its future—one that Cade might be part of some day.

Neil's cousins led them to a side chapel where slabs of stone marked graves with names etched in Latin, some dating back nearly four centuries. "You're related to all of these people?" Cade asked, brushing his fingers gently across one of the inscriptions, as though afraid to disturb whole centuries.

Neil nodded. "Every one of them. My blood's been here longer than most countries have even existed." He smiled faintly, though there was weight in his tone.

He studied Cade's profile against the chapel as his backdrop so that he could sketch it later in his book.

Chapter Sixteen.

Neil woke on a pull-out sofa to the clatter of dishes in the kitchen and the voices of cousins already arguing cheerfully over who made the better coffee. The sound echoed over the tile floors. For a moment, he didn't want to move. Naples wasn't just a city on a map anymore—it was faces, laughter, and warmth. A kind of belonging he hadn't known he'd been missing.

By the time he and Cade stepped into the kitchen, the table was already crowded with plates of pastries, ricotta drizzled with honey, and fruit piled high. His aunt kissed both his cheeks, then Cade's, as though he'd always been part of the family.

"Neil, you come back," she said in slow but clear English, pressing her hand to her chest. "This is... your house too." She pressed her palm to Neil's chest and then to Cade's.

Neil nodded, "*Grazie per tutto*. I will."

When they finally left, his family insisted on walking them to the hotel. Cade lugged his backpack, grinning as one of Neil's younger cousins kept peppering him with Italian phrases to repeat, all of which made the others howl with laughter.

At the hotel overhang, Neil's aunt caught his face in her hands and kissed his forehead. "*Sei un bravo ragazzo. Non dimenticare.*"

"What'd she say?" Cade asked once they stepped into the lobby.

Neil smiled faintly. "That I'm a good boy. And not to forget."

Cade studied him, then bumped his shoulder. "Did you tell her that you're **my** good boy?"

"Shush, you." Neil blushed through a smile but didn't turn away from Cade, bumping his shoulder.

When they rejoined the school group at the hotel later that afternoon, there were curious looks, teasing comments about Neil "ditching" for family time, and a few raised eyebrows at Cade for tagging along. Neil didn't feel defensive. He just smiled, shrugged, and let Cade throw an arm casually around the back of his chair during dinner as if to say, "Yeah, we were together."

Later that night, after the noise of the hotel dinner and the shuffle of students taking Instagram photos of their food and peeling off to their rooms, Neil and Cade slipped onto a quiet balcony overlooking the Naples streets.

Neil leaned against the railing, still processing the day. "I can't believe I finally met them," he said softly. "My mom used to tell me stories about those cousins like they lived on another planet. And now? They're just... real. Loud and affectionate and impossible to keep up with, but real."

Cade smiled. "They were crazy about you. I think I got, like, fifteen kisses just by being in the same room."

Neil laughed, then glanced sideways. "What about your family? You always make it sound like they've been in Tennessee since granite was magma."

Cade shrugged, pausing with a bit of discomfort. "Pretty much. My dad's side has been in West Meade since before Nashville was even Nashville. I think they called it The Cedar Bluffs back then. Antebellum family, old traditions, the whole thing. We even had a real plantation." Cade scrunched his face in discomfort. "I know that's not great, but apparently we were the shit about a hundred and fifty years ago."

Neil arched a brow. "So you're secretly Southern royalty like the... um... Beauregards?"

Cade smirked. "Descendants of John Harding, actually. You know the winery in Belle Meade?"

"Yeah," Neil answered.

"That was the family plantation. We have a family gathering there every few years. And if by 'royalty' you mean endless charity dinners, horse farms, and hearing my grandma say 'bless their heart' about people she absolutely hates, then yeah."

Neil grinned. "I'd pay money to see you in one of those bow ties they all wear."

"Don't," Cade groaned, tipping his head back. "I have trauma-bonded friends from the cotillions."

Neil nudged him with his shoulder, quieter now. "Still, it's still kind of cool in a historical way. Deep roots."

Cade glanced at him, expression softening. "Yeah. We are so cool that my family volunteered for a war that couldn't be won over a bullshit cause. Then there are expectations. Everyone had already decided what kind of Riley I'm supposed to be before I even got to choose.

You're so lucky to have a family that shows affection. No one in my family acts like they even like each other, and dinner is the quietest event you can imagine."

The words hung there between them. Neil felt the weight of them, the contrast to his own day of open-armed welcome.

He reached for Cade's hand and squeezed it. "Maybe this trip's about finding out who you want to be instead."

Cade's thumb brushed against his knuckles, a slight, grateful pressure. "Maybe it is. The truth is... West Meade sounds better on paper than it feels. Everyone knows your last name, your GPA, and the kind of car your dad drives. Feels like there's this mold you're supposed to fit into, and if you don't, you're just... disappointing the family tree."

Neil's grin faded into something gentler. "That's a lot."

"Yeah." Cade shrugged, his voice quiet.

Just as Cade squeezed his hand again, the balcony door creaked open.

"Neil?"

He startled, quickly letting go. His friend Chloe from the safety team poked her head out, her auburn hair frizzing in the night air. "I thought that was you. Didn't know you'd snuck off."

Neil exhaled, trying not to sound guilty. "Uh, hey,

Chloe. You know Cade, right?"

She smiled. "Oh, I know Cade. Everyone knows Cade. Hi, Mr. Soccer. How are the eyes?"

Cade chuckled, tipping his head. "Healing. Still feels weird sometimes, but I'll live."

"Good," she said warmly, then turned to Neil. "We've got a safety team meeting in the lobby in, like, ten minutes. Larkin wanted me to remind you."

Neil nodded, already scrambling for an excuse. "Yeah. Um... actually, I was hoping to stick with Cade tonight. Just in case, you know, his vision gets blurry when he walks back. The streets here can get crowded."

Chloe studied them for a moment, then smirked as if she saw through him. "Right. Sure. Well, tell the others you were on Cade duty. That'll play." She gave a little wave and slipped back inside. "I'll check back in with you tomorrow with my notes."

The door clicked shut, leaving them in silence.

Neil turned, wide-eyed, and Cade burst into laughter. "Oh my God, she totally knew."

Neil groaned. "We sounded so sketchy. Like we're hiding contraband."

Cade was still laughing, shoulders shaking. "Relax. Act like we just got away with something."

Neil couldn't help it—he started nervously laughing

too, the sound tumbling out of him until his stomach hurt. When it faded, they were left in the glow of the street lamps again, a little freer, a little lighter, like the world was secretly conspiring in their favor.

Cade smirked. "So what about your family?"

Neil grinned. "Well, I grew up in Green Hills. So... historic brick houses, professors mowing their lawns in khakis, and grad students drinking bad coffee at all hours."

Cade laughed. "That tracks. You've got the smart neighborhood energy. The kind that would actually read the community newsletter."

"No...," Neil said, grinning wider. "Okay, maybe once."

They both laughed, but the sound softened as Cade looked down over the railing, fingers drumming against the iron.

The city noises filled the pause. Neil reached out, brushing Cade's hand where it rested on the railing. "You don't have to live anyone else's script."

Cade looked at him, his expression caught between surprise and relief. "Yeah? And what if I don't even know what my own script looks like yet?"

Neil gave a small smile. "Maybe that's what this trip and university are for."

Cade leaned heavily against the railing, his voice turning wry. "Telling my dad I'm dating a boy should solve all of that."

Neil blinked, pulse skipping. He forced a light smile, playing along. "Oh, so you're dating a boy, are you? What's his name?"

Cade didn't miss a beat. He turned his head just enough, his eyes catching the glow from the streetlights. "Neil," he said quietly. "His name is Neil, and he's perfect."

"He must really be something." Neil's breath stopped. The city noise seemed to fade—the scooters, the laughter, even the clatter of dishes from inside. It was just Cade, saying his name like it was the only thing that mattered.

"You told your family I was your boyfriend, so that means you decided we were dating first."

Neil's humor faltered, his voice softer now. "You don't play fair."

Cade's smile curved slowly and with certainty. "I mean, it's working in my favor, so far."

145

Chapter Seventeen.

The train hugged the coastline, winding past cliffs that seemed to spill straight into the sea. The windows framed an endless expanse of cobalt water, dotted with white sails like careless brushstrokes. Neil pressed his forehead to the glass, grinning like a kid.

"Okay, I take it back," he said. "Italy's not real. Somebody painted this."

Across from him, Cade stretched his long legs into the aisle, sunglasses tipped down the bridge of his nose. "You said that in Venice."

"And Florence. And Rome," Neil admitted. "But this is worse. This is... like the travel brochure they'd never let you believe because it's too perfect."

Cade tilted his head, listening to the rumble of the train and the distant crash of surf whenever they dipped closer to the water. "Describe it for me."

Neil turned from the window, caught off guard. "What?"

"Describe it," Cade repeated, his voice low and deliberate. "Like you did in England and France. Pretend I can't see it." Cade closed his eyes.

For a moment, Neil forgot he had done that before, then let out a breath. Cade didn't need him to describe anything anymore—the bandages were gone, his vision intact. But he wanted Neil's voice anyway.

Neil swallowed, heart thudding, and said softly, "Alright. The water's so blue it looks like the sky flipped upside down. The houses on the cliffs are painted in colors you'd never think to put together—peach, lemon, that kind of old terracotta red. And somehow it works. And it smells like salt and sunshine and... I don't know..." he slowed his speech as he looked back at Cade with his eyes closed, wanting to kiss him, "...possibility?"

Cade smiled, leaning back with his eyes still closed. "See? Better than a guidebook."

Neil ducked his head, heat rising to his face. He wasn't sure if Cade meant the scenery—or him. Cade felt lucky. Neil felt grateful.

Neil sat silently, thumbing through his phone.

"What's going on over there? Your face is all scrunched up," Cade said.

"Is it? I just scrolled past one of Kyle's posts."

"Everything okay? Do I need to kick someone's ass?"

"Yeah." Neil paused. "I mean, I guess I know why he broke up with me."

"What's up?" Cade asked.

Neil turned the phone around and showed him a photo of two guys kissing with the caption:

kyle_of_art
2♥s

"Oh noooo," Cade said sarcastically, which felt like an odd response to Neil, who scrunched his eyebrows. Cade took out his phone and said, "And... send."

"What did you just do?" Neil asked just as his phone notifications dinged.

Neil opened his phone to find that Cade had posted a photo of them in Naples at the Cathedral with the caption: "Looks like a great place to get married. xx"

"Cade!" Neil laughed. "The rumor mill is already on

fire, my dude."

Cade laughed briefly, but with a cackle. "Let *Kyle* see what he lost."

"Maybe this guy will find his weird coffee orders charming."

Cade looked puzzled. "Weird coffee orders?" he asked.

"Yeah, when he orders coffee, it's like an event. **'Venti iced americano, five shots decaf with almond milk, extra ice, eight honey, seven matcha, double blended, double cupped,'** and often has it split into two tall cups, thinking his guy (that was previously me) will love it as much as he does."

"*Bruh*. That ain't it," Cade said.

The train slid into the station, brakes screeching against the rails, and by the time the group spilled onto the platform, the heat and light of the Calabrian coast seemed to wrap them in a new world.

The air smelled different here—saltier, brighter, like lemon rind and sea spray. Houses clung to cliffs in impossible stacks, their pastel walls sun-faded but still proud. The Mediterranean glittered at the bottom of it all, as if it had been poured freshly just for them.

Neil adjusted his backpack, stealing a look at Cade. "Told you Italy's not real," he murmured.

Cade smirked, sunglasses shielding his eyes. "I'm still waiting for you to prove it isn't created in Photoshop." He smiled confidently and lovingly at Neil.

By the afternoon, the group had trekked down to the Reggio di Calabria's *Arena dello Stretto* stone steps that felt endless, finally spilling onto a small beach tucked between cliffs. Shoes were abandoned, bags dropped, and shirts peeled off and thrown into unceremonious piles. The sea was a shock at first touch—cold enough to bite—but soon laughter and shouts bounced off the rocks as the seniors flung themselves into the waves with the deep scent of Italian cologne, somehow.

Neil lingered ankle-deep, squinting out at Cade, who had waded in with easy confidence, water lapping at his waist. "Come on!" Cade called, splashing water in his direction.

Neil groaned dramatically, "Peer pressure is real," before diving in. The water rushed around him, clean and startling, leaving him sputtering and laughing at the same time.

When he surfaced, Cade was closer than expected. The sunlight flickered across his face, droplets clinging to his hair. "See? Worth it."

Neil found himself smiling too hard. "Yeah. Worth

it." Neil said, looking at Cade with wonder.

Later, stretched out on warm rocks to dry, Cade tilted his head toward him. "You've got something in your hair."

Neil ran a hand through it. "Pretty sure I've got half the sea in my nose and... other places too."

Cade chuckled and, naturally, reached over to firmly—ploddingly—ruffle Neil's hair. The touch was brief, casual enough to pass for nothing—yet it lingered, like sunlight on Neil's scalp.

As the tide pressed against the rocks and the group grew louder behind them, Neil closed his eyes, just for a second, and let himself imagine: maybe this was what it meant to belong to someone. Plus, Neil found it stimulating to see Cade shirtless in the sun, rather than the fluorescent glow of the hotel showers.

"You look terrific," Cade said, embarrassing Neil just a little.

"Thanks," Neil said, unsure where to go with the compliment.

They climbed back up from the beach just as the sun began to sink, painting the cliffs in molten orange. The air had cooled, carrying the scent of salt and frying garlic from the cafés above. The group drifted in different directions, some off for food, some back to the hostel, until it was just Neil and Cade trailing along the narrow street that skirted the water.

The path was quiet, lamplight beginning to bloom in soft golden circles. Waves slapped against the rocks below, steady and patient.

Neil broke the silence first. "Do you ever notice how the sea sounds different at night? Like it's not trying so hard. Just... breathing." He spoke as if he were breathing pure oxygen.

Cade smiled faintly. "Do you always describe things like that?"

Neil shrugged and shook himself, suddenly self-conscious. "Sorry. You have me in colorful description mode."

"Don't be sorry." Cade's hand brushed against his as they walked, casually, maybe even accidentally—but then it lingered. Their fingers found each other's without discussion and connected back to back.

For a few minutes, they walked like that, the hush of the sea filling the spaces between words. Finally, Cade spoke. "This whole trip, I thought I'd hate being cut off from everything. No tech, no soccer, no... whatever else I usually hide behind. But it's been the opposite."

Neil squeezed his hand lightly. "Same. I've barely looked at my phone. What's been the opposite?"

Cade slowed, turning to face him. The lamplight caught in his eyes softened them. "You. Us. Somehow, not seeing you... It was actually what *let* me see you. And now—" He broke off with a small laugh, shaking his head. "Now I don't want to stop. I'm... blind-sighted, I guess."

Neil internally flinched, completely caught in Cade's tenderness. His words were tangling in his throat. He wanted to agree, but the moment seemed too delicate for clumsy honesty. Instead, he leaned against the railing, looking out at the silver stretch of sea, and let their joined hands speak for him.

The waves whispered against the rocks. The lights of fishing boats flickered on the horizon. Neil felt no need to rush past the silence. He decided that simply being with Cade and sharing that moment in Italy was his best response.

They walked further down the promenade, hand in hand, until the sound of the group had faded completely. The lamplight blurred on the water, turning the sea into a sheet of molten gold.

Cade squeezed Neil's hand. "Feels like we slipped out of time."

Neil smiled. "Nope. Don't jinx it."

"Neil!" A voice cut through the night, bright and familiar.

"Too late," said Neil as a joke.

Both of them flinched, almost guiltily, before spotting Larkin Collins—the kind of classmate who made the honor roll look like a competitive sport—pacing toward them with a notebook clutched to her chest. Her sandals clacked with purpose against the cobblestones.

"There you are," she said, adjusting her glasses. "We're trying to finalize tomorrow's safety assignments, and you completely skipped the prep meeting."

Neil straightened, like he'd been caught sneaking out past curfew. "Sorry—I got sidetracked."

Larkin's eyes narrowed briefly, then to Cade, still standing close. "I see." Her tone softened slightly. "Well, don't let it happen again. Some of us are relying on you."

"I'll be there," Neil promised.

"Good." She gave Cade a brisk nod, as if he were a new variable she had no time to process, then spun on her heel and disappeared up the hill.

Cade exhaled, a laugh bubbling out of him. "She terrifies me, and I've only said one word to her, ever."

Neil shook his head, grinning now that the tension had passed. "She terrifies everyone. She once asked for extra credit on a final exam she already aced. Plus, she has way more ambition than I do at the moment to fight for valedictorian. I think I'm going to have to settle for number two."

"She radiates Elle Woods energy," Cade said. "What's the word for that?"

"*Officious*," Neil said, nudging Cade's shoulder. "Annoyingly domineering. Usually in a petty way." He paused, squinting at Cade. "I'm kind of shocked you even know who Elle Woods is."

Cade smiled, unbothered. "What would you call me if I were... *pleasantly* domineering?"

Neil echoed the phrase, testing it. His smile turned deliberate as his hand slid to Cade's bicep.

"Steadfast."

"Resolute."

A beat.

"Strong."

Cade swallowed, suddenly out of words. He reached for Neil's hand again—slow this time, careful, as if giving Neil space to pull away.

Neil didn't.

Instead, he leaned in and kissed him.

It startled them both—how natural it felt, how inevitable.

Neil noticed how easy that was now.

And Cade felt it too—the spark he'd carried for years catching all at once, bright and undeniable.

Chapter Eighteen.

Neil sat in a cramped hostel dining room that had been converted—at least for the morning—into "Safety HQ". A whiteboard leaned crookedly against a chair, half-covered in bullet-point reminders: *Buddy system—emergency contacts. Head counts at every stop.*

Within his academic group, Neil knew he was well-liked. Everyone was always happy to see him, and several touched his arm as they walked past to say hi.

Larkin Collins stood at the front like a general addressing her troops, her voice brisk and efficient. "We've got two days remaining before our Rome departure, and I want zero incidents. That means clear roles. Neil, you'll cover Group B transitions—head counts at every departure, check-ins at arrivals, especially when we're moving between bus and train."

Neil nodded, dutiful as ever. "Got it."

"Also, don't forget the First Aid kits. Someone misplaced the bandages last time, and—" her gaze flicked over him pointedly "—I think we all remember how that went."

A ripple of laughter went around the table. Neil jokingly ducked his head, fighting a smile. Yeah, *hard to forget.* "Sorry."

"You had a lot on your plate those first few days. You get a pass," she said, like a pardon.

He scribbled notes in his already meticulous planner, letting the others argue over flashlight batteries and evacuation routes. His mind, however, wasn't on the checklist. It was still back on the promenade, Cade's hand warm in his, the salt wind in his hair.

When the meeting finally adjourned, Neil was halfway out the door when a low voice teased behind him:

"Teacher's pet."

He turned, and Cade was leaning in the doorway, sunglasses tucked into the neck of his shirt, a grin tugging at his mouth.

Neil rolled his eyes. "I'll have you know, it's Safety *Captain* to you."

"Oh, excuse me," Cade said, stepping closer, lowering his voice so only Neil could hear. "*Safety Captain.* Does that mean you're responsible for keeping me alive through the mean streets of Italy?"

Neil tried not to smile, but it cracked through anyway. "And beyond. That's the job description, but you might be a challenge, based on your record of injury."

Cade's grin softened, his hand brushing Neil's as they fell into step together down the hall. "I'd say I'm in pretty good hands."

The safety group finally broke up, the whiteboard squeaking as Larkin scrubbed the last reminder about "hydration accountability." Neil slipped out, planner hugged tight to his chest.

Cade fell into step beside him. "Do you get a badge? Or like... a whistle? Because I'd pay to see you blow a whistle at people."

Neil groaned with a smile. "Please stop."

Cade nudged him in the ribs. "What? I think it's hot."

Neil shot him a look. "You're just poking fun at me for being responsible."

Cade didn't miss a beat. "What? No. You're sexy as hell when you're responsible."

Neil actually tripped, catching himself against the wall. "Excuse me?"

"Sexy," Cade repeated, grinning wider, "as hell."

Neil shoved his shoulder, harder this time. "Cringe."

Cade staggered a step back, clutching his chest like he'd been shot. "Wow. Safety Captain assaults an innocent student. Extra, extra."

Neil tried not to laugh, turning down the corridor, but Cade chased after him, bumping his hip into Neil's.

"Come on," Cade teased. "Admit it. You love it when I say it."

Neil fought a smile. "All you've proven is that your brain melted in the Italian sun, and yeah... I really do... like it a lot, I mean."

"Nice," Cade said, leaning closer, his voice dropping an octave. "But melted brain or not... you're still hot."

Neil shoved him again, but this time Cade caught his wrist, tugging him close until their shoulders bumped. "Dangerous move, Safety Captain," Cade murmured.

Neil shook his head, flustered but grinning. "Well, that explains why it's so *hot* in here."

Cade raised an eyebrow. "Neil, we're literally outside."

"Yeah," Neil shot back, his lips twitching, "and it's still hot in here. Case closed. Do I really want to point out that I like it when you pull me in like this?"

Cade laughed so hard he nearly walked into a doorway. "You are so unhinged," he said, throwing an arm around Neil's neck in a loose headlock.

Neil squirmed but couldn't stop smiling. "I guess that makes me sexy and dangerous. A double threat."

Cade ruffled his hair before finally letting him go. "Triple threat if you count how good you look being mad at me."

Neil shoved him one last time, but it only made Cade laugh harder, the sound echoing down the hostel hall.

Cade still had Neil in a loose headlock when someone cleared their throat from down the outside corridor.

"Ahem."

They both froze. Standing by the stairwell was Jordan Kim, another Safety Team recruit, arms folded with all the authority of a traffic cop. His neon-orange lanyard bounced against his chest as he raised an unimpressed eyebrow.

"Safety Captain," Jordan said flatly, "is that how you enforce the rules? Horseplay and chokeholds?" He snapped the rubber band around his wrist and flinched, which felt like a unique reward to himself, somehow.

Neil flushed red, shoving Cade off of him immediately. "It's not—I wasn't—he started it."

Cade grinned as if he'd just been crowned king. "Correction: Safety Captain assaulted me. You're my witness."

Jordan sighed, like he was already over it. "Whatever this is, take it away from others. Some of us are trying to keep people alive, not... whatever you two are doing."

Cade leaned against the wall, unbothered. "What we're doing is team bonding. Very important for morale. Lighten up, cadet."

Jordan shook his head but smirked faintly as he turned for the stairs. "Fine. But if Larkin asks, I didn't see a thing. Safety Team solidarity."

As soon as he disappeared, Cade burst out laughing, doubling over. "Oh my God, you should've seen your face."

Neil glared, still pink. "Is that how people see me? Like a Trump ICE Agent?"

"Absolutely not," Cade answered.

"Just so we are clear, about the teasing—"

"Yeah?"

"You have exactly five decades to stop doing that. All of that," Neil said.

"Sir, Yes, Sir!" Cade answered with enthusiasm.

Neil groaned, but despite himself, he was smiling again. "I know you think this is a joke, and you're very hilarious, but this is like me running out on the soccer field in the last three minutes of the game and deflating the ball."

"I'm sorry. You're still sexy as hell, though," Cade shot back.

Neil saw a tennis ball, picked it up, and threw it down the hall to shut him up.

"Fetch!"

"Now, that was rude," Cade said. "I'm well aware that your friends call me a golden retriever, but I like it a lot that you're starting to find your inner boss."

The two leaned against the stone railing, the late-afternoon sun casting a glow across the Tyrrhenian Sea. The water shimmered endlessly, and Neil shaded his eyes, pointing toward the faint shape that hovered on the horizon.

Neil looked at Cade's eyes, checking if any of the blood that had pooled was subsiding.

"Your eyes are looking better. Are they sensitive? The red is starting to turn to that brownish-yellow color, like it is clearing up on its own."

"Yeah, still a bit sensitive but much better."

"Good." Neil pointed, "Out there, that's Sardinia," he

said softly, referencing the watery edge of the horizon. He had a little awe in his voice. "On a clear day, you can just make it out, I bet."

Cade squinted, then tilted his head. "So that's where sardines come from?"

Neil blinked, then laughed. "Funny, and yes—they used to be abundant there. But they're not even as common in Sardinian cuisine now as they are in other Mediterranean places."

Cade wrinkled his nose like he'd been served bad cafeteria pizza. "Yeah, not exactly heartbroken about that. Sardines are gross."

Neil's mouth dropped open. "Gross? Even on a salad?"

"Especially on a salad."

Neil looked horrified. "Don't ever say that in front of my mother. You'll be excommunicated from dinner forever."

Cade chuckled, nudging him with his shoulder. "Guess I'll survive. Wait. I get to meet your mother? Things are moving faster than fast with us."

"You won't survive, actually," Neil shot back, only half joking. "Proper sardines are full of good fats, proteins, minerals... they're practically a superfood." His tone grew playful, a spark in his eyes. "One day, I'll make you something with sardines, cooked the right way. Then you'll see."

Cade groaned dramatically, as if Neil had threatened him with poison. "If this is your idea of romance, Safety Captain, we're doomed."

Neil smirked, watching the sea glint in Cade's sunglasses. "You'll thank me later."

Cade sighed, the corners of his mouth twitching upward. "I'm already thanking you now. But if I end up liking sardines because of you, I'll never live it down."

"Good," Neil said, still grinning. "Whatever it takes. Next, you'll be fighting me about anchovies on pizza."

Cade started to say something, and Neil made a grunting noise to stop him.

Chapter Nineteen.

Traveling southward, curving along the cliffs where the Tyrrhenian Sea caught the morning light like a handful of diamonds tossed across the waves. Neil pressed his forehead to the glass, watching fishing boats scatter white wakes through the blue. He thought he'd never tire of Italy, of the language, or of the way the air seemed to shine with history. But what struck him most was Cade, slouched across from him, grinning as if he'd finally figured something out.

"I like it when you stare," Cade said without opening his eyes.

Neil was definitely looking at Cade. "I'm looking at

the sea."

Cade cracked an eye open. "Sure. The sea, that sexy horizon."

Neil groaned, throwing a balled-up napkin at him. "Uh-huh."

"Sexy and impossible," Cade teased, catching the napkin before it hit the floor. Then he stretched, leaned forward on his elbows, and dropped his voice so no one else could hear. "Admit it, Erickson. You missed me at that safety meeting yesterday."

"You crashed that meeting."

"It was basically already over." Cade tapped his knee against Neil's under the table. "Probably even made a sardine agenda item just to cover for it."

Neil's ears went pink. "Please don't ever say 'sardine agenda' again."

Cade laughed so hard that the teacher two rows back shushed them. He covered his mouth but kept chuckling, leaning closer until his shoulder brushed Neil's. "One day you're going to crack, and I'll win. You'll cook me sardines, and I'll fall in love."

Neil tried not to smile, but laughed anyway, eyes on the window. "Idiot. I don't cook sardines."

"Sexy as hell, though," Cade whispered, just loud enough for only Neil to hear.

Neil finally looked at him, sunlight catching Cade's blue eyes, and felt that now-familiar panic in his chest—panic that maybe this was real, and perhaps it was worth the risk.

The train pulled into the station at Salerno just as the sun slid higher, warming the tiled roofs to a glow. The group spilled out onto the platform, their voices bouncing in a dozen directions—half of them already chasing snacks and trinkets, the other half fumbling with cameras.

Neil and Cade hung back, keeping pace with each other as the teachers corralled everyone toward the day's excursion.

"You'd think half these people had never seen sunlight," Cade murmured, tugging his baseball cap lower.

Neil smirked. "That's because most of them haven't been forced to stand on a farm for hours in August hayfields."

Cade elbowed him gently. "Are you calling me country?"

"Not all of us live on thirty acres in West Meade."

Cade looked at him, a playfully stunned expression on his face.

Neil gasped theatrically. "That's rich, *literally* rich."

They wandered out into the cobbled streets, the sea glinting in the distance. Palm trees framed boulevards where scooters passed like bees in a hive. Street vendors hawked postcards, sun hats, and—of course—platters of grilled sardines.

Cade stopped dead at the smell. "Oh, no. Not this again."

Neil grinned, tugging his sleeve. "Yes, this again. The sea provides, Riley. One day you'll be grateful."

"I'll be grateful when the sea provides pizza instead," Cade muttered.

"Blasphemy, although we did briefly discuss anchovy pizza." Neil held a hand to his heart, pretending to stagger. "Never mock tiny canned fish where my nonna can hear you. You'll meet your end, ironically, in a can. Hey, look, they sell cowboy hats here," Neil announced. He put one on Cade's head. "There's the Cade we all know and ad—"

"And what? Adore?" Cade stood there in the hat and stared at Neil through his sunglasses. "I'd buy all of these hats if that's what it took for you to legitimately say that."

"Just that one will do," Neil said, shelling out thirty-four euros. "Pricy Stetson hat."

"I hope I'm worth it. " Cade said, pausing to say, "You've taken really good care of me on this trip. I'll pay for my own hat."

"As you wish, Cade Riley Devereaux-Beaumont," Neil said in an aristocratic Southern voice.

Cade started quoting Foghorn Leghorn from Warner Bros. to poke fun at himself.

"It's actually just **Caden Walker Riley.**

Neil nodded solemnly. "Tragic. I already monogrammed the sterling."

Cade's laugh echoed off the old stone walls, and a few classmates glanced their way. He leaned closer, voice low just for Neil: "Never monogram the sterling. I have so much to teach you."

"On God," Neil responded, in agreement.

They fell into step along the seaside promenade, where the Tyrrhenian sea spread out endlessly before them. Children chased soccer balls between the benches, and the air smelled faintly of lemon and salt. Cade tilted his head back, closing his eyes to the sun, his face slack with a kind of peace Neil hadn't seen before.

"Do you ever think," Cade said after a long silence, "that this is the kind of day you'll remember when you're old? Like—this exact moment?"

Neil looked at him, heart twisting. "Yeah. I think about that a lot, strangely."

Cade cracked one eye open, a slow smile creeping

across his face. "Really? You're such a sap."

Neil grinned back, bumping his shoulder. "Sexy as hell, though. You said it."

They both dissolved into laughter, tangled together against the rail while the sea sparkled below.

"You say 'sexy as hell' so much that we might have to make a drinking game out of it," Neil said.

The group gathered at the base of an old fountain, where a guide with a red flag tried valiantly to make herself heard over the din of chattering high school seniors. Cameras clicked, a soccer ball bounced dangerously close to the water, and someone shouted that the gelato stand up the street had a Nutella flavor.

Neil and Cade sat on the edge of the fountain, knees nearly touching, watching the chaos unfold and snickering about feeling fortunate not to be in charge of these hooligans.

"So," Cade said, tilting his head toward Neil, "college apps. Where are you headed after all this?"

Neil made a face. "That's assuming I get to decide."

Cade raised a brow. "Parental expectations?"

"Mm-hmm." Neil traced the worn stone under his hand. "My dad has a chain of grocery markets: Giordano's. It's my mother's family business. The plan is for me to come back to Nashville, get a business degree, and take it over. End of story."

Cade whistled softly. "Doesn't sound like much of a choice."

"It's not." Neil shrugged, trying to keep it casual. "Don't get me wrong—I love parts of it. The markets are kind of the heartbeat of our neighborhoods. But... sometimes I wonder if it is the right future for me. Anyway, it will work out."

Cade was quiet for a beat, then nudged him with his knee. "You'd run it better than anyone, though. Probably modernize the place. Maybe put sardines on every shelf."

Neil laughed, but there was a pang in his chest. "And plenty of other things that you think you hate or prejudge. And you?" Neil asked, shifting the spotlight. "Where are you supposed to end up?"

Cade sighed, tipping his head back against the sun. "Stuffy Southern university of Dad's choosing. Business degree. Then straight into the family firm. He's already got my office picked out."

Neil frowned. "So... basically the same deal as me."

"Yep," Cade said, his smile thin. "Different product, same cage. But hey, at least we are in the same city if we follow the rules."

They both sat in the piazza's noise for a moment,

watching classmates scatter in every direction. Then Cade leaned closer, his voice low so only Neil could hear:

"Do you ever think about just... not doing it? Running away from all of it?"

Neil glanced at him, caught by the intensity in his eyes. "Sometimes."

"Yeah," Cade said softly. "Me too."

Their classmates shrieked over the soccer ball rolling into the fountain, and the moment broke. Neil and Cade both laughed at the chaos, but something lingered in the space between them—a shared secret, heavier than the noise around them.

Chapter Twenty.

Mads Chandler
Sophomore year, Penderton Academy AP Social Hall

Mads slumped against the lockers, hood up, knees drawn in, her usual sparkle noticeably dimmed. No Sour Patch Kids. No commentary. No unsolicited life advice. Just stillness—unnerving in a girl who didn't believe in *still*.

Jenna rounded the corner with a stack of notebooks and froze.

"Oh my God," she said softly. "Mads? Are you okay?"

Mads didn't look up. "I'm fine."

Jenna blinked. "That 'fine' sounded like it's been chewed up in an emotional blender."

Sophie arrived next, her eyes widening. "Oh, honey,

what happened? Who do I have to fight? I'll swing on a teacher."

"No fighting." Mads tugged her hood farther over her face. "The world was too loud today. My brain feels like a radio stuck between stations."

Sophie, heart-first as always, leaned down and opened her arms. "Come here. Let me just—"

Before she could close the distance, Neil slid in between them with the reflexes of someone trained in Mads Chandler Management and took the hug from Sophie.

"Whoa," he said. "Don't hug her. Hug me instead."

Sophie blinked. "Why not? She looks like she needs one."

"She does," Neil said gently, crouching beside Mads, "but not like that."

Mads exhaled shakily. "Thank you."

Jenna's eyebrows knit together. "What do you mean?"

Neil pointed lightly to Mads without touching her. "When she's overstimulated or overwhelmed, surprise physical contact makes it worse. Think... adding fireworks to a house fire."

Mads nodded under her hood. "Hugs are great when I'm normal me. Not great when I'm radio-static-me."

"Oh," Sophie said, pulling her arms back, guilt flickering in her expression. "I didn't know."

"It's okay," Mads mumbled. "You meant well. You're like a Disney character who hugs first and asks questions never."

Neil cracked a tiny smile. "That is actually shockingly accurate. You are kind of an adorable Disney character."

He sat beside her, a careful few inches of space between them. Not touching—just present.

"Do you want anything?" he asked. "Water? Quiet? Someone to glare at people for you?"

"Just sit there," Mads whispered. "You're good background noise."

Sophie and Jenna exchanged looks—soft, relieved ones.

"Okay," Sophie said quietly. "We'll just... stay nearby. No touching."

Jenna nodded. "And we'll threaten anyone who comes within five feet."

"Aw," Mads muttered. "My tiny, terrifying army."

Neil rested his elbows on his knees. "We're not going anywhere."

Mads let out a long breath—one that sounded like she'd been holding it all day—and for the first time since they found her, her shoulders relaxed an inch.

"Thanks," she said. "And Neil?"

"Yeah?"

"You're the only person who doesn't make my brain feel like a shaken soda can."

Neil's expression softened, just for her. "That's because I read the manual."

Jenna blinked. "There's a manual?"

"There is," Mads said, finally pushing her hood back and revealing tired eyes. "Neil wrote it."

"I just did the research and wrote some notes," Neil clarified.

Sophie smiled, warm and relieved. "Then we'll read the manual too."

Mads nodded once, the corner of her mouth lifting.

"Good. Because this radio-static stuff? It sucks."

Neil stayed right where he was, quiet and steady.

"Yeah," he said softly. "But we've got you."

Chapter Twenty-One.

The next morning dawned bright and chaotic, as mornings on the trip usually did. Backpacks clattered against narrow train aisles, someone shouted about losing a passport, and the teachers were already stressed before breakfast trays had even been collected. Neil was in charge of the lost phone log, and the list was growing longer by the day.

Neil shouldered his bag, weaving through the crush of bodies, when he spotted Cade in the middle of it all—half-smiling as a classmate begged him to help decipher a ticket stub.

"Tell me again why we're trusted to cross

international borders as a group?" Cade muttered when Neil reached him. "Half of them can't even manage pocket euros."

"Maybe that's why the safety team exists," Neil said, deadpan.

"Good point," Cade said, then leaned in. "Though I feel safer when it's just you."

Neil rolled his eyes, heat rising in his ears. "Don't start with me this early."

They shuffled with the group into the bustling station, swept along by the current of commuters. Vendors shouted over the din, the scent of espresso and warm pastries curling through the air. A few classmates broke away toward a kiosk selling glossy postcards, and one girl waved a train-shaped pen as if it were a holy relic.

Neil laughed under his breath. "You'd think none of us had been outside of Tennessee before."

"Hey," Cade said, catching his arm, "don't knock it. I'm about two seconds from buying that pen myself. Half this crap you can get on Music Row back home."

Neil gave him a mock glare. "You're supposed to be the dignified one."

Cade grinned, tugging his cap lower. "Nah, that's your role. I'm just here for the Cool Ranch Doritos and enormous Pringles tubes."

As if on cue, a teacher clapped her hands and announced in brisk tones, "All right, group, line up—we've got a walking tour this morning, so fuel up now if you haven't eaten."

Groans rippled through the students, but Cade turned to Neil, smirking. "Fuel up, huh? Think they've got sardines around here?"

Neil gasped theatrically. "You dare insult Italian breakfasts with that comment?"

"Not insulting," Cade shot back. "I'm just keeping my options open."

"Keep it up, and I'll tell my cousins you refused their feast," Neil said, nudging him forward in line.

Cade chuckled, shoulders brushing Neil's as they were herded out of the station into the bright swirl of morning. He popped Neil on the behind. "Wow. Dat azz."

For all the noise and motion around them, it struck Neil how easy it was to fall into step with Cade—like no matter how loud the group got, they kept their own quiet rhythm.

The teachers shepherded them out into the streets, where the guide with the red flag was already waiting. "Stay close, *ragazzi*!"[1] She called out to the slacker boys in brisk English, waving the flag like a lifeline. "We move

[1] *ragazzi*: boys

179

quickly, yes?"

The group shuffled into motion, a ragged snake of Penderton logos and sneakers weaving through cobbled streets older than their country.

"Stay close, *ragazzi*," Cade whispered firmly in Neil's ear, mimicking the guide's lilting tone. "That means you have to hold my hand."

Neil shot him a look and said, "*Ragazzo*," but Cade's grin was so shameless that Neil almost tripped. "Woof. Don't get me excited, or I may faceplant," Neil responded.

"I've got you, babe," Cade said, supporting Neil with his arm. "You're walking next to your man."

Neil tried to focus on the guide's monologue about ancient aqueducts, but Cade kept leaning closer with a running commentary:

"That fountain definitely has diseases."

"I swear that statue looks like your cousin."

"Do you think they built this entire piazza just for vendors?"

By the time they paused at a towering church, Neil's sides hurt from laughing. The group clustered around the guide, craning their necks at the ornate façade, snapping pictures like the world would end without them.

Neil murmured, "This is incredible."

Cade tilted his head, listening more than looking. "Describe it to me."

Neil blinked. "You can see now. You don't need me to."

"Humor me," Cade said softly.

Neil swallowed, then said, "It's like... stone lace. Every inch is carved and alive, like it's breathing. You can feel the history just standing here."

Cade's expression softened, his eyes on Neil more than the church. "Nice."

Before Neil could respond, one of Cade's friends from the soccer team called out, "Hey, Riley! Are you actually paying attention or just flirting your way through Italy?"

Cade didn't miss a beat. "Both!" he shouted back, grinning, and blew the player a kiss.

The group roared with laughter, the guide sighed audibly, and Neil went red to the roots of his hair.

As they moved on, Cade leaned close again. "Worth it," he whispered.

Neil couldn't stop smiling.

By the time the guide released them for a short break, the group scattered like marbles across the piazza—some chasing food, some bartering for trinkets, some collapsing dramatically onto shaded benches.

Neil lingered at the edge, stretching his legs, when Cade tugged at his sleeve.

"C'mon," he said quietly. "Too many people."

They slipped down a side street, away from the chatter. The noise dimmed instantly, replaced by the hush of their footsteps against sun-warmed stones. Laundry fluttered overhead on clotheslines, and a cat stretched lazily in a patch of light.

Neil exhaled. "Much better."

Cade leaned against a wall, arms crossed. "You know, this is the first time all day I haven't felt like part of a cattle drive."

Neil grinned. "You're just mad the guide didn't wave the red flag for you personally."

"You are being *ridonculously* hot today," Neil confessed.

"Oh yeah? How so?"

"Oh, I think you know what you're doing. Standing up for both of us like you're doing, and talking to me through that incredulous grin."

A cat darted into a doorway, the breeze carried the faint smell of bread from somewhere down the alley, and Neil realized he was smiling so hard it hurt.

Before either of them could say more, a teacher's voice echoed faintly from the piazza: "Penderton group!

Five minutes!"

Cade groaned. "And back into the cattle drive we go."

Neil laughed, but as they headed back toward the noise, Cade brushed his hand lightly against Neil's, letting it linger just a second longer than casual, just to drive him a little wilder.

Chapter Twenty-Two.

The Calabrian streets glistened with late afternoon light, the kind that turned the stone buildings honey-gold and made every corner feel like a painting. The Penderton group shuffled out of a basilica, rumbling with chatter about the ceiling frescoes and the fact that two kids had tried to sneak food inside.

Neil lingered behind, shoulder to shoulder with Cade. Somehow, without ever planning it, they always drifted a little apart from the crowd, as if the city itself conspired to carve out space just for them. Narrow streets stretched ahead, golden light pooling against shuttered windows, and the air carried the scent of warm stone and sunshine.

"Feels like we've been walking for hours," Cade muttered, tugging his cap lower. "Think they'd notice if we slipped away for a coffee?" Neil's smile curved, soft and knowing.

"Adorable—you'd be asleep in ten minutes, even with the caffeine."

"Which would make it worth it," Cade said, his arm drifting against Neil's. The touch was light, fleeting—and yet Neil felt it everywhere. He let the thought linger, impossible to shake: Cade asleep on his shoulder, the city still moving—a moment Neil knew he could love forever.

They rounded a corner into a quieter street. Up ahead, the group drifted on, Penderton school jackets bright in the sun, phones lifted in photo mode, capturing anything that stood still long enough. But here—just here—it was only the two of them.

A street musician leaned in a doorway, coaxing a tender rhythm from his guitar. The notes lingered in the warm air, wrapping around now familiar scents and the soft dust of old stone, as if the city itself had slowed to frame the moment for them.

Cade's smile touched his voice as he answered, softer than the music. *"This is even better."* Italy offered them its small mercies: a guitar's slow rhythm, the scent of coffee, and a street corner that belonged only to them.

For a few glorious steps, everything was perfect: warm hand in hand, the city unfolding around them, a secret made solid. Neil's heart felt too big for his chest.

Then—

"Riley!"

The jeer cleaved the moment in two.

They froze. Up ahead, three of Cade's "friends" turned, grins sharp as knives. One arched his brows, elbowing the third.

"Well, well," Buddy Fowler drawled. "Guess you've been keeping busy."

Laughter spilled back down the street—not cruel, not yet, but loud enough to ripple outward. A gasp, a whisper, the static passing down the line. Even a tourist family slowed, the son staring before being hurried along.

Neil's stomach dropped. His chest hollowed. Every instinct screamed: vanish. Not worth the air it would cost.

But Cade caught the flicker of dread in Neil's eyes and refused to yield. He squared his shoulders, jaw hard as stone. His voice carried back, steady, unshaken:

"Yeah. I have."

Then, without hesitation, he hooked Neil's hand into the front pocket of his jeans and laid his other hand firm on Neil's well-defined bicep—a bold, claiming, and beyond-his-years masculine gesture that dared anyone to challenge him.

Neil's chest swelled, pride and heat colliding inside him. In that instant, they weren't two boys—they were one undeniable force, unflinching, untouchable.

The bullies faltered. Their laughter stumbled into awkward noise. "Okay, man, whatever," Buddy muttered. They turned back toward the piazza, but it was too late—the whispers had already spread like fire.

Neil felt eyes burning into him from every side, but Cade had turned humiliation into defiance—into something dazzling, protective, and unimpeachably hot.

"Are you okay?" Cade asked.

His throat went dry. "You didn't have to—"

"You keep saying that, but yeah, I did," Cade said, softer now, just for him. He brushed Neil's hand again, reclaiming it from his pocket as if it were a vow in his hand. "I'm not letting anyone take this from us."

Neil swallowed, a storm of fear and exhilaration in his chest. The secret was out now, and there was no putting it back.

He steadied his voice. "I'm only going to say this

once."

Cade braced, eyes steady, nervous. "Okay."

Neil held his gaze until Cade almost broke. Then he dropped it, low-toned and certain:

"You have never been hotter. And I can't even say in public what I want to do to you right now."

Cade's grin went feral, hungry. "Bet! Well, I like hearing that!"

Neil laughed with sexy, ragged adrenaline. Cade's grip tightened, pulling him closer, and for one breathless instant, the city dissolved—their whole world reduced to golden light, cobblestones, and the heat blazing between them.

The rest of the walking tour blurred for Neil. Every time he glanced around, he caught someone whispering or looking at Cade with raised eyebrows before pretending to study their guidebook.

By the time they trudged back to the hostel, Neil's nerves were frayed raw, not just from the incident that had triggered it, but also from Cade's response. It would take Neil hours to cool down. If he were to get Cade alone, he wasn't even sure what he would do, having little experience, but he knew it would be fun.

Dinner was loud—long tables, cheap pasta, classmates

trading stories about near-pickpockets and souvenir scams. Neil slid into a seat near the edge, hoping to disappear. But then Cade dropped into the chair beside him, tray clattering.

And without hesitation, Cade placed his hand on Neil's out in the open.

The noise around them didn't stop exactly, but it changed. A ripple passed through the room, subtle but sharp. Heads turned. Conversations faltered.

Neil didn't freeze. He didn't want to pull away or to vanish under the table.

Cade sat back casually, fork in his free hand, expression daring anyone to say something. Cade now knew the power he had. They both knew that Neil was not a weakling. He was 5'10" and well built; he could back Cade up if any confrontation ever really happened. But what was now clear was that Cade's protective nature brought out the animal in Neil, and he planned to exploit it someday—hopefully soon. He didn't share this with Neil. Not yet.

"Dude," one of his basketball friends muttered across the table, "are you for real right now?"

"Yeah," Cade said, calm as if he were talking about the weather. He took a bite of pasta, still holding Neil's hand tight.

The silence stretched, then someone at another table laughed nervously, muttering something Neil couldn't catch. Soon the din picked up again, but sharper this time, edged with glances and whispers that prickled down Neil's spine.

Neil forced himself to eat, but his stomach was in knots. As was apparently normal, Cade took a good thing too far. Subtlety was not mastered. Was Cade really doing this for him—or was Neil just a convenient way to shock his friends, to rebel in the most outrageous way possible? Now, with so many incidents, Neil began to question whether Cade was intentionally causing these confrontations to get the attention that came with his actions.

Later, in the hallway outside their room, Neil pulled his hand free. "What was that?" His voice cracked, and he sounded sharper than he meant.

Cade frowned. "What do you mean?"

"You—" Neil gestured vaguely, too wound up to form a coherent sentence. "At dinner. The... display."

Cade leaned against the wall, arms crossed. "You mean holding your hand?"

"You know what I mean. It's starting to feel like—like you're making a point. Like I'm a prop in some act of defiance."

The words hung between them, heavier than the stones in the walls.

Cade's jaw tightened. "Neil, I wasn't using you. I wanted to hold your hand. So I did."

Neil's heart hammered. "There's a big difference between standing up to a pack of bullies and intentionally antagonizing someone."

Cade's expression softened, but his voice stayed steady. "What?"

Neil looked away, staring at the scuffed floor tiles, torn between the dizzy rush of Cade's boldness and the gnawing fear that he'd wake tomorrow to gossip and regret.

For the first time since the bandages came off, he didn't know which way Cade would tilt—toward him or back toward the safety of his old life once this act of defiance settled in the dust. Would he leave Neil to clean up the mess on his own? Neither of them shared their thoughts or fears.

Everything was happening so fast.

Chapter Twenty-Three.

The train traveled on, steady and hypnotic, like the world itself had slipped onto rails. Outside the window, the villages of stone houses that seemed too old to be real, then another stretch of farmland lit gold by the sinking sun.

Cade had drifted off beside him, his head tipped just enough that his hair brushed Neil's shoulder, the slow rise and fall of his breathing syncing with the sway of the carriage. It should have been perfect. For Neil, though, stillness had a way of dredging up ghosts.

His reflection in the glass was too easy a canvas for his memories of everything that went wrong with Kyle back in August.

The memory arrived in fragments, uninvited: Kyle's lopsided grin at the arcade, the thrill of a text that only came at midnight, the charged hush of local library tables where their knees brushed like accidents. Neil had thought those moments meant something. That being wanted in secret was better than not being wanted at all.

But then came that last conversation, still sharp as broken glass:

"Look, Neil," Kyle had said, voice clipped, eyes darting past him to a hallway already empty. "I can't give you what you want."

Neil had stared at the carpet, searching for words, finding only the lump in his throat. "What is it that I want? How would you know if you've never asked?" he'd whispered. "We actually have to have that discussion before you can say that, Kyle."

Kyle's sigh had been heavy and impatient. "You knew what this was. It was supposed to be easy."

Easy. That was the word that had gutted him. As if caring had been some kind of crime, or even difficult. As if Neil had broken the rules by wanting to be seen or cared for.

A field rushed past the window now, its rows sharp and deliberate, and Neil thought about how Kyle had always kept everything in rows, too—neat compartments. Neil had been tucked into one of them, safe until he wasn't.

Beside him, Cade stirred slightly, his hand falling open on the armrest, fingertips brushing Neil's as he napped.

Cade didn't keep him compartmentalized. Cade reached for him on crowded streets, unashamed, laughing when their hands met. Cade didn't shrink when Neil's voice shook. He leaned closer. He held on tighter.

The trap had never been Kyle, not exactly—it had been Neil convincing himself that half of someone was enough. That secrecy was proof of love.

He couldn't do that again, not with Cade. If this— whatever this was—had a chance, it had to be honest. Real. Messy, maybe, but out in the open.

Neil turned his palm and carefully held Cade's hand. Cade didn't wake, but the small weight of his hand anchored Neil, steadier than the rails beneath them.

The glass showed their reflections side by side, blurred by the streaks of light racing past. For the first time since August, Neil didn't feel like he was carrying the wreckage alone.

The last time Neil saw Kyle, it was in the parking lot of a strip mall halfway between their houses—neutral ground. The kind of place that didn't belong to either of them, where the only witnesses were a Dollar Tree and a shuttered laundromat.

Neil had biked there in the July heat, still hoping Kyle had changed his mind, that this wasn't what it felt like. But Kyle was already leaning against his car when he arrived, arms crossed, sunglasses hiding his eyes.

"Hey," Neil said, forcing brightness into his voice.

"Hey." Flat, final, from Kyle.

Neil set his bike on its kickstand, suddenly aware of how ridiculous it looked beside Kyle's car. He'd never felt the difference between them more. His bike probably cost more than Kyle's car.

Kyle cleared his throat, shifting his weight. "Look, Neil... we can't keep doing this."

The words snapped the air between them. Neil's pulse stumbled. "What do you mean?"

"This—us," Kyle said, waving a hand like he could brush it all away. "It doesn't work. You're starting school again, I'm starting mine. It's too much."

"That's it?" Neil asked, voice rising. "Because classes are starting?"

It should have been a conversation, a back-and-forth. Instead, it was a closing statement. Neil knew it the moment Kyle reached for his keys, ready to drive off and let this be the end.

"You could've called," Neil muttered, hating the crack in his own voice. "Instead of dragging me out here."

Kyle hesitated for just a second, then slid into the driver's seat. "I'm sorry," he said, but it sounded practiced, like the line had been rehearsed.

The car pulled out of the lot, leaving Neil standing beside his bike, the cicadas shrieking in the August heat.

He gripped the handlebars until his knuckles went white. For weeks, he'd been telling himself he'd mattered to Kyle, even if it was complicated. Now the truth landed heavily: he'd only ever been convenient.

The email reminder pinged at nine that night: Final Deadline for Penderton Senior Trip—24 hours left to register.

For weeks, Neil had ignored it. He'd told himself he'd stay home; that summer would be about Kyle—late-night drives, movie marathons, maybe even figuring out what they were to each other. But that was before the parking lot, before the easy shrug of "it's too much," before Kyle's taillights disappeared down the road.

Now, the thought of staying in town felt unbearable. Every street corner, every empty parking lot, and every diner booth would echo with Kyle's absence. All of his friends would be away in Europe. Neil didn't want reminders. He wanted distance. He wanted an ocean of it.

He stared at the glowing registration form on his laptop. The cursor blinked like it was daring him.

"Anywhere but here," he whispered.

His fingers moved before he could talk himself out of it—typing in his information, clicking through payment screens, watching as the confirmation page finally appeared.

Congratulations! You're going to Europe!

Neil leaned back in his chair, heart still heavy but beating a little faster. He didn't know what the trip would bring, only that for the first time in weeks, he had something to look toward instead of back.

He texted Jenna:

Neil
Any space on the Europe safety team?

Jenna
Are you going? The deadline is tomorrow.

Neil
Yup. Just booked it. Kyle dumped me, so I could make myself useful.

Jenna
OH NO! I'm sorry, but I'm not sorry you're going to Europe with us.

Neil
Thanks

Neil immediately pulled out his university planner and added the safety board participation to his list of extracurricular activities for his university applications.

"Good ole trusty and reliable Neil Erickson. That's me," he said as he wrote. "That's my lore. You can *always* count on, anticipate, and predict... me."

Back to the present day on the train, Cade was asleep against his shoulder, and Neil watched the hills drift by, half-awake himself. The scenery turned into memories of Kyle—quick flashes of what used to feel like everything— their time together had been short but loud, impossible to forget. As the train carried him farther from it all, Neil made a choice: to leave those moments where they belonged, and let himself believe in something better— with Cade.

He couldn't help but let himself think that if the relationship went sour with Kyle, it might happen with Cade. Maybe he should guard his heart a little longer.

Chapter Twenty-Four.

Breakfast was tense. The hostel's cafeteria clattered with trays, scraping chairs, and the burnt-toast smell of industrial toasters that seemed to ruin every slice. A faint chatter filled the room while Neil grabbed a plate for the buffet. The air felt thick, charged—like a storm that hadn't broken yet.

At the far end of the room, Cade's friends sat bunched together, their voices pitched low but their eyes flicking toward him with not-so-subtle precision. They weren't good at hiding their judgment; they wanted Cade to see it. To feel it.

Finally, Tyler—the loudest, broadest, and most

predictable of the soccer bunch—slammed his *succhi*[1] down so hard the straw bent. He leaned across the table, squaring off as if this were practice and Cade was the target. Tyler had always been a rude, oafish cowboy wannabe, stomping around like the world owed him a dust cloud.

"Alright, Riley. What's going on?"

Cade didn't flinch. He sat with his arm draped lazily over the back of the adjacent chair, posture calm but dangerous, like a lion pretending it wasn't hungry. "What's it look like?"

"It looks like you're pulling some stunt," Tyler shot back, his voice just loud enough to make the kids at the next table over perk their heads up. "First, you ditch us when you're patched up, then suddenly you're glued to... *him*."

Cade stiffened, not at the word itself, but at the bite Tyler put into it. Neil's name wasn't even necessary. *Him* was enough to mark Neil as *other*.

The optics may be wrong, Neil had once warned him. Cade knew it. But wrong or not, Cade wasn't about to let anyone tell him who to sit beside, who to walk with, or who to care for. He wanted to be Neil's protector, not because Neil couldn't handle himself—Neil had proven

---

[1] *succhi*: juice

that plenty—but because Cade wanted to. Because he wanted to be his man.

Buddy Fowler chimed in, nervously twirling his spoon. "Is this about the prank? You're still pissed, and this is your way of screwing with us? Because, Bubba, it's not funny anymore."

Neil froze in the doorway, half-hidden behind the wall, tray balanced in his hands. He hadn't stepped inside yet, hadn't claimed a seat. From where he stood, he could hear every word, and each one sliced deeper.

That was it, wasn't it? Cade wasn't choosing him. Cade was making a statement. A middle finger to the friends who'd left him behind. Neil's throat tightened at the thought. He was a symbol, not a person.

But Cade's jaw was set now, his eyes locked like crosshairs on Tyler. "This isn't a stunt."

Tyler snorted, leaning back with a derisive laugh. "Come on. You're Cade Riley. Girls line up for you. And now you're—what—swooning over the gay safety book-boy? Give me a break. No one is buying this act."

The words landed like a slap. Neil's chest hollowed out, his tray pressing into the wall as if he could disappear into it. His knuckles whitened against the plastic edge, every instinct screaming at him to bolt, to vanish before Cade answered and shattered whatever fragile hope he had left.

But Cade didn't shrink. He didn't fumble or dodge. He leaned forward, eyes stern, voice steady as stone. "Yeah. I am. Got a problem with that?"

The table went silent. Forks paused mid-air, and conversations stuttered into nothing. A few heads turned from nearby tables, and someone—maybe one of the girls who always hovered near Tyler—snickered nervously, like the silence demanded a release.

Tyler shook his head slowly, muttering like a man who couldn't win the fight but needed the last word. "You've lost it, man." He shoved his tray aside, the chair screeching against the floor as he stood. He stalked off without looking back, the others trailing behind him in a whispering clump.

Cade sat back, exhaling through his nose, not triumphant exactly but unyielding. His chest rose and fell as if he'd just sprinted across a field. He looked satisfied, sure—like he'd won something important—but under it all was a shadow, a flicker of worry. He felt like he'd lost something too. And as he stared across the cafeteria, his jaw softened with one quiet thought: *Where's Neil?*

Because Neil wasn't beside him. Not where he should've been.

Still hidden at the edge of the doorway, Neil's pulse thundered. His chest was tight with a mess of feelings he couldn't untangle fast enough.

On one hand, Cade had been brave—no hiding. No excuses. Fearless in a way Neil never dared hope for.

But on the other hand, was it bravery—or just another reckless middle finger to the world? Was Neil the message, not the meaning? The perfect weapon: convenient, available, and, if necessary, expendable?

Neil's heart whispered what he wanted to believe—that Cade cared, really cared, that he meant every word he'd just said.

But his head spun with the darker possibility. Cade Riley was fearless, yes. But fearlessness without thought wasn't always noble. Sometimes, it was reckless. And Neil, standing there with his tray gone cold, wasn't sure if he was the boy Cade wanted... or the collateral damage Cade was willing to risk.

Chapter Twenty-Five.

Neil kept his head down the rest of the morning, blending into the Penderton Advanced Placement herd as they wound through another Roman piazza. Every laugh and whisper behind him felt sharp, like it might be about him. About them.

He slipped further back, letting classmates buffer the space between himself and Cade. It wasn't difficult—Cade belonged in the center, his tall, muscular frame soaking up attention like sunlight. Neil stayed in the shadows, safe, invisible.

By lunch, he ducked into a café with the safety team. He laughed when they laughed and nodded at talk of train schedules, but inside, his stomach was in a knot, pulling tighter with every breath.

Boyfriend or prop?

When Neil spilled back onto the street unknowingly ahead of his friends, he thought he would disappear into the tide of seniors, but Cade wouldn't let him.

"Neil!" His voice cut above the chatter.

Neil didn't turn. He lengthened his stride, slipping down a narrow alley shaded by ivy and laundry lines that fluttered like flags.

Jenna saw it from inside the café. Neil hadn't mentioned anything, but she knew something was going on when Neil was spending time with his friends without Cade. Like her classmates, she was enjoying the rom-com of the Cade-Neil show, but she had a seat a lot closer up front than most.

"Neil!" Footsteps closed in. A hand caught his arm and spun him gently around.

Cade, breathless. Sunglasses tilted, hair mussed from running. "What are you doing? You've been dodging me all morning."

Neil's throat went dry. "I'm giving you space."

"Space?" Cade frowned. "I don't want space."

Neil forced a brittle laugh. "Maybe because I don't want to be the punchline for your performative romantic attention and sudden rebellion from your friends."

Cade blinked, stung. "Is that what you think this is?"

"Isn't it?" Neil's voice sharpened. "They ditch you after the prank that got you hurt, you get stuck with me, and suddenly I'm your perfect weapon. You hold my hand at breakfast, at dinner—you don't care if I get burned for it because it makes you look and feel fearless."

Silence thickened, broken only by the passing of a scooter at the alley's mouth.

Cade stepped closer, voice low, stripped of bravado. "Neil. Look at me."

Neil looked at him, against his better judgment.

A soft rumble of thunder made its presence known. Neither seemed to acknowledge it.

Cade's jaw was tight, but his eyes—his blue eyes burned steady. "I don't care about them. I care about you. I held your hand because I wanted to. You think I'd chase you through half of Italy if this weren't real?"

Neil's chest ached. "Then why does it feel like I'm just... convenient to you? Why is everything either zero or a hundred? You keep saying it doesn't matter what they think—but what if it matters to me?"

Cade shook his head. "It matters. I was just trying to be protective." Cade paused to look at Neil. "This started because you showed up when no one else did. Honestly, it started way before then. I kept going because—" His voice cracked, softening. "—because I didn't want it to stop. I **don't** want it to stop, Neil."

Both ignored the rain falling. Neil's pulse thundered to match the rain. He wanted to believe. God, he wanted to. There was absolutely no reason for this to be happening. He was in Europe to get over Kyle, who became non-existent when Cade looked at him and remained so thereafter.

Cade touched his arm, grounding him. "Please. Don't pull away. I need you. Please understand, this is my first 'hello'. Teach me how to be better at this?"

And then—music, sending a divine message from an open window with an echo.

♫ *Si sono incontrati in un luogo affollato...*
(They met in a crowded place)...

Neil's breath hitched. He remained quiet as he listened to the song, and a tear came down his left cheek, masked by the water coming from his wet hair. They both heard the music, but only Neil could translate the lyrics.

♫ *Sai che lo ami e non puoi lasciarlo andare.*
(You know you love him and you can't let him go).

♫ *Da qualche parte dentro di te sai che anche lui ti ama.*
(You must know by now that this love is predestined).

Neil looked at Cade, still saying nothing.

"Neil, what does it mean?" Cade's thumb brushed Neil's wrist, insistent.

Neil felt the vocals as if they were a divine message from somewhere beyond, somewhere greater.

> ♫ *Ormai dovresti sapere che questo amore è predestinato.*
> *(By now, you should know that this love is predestined).*

"It means—" Neil paused because he couldn't say what he really felt yet. He didn't understand why he felt love for Cade already, but he surely wasn't going to make himself more vulnerable in this moment.

Cade leaned closer, breath trembling. "I'm here, Neil."

Neil's heart betrayed his sensibilities, and his feelings broke free in his voice.

"It means that I trust you. Please don't break that trust, Cade."

The chorus exploded just as Cade kissed him.

The kiss was trembling at first, then urgent—sweet, desperate, inevitable—public, but undeniably theirs. They were soaked with the emotion of the rain.

When they finally broke apart, foreheads pressed together, Cade whispered with a faint, crooked smile, "Still think you're just a prop?"

Neil's body shook with a mix of fear and joy. His

voice came raw, wrecked:

"You're either everything I've ever wanted, or you're going to destroy me, Cade."

"I'd rather be your everything," Cade said with optimism.

"You better fucking be worth it," Neil softly demanded. He had plans for his life, and he knew if Cade didn't grow up just a little, he could derail everything in the long term.

Above them, the song belted into the Italian sky, echoing off stone walls as if the whole city was making its case for them to be together.

Jenna and the rest of Neil's friends, who he had been with earlier, all watched from the window of the cafe, where they could see them at a distance. They were so happy for both of them, but especially for Neil.

"He deserves this," Sophie said. "Plus, I love this song."

"Ah, *Amore Predestinato*...predestined love. So sweet," Jenna added.

Mads popped the last bite of carrozza into her mouth and mumbled, "I'm going to need one of you to drop a set of bagpipes on my face."

"Gurrl, I'll do it," Kip said under his breath.

Chapter Twenty-Six.

Kip Wendell

If Penderton Academy had a weather report, Kip Wendell, often using the name "Kipwen" would be listed as **partly cloudy with a 90% chance of drama.**

He didn't walk down hallways; he breezed. He didn't raise his hand in class; he *flourished* it. His hair—usually bleached within an inch of its life—seemed to defy gravity, physics, and common sense. He accessorized like someone dared him to be unforgettable. And he always, always took the dare.

And yet, if anyone asked him—*anyone*—Kip was straight.

"Straight as an arrow," he'd say with a wink so

exaggerated it negated the statement completely.

Everyone assumed he was joking.

Kip wasn't sure he was.

Kip grew up with two sisters who treated the living room as a stage and him as their third understudy. There were dance routines, impromptu talent shows, and an annual competition called *Wendell Family Idol*, which was rigged in favor of whoever had the most glitter.

The Wendell parents encouraged creativity to a fault. His mother, an interior designer, believed color palettes were emotional states. His father, a chef, spoke about spices like they were characters in a romance novel.

"So of course," Kip liked to say, "this is how I turned out."

Flamboyance wasn't rebellion. It was his inheritance.

But sexuality? That was... different. Complicated. Undefined.

When Kip arrived at Penderton in ninth grade, he had no interest in labels. He knew what he liked: fun, chaos, attention, making people laugh, and occasionally making people gasp.

He flirted with girls because it was easy—effortless, even. They called him adorable, ridiculous, and charmingly unhinged. He liked the reactions. He liked the attention. He liked the theatrics of it.

But he also liked it when guys laughed at his jokes. When they fist-bumped him. When they hugged him in that bro-ish, effortless way that seemed casual to everyone except him, who felt something tug just a little too long.

He never said anything about it.

He wasn't ready to.

That was when he met **Neil Erickson**, who was quiet, observant, and so nervous about his sexuality that Kip could practically see the smoke coming from the boy's ears. Kip liked him instantly.

And when Neil came out sophomore year, Kip watched his world rearrange itself—watched him get braver, watched him step into something he'd been afraid of.

Kip celebrated him loudly, obnoxiously, and proudly.

But Kip didn't say a word about himself.

Why claim to be straight?

Because for Kip, claiming he was straight was easier than claiming anything else.

Straight meant no one asked questions.

Straight meant no one waited for him to explain feelings he didn't understand.

Straight meant he wasn't disappointing the parade

of girls who thought he was safe because he wasn't "like that."

Straight meant he didn't have to confront the quiet truth gnawing at him:

He wasn't sure he was.

He wasn't sure he wasn't, either.

So he floated. Somewhere in between. Loud on the outside, uncertain on the inside. A disco ball full of shattered pieces reflecting in every direction.

When Jenna once asked him casually, "Do you even like girls?" Kip had answered:

"Absolutely. I like everyone. I'm an equal-opportunity problem."

Which was true. Just not the whole truth.

The first crack in Kip's "straightness" came junior year at a Penderton soccer game. AJ Collins—golden, grinning, infuriatingly handsome—had just made a game-winning kick, and the stands erupted.

Kip shouted the loudest.

But when AJ jogged past the bleachers, grinning up at the crowd, he made eye contact with Kip. Only Kip. Gave him a playful salute. Ran on.

And Kip's stomach did something stupid and traitorous. He didn't mention it to anyone.

Not Mads, not Sophie, not Neil.

Especially not Neil.

He just lay awake that night staring at his ceiling, absolutely furious that AJ Collins' dumb, beautiful face was messing with his entire sense of self.

But his official stance remained:

Still straight.

Very straight.

Unreasonably straight.

Possibly the straightest person alive.

Except... maybe not.

Is Kip straight?

The truth?

Kip didn't know.

Not knowing made him uncomfortable. Uncomfortable made him deflect. Deflecting made him theatrical. Theatricality made people assume he was gay, which made him deny it harder.

It was an exhausting cycle.

But Kip had gotten very good at exhausting cycles.

He wasn't ready to claim a label.

He wasn't ready to abandon one, either.

He wasn't ready to say he liked boys.

He wasn't ready to say he didn't.

What he was ready for—what he knew deep down—was this:

One day, when he figured it out, his friends would accept it.

Neil would. Sophie would. Mads definitely would.

Jenna would roll her eyes and say, "Finally."

He knew this.

But he didn't know himself yet.

And for now, that had to be enough.

That night, as the Fab Five sat around Mads' backyard fire pit—Neil pressed close to his boyfriend, Josh, Sophie quietly content, Jenna on her phone, and Kip loudly critiquing everyone's s'more technique, caught himself staring at AJ.

AJ, who had stopped by unexpectedly in the school courtyard earlier that day, who had flopped onto the grass beside him and Sophie like it was the most natural thing in the world. Who now nudged him and said, "You're weird, dude. But in a good way."

Kip swallowed hard.

"Straight," he reminded himself silently. "Super straight."

But his heart whispered something else.

Maybe. Maybe not. Maybe yes. Maybe later.

He wasn't ready to know.

He enjoyed being unique.

Chapter Twenty-Seven.

The walk back to the hostel felt like moving underwater. The cobblestones glowed under the street lamps, coastal Italy existing around them like nothing extraordinary had just happened—even though Neil's lips still tingled, even though his heart hadn't found its regular rhythm since Cade kissed him.

They turned a corner and passed a group of classmates clustered under a trattoria awning. The whispers started immediately, rippling through the group like static. Neil heard his name once, Cade's twice. No one said anything to their faces, but the heat of being watched clung to them all the same.

Neil shoved his hands into his pockets. Cade didn't flinch. He walked taller, almost smug, like he'd been waiting for this.

Then Neil's phone buzzed. And again. Cade's too.

Neil fished his phone out of his damp pocket and froze. On Instagram, someone had already posted a blurry-but-undeniable photo: him and Cade in the alley, leaning in, caught mid-kiss in the rain. The caption was a string of heart emojis, and the video looped with *Amore Predestinato* blaring in the background, synced up almost perfectly to the moment their lips touched.

Neil's stomach dropped. His first thought: *we're ruined*. His second: *it looks... kind of amazing*.

The photo wasn't staged, but it might as well have been.

Cade and Neil, kissing in a narrow side alley just off the cobblestone street, sunlight spilling over the wet, storm-lit stones. Cade had one hand pressed to the wall beside Neil's head, the other resting at Neil's waist. Neil's chin was tilted up toward him, lips parted, and eyes closed like he was weightless.

Behind them, the blur of the coastal town stretched away—whitewashed buildings, flower boxes spilling color from balconies, and a slice of blue sea at the edge of the frame.

It was breathtaking in its imperfection: Cade's shirt half-untucked, Neil's curls messy from the salt air and rain, their shadows long across the stones.

Posted to Instagram by a classmate, it looked less like a tourist snapshot and more like a movie still—two boys caught in the kind of kiss people only dreamed about.

The caption was simple, careless, and damning:

pendertonkid
Italy is for lovers.   #CalabriaNights

Within minutes, hearts and shocked-face emojis flooded the comments, classmates tagging each other, sharing it faster than Neil could process.

For everyone else, it was gossip.

For Neil, it was exposure.

For Cade, it was liberation.

sarahbeth23 3m
UM ••••••

trevorrules 3m
called it.

mallorygrace 4m
wait is this for real???

jennydrinksespresso 6m
ngl this is hotter than anything I've seen in a movie

He turned the screen to Cade, voice tight. "Is this— good or bad?"

Cade studied the post for a moment, then huffed a laugh. "Looks mostly supportive. Celebratory, even." He scrolled through the comments—some wide-eyed, some cheering, and a few jokes in bad Italian. "Either way..." He handed the phone back. "I like it."

He paused, his voice dipping quieter as he looked at Neil. "How about you?"

Neil's pulse thudded in his ears. The world already knew now. The whispers, the photo, the song—they weren't hiding anymore.

He swallowed. "I... think I like it too."

Cade's smile widened, easy and sure. He bumped Neil's shoulder as they kept walking, like that settled it.

But Neil's chest still ached with a knot of nerves, tangled up with something brighter: relief.

By the time they reached the hostel lobby, the whispers had turned into something bolder. A small cluster of classmates broke off from the couches where they'd been scrolling their own feeds.

"Yo, that was you two?" one of the guys from Neil's econ class asked, grinning widely. "Legendary."

A girl from the art club laughed, clutching her phone. "Seriously—falling in love in Italy? Who even gets to say that? You're like in a movie, and we are all extras."

Neil's face flushed hot. He opened his mouth to argue—to say *love* was a pretty big leap from a kiss in an alleyway—but Cade beat him to it, grinning like it was the most natural thing in the world.

"Guess we got lucky," Cade said smoothly, slinging an arm across Neil's shoulders.

Neil's stomach twisted. Lucky, yes. But in love? He wasn't ready to stamp that word on what was happening—not yet, not with his heart still whiplashing between panic and exhilaration.

Still, the smiles around them felt startlingly genuine. Not cruel. Not mocking.

"You're trending in our class group chat," another student chimed in. "Like, half the comments are jealous. You know that, right?"

Neil blinked. For three and a half years at Penderton Prep, he'd been wallpaper—competent, reliable, but not the kind of guy anyone whispered about at breakfast. Now people he barely knew were clapping him on the back, saying things like, "Good for you, man," or "Didn't see it coming, but I like it."

Cade leaned down, close enough for only Neil to hear. "Told you. Italy's got our backs."

Neil tried to smile, but his thoughts were in a tangle. Cade seemed to be thriving in the spotlight, but Neil wasn't sure if he could live up to the version of their story everyone else was already writing.

The crowd of congratulations eventually thinned, but Neil still felt eyes on them. Every laugh and every grin aimed their way made his skin tingle, as if he were under a spotlight.

When they reached the lobby, Neil tugged gently at Cade's arm. "Do you want to head upstairs? I... kinda need to find the... washateria."[1]

Cade gave him a look, all raised eyebrows and sly grin. "Laundry. That's your grand escape plan?"

"It's practical," Neil said, already steering him toward the stairwell. "And somebody has to wash your sandy socks."

The hostel's laundry room was small, tucked in the basement with one rickety washer and dryer. Neil combined their clothes into a single load—shirts, socks, jeans, everything thrown together without a second thought. Cade leaned against the machine, arms folded, watching him with that maddening grin.

"You just... mixed mine with yours?" Cade asked.

Neil shrugged. "What, are your boxers too good for my T-shirts?"

Cade's grin widened. "Nah. I think I like it. Our stuff is all tangled up. Feels... official."

Neil froze for half a second, heart banging in his chest. Then Cade tugged him upright, caught his wrist gently in his hand, and kissed him.

It wasn't cautious like in Paris or stolen like in Rome. This kiss was heat and certainty—Cade's hand sliding up the back of Neil's neck, Neil clutching his shirt like he'd fall without it. The washer rattled to life, a loud metallic

[1] Washateria: laundromat, hotel laundry room.

thrum giving them cover.

Halfway through, Cade broke away just long enough to fish his phone from his pocket. Neil frowned, breathless. "Seriously? You're checking your Insta now?"

"Not checking." Cade grinned, tapping his screen. The familiar notes of *Amore Predestinato* filled the little basement, bouncing off the concrete walls. "Downloaded it. Along with a few others. Figured we needed a playlist."

Neil's laugh came out shaky, half disbelief, half joy. "You—made us a soundtrack?"

"Damn right," Cade said, pulling him back in. "Laundry room dance floor. Come here."

"You are just too good to be true, Cade."

The song swelled, their kiss deepening with it. Salt air drifted faintly through the cracked window, mixing with the warm, dizzy closeness of Cade's mouth on his. By the time the chorus hit, Neil wasn't sure where his heartbeat ended, and the music began.

When they pulled apart, foreheads pressed together, Cade whispered, "Laundry was the excuse. But this? This was always the plan."

Neil chuckled, breathless. "You're a terrible influence."

"Or the best," Cade said, hitting repeat on the song before kissing him again, the washer clattering like applause in the background.

Chapter Twenty-Eight.

Dinner was loud and crowded, filled with the aroma of garlic and olive oil and overlapping conversations. Kids were snapping photos of their food with phones, making shutter sounds every millisecond.

Neil tried to focus on his pasta, but he could feel it in the air—everyone knew.

"Hey," one of their roommates announced, grinning over a slice of pizza, "we figured we'd crash with other friends tonight. Give you guys the room."

Neil almost dropped his fork. "Please don't feel like you need to do that—"

"It's the perfect excuse to party all night," another

chimed in. "Win-win. Maybe we will get lucky, too."

The laughter around the table drowned out any protest Neil might have made. Cade just squeezed his knee under the table, his grin mischievous.

Back in their room, it felt twice as big without the clutter of voices, messy classmates, and bags. Just them, the ceiling fan's steady whir, and a neat pile of clean laundry.

Neil tried to busy himself, folding shirts with a precision that could have earned extra credit. Cade sprawled across his bed, iPad balanced against a pillow.

"What are we going to watch?" Neil asked.

Cade scrolled lazily. "*Heartstopper? Sex Education?* Fitting, right?"

Neil rolled his eyes but couldn't hide his smile. "I'm sensing a theme."

For a while, it was domestic: folding, teasing, pretending to watch whatever was on the iPad. But beyond laundry, Cade and Neil found themselves sitting closer, shoulders brushing, then hips.

If anything notable happened on screen, neither Cade nor Neil would have noticed. They just weren't watching it anymore. Cade was watching Neil, and Neil was pretending not to notice.

"You fold laundry like someone's grading you," Cade

teased, voice low, eyes warm.

Neil gave a nervous laugh. "Years of practice. Why does that make me question if you do laundry at home at all?"

"We can talk about my laundry habits another time." Cade slid the neat stack of shirts aside. "I think we've done enough laundry for one night."

"What's this 'we' shit?" Neil chuckled.

Neil barely had time to breathe before Cade leaned in from behind, catching his mouth with his from the side. It was different this time—deeper, more urgent, yet domestic, as if it happened all the time. Cade's hand slid to Neil's jaw, tilting his face, and Neil let himself melt into it, fingers curling in Cade's shirt.

The kiss stretched, grew, and turned into two and then three buttons being undone, until Neil lost count. Cade pulled him down with him, the bed dipping beneath their weight. Neil's heart hammered so hard he could feel it in his throat, but he didn't stop. Couldn't.

"Can I touch you?"

"Yeah."

Cade's hands traced cautious but specific paths— Neil's shoulder, his arm, his waist—pausing just long enough for Neil to nod, to breathe yes without saying it. Neil touched him back, shy at first, then braver, like they were learning each other in a language only they could speak.

The movie flickered on, forgotten. The pile of folded laundry slipped to the floor, unnoticed.

When they finally paused, both breathless, Cade whispered, "You know what's crazy?"

"What?" Neil murmured, lips still inches away.

"That this feels... easy. Like I've been waiting to get here with you."

Neil took a deep breath, not with panic this time but with something dizzy and light. "Yeah," he whispered back. "Me too."

"I love feeling like I am protecting you... us, really, earlier today," Cade said, holding him firmly.

"Yeah? You like protecting your *ragazzo?*[1] *Fidanzato?*[2]

"I do. I like it a lot. I liked it even more when I hooked your hand on my jeans' front pocket, and you left it there, like it belonged where I put it." Cade nuzzled up to Neil.

"I really liked that a lot too," Neil said. "You make me feel really... special."

And then the night belonged to them—no interruptions, no whispers, just the whir of the ceiling

[1] *Ragazzo:* boy

[2] *Fidanzato:* boyfriend

fan, the salt air drifting through the window, and the steady rhythm of two boys discovering how much they wanted each other.

Cade stopped himself after things became too hot between them.

"I didn't ask first if you were okay with making out. I'm sorry."

"Cade, it's fine. Thank you for considering me, though."

"I've just done so much that was wrong in my approach with you. I want to do things right from now on." Cade paused, looking at Neil strangely. "Did I just make this weird?"

"Hey, I like weird." Neil teased, slightly embarrassing Cade. "How about we make it my responsibility to say something if I'm uncomfortable? Would that work?"

"Yeah, I like that. So can I—"

"Oh, shut up and go back to what you were doing," Neil jokingly demanded.

Cade quickly moved to kiss Neil on his back, close to the waistline of his shorts, moving his shirt up to drag his tongue up Neil's spine to his neck.

"How about that?" Cade asked softly at Neil's right ear, then down to lick his neck below his ear and forward to his collarbone.

Neil pulled his shirt over his head,

"I think you're on to something," Neil said.

The next morning, Neil woke to sunlight sneaking through the thin curtains and the faint crash of waves outside. For a second, he didn't remember where he was—until he shifted and realized Cade's well-developed arm was slung heavily across his chest.

Neil froze, then let out a quiet laugh. Cade was practically draped over him like a human blanket, hair sticking up in every direction.

"Morning," Neil whispered, testing the waters.

Cade groaned, pulling the pillow over his head. "Nope. Illegal. Mornings are banned."

Neil chuckled, trying to wriggle free. "I can't breathe, you know."

"You'll live," Cade mumbled into the pillow to avoid morning breath. "You're sturdy."

Neil shoved at him lightly. "And you're dead weight."

Cade peeked out with one eye, still half-asleep, grinning. "Dead sexy weight, though."

Neil rolled his eyes, but the heat crept up his neck anyway. "You really think you're funny, huh?"

"Think?" Cade yawned. "I know."

"Your cockiness is growing on me. It's starting to become sexy, and that's dangerous."

They wrestled lazily until Cade finally sat up, rubbing his face. He stayed sprawled on the bed, reaching for his phone on the nightstand.

A few seconds later, music drifted softly from the tiny speaker. Neil blinked in recognition as the opening chords of a Mellow Casualty song filled the room.

"Really?" Neil asked, though his lips were tugging into a smile.

Cade stretched, unapologetic. "What? It's a vibe. Morning soundtrack. Just us and the sea."

"I'm just surprised you want something this happy-sounding while complaining about mornings," said Neil. He shook his head and shrugged, but the warmth in his chest spread as the chorus floated through the sunlit room.

Cade sang along off-key, grinning like a fool. He wrapped his arms around Neil from behind and started softly singing along while gently bouncing him.

"OMG, you're so cringe," Neil laughed. "And ridiculous."

"Ridiculously charming," Cade countered, nudging Neil with his foot.

"I might have to jump you again," Neil sighed, faking

exasperation, but he couldn't stop the grin. The night before lingered between them—unsaid, but there in every glance and lazy brush of contact. And with the song looping in the background, it felt like the morning was theirs alone, stitched together with sunlight, music, and something neither of them was quite ready to name.

"Your voice says 'red flag,' but everything else is giving me 'green flag,'" Cade said confidently through a yawn.

Neil paused, then pounced on him and kissed his cheeks.

"It's all green flags," Neil said, enjoying Cade's megawatt smile.

The last night before Rome was all fire and bass. Someone had dragged massive speakers down to the sand, and the bonfire flared high enough to rival the stars. The music thumped—electronic, hypnotic—and the whole group gave in, bodies moving in the dark like the sea itself had pulled them into its rhythm.

Neil and Cade didn't mean to steal the spotlight, but once Cade tugged Neil into the circle of firelight, there was no stopping them. Both shirtless with bare feet in the sand, arms wound around each other, laughter sharp and bright—they moved like they'd rehearsed it for years.

Neil leaned back, Cade caught him at the waist, and for a split second, it looked like a scene from a movie that everyone secretly wanted to be in.

Phones went up. Flashes sparked. By the time they collapsed in front of a log to lean up against, sweaty and breathless, Neil's phone was buzzing like a cicada back home. He glanced at the screen and froze.

There it was: a blurry, firelit photo of him and Cade mid-dance, Neil's head thrown back in laughter, Cade looking at him like nothing else in the world existed. The caption read:

A Riley–Erickson romance is the love story we didn't know we needed. Look how perfect these two are for each other. Who had this on their bingo card? #notme

Neil shoved the phone at Cade, his face hot even in the night breeze.

Cade read it, then grinned wide enough to split the world in two. "They're not wrong."

Neil tried to groan, tried to act embarrassed, but it came out as a laugh. "We're literally trending as someone's dream couple. Do you know how surreal that is?"

"Yeah," Cade said, tugging him back toward the fire as another beat dropped. "But surreal is my favorite place to be with you."

And just like that, Neil gave in—laughing, dancing, and not caring who watched. The night belonged to them.

"Do you effing care?" Cade asked.

For once, Neil didn't feel like ducking his head or pretending it wasn't about him. He slipped the phone back into his pocket and grabbed Cade's hand, tugging him toward the firelit circle where the beat had shifted, hot and fast.

Neil mouthed silently to Cade, *I don't effing care.*

The opening of the Italian Tarantella blasted through the speakers, and the crowd whooped as dancers clapped in rhythm. Cade raised his eyebrows, as if to say, *"Really? Tarantella?"* But Neil only laughed and pulled him in tighter.

"I love how you have embraced my Italian roots," Neil said.

"That sounds like code for 'pull my hair, Daddy,'" Cade said with a mischievous grin.

Neil laughed, but didn't give Cade the response he wanted.

"Now if there was only music that represented pasty white WASPy culture," Neil verbally jabbed.

"You might be Tarantella, but I'm anything by Ian Randall," Cade fired back.

"You're way hotter than a Nashville legend like Ian Randall."

"Oh, really?" Cade's eyes narrowed. His smile widened as he sang a few lyrics from country music star Ian Randall's hit song. "Chasin' You," he sang over the music, grabbing Neil's belt loops.

They spun, collided, hands locked, moving together in a wild, joyful blur. Classmates clapped and cheered them on, and Neil—who used to shrink from attention—leaned into it. He didn't care how many phones were up or how many flashes went off. When Cade dipped him low and kissed him like the sea might rise to meet them, the crowd roared like they were in on it.

Neil broke away only long enough to grin against Cade's cheek. "Let's see what photos we get out of this tomorrow—" he kissed him again, heat and rhythm and laughter all tangled together—"and what the comments will be."

Cade just laughed, pulling him close as the music pounded and classmates circled tighter, chanting their names. Neil had never been so seen in his life. And he'd never felt freer at the same time.

By the time the bonfire was low in the photos and most of their classmates had wandered off toward their hostel, Cade and Neil were still on the sand, the glow of someone's forgotten speaker cycling through moody house beats.

By morning, after they put their devices in daily mode, their phones were buzzing like broken alarm clocks. Every time Neil cleared one notification, three more popped up. "This is insane," Neil muttered, thumbing through the feed. "Okay, listen to this—"

choirgurl88 33m
The Riley-Erickson power couple era begins.

ballislife23 36m
Not me crying over this like it's the season finale of a Netflix show.

latte_queen 44m
I thought this was fake at first, but then realized, nope, this is our reality now. Iconic.

tennissara 45m
Forget prom kings. Give them the presidency already.

ohsnapitsmaddie 53m
The way they're not even hiding. We LOVE growth!

countryroads45 55m
Ok, but tell me who choreographed that kiss because it deserves an Emmy.

cappuccino_girl 56m
Um. How 'bout No

Neil chuckled, scrolling down, but Cade was watching him instead of the screen, chin propped on his hand.

"What?" Neil asked, catching his stare.

"Keep reading," Cade said softly. "I don't even care what they say. I just like hearing you reading through them."

Neil rolled his eyes, cheeks warming. "You're mental, and I'm here for it."

"I'm mental for you," Cade answered, leaning back with a grin while Neil shook his head and read another. "You are the hottest when you realize people are seeing you, and I bet no one knew you had such a hot body until last night when we tucked our shirts through our belts like we were at Coachella."

Neil pretended to ignore him. He just smiled.

He kept scrolling, half laughing, half mortified. "Okay, this one—listen. '*The way Cade Riley used to only date cheerleaders, and now he's got Neil Erickson? Upgrade.*'"

Cade sat up straight, feigning outrage. "Excuse me? I am the upgrade. Clearly."

Neil smirked. "Mhm, that's not what @tinybutmighty thinks."

"Who even is that?" Cade shot back. "Sounds like a

hamster account."

Neil lost it, laughing so hard he nearly dropped the phone. "A hamster account? Really? That hamster thinks you are an arrogant jock."

"I'm serious. Nobody with that username gets to call me anything but an upgrade," Cade said, crossing his arms but fighting a grin.

Neil, still laughing, nudged him with his shoulder. "You're fearless, fighting with hamsters online."

"Oh, I'll fight whoever I have to." Cade leaned closer, voice dropping just enough to make Neil's pulse jump. "Now give me one where I get to defend you."

Neil rolled his eyes and tried to scroll again, but Cade was already leaning in. "Cade, I'm reading—"

"Not anymore, you're not."

And before Neil could argue, Cade kissed him—quick, sure, stealing the last word as always. Neil sighed against his mouth, smiling despite himself.

"Fine, I guess I'm not," Neil muttered when they finally broke apart. "For the record, you're definitely an upgrade in my book."

"Damn right," Cade said, tugging him in for another kiss. "Thank you, Kyle! He's mine now!"

Flashback to the night before.

Neil scrolled again, the light from his phone catching his grin. "Okay, last one. 'A Riley-Erickson romance is literally cinematic. Somebody call CRAVE.'"

Cade stretched out beside him, propped up on one elbow, watching Neil more than the phone. "See, they're not wrong."

Neil snorted. "Oh, please. If our lives were a show, you'd be the flashy lead. I'd be... the quirky side character who gets canceled after season one."

Cade reached over, plucked the phone from his hand, and tossed it gently into the sand. "Correction—you're the only character worth watching."

Neil laughed softly, shaking his head, but the warmth in Cade's eyes made his chest tight. "You're so dramatic."

"Guilty." Cade leaned closer, his voice low now, threading into the rhythm of the waves. "But also right."

Neil hesitated, then rested his forehead lightly against Cade's, breathing in the salt and smoke in his hair. "Fine. You win."

"Damn straight I do." Cade's smile brushed against Neil's lips before the kiss actually landed—slow, lingering, the kind that felt like it left a spark behind. "I mean, damn *gay* I... whatever," he chuckled.

When they pulled back, Neil exhaled, half laughing. "You know this is going to be everywhere by morning, right?"

Cade smirked, pulling him closer. "Good. I hope they enjoy the show."

And with the surf whispering around them, Neil stopped caring about tomorrow's photos, or comments, or anything at all—except the guy who had just made the world feel this small and this huge all at once.

Chapter Twenty-Nine.

Now, it was just... normal.

They were *together*, and everyone seemed to accept it without question.

On the platform in coastal Italy, backpacks slung over their shoulders, they blended into other students waiting for their train. The air was heavy with sunscreen, voices tumbling over each other as they chattered about souvenirs, grades, and the long flight home.

Neil felt Cade brush against him, their arms touching, not by accident. Cade didn't pull away, and neither did Neil.

"Feels weird, doesn't it?" Cade murmured.

"What does?" Neil asked.

"Being... us, and it being celebrated by people we don't even know."

Neil glanced around. He caught one classmate's eye—someone who'd teased them just days earlier. She smiled, gave a little wave, and went right back to her conversation.

"Yeah," Neil admitted. "Weird. But kind of nice."

They boarded the train side by side, sliding into a double seat without hesitation. This time, no one tried to swap or make a joke. They were left in peace, the countryside blurring past the windows as the train carried them north, toward Rome, toward the end.

Neil leaned back, the rhythm of the train settling into his bones. Cade stretched, his knee bumping Neil's, and left it there. They traded small talk about the trip, about what they'd miss, and about the food they wished they could smuggle home.

But under the words sat something heavier. Something neither of them quite dared to say.

Neil caught himself watching Cade laugh at his own dumb joke, and the thought came uninvited—*I love you.* It was so strong, so startling, that he had to look away, staring out at the blur of fields until his pulse steadied. It just wasn't the time, and he wanted Cade to say it first.

Beside him, Cade's smile faltered into something softer, almost thoughtful. He looked at Neil, as if he might be thinking the same thing.

But neither of them spoke it aloud. Not yet.

Instead, Cade reached for Neil's hand under the table, their fingers locking together easily and naturally, like they'd always done it.

The train rattled on toward Rome, toward flights and families and futures that neither of them had figured out yet. But for now, here, on this train, they were a couple, and that was enough.

By late afternoon, the train pulled into Rome, its brakes screeching against the rails. The group shuffled off in a blur of luggage and yawns, everyone processing the low-grade energy of students who knew the trip was nearly over. Tomorrow meant planes, airports, and real life.

But tonight? Tonight was theirs.

After a quick hostel check-in and a half-hearted dinner in the standard room, Neil and Cade slipped away. Nobody questioned it anymore. Nobody teased them.

The Roman night wrapped around them like warm velvet as they wandered through the streets, backpacks light, shoulders brushing. Street lamps cast golden halos on cobblestones, and the sound of scooters punctuated the night.

"So, one last adventure," Cade said, grinning as he gestured down a narrow alley that opened into a plaza. "Where to?"

Neil thought for a moment, then smiled. "The Trevi Fountain?"

"Touristy," Cade teased, but he didn't complain. "Verbal shrug."

When they reached it, the fountain was glowing, lit up like a dream. Tourists milled about, some tossing coins, some snapping pictures, but the crowd wasn't overwhelming this late at night. The rush of water drowned out most of the chatter, giving the place a kind of intimacy.

Neil fished a coin from his pocket and handed it to Cade. "Tradition says if you throw it in, you'll come back to Rome someday."

Cade smirked. "And if I don't throw it?"

"Then maybe you won't," Neil said. "But why risk it?"

Cade considered him, then closed his hand over the coin. "Only if you do it with me."

So they stood side by side, fingers brushing, and tossed their coins into the water. The splash was small, lost in the fountain's roar, but it felt enormous. Then they heard a cheer.

"Viva gli sposi!"

"Cin Cin!"

Several in the crowd turned to Cade and Neil and applauded.

"What is happening right now, Neil?"

"Perché ci applaudite?" Neil asked a friendly woman, clapping. (Why are you applauding?)

"Le vostre monete sono atterrate insieme. Vi sposerete," she said.

"Grazie," Neil responded, but with a shocked look.

"Neil? Are you okay?"

"Yeah," Neil said almost breathlessly. "Our coins landed together in the water."

"Oh?" Cade chuckled.

"The lore is that if two people's coins land together, they will be married. They are wishing us congratulations, even though it translates to bride and groom," he chuckled.

"Aw, well, that's kind of hilarious and... beautiful."

Neil knew what was coming. He already knew Cade well enough to see it. "Oh, here it comes, ...Cade!?"

Cade kissed Neil in a *big production* way, mostly because he thought it was romantic, but also for Neil to feel more applause. There were a few groans, but mostly celebratory clapping and cheering.

They lingered there for a few more moments, leaning against the balustrade, the glow of the water painting their faces. Neil felt Cade's hand find his again, their fingers tangling naturally. As they began to leave, Cade said loudly, while raising one arm in the air and making noise like Americans often do, "We are leaving to get married now. Thank you! Thank you all."

Neil had started to learn not to be so embarrassed by Cade's productions. It was fine. He was starting to appreciate Cade's bombastic method of living life loudly.

"You know," Cade said quietly, almost lost in the rush of water, "if we really do come back to Rome... I definitely want it to be with you."

Neil's chest tightened. The words weren't "*I love you,*" but they felt dangerously close. He swallowed hard, forcing a smile. "Then you'd better start saving."

Cade laughed softly, leaning closer until their shoulders pressed together, until Neil could feel the warmth of him even in the cool night air.

"Rileys don't *save.*"

That was Neil's first flag that Cade might have a different financial approach to the world.

They walked the Via della Stamperia until the stars

above Rome looked sharper against the black sky. Then they turned back toward the hostel, their hands still linked, their steps in sync, their silence conveying all the things neither of them dared to speak aloud yet.

"You are really growing on me, Cade."

"I'm not mad at that," Cade said playfully.

Chapter Thirty.

The morning air at Fiumicino Airport in Rome smelled faintly of the ancient stone and jet fuel, sharp and bittersweet all at once. Fiumicino Airport pulsed with travelers—families dragging sleepy children, tourists clutching souvenirs, and businesspeople tapping furiously at phones. Through it all, Penderton Academy's seniors shuffled in a slow-moving herd, a trail of matching hoodies and overstuffed carry-ons snaking through the terminal.

Neil felt the weight of every step. Not from his backpack—from this. The leaving. Each stride tugged him further from the magic of cobblestones and piazzas, from fountains and ruins and stolen moments that had made the trip feel like something out of a film.

Beside him, Cade yawned into his fist, bleary-eyed, his other hand brushing against Neil's as if by instinct. They didn't hold hands here—not in the middle of the bustling terminal where cameras flashed and classmates jostled—but the space between them still thrummed, alive with memory. The Trevi Fountain shimmered in Neil's mind: silver coins arcing, water spilling, promises left unsaid but felt in his bones.

At the check-in counter, one of the teachers clapped her hands and called out in a harried voice, "Penderton seniors—group check!" Groans rippled across the students like a wave, the collective dread of early flights and long queues.

"Neil!" Jenna called out. As she walked up, she handed their boarding passes to him and Cade. "I wasn't able to move Cade back to our section, but I was able to get you two together. You'll just have to sit around with some of the Soccer guys. I hope that is okay. It's the best they could do."

"One hundred percent. Thank you, Jenna." Neil hugged his friend.

Cade tapped her on the shoulder lightly and said, "Thank you."

"The aisle seat will probably stay vacant, so at least you have the whole row," she said.

"Rome's really kicking us out," Cade muttered, his voice low enough that it was just for Neil.

Neil smirked, though the gesture felt heavy on his lips. "Guess we'll just have to come back someday."

Cade glanced at him, his grin softer this time, private in a way no one else would notice. "With you, yeah. We will come back and visit your family again."

The line shuffled forward, the teacher herding them like cattle toward the security checkpoint. Beyond the massive windows, the city glittered in the morning light—domes catching fire from the rising sun, spires stabbing skyward, and laundry flapping from balconies as if Rome itself were waving goodbye. Neil drank it in one last time, the ache deepening. He wished, just for a heartbeat, that he could freeze time right there: Rome at his back, Cade at his side, the future still waiting.

But the line moved, and the airport swallowed them whole. By the time he blinked, Italy was behind them.

On the plane, exhaustion draped itself over everyone like a heavy blanket. They sank into their seats side by side, Cade sprawling with careless ease, Neil clutching the thin airline pillow like it might anchor him. Cade tilted his head back with a groan. "Ten hours home."

That's when the flight attendant appeared—mid-thirties, Italian, with a smile both polished and real. His eyes flicked from their joined hands (quickly dropped) to their faces. The pause stretched just long enough to thrum.

"You boys together?" he asked quietly, his accent softening the words.

Neil's stomach tightened.

Cade opened his mouth, already fumbling for something vague, but Neil beat him to it. He slipped into Italian, voice steady, surprising even himself:

"Sì. *Grazie per averlo notato.*"
(Yes, and thank you for noticing).

The man's smile warmed instantly. He leaned closer, switching languages so no one nearby could eavesdrop: "Your Italian is so good! Don't worry. You've got the family look. Italy always takes care of its own."

Neil flushed hot, unprepared for the kindness. Cade, who didn't need a translation, figured it out anyway, grinning wide as he slid his hand to squeeze Neil's bicep. "See? Even the flight attendant is rooting for us."

With a conspiratorial wink, the man slid two extra bottles of water, a spare blanket, and upgraded headphones onto their tray table. "Family treatment," he added in English, before moving on down the aisle.

Cade chuckled, nudging Neil's shoulder. "He's funny! You've got connections everywhere, don't you? Naples, Rome, even thirty thousand feet in the air."

Neil ducked his head, embarrassed but smiling. "It's not me. It's just... an Italian thing."

Cade studied him, expression softening into something more profound. "No. It's you. You make people want to look out for you." He hesitated, then added in a quieter tone, almost to himself, "Including me."

Neil looked at him lovingly from the window seat. "Aww. You want to take care of me?"

"Yes. I do."

"Lucky me," Neil said.

The engines rumbled, vibrations shivering up through the floor. The cabin lights dimmed, washing the space in twilight. Their hands found each other again, bold this time; the armrest slid up and was forgotten. Thanks to the attendant's small mercy, the aisle seat was left empty. Cade shifted, stretching long legs into the open space, while Neil let his head fall gently against Cade's shoulder.

For a while, neither spoke. Neil's breath evened out, drifting toward sleep, the warmth of his weight anchoring Cade in place.

Ten hours to go. Ten hours until home. Cade let his

head tip against Neil's, the faintest smile playing at his mouth. Nashville loomed ahead, and with it, a thousand question marks: his parents, his brother, and the inevitable fallout. But beyond that, he saw it already—his Citroën rolling through the city, Neil in the passenger seat, music blaring, dinner dates downtown, late-night shows where Neil would tilt his head back and laugh like he meant it.

These thoughts filled Cade's chest until it almost ached.

Whatever came next, he couldn't wait to find out.

Cade got up to use the lavatory. Once inside, he secured the door behind him, looked in the mirror at himself, and felt proud of what he accomplished on this trip. It all hit him at once, and he had an emotional moment in private. Cade returned to his seat to find Neil asleep. He took his hand and gently kissed it, hoping he wouldn't wake him. Neil curled to Cade's shoulder most sweetly, and Cade felt like the happiness might break his chest.

Chapter Thirty-One.

The airplane cabin lights flickered back to life, signaling breakfast trays and the slow shuffle of students stretching awake. Neil blinked against the half-light, disoriented for a second until he felt the steady rise and fall of Cade's chest under his cheek.

"Morning," Cade whispered, voice still thick with sleep.

Neil sat up a little, rubbing his eyes. "How long was I out?"

"A couple of hours. You drool, by the way."

"I do not."

"You totally do," Cade grinned, brushing an

imaginary smear off his T-shirt.

Neil groaned but smiled, leaning back against the seat. Then it hit him—harder than the turbulence had all flight. "Cade... our parents."

Cade's grin faltered. "Oh. Right. Parents. Pickup at the airport."

They both went quiet for a beat as the plane continued home. Around them, classmates were already comparing souvenirs and snapping blurry sunrise photos through the windows. Normal. Easy.

Neil finally broke the silence. "So what's the plan? Do we... walk out together? Pretend we're just seatmates? Do we..." He trailed off, not sure how to finish the thought.

Cade tilted his head, considering. "Honestly? I don't want to pretend, not after all this. But maybe we don't need to announce anything either. We can just... be together. Let them figure it out."

Neil's heart thudded. He wanted to believe that would be enough—that his parents, Cade's parents, and their whole separate worlds would just... fall in line. "And if they don't figure it out?"

Cade gave a little shrug, his hand finding Neil's. "Then we'll make them. But either way, I'm not stepping off this plane and pretending you don't matter."

Neil looked at him, at the determination in Cade's tired eyes, and felt something shift inside him—equal parts terror and hope.

"Okay," Neil whispered. "Then we need a united front. No awkward 'uh, we just sat next to each other for ten hours' nonsense."

Cade smirked. "Deal. United front. Starting with breakfast, because if they serve me one more cold croissant, I'm calling the embassy."

Neil laughed, the tension breaking for just a moment as the flight attendant slid their trays onto the table. But even as he unwrapped the foil, his mind spun on repeat: *airport, parents, together.*

Cade went quiet for a long moment, pushing the sad little croissant around on his tray. Then he glanced at Neil, his voice lower than it had been before. "You know what's wild? I never even asked if you are out to your parents."

Neil's smile was slight but sure. "Yeah. I told them last year. It wasn't this huge thing—it was just... me, and they love me. They'll love you, too. That's not even in question."

Neil swallowed hard, trying to let the words land. He really wanted to hear Cade say he loved him someday. Another thought pressed in, heavy as the stale cabin air.

Cade's family—West Meade, Southern tradition, silver picture frames lined with legacy. *Old Nashville money.*

And him? He came from Green Hills, from a family who'd built their success one store at a time. Giordano's Market—aisles of imported olive oils, handmade pastas, and produce so fresh that his dad still boasted it could "outshine Kroger any day of the week." They were proud of what they'd built, proud of their Italian roots.

But would Cade's family see it that way?

Neil forced a smile and sipped his orange juice, saying nothing. It wasn't that he doubted Cade—but acceptance was an entirely different matter, nor should it be expected.

Cade leaned closer, brushing his knee against Neil's under the blanket. "Hey. You're quiet. You okay?"

"Yeah," Neil lied softly. "Just... thinking about home."

Cade squeezed his hand. "Me too. But whatever happens, we've got this. You and me."

Neil nodded, trying to believe it. Outside the window, the Atlantic stretched endlessly below, a ribbon of light just beginning to bend across the horizon. A few more hours to go—and then the real test would begin.

The airport had that restless air that always made

Neil feel small. Penderton students spilled out of the jetway in a loud, clumsy wave, dragging carry-ons and shouting about missed connections, as parents waited in the pickup lanes.

Neil lagged at the back, Cade's shoulder brushing his as they walked. Cade still wore sunglasses—more out of habit than necessity now—but his eyes flicked toward Neil often, like they were checking that he hadn't vanished.

The bubble had popped. Europe was gone, replaced by fluorescent lights, Department of Homeland Security announcements, and the weight of home.

Neil tugged his duffel higher on his shoulder, pulse ticking faster. "Well," he said, forcing a laugh, "back to reality."

Cade grinned, careless as ever. "Good thing I like reality better now."

Neil's throat tightened. "Yeah, but—this isn't Paris. People here..." He trailed off, glancing at the crowd ahead. Already, classmates were peeling back into familiar clusters, laughter echoing, secrets traded in whispers. Nashville remembered everything.

Cade slowed, letting the others move on ahead. When they reached the baggage claim carousel, he hooked a hand around Neil's wrist. "You're doing it again," he said softly.

"Doing what?"

"Acting like I'm gonna peel off the second someone looks at us sideways." He squeezed gently, pulling Neil's gaze back to him. "Newsflash: I'm not. Paris wasn't a bubble. It was me finally not being stupid about what I wanted."

Neil blinked, the words sinking like stones in water. "And what happens if everyone else makes it impossible?"

Cade leaned in, close enough that only Neil could hear. "Then screw everyone else. I picked my seat on the train, didn't I?"

Neil wanted to believe him. God, he did. And when Cade's grin broke—bright, stubborn, unshaken—something in Neil loosened.

Still, as their classmates shouted and parents waved from the railing, Neil couldn't stop the worry chewing at him: Paris had felt like a secret miracle. Nashville felt like a test.

But Cade was still holding his wrist, steady as ever.

"Hey," Cade said. "One last kiss before the parents trample everyone.

Neil tilted his head up to kiss Cade and added a strong hug.

"Here we go! Back to reality," Neil added.

The terminal rang with the kind of chaos only international flights could conjure up—luggage carts weaving, kids whining, overhead announcements rattling through bad speakers. The line for customs had crawled, and by the time Neil and Cade stepped through the sliding doors into the arrivals hall, the crowd of waiting parents surged forward like a tide.

There were squeals, hugs, camera flashes, and backpacks exchanged for rolling suitcases. Moms cried. Dads awkwardly patted shoulders. The sea of reunion blurred together—except in one corner.

Neil's parents spotted him instantly; his mother waved so wildly that she nearly dropped her purse. His dad's grin split wide, proud and relieved. Neil smiled, tugging his bag closer, heart catching in his throat.

But then—no Cade parents. No tall Southern mother in pearls. No stern father with a handshake sharp enough to cut glass. Instead, Tilda stood with quiet authority and a kind smile.

Tilda, whom Neil had only ever heard about in Cade's offhand comments—his former governess turned house manager, the one who ensured his life actually ran smoothly while his parents floated on dinner party yachts and worldwide business trips.

"Caden Walker Riley," she said as he reached her, the familiar European voice lilting with affection. She pulled him into an embrace before he could even reply. "You've gotten taller again. When will you stop growing, hmm?"

Walker, Neil noted. These were details Neil hadn't thought about since Salerno.

Cade laughed, relief breaking across his face like sun after rain. "Tilda. You didn't have to—"

"I most certainly did. Your parents couldn't rearrange their schedules." She gave a look that suggested she'd argued otherwise and lost. Then she cupped his face, carefully checking the still-healing skin around his eyes. "And you've been through enough without them."

Neil stood just behind Cade, watching, trying not to stare too openly. It was warm, but not the scene he'd expected. Cade's parents hadn't come. They'd sent someone else. Someone who, yes, clearly loved Cade, maybe more fiercely than his actual family. But still.

Tilda's eyes flicked to Neil then, sharp but kind. "And you must be the boy who's been looking after him."

Neil swallowed, offering his hand. "Neil Erickson, ma'am."

Tilda's expression softened immediately, a hint of a

smile tugging at her mouth. She ignored his hand and pulled him into a hug instead. "Thank you for keeping him in one piece. Truly."

Behind them, Neil's parents were already waving him over, their faces alight with curiosity. Neil hesitated, torn in two directions—toward his family, toward Cade.

Cade noticed. He leaned closer, whispering just for him. "Go on. They've been waiting. Text me later."

"Who is that lady, Mom, and why did Neil stop to talk to them first?" Neil's sister Isabella asked in her young voice.

"I don't know, honey," Mrs. Erickson answered. "I think we might find out, though."

But Neil lingered a second longer for a hug, the ache in his chest settling heavy. Cade deserved more than being picked up by an employee. He deserved parents who showed up.

Neil forced a smile anyway and turned toward his family, but the thought clung to him: If his parents couldn't show up here, how could that affect Cade in the future? Or worse: how could the past affect him?

Neil's parents were a wall of joy—his mother pulling him into her arms so tightly he thought his ribs might crack, his father clapping him on the back, his sister, Isabella, snapping pics while their little brother, Maxx, bounced up and down, chanting, "Neil's home! Neil's home!"

They shepherded him through the terminal with luggage trailing behind, the smell of airport coffee and fried food giving way to the comfort of their minivan. Once inside, Neil leaned back against the seat, letting the noise of his family wash over him.

From the driver's side, his mother's eyes flicked up to the rearview mirror. "*Tesoro*, who was that woman you were talking to with your friend? She hugged you both like she knew you forever."

Neil exhaled. "That was Tilda—Cade's former governess. Well, house manager now. His parents sent her to pick him up instead," he said sadly. "That seems... upsetting."

His mother frowned, her knuckles tightening slightly on the back of the seat. "Instead?"

"Yeah." Neil looked down at his hands, twisting them together. "He got hurt overseas, Mom. He went to the hospital and left with his eyes bandaged for four days. His parents didn't even call."

A quiet hush filled the van. His sister lowered her phone. Even his little brother went still. Neil came from a family that had no concept of parental absence, let alone neglect.

Neil's mom reached back to him, her hand finding his knee and giving it a firm, tender squeeze. "*Oh, tesoro mio.* Some parents… some parents just don't know how to be loving. Not every family shows the same amount of love that we do." Her husband reached over to touch her back in a gesture of solidarity.

Her voice was warm, steady, and confident. Neil blinked rapidly against the sting behind his eyes, letting her words envelop him like a blanket.

Through the window, Nashville rolled by in the late-afternoon light—familiar streets, familiar skyline. But Neil's mind lingered on Cade in that other car with Tilda, wondering what it must have felt like to step through the airport terminal and find not his mother, not his father, but someone on the payroll.

Neil sat back, his family's voices bubbling around him, and made himself a silent promise: Cade would never doubt he had someone who showed love for him. Not as long as Neil was in his life.

Chapter Thirty-Two.

The Erickson house ran well into the evening. Laughter spilled from every corner, his grandmother insisting everyone eat another *polpetta*, or meatball, as Neil would call it. His grandfather retold the story of how he'd once outbid a man at the produce market in Naples, as if it were a war victory. Plates piled high with pasta, roasted chicken, and fresh bread disappeared as fast as they were set out; that wasn't even to mention the antipasto, which was gone as soon as it hit the plates.

Neil felt full in every sense—his stomach was heavy, his heart was overwhelmed, and his head was already aching from jet lag. When the last of the tiramisu was finished, and the espresso cups clinked empty, his father pushed back his chair with a satisfied sigh.

"Well," Mr. Erickson said, clapping his son on the shoulder, "I think your mama deserves the final word tonight." He kissed her cheek, then glanced at their daughter. "Come on, sweetheart. Help me entertain Nonna and Nonno in the living room."

They left, and suddenly the kitchen felt still—just Neil and his mother, the scent of coffee lingering, the dishes stacked high but forgotten.

She turned to him, her eyes sharp but soft. "*Tesoro mio.* Tell me—was everything truly okay in Europe?"

Neil hesitated, tracing the rim of his espresso cup. "Mostly, yeah. It was... more than okay, actually."

Her gaze narrowed slightly. "And the boy? The one at the airport. The one with the... *governante*?"

Neil's throat tightened. "Cade. His name is Cade Riley. He's—" He stopped, fumbling for words while resisting the urge to smile widely. "He was one of the seniors on the trip. We didn't really know each other very well before, but then... something happened."

"Something?"

"He got hurt," Neil explained, his voice low. "A prank went wrong. He had to have his eyes covered for four days, and I got assigned to help him get around. At first, it was just a responsibility. You know—safety team. But then..." His voice wavered. "We spent every day together. Every night. Talking, walking, holding hands. And somewhere in there, it stopped being an assignment."

His mother tilted her head, listening. "Kids can be so cruel with what they think is funny."

"I think... I care about him," Neil admitted. "More than I expected. More than I can say. But his parents—" He shook his head. "They didn't even come to the airport. Just sent Tilda. I don't know what it means for him or for me. Or for us."

For a long moment, his mother said nothing. Then she reached across the table, her hand warm and sure over his.

"*Amore* is never simple, *tesoro*. But if this boy made your heart feel lighter when you were far from home... then that is no small thing. That is real."

Neil looked at her, the knot in his chest loosening just slightly.

"*Come può qualcuno dare amore...?*" Neil asked, "*Se non lo sa dalla sua famiglia?*" (How can someone give love, if he doesn't know it from his family?)

She smiled faintly, brushing his hair back as she had when he was little. "If his parents cannot see their son as a treasure, then that is their loss. Not yours. Not his."

Neil swallowed, blinking fast, and whispered, "*Grazie, Mamma.*"

"Always," she said softly, giving his hand one more squeeze. "If he is deserving, he will learn love from you."

The Riley house stood tall and perfect in West Meade, every window glowing like a scene from a magazine spread. From the outside, it looked like the kind of home that never knew a day of trouble—white columns, sprawling lawn, roses trimmed within an inch of their lives.

Inside, it was silent. Too silent.

Tilda clicked on the entryway door latch and set Cade's suitcase down with practiced ease. "Home," she said gently, her voice carrying the weight his parents' should have.

Cade lingered just past the threshold, his eyes catching on the framed portraits along the hall—his father in tuxedo after tuxedo, his mother at charity galas, himself as a boy in stiff bowties, smiling because Tilda had told him to.

"Where are they?" Cade asked, but he already knew.

"Your father had a business dinner," Tilda said, hanging up her coat. "Your mother is with her sister in Charleston." She looked at him with a quiet apology.

"They both send their love."

Cade huffed a humorless laugh, dropping onto the bottom stair. "*Right*. 'Their love.'" He rubbed his eyes, still tender from the bandages. "I spent ten days across Europe, nearly blinded, fell in—" He stopped himself short, clenching his jaw. "And they couldn't even come to the airport."

Tilda sat beside him, her hands folded neatly in her lap. "You don't need their performance, Cade. You never did." She tilted her head toward him, her voice softening. "What matters is that you came home with more than you left with. You look different. Lighter."

Cade stared at his shoes, heat rising in his face. "You think?"

"I know." She gave him a small smile. "Who is he?"

Cade's head snapped up. "What?"

"Caden Walker Riley," she said, amused, "I raised you. I know when you've got a secret. And I know when it's a good one."

Cade's lips twitched into the faintest grin. He didn't answer outright, but the color in his cheeks betrayed him.

"Neil. He's just... the *best*, Tilda."

Tilda patted his knee, satisfied. "Good. I like seeing that look on you." She rose to her feet, smoothing her skirt.

"Now, go upstairs. Rest. You've had enough travel and drama for one summer. I'll make you something to eat."

As Cade trudged up the grand staircase, he glanced back once more. The house still felt cavernous and cold, but at least Tilda's presence warmed the edges. And in the quiet of his room, his mind returned to Neil—Neil's laugh, Neil's hand in his, and Neil's voice promising him he wasn't alone. He missed his tight spaces with Neil and preferred them to this cold cave he lived in.

Cade didn't feel entirely abandoned in that house with Tilda there and Neil a text away.

Cade lay sprawled across his bed, suitcase still half-unpacked on the floor, staring at the ceiling fan as it spun in lazy circles above him. His phone buzzed on the nightstand. A message from Neil.

Neil
Hey. You good?
Did you eat yet?

Cade grinned faintly and typed back, thumbs moving slowly, carefully.

Cade
Tilda's making me dinner. Like old times.
I'll be fine.
What about you? It feels weird to text you,
btw.

Neil
lol yeah my family made a big dinner. I'm
stuffed and just wanted to check
on you.

He sent it, then slipped the phone down on the table with a sigh.

His mother, drying her hands on a towel, turned to study him. "Is it him?" she asked gently.

Neil nodded. "He's fine. Tilda's cooking for him."

Her brow furrowed. "But not his parents."

Neil's silence was enough of an answer, confirmed with a sigh.

His mother came closer, setting her hand on his shoulder. "Tesoro, tell him to come here next time. I'll feed him. I don't care if he's from fancy West Meade or Mars— if he is important to you, he has a place at this table."

Neil's throat tightened. He nodded, grateful, though he didn't send the message. Not yet. Cade was proud, and this was fragile ground. But still, knowing he had his mother's full welcome eased something in him.

His phone buzzed again.

Cade
I keep thinking about Paris. About us.
It feels weird to be back here without you

Neil smiled down at the screen, warmth flooding

through the ache inside him.

Neil
Same

He hit send before he could overthink it, leaning back in the chair. In the quiet sounds of the Erickson kitchen, with his mother watching him like she already understood, Neil felt the first threads of *home* start to weave themselves around Cade—even if Cade didn't know it yet.

Neil
If I had known your parents weren't going
to be home, I would have brought you
home with me.

Cade
That's a nice thought, but this is normal.

Neil
What about your brother?

Cade
I have no idea where he is either. He's
probably off with his girlfriend. Tilda said
dinner is ready. I'm going to go downstairs
and eat with her. Visit with your awesome
family. TTYL 🖤

271

Chapter Thirty-Three.

Late morning in Green Hills smelled of cut grass and honeysuckle even in September, the kind of neighborhood rhythm Cade Riley had only seen in drive-bys on his way downtown. The streets curved under tall sycamores, their branches intertwined, forming canopies that mottled the sidewalks with shade. Porch swings creaked with the slow ease of late summer, sprinklers hissed across front lawns, and someone down the block was already grilling hot dogs as if it were a holiday.

Neil was on the porch swing with his little brother, Maxx, both barefoot in shorts and T-shirts, the picture of a late summer morning without effort. Neil nudged the swing higher with his heel, Maxx's laughter carrying through the heavy air, while the sound of cicadas filled the spaces between.

Cade eased the 1967 *Bleu Antarctique* Citroën DS21 Chapron Serie 2 Cabriolet, a very special French classic, to the curb, the sun catching the silvery blue and cognac leather until it gleamed like polished armor. Against the quiet, standard sidewalks and weathered driveways, the car shimmered like it had been airlifted in from another world. He cut the engine, listening to the tick of cooling metal, as the car lowered evenly. He wondered if it looked too loud here—like a movie set piece shoved into the wrong scene.

Neil stood, eyebrows arched nearly into his hairline. "Are you serious? You parked that on my street?"

Cade slid out, pulling his sunglasses free and squinting into the Tennessee sun. "Is it okay here? I don't want to... you know, be that guy who blocks a neighbor's view of their azaleas."

Neil barked a laugh, quick and genuine. "You're in luck. Azaleas only bloom in the spring."

"Really??" Cade responded, glancing up and down the street. Two-story houses, gabled roofs, shaded porches—every one of them lived-in. The kind of lived-in that smelled like pasta sauce simmering on Sundays and grass stains ground into jeans, not lemon polish and silence. Neil's house was lovely—probably worth at least two million in this zip code—but it wasn't showy. It was warm. It breathed. It *breathed* with family in a way Cade's West Meade estate never managed, even with its ten-million-dollar-plus curated perfection.

From the doorway, Neil's mom leaned against the frame, a towel casually slung over her shoulder, her eyes amused yet kind. Cade straightened immediately, as if he were meeting royalty.

"Good morning, Mrs. Erickson," he said, almost too formal. "Thanks for letting me stop by."

Her smile was wry but warm. "Good morning, Cade."

"Why does your car sit down when you get out of it?" Maxx asked.

"It's called a hydropneumatic suspension."

Maxx looked puzzled.

"It means there's fluid that drains out when the pump turns off. I'll take you for a spin sometime," Cade said. "I'll show you."

"Cool. It looks like a camel," Maxx responded.

"Yeah, I guess it does. Good call."

Neil rolled his eyes, but the smile tugging at his mouth softened everything. "Come in."

Inside, the air was cooler, carrying the smell of toast

and something sweet—jam maybe—mixed with detergent and faint traces of Maxx's crayons scattered on the dining table. The family lived here in every corner: mismatched picture frames on the wall and an abandoned soccer ball half-kicked under the couch. Cade tried to blend into it, to slip into the rhythm of this house more than he ever cared about fitting into the marble hallways of his own.

Through the kitchen doorway, Neil's mom busied herself with jars of jam, the towel now looped at her waist. Mr. Erickson hovered near the window, arms crossed, gaze flicking between the Citroën outside and his wife inside. He looked up from his phone. He had googled the car.

"Who buys their seventeen-year-old a ninety-thousand-dollar rare classic French car?" he asked quietly, a trace of disbelief in his voice.

She shrugged without looking up from her work. "The kind of parents who don't know what else to give him."

Cade accidentally caught the words reverberating from the kitchen. He still had a heightened sense of hearing since the accident. His chest tightened. He forced a polite smile as he followed Neil up the steps to his room. The truth hit harder than he expected.

He wasn't sure he cared about the car, or the money,

or the house he came from. Standing in the upstairs hallway, stepping into this life that smelled like cut grass and honeysuckle and family, he realized something with startling clarity: He didn't want to fit his Citroën into the neighborhood. He wanted to blend himself into Neil's world.

As he trailed Neil inside, his heart beating faster than he'd admit, Cade thought—for the first time in a long time—that he was walking toward a life he actually wanted.

The Erickson house wasn't cluttered, exactly, but there were family photos on the walls, shoes kicked near the door, and someone laughing from another room. It felt... lived-in.

Cade glanced around, smiling despite himself. "I like your house," he said.

Neil looked back at him, a skeptical expression on his face. "Really?"

"Yeah." Cade nodded too quickly, then rushed on. "It's, um, cozy. You know. Kinda small but in a good way—"

Neil raised an eyebrow. "Small? It's like five thousand square feet. Now I'm curious how big your house must be to call this small."

Cade froze, realizing the hole he'd just dug. "No, no,

not small-small. I mean... compared to mine. Which is ridiculous. It echoes. Like, I swear I could have a medical emergency in the living room, and someone upstairs would never hear me."

Neil bit back a laugh. "So my house is tiny, but yours is an abandoned cathedral?"

"I guess," Cade said, chuckling and relieved. "Your house feels like a home."

Neil's shoulders softened at that, his teasing fading. "Okay. That's fair."

Cade shoved his hands in his pockets, suddenly sheepish. "Sorry, I didn't mean it to sound... insulting. I just—when I walked in, it felt good here. Warm. Yours is the kind of house people want to come back to."

Neil studied him for a moment, then gave a crooked smile. "That's the nicest way anyone's ever called my place small."

Cade laughed, brushing his knuckles against Neil's arm. "You knew what I meant."

"Uh-huh," Neil said, grinning now. "I'll let you dig yourself out of that one."

Just then, Neil's mother appeared from the staircase, calling, "Cade, are you hungry? Sit. I'll fix you a plate."

Cade straightened up, suddenly as polite as a Sunday school student. "Yes, ma'am. Thank you, ma'am."

Neil rolled his eyes, leaning close to whisper, "See, now you're just showing off."

But Cade wasn't. He was trying—awkwardly, earnestly—to belong.

Cade sprawled across Neil's bed, phone pressed to his ear, a hopeful grin tugging at his mouth. Neil sat at the desk nearby, pretending to flip through a summer reading book but really just watching him, listening.

"Hey! Yeah, it's me," Cade said, voice warm, brighter than Neil had ever heard it. "We just got back yesterday. Paris was insane. No, like—actually insane. You would've loved it. I was able to see all of Italy."

A pause. Cade's smile faltered just slightly. "Uh-huh. No, I'm home now. Just wanted to let you know. I've got stories to share and some news. I—"

Another pause. Cade's fingers tightened around the phone. "Right. Yeah. I know you're busy."

Neil stared, heart pinching.

"Sure," Cade said after a beat. His voice had dropped a notch, that earlier glow dimming. "I'll let you go. Yeah. Love you too."

He hung up, tossing the phone aside in frustration. For a second, silence filled the room. Then Cade dragged a hand over his face and let out a shaky laugh that wasn't really a laugh.

"Guess the Eiffel Tower isn't as interesting as whatever charity gala they've been to in Singapore or Dubai or—God, who even knows." He blinked hard, like he could force it away. "They didn't even say where they were. Tilda told me they were in Charleston, and I didn't get to tell them about us."

Neil pushed his book aside and moved to sit on the edge of the bed. "Cade..."

"It's fine," Cade said quickly, but his voice cracked. He pressed his palms to his eyes. "It's just—every time, I think maybe they'll want to hear about me, and every time it's like... I'm a commercial break in their actual lives."

Neil felt Cade's frustration. He wanted to fix it, but there wasn't a fix for parents who didn't listen. He settled for reaching out, his hand brushing Cade's arm. "They're the ones missing out. Not you."

Cade exhaled, shaky. "I mean, your mom asks if I've eaten. Your dad wants to know what soda I like. It's stupid, but I have been here exactly once, and it feels like your family actually... sees me more than mine ever has."

"That's not stupid," Neil said. "My family is awesome. Don't compare anything to my parents. It's not fair." Neil tried to joke to help lighten Cade's load. He didn't want to overload Cade or further pin the fact that his parents just weren't there for him or his brother.

Cade tilted his head back against the headboard, eyes shining. "Other than my brother, you and Tilda are it. The only ones who feel like... home." His throat clenched. "I just want to be here all the time. Why don't I want to go back to my house unless I have to?"

Neil's breath hitched. The vulnerability in Cade's voice cut right through him, sharper than any of the banter they usually traded. He reached for Cade's hand.

"You don't have to explain," Neil said softly. "You're not a commercial break here. We all adore you."

Cade's hand squeezed back, grip fierce, like he was holding onto that promise for dear life. Neil hugged Cade tightly.

In the stillness, Neil realized something: Cade Riley, who everyone thought had everything, had been looking for family all along. Somehow, unbelievably, Neil could offer him what he wanted and what he needed. The mystery of Cade's sadness was starting to reveal itself.

Chapter Thirty-Four.

They'd just finished lunch when Cade's phone buzzed on the table, screen lighting up between the remains of pasta bowls and Neil's little brother's fingerprints. Cade swiped it up, thumb hovering, and let out a half-groan, half-laugh.

"What?" Neil asked, still leaning back in his chair.

Cade tilted the phone toward him, as if it were both a treasure and a curse. "Invitation. Brentwood. Tonight."

Neil squinted at the text:

Cal Cronwell
Party. My place. Spread the word to cool people. 8 tonight.

"Who is Cal?" Neil asked, looking at the text header.

Cade looked at Neil with an extra cheesy smirk.

Neil's jaw dropped. "Wait—Cal Cronwell, as in Kirk Cronwell's son?"

Kirk Cronwell had become one of the top country music artists of all time.

"The one and only," Cade confirmed. "And knowing Cal, it won't just be a party. It'll be... epic. Kirk probably won't be there, but every Nashville royalty kid within thirty miles will."

Neil blinked. Brentwood was Jenna's neighborhood, which meant sprawling estates with gates taller than people, driveways longer than highways, and neighbors who casually bumped into Reba McEntire at a neighbor's kitchen table. Green Hills felt like a small planet compared to that galaxy. "How are you even friends with Cal?"

"I'm not," Cade said honestly, tossing the phone down again. "We just... orbit. Same type of prep schools, same country club dinners. It's one of those invitations that finds its way to your phone whether you want it or not."

"Yeah, but I go to your prep school, and I don't know Cal Cronwell. You're... going, right?"

Cade hesitated. "Not alone." He glanced at Neil, expression softening. "What if you came with me? Might be worth it. We could crash a Brentwood party together.

Please let me take you, Neil. Plus, isn't it your birthday?

"I swear I'm going to knock Maxx out. Did he tell you?"

"I saw it on the kitchen calendar. Why didn't you tell me? I texted some friends about what was going on tonight, and that's why I got the Cronwell invitation, probably."

This wasn't a scene Neil was comfortable with, but with that charming accent Cade had and how he milked it a little thicker when he was asking Neil, how could he say no?

Neil snorted. "I'll blend right in at Kirk Cronwell's mansion. Let me just grab my rhinestone boots and monogrammed Yeti cooler. Sadly, I'm between Bentleys."

Cade grinned, nudging him under the table. "You'd be surprised. You're a Dean's List guy with perfect hair. They'll assume you're someone's cousin from out of town."

Neil gave him a look. "Danielle de Barbarac?"

"What?" Cade asked.

"Never mind."

"I don't want to go if you're not there, especially on your birthday. Legendary country music royalty aside, the whole thing's just noise without you."

Neil tried not to let his face give away how that landed. "You're dangerous when you talk like that... and I'd go anywhere with you."

"Then say yes before I make it worse, darlin'," Cade teased, thickening his accent even more.

Neil sighed, though the smile was already tugging at his lips. "Fine. But if someone starts line-dancing in a cowboy hat, it might be me. Also, don't tell anyone it's my birthday. I don't want to look like I'm making a big deal about myself at a party like that."

Cade grinned, victory glowing in his eyes. "Deal. Just don't say no when they hand you the red crystal."

"Red Crystal?" Neil asked.

"A red Solo cup. It means you're part of the crew."

Neil wasn't sure why he even bothered rummaging through his closet—jeans, button-down, sneakers. Simple. Comfortable. His mom had always said he looked best when he wasn't trying, and Cade seemed to agree.

"Perfect," Cade said the second Neil finished dressing. "Ta-dah! No hesitation, no fuss. Just *perfect*."

Which made Neil flush in a way that no mirror ever did.

Minutes later, they were gliding down Hillsboro Pike with the top down on Cade's Citroën, leather still holding the faint scent of cologne and salt air from Italy (for reasons unknown) and a little charm left over from Europe. Neil glanced sideways at him, his hands loose on the wheel, his hair catching every passing light through the curved windshield. And he thought—not for the first time—how the hell had he ended up here? *Me, Neil Erickson, Dean's List grocer's kid, sitting shotgun while Cade Riley chauffeurs me to Brentwood like it's the most normal thing in the world.*

The gates of the Cronwell estate loomed like something out of a gothic film, iron bars curling into ornate spirals. Security leaned in, stone-faced, the light flooding Cade's hands as he casually lifted his phone and flashed the text. "We're on the list," he said, in an aristocratic tone only bestowed by southern birth.

The guard waved them through as the gates groaned open.

The driveway curved forever, lined with lanterns, until the mansion appeared—its lights blazing like it was built just to remind Nashville who really had money. Dozens of cars were already parked, music pulsing faintly from inside. Cade pulled into a spot like he'd done this a hundred times before, killed the engine, and glanced over at Neil as the car lowered automatically.

"Ready?"

Neil swallowed and nodded. "Sure. Totally. This is... cool."

Cade grinned and pushed his door closed behind him. "That's the spirit."

Led Zeppelin's *Kashmir* billowed out of the front door into the front motor court, making their entry to the party increasingly ominous. The Italian fountain's lights had been programmed to rotate through all the colors of the rainbow. Cade and Neil found this amusing and joked that it was lit up to welcome them.

Inside, the place was alive—laughter spilling down hallways, country and pop songs battling through expensive speakers, clusters of kids holding Solo cups in one hand and phones in the other. Neil hadn't even adjusted to the noise when Cade was already being clapped on the shoulder by some guy in a backwards cap, with two more calling his name from across the room.

Neil realized something quickly: Cade wasn't just known here. He was expected to be part of the furniture. And yet... something was different.

Cade laughed, nodded, and tossed back greetings, but not once did he stray more than a step from Neil. When one girl squealed and pulled him toward the kitchen, he held his ground, tugging Neil closer by the wrist.

Neil's stomach flipped. Cade wasn't loud, wasn't reckless, and wasn't the wild-eyed life of the party Neil suspected him to be. He was measured and grounded—like he wanted everyone in the room to know exactly who he'd walked in with.

For Neil, this was both thrilling and terrifying. Neil was confident, but this was a new level, and not his typical cast of characters.

They hadn't been inside more than five minutes before Cade was swept into a loose circle near the grand staircase; a couple of guys Neil vaguely recognized from Penderton, plus a girl in boots that looked like they'd been designed for a red carpet, not hardwood floors.

"Kip wore boots like that once, and dented the floor," Neil said to Cade.

"Cade Riley!" one of the guys named Mark called, raising his cup. "Didn't know you were back stateside yet. Saw your Insta. Europe looked wild, man."

"Yeah," Cade said easily, sliding his hand briefly against Neil's back like a grounding wire. "It was."

Before Neil could disappear into the wallpaper, Cade gestured toward him. "This is Neil Erickson."

Neil braced for the usual look—the once-over, the subtle math of *who are you* and *why are you here?* But instead, the girl's face lit up.

"Neil? *Governor's List*, Neil?"

Neil blinked. "Uh... yeah. Governor's *award*."

"Oh my God," she said, practically bouncing. "You're the one who crushed that regional debate final last year, right? My cousin goes to your school—he said you're, like, scary smart."

"That's me. Mister Scary," Neil laughed.

The guys chimed in, half-grinning. "That's you? I thought you were just a name on the board, dude. Nice to meet you."

"I'm Iris, by the way," the girl said.

Neil felt his ears burn. Compliments weren't rare, but in Cade's orbit, they felt different, as if he were a phantom that didn't exist on their side of the mirror.

Cade shot him a smug grin, leaning close to murmur, "Told you you'd mesh."

Neil elbowed him lightly and smiled. "Mesh... isn't the word I'd use."

But Cade only smiled, proud and easy, and Neil realized that he wasn't here as Cade's tagalong. He was here as Cade's *pick*. And everyone seemed to know, yet didn't precisely know anything.

The music shifted—some remix of a Luke Bryan song with way too much bass—and Iris, the girl with the runway boots, leaned closer, curiosity flashing across her face. She pulled Neil away from the group.

"So... I hope it's okay to ask, but are you dating Cade?" Iris asked in a Clarksville accent, smooth as if she were asking whether he preferred Coke or Pepsi. "No smirk, no edge. Just curious."

Neil froze. His mouth opened, but no words came out.

Then she snapped her fingers. "Wait—duh. Instagram. I saw it last week. That picture with the song over it? *Amore Predestinato* or whatever?" Her grin widened. "That was you two, wasn't it?"

Neil's stomach dipped—half panic, half awe. He decided to have fun with it. Why not?

"I haven't decided if you're my instant friend or just a bisshhh, but either way you're fun," Neil said. Iris laughed, and then Neil laughed.

"I'm your friend, gurrrrl," she said. "Ya stoopid bissh."

"Stoopid bishhh..."

Neil just played along with the stereotype.

But before he could stammer out a response, she added, "That was actually really cool. Like, iconic, you know? Nobody ever does anything that bold around here. People just post their vacation tans or their dad's boat.

But you two—" she gave a little clap, "—trendsetters."

A guy walked up beside her, clearly one of her friends, and nodded. "Yeah, I saw it too. Props, man. Took guts. Name's Gud."

"Your name is 'Good'? Did I hear that right?" Neil asked.

"Yeah, I get 'G-O-O-D' on my Starbucks cup a lot, but it's 'G-U-D.' Comes from having a hillbilly, freak-show religious politician grandmother," he said.

All three said, "Misha Blackpot," in unison, and laughed.

"Two things that I've noticed since Penderton Academy are: One, everyone has interesting names, especially if their parents are odd. Two, no one seems to know where their parents are," Neil said. "And then there's me, with two parents still together who are probably going to text me within the next ten minutes."

"Yeah, it's just part of the culture, sadly," said Gud.

Neil felt a sense of relief, but the words eventually came out. "What is happening right now?" he laughed a little, looking silly after having only one drink. Was he making friends in this circle of kids he thought were shallow?

Alone with Cade for a moment, Mark nudged him. "So you're hanging out with the smart kids now. Very mature of you."

Cade shrugged. "Yeah, they're actually pretty cool."

Mark lowered his voice, clearly dying to spill something. "FYI, AJ's been on a whole soft-launch arc with his feelings for one of Neil's friends."

Cade blinked. "AJ? Really? He hasn't said anything to me. He's been in that situationship with Savannah for months."

"Well," Mark said, leaning in like he lived for this, "he's been talking about Sophie McCallister way more than Savannah Holt lately."

Mark tapped his cup to Cade's longneck bottle, leaving Cade with a surprised look.

The group moved on seamlessly, asking about Europe, about trains, and about which cities were worth the hype. To them, it was settled: Cade and Neil were a *thing*. And somehow, that was more disorienting than if they'd laughed.

Neil forced a smile as he answered questions, but inside he was electrified with excitement. Supportive as it was, it also meant people were watching, talking, maybe celebrating, maybe not—but definitely watching.

Neil couldn't decide if that thrilled him or terrified him.

It didn't take long for the whispers to ripple closer.

Someone from Cade's soccer team sidled up with a half-grin that didn't quite reach his eyes.

"So, it's true then? You and Neil?" he asked, his tone dangling between teasing and challenge.

"I gotta say," said Buddy Fowler, making himself known from the back of the group, "I didn't see that one coming, Riley. Thought you were more into—" he gestured vaguely at the girls around them, "—this scene."

The laughter that followed wasn't cruel, but it was enough to tighten Neil's body. He wanted to shrink back into the wood-paneled walls and pretend none of this was happening.

But Cade didn't flinch. He squared his shoulders, eyes scanning the crowd, and for a heartbeat, Neil thought he was about to launch into some snappy comeback.

Instead, Cade turned, slid a hand along Neil's jaw, and kissed him.

Not just a peck. Not something you could laugh off as a dare or a joke. It was full, deliberate, and passionate—every ounce of defiance poured into it. The room seemed to exhale all at once, some gasping, others hooting, and a surprising number of them applauding.

When Cade pulled back, his wrist still resting against Neil's neck, he looked straight (pun intended) at the guys who'd been needling him. His voice was even, almost casual.

"Yeah. We're together. And if anyone has a problem with it..." He let the pause hang, a smirk tugging at his mouth, "...you can take it up with me, fuckers," and he let out a laugh.

The challenge landed heavily and humorously, but, of course, no one stepped forward. A couple of heads shook. Buddy muttered, "Respect," before slipping back toward the kitchen.

Neil's heart was slamming against his ribs. He should've been mortified and should've hated every eye in the room on him. But instead, he was lit up. The boldness of Cade's gesture, the sharp edge of his voice, the way he claimed him without hesitation—it sent a shiver through him. Neil didn't drink a lot, but the one drink he had, combined with what Cade just did... He wanted to be ALONE with that boy... right now!

Maybe he wasn't a wallflower anymore. Maybe Cade Riley had just set him on fire.

They rounded the corner into a massive living room that looked like a movie set. And there—holding court near a fireplace, slightly taller than most eighth graders—was Cal Cronwell.

He looked exactly like someone named Cal at a mansion party would look—perfect suit, perfect hair, a glass of something sparkly in his hand, and an audience hanging on every word.

Cade hesitated. "Okay... we should say hi."

"We should? Why?" Neil whispered urgently. "Who are we? Why are we here?"

"Because he invited everyone," Cade said. "And it's weird to avoid the host."

Neil swallowed. "Future reference: I am pro-avoidance."

Cade laughed and nudged him forward.

Cal spotted them approaching and broke into a welcoming—if slightly amused—smile.

"Riley!" he said, lifting his glass. "Haven't seen you all night. Thought you'd ditched us for the rooftop pool."

"We don't... have a rooftop pool," Cade said.

Cal smirked. "Exactly."

He turned to Neil. "And you brought someone new. I approve aesthetically already."

Neil almost choked.

"This is Neil Erickson," Cade said, suddenly a little stiff. "He was... uh... on the trip with us."

Cal extended his hand with a dramatic flourish. "Cal Cronwell."

Neil shook it, trying not to overthink whether his palm was sweaty. "Hi. Um. Nice house."

Cal grinned. "Thank you. It tries very hard."

Cade snorted.

Cal eyed Neil—curious, but friendly. "So, Neil, how did Riley convince you to wander into a den of inherited wealth and questionable taste?"

"Oh, him? No, I tailgated the catering trucks," Neil said before he could stop himself.

Cal laughed—genuinely. "Excellent survival instinct. You'll go far here."

Neil felt his shoulders loosen a fraction. "Your Italian table might actually be the main event tonight. Giordano's would be proud."

Cade looked at Neil—noticing the shift—and gave a tiny smile.

Cal continued, gesturing broadly with his glass, "Welcome to the circus. A lot of it probably did come from Giordano's. We love that place, obviously, you're a fan."

"Yeah, you could say that," Neil responded. "My mother is Gianna Giordano Erickson."

Cade raised an eyebrow at Neil.

"Well then, we now know where you get your good taste, my friend," Cal said.

"Drinks on every table, food in every corner, and at least four rooms you should absolutely not enter unless you want to see something emotionally scarring."

Neil blinked. "Is that a joke?"

Cal paused. "Mostly."

"Cal," someone called across the room, waving a designer clutch. "Come approve my cousin!"

Cal rolled his eyes. "God help me. Gentlemen, enjoy yourselves. Neil, if the crowd overwhelms you, the east conservatory is quiet this time of night. And has excellent acoustics if you feel like screaming."

And with that, he swept away.

Neil let out a breath. "Okay. He's... a lot."

"He's Cal," Cade said simply. "This was actually pretty tame. Well done, by the way."

"Thanks! I get my conversational theatrics from my mother."

They drifted deeper into the room, the chandelier glittering above them. Cade's elbow brushed Neil's—just a soft touch, probably accidental, but warm.

Neil didn't step away.

Cade put his right arm around Neil and lifted him in a hug. Then he looked lovingly at him.

Neil laughed, tension finally breaking. "And here I thought I'd be wallpaper tonight."

Cade leaned close, murmuring just for him. "You have never been wallpaper, no matter how hard you have tried to be. It's all been an illusion. You might be walking at a slant[1], though."

Iris appeared out of nowhere, like she had known Neil all of her life, with the distinct smell of too much whiskey.

"Hey, gurl," she said. "I've got this guy who keeps texting me, and I can't block him because... well, long story. How do I get rid of him? I think he's *reeeaaally stoopit.*"

Neil was used to these questions; it's just a part of being gay. Some girls use gay guys as an on-call therapist. Why? No idea, since most gay guys didn't go on their first date until college. So, as they do, Neil made up a goofy response.

"Okay, so if you want to find out how dumb he is, here's what you do: text him back and tell him that you need to be honest with him about something sensitive. He's going to perk up and be ready to be there for you."

"Okay. Uh huh."

"Now, make sure all of this is in text. This isn't a voice conversation."

Cade was intently paying attention, enamored by

---

[1] *Walking at a slant:* You're drunk.

what he couldn't see coming.

"Type: **I am illiterate. It's so embarrassing,**" Neil continued. "Now, if he wants to help you, he's stupid. If he turns on you and tells all of his friends, you've wiped out a whole swath of stupid people from your dating pool."

"I don't get it. Why?" Iris asked.

Cade's mouth was agape at what he was witnessing.

Neil briefly looked up at Cade, then back to Iris.

"Look at me," Neil said to Iris. "His friends are going to ask him how he knows this, and he's going to show them the text." Neil paused to wait for her to get it.

"Okay, I'll do it right now. Thanks, Neil."

When she was gone, Cade laughed. "She didn't get it, did she?"

"No, she absolutely did not," said Neil. "Maybe she should just go out with him."

Cal Cronwell's Brentwood mansion pulsed like it had a heartbeat. Music rattled the windows, bass rolling through the walls like thunder. In the great room, Cal had cleared the furniture, strung colored lights across the rafters, and turned polished hardwood into a dance floor.

Cade leaned close, his breath brushing Neil's ear.

"Welcome to Brentwood."

Neil tried to laugh, but it snagged in his throat. The room was a crush of bodies, lights flickering like fireflies. He should've stayed at the edge, clipboard in hand, cataloging chaos from a safe distance. But Cade's hand found his, tugging him toward the center.

"Cade—"

"Trust me," Cade said, his grin flashing in the strobe lights.

The song shifted, synths climbing, bass dropping heavy, and Cade pulled Neil in close—hands sliding to his hips, guiding him into the rhythm. At first, Neil moved stiffly, awkwardly, but Cade's body pressed confidently against his, leading, coaxing, and steadying.

"You're fine," Cade whispered, so close Neil could feel the words against his skin.

"Actually... you're better than fine."

Neil's cheeks flamed. "I'm not—"

"Shh." Cade's forehead brushed his temple. "Just let go. I've got you."

And Neil did. For just a moment, he forgot the crowd, the house, and the million eyes that could be on them. He moved with Cade, heart hammering, body catching the rhythm in ways he didn't know it could.

The song's chorus hit, lights flared, and Cade spun

him—quick, dizzying—before catching him back against his chest. Neil laughed breathlessly, and Cade's hand slid up to cradle his jaw, the thumb brushing just under his ear.

The music, the crowd, the mansion—all of it blurred into nothing.

Then Cade kissed him.

"Happy birthday," Cade said.

It wasn't tentative, or hidden, or stolen in the dark. It was bold, right there on Cal Cronwell's hardwood dance floor, under the flood of colored lights and the roar of bass. For a split second, Neil's brain screamed that everyone could see—but Cade didn't care. His lips were warm, certain, and lingering until Neil forgot to care too.

Back on the dance floor, Cade pulled back just enough to whisper against Neil's lips, "See? Told you you could dance."

Neil couldn't even find words. He just laughed, dizzy and alive, as the music surged again and Cade drew him closer, daring the whole dang room to watch.

Back in Italy, Neil had already started to fall for Cade's boldness. Cade didn't shrink from the world—he met it head-on, daring anyone to challenge him. At first, Neil had worried that confidence might look like arrogance, even bullying. But he'd learned better. Cade's edge wasn't about pushing people down; it was about refusing to hide who he was, about claiming joy and fighting for it when he had to.

To Neil, nothing was sexier than that. Not Cade's easy grin, not his ridiculous good looks—though those didn't hurt—but the way he lived unapologetically, like he... or they, were more than enough. Neil knew Cade would stand up for him just as fiercely, and the thought turned his knees to absolute jelly.

"Wanna get out of here?" Cade asked.

"Uh-huh," Neil responded in a way that sounded like *anything for you.*

Chapter Thirty-Five.

They slipped out the side door, the bass of the party trailing after them like a distant heartbeat. Cade's car waited patiently, sleek and gleaming under the lanterns, like it belonged more on a runway than in a driveway.

Neil slid into the passenger seat. The leather was warm against his back, the air faintly scented with Cade's cologne and the trace of bonfire smoke clinging to them from the party. His pulse still hadn't settled—from the kiss, from the stares, from Cal Cronwell's unexpected elevated hospitality. He felt raw, lit up, as if the night were writing something new in permanent ink.

Cade started the engine, and the low purr filled the

302

cabin as the car rose about a foot from its relaxed lower position. Behind the wheel, with one arm resting easily, Cade looked older—confident in a way that Neil couldn't help but stare at. He wondered what he would look like at thirty, then forty.

"Are you okay to drive?" Neil asked carefully.

Cade flashed a grin. "I've had half a beer. Mostly just carried it around so nobody would shove another one at me. Figured I should keep my act together tonight."

Neil's chest tightened. "For me?"

"Yeah," Cade said, glancing at him with that easy certainty. "For us."

He flicked on the Bluetooth, and a sweet country song by Megan Moroney poured from the speakers— aching vocals spilling into the dark, the lyrics spinning too close to how Neil felt.

"I sometimes drink too much, and I have never wanted to be fully present before, but now I do... when I'm with you," Cade said before he started to sing along.

Neil's breath caught. Cade's sweetness and the song—the rise, the longing—made the night feel unreal, like a movie he didn't want to end.

Cade kept singing. And, unfairly, he could really sing. Of course, he couldn't resist changing the lyrics.

♫ ***"Oh my God, I think I'm gay!"***

Neil groaned, laughing so hard he had to clutch the handle above the door. "Fuuuuuuuuuuqq—not you out here being cute as a whole puppy!"

Without thinking, he disengaged his seatbelt and leaned over the console to kiss Cade on the side of the mouth, quick but fierce.

"Oh my God, put your seatbelt back on," Cade said through a grin as he slowed the car down. "Gotta keep my babe safe." He reached over and squeezed Neil's knee, thumb brushing just enough to make Neil shiver.

Cade was cheesing so wide that it set off his own laugh, his shoulders shaking. He loved it when Neil made noise about him—when Neil admitted out loud that he liked him and wanted him.

"Also—thank you for not being one of those guys who peel out of parking lots just because the car can," Neil said, exhaling, still giddy. "You know what you are? Quiet luxury."

"Quiet luxury?" Cade arched a brow. "How much have you had to drink, sir? No one has ever accused me of being quiet, ever!"

Neil laughed, dropping his head back against the seat. "Excuse me, I only had one. Who are you?" The words came out more awestruck than he meant, so he chuckled to cover it.

Cade downshifted, the engine answering with a low growl. He flicked his gaze over, just long enough to make it count, and winked.

"I'm your **boyfriend**, that's who."

Neil's breath stalled. *Boyfriend.* The word wrapped around him, startling and thrilling and terrifying all at once. It was casual and tossed out there, but Cade meant it. Neil could feel it in the way Cade's hand hovered, waiting.

Neil slid his fingers into Cade's without hesitation. Their hands fit, palm to palm, warm and sure.

A Rufus Du Sol remix of *On My Knees Again*, spilled into the car, the bass thrumming under their skin.

Cade laughed and pressed the accelerator; the car surged forward. He took back his hand and placed it on the steering wheel. The song swelled as the city blurred outside the windows—streetlights streaking the sky gold, the night unfolding wide around them.

"Say I'm your boyfriend," Cade commanded playfully as he stared straight forward, focused on the road.

Neil yelled, loud enough to echo down Granny Smith Pike. "YOU'RE MY BOYFRIEND!!!!"

Cade floored the car, and it pushed Neil back, heart pounding, caught somewhere between disbelief and joy, thinking that this—this rush of music and headlights and Cade's fun command—wasn't just a moment.

This was the start of everything.

They coasted into Neil's neighborhood, headlights sweeping across familiar lawns and mailboxes. The adrenaline of the party, the kiss, the drive—it all hummed in Neil's chest, but softer now, like the song was fading into a slow reprise.

Cade pulled into the driveway and cut the engine. Silence fell, thick and sudden, broken only by the engine cooling and the distant chirp of crickets.

Neither of them moved.

Neil unbuckled, fingers fidgeting with the strap. "So..." He glanced at Cade, then away. "That was... fun."

Cade leaned back against the seat, one hand still resting loosely on Neil's knee. "Yeah. I loved every minute of it."

Neil's laugh came out nervous and thin. "Good," he echoed. His throat worked, words catching. "You know, tomorrow people might—"

"Don't," Cade cut in gently. He turned, blue eyes steady on Neil. "Please don't ruin it with tomorrow yet. Tonight's ours. Promise me you'll wait to look at Insta until morning."

"Okay," he said softly. Neil's chest went hot. Cade had a way of cutting through his spirals like that—taking the moment and pinning it down, making it feel real and safe.

For a second, neither of them spoke. Then Cade

tilted his head, a grin tugging at his mouth. "I'm still waiting, you know."

Neil blinked. "For what?"

"The *official* boyfriend kiss. You climbed over the armrest earlier, but I was trying not to drive us into a tree."

Neil laughed, shaking his head. "You're a nut."

"Yeah," Cade said. "But I'm your nut. I mean, I'm yours," he laughed nervously. "I mean, I'm nuts for you."

The awkward words hit so deep,

Cade's face changed back into that commanding look. "Kiss me," he said.

Neil didn't think—he leaned across the console again, slower this time, and kissed him properly. No rush, no headlights streaking by. Just warm leather, a quiet night, and Cade's hand slipping up to cradle the back of his neck like it belonged there.

When they finally pulled apart, breath mingling in the stillness, Cade grinned. "Now that's official. Also, if my car were bigger, I'd probably have already pulled you all the way onto my lap by now."

Neil groaned, dropping his forehead against Cade's shoulder, but his smile betrayed him. "You're not right."

"And yet," Cade said, squeezing his hand, "you keep showing up."

"Also, cheers on your new, bigger car. That's going to be great. Even though I love this beautiful Citroën."

"Yeah? What would I get?"

"How about a sketchy old white van?"

"Maybe a sprinter. I would never ask you to get in an old white van."

"Okay. Sprinter it is. Big enough to carry a dog around, too."

"Yeah, I'd love to co-parent a dog with you," Cade said. "We can name him Romeo."

Neil didn't argue. He just sat there, soaking in the quiet, knowing that when he finally walked inside, the world would tilt back into its ordinary state. But here, in the dark car with Cade's arm brushing his, *ordinary* didn't stand a chance.

A flick of light cut across the car. The porch light clicked on.

Neil froze. He didn't have to look to know it was his mom—probably at the kitchen window, wondering why Cade's car was loitering in the driveway at midnight.

Cade pulled back, a sheepish smile creeping across his face. "Guess that's our cue."

Neil let out a strangled laugh. "She's going to kill me."

"Worth it," Cade whispered, pressing a quick kiss to

Neil's temple before reaching for the keys. "I hope you had a good birthday."

"I did, thank you. But, worth it even if she kills me? Some boyfriend you are. By the way, when do we get to celebrate your birthday?"

"We already did."

Neil looked puzzled.

"Remember when we kissed in the rain in Calabria?" Cade looked at him lovingly.

"That was your birthday? Cade! We could have celebrated that in Italy?"

"Honestly, it was the best birthday... ever. One of my favorite days, actually."

"You don't strike me as the type to let your birthday go unnoticed, Cade."

"I'm not, and it didn't. Go spend some time with your mom before she hates me for taking you away on your eighteenth birthday."

"Night, Cade."

"Night, babe."

Neil sat there for one more breath, heart hammering, caught between terror and euphoria. Then he opened the door, the warm porch light spilling over him like a spotlight, and stepped back into the real world.

Cade put on a song that put everything in perspective

for him on the way home: *Something About You* by Elderbrook & Rudimental. Usually, he would be drunk and calling Ryan when he was this happy, or even when he was very sad, to come get him. Not tonight. Something about Neil... kept him from drinking.

Neil slipped inside, shoes soft against the hardwood. The house smelled faintly of laundry and whatever leftovers his mom had reheated earlier. He half-expected a lecture waiting by the door, but instead, his parents were camped out on the couch, the TV muted, a lamp throwing soft light across the room.

His mom tilted her head. "You seem like you had a good night."

Neil froze for a beat, pulse still racing from their moment in the driveway. Then he managed a nod, tugging at the hem of his shirt. "Yeah. It was... good."

His dad chuckled. "That's all we get? "Good?"

Neil shrugged, trying to hide the grin tugging at his face. "There was a party. Music. Dancing. That's pretty much it." He hesitated, then added, softer, "But... yeah. It was excellent. I met Cal Cronwell. He was really nice."

They exchanged a look—one of those silent parental conversations Neil had grown up resenting. But this time, when his mom's eyes flicked back to him, her smile was warm.

"I don't think I've ever seen you quite like this," she said gently.

Neil ducked his head, cheeks burning, but he couldn't fight the smile breaking wide across his face. "Guess it was just... a good night."

"More than good," his dad murmured, almost to himself.

Neil mumbled a quick goodnight and escaped upstairs, heart still galloping. Behind him, his parents lingered in the glow of the muted TV, both knowing—without saying—that something had shifted in their son that night.

"You should know, son," his dad said, "We really like what Cade brings out in you."

"It's obvious he makes you very happy, and you know how much we love that," his mother said.

"I love you both so much," Neil said.

He hugged his parents and then ran up the stairs, happier than he had ever remembered being, narrowly avoiding breaking out in happy tears. The night couldn't get any better for him to have their approval.

Neil shut his bedroom door with a soft click and collapsed backward onto his bed, still fully dressed. The mattress sighed under him, the room dim and familiar, but everything inside him felt lit up, like he'd smuggled the night home in his chest.

The smell hit him first. Cade's cologne—warm, sharp, with a scent like cedar and citrus—clung to his shirt where Cade's arm had brushed against him, faint but undeniable. Neil pressed his face to the fabric, inhaled, and felt his grin break wide all over again. Cade was everywhere: in his ears, in the burn on his lips, and in the way his pulse wouldn't calm down.

Tonight had been impossible. The party, the car, that ridiculous lyric change, Cade's hand on his knee, and then—*boyfriend*. Said like it had always been true. It felt different from when it was said in Italy. Now it was said in the real world. in *his* real world.

Neil rolled onto his side, burying his smile in his pillow, muffling the laugh that bubbled out of him. He couldn't remember ever feeling like this before—like his whole body was a secret he couldn't contain.

His phone buzzed on the nightstand—one new text.

Cade
Still thinking about that kiss. You're in so much trouble, but you're still my good boy.

Neil groaned into the pillow, kicking his feet like he was twelve. He typed back, erased it, typed again.

He stared, then added, "Goodnight, boyfriend."

The reply came instantly, like Cade had been waiting for it.

Cade
Goodnight, seeing-eye boyfriend.

Neil set the phone down, lying back with his hands over his chest. He smelled Cade on his shirt. He didn't want to wash it or have the night fade.

Downstairs, his parents' voices murmured. Outside, the street was quiet. But here, in the cocoon of his room, Neil let himself believe it.

Cade Riley had called him his boyfriend. And Neil had never wanted tomorrow to come so badly.

In Cade's room, he dropped his keys on his desk and fell face-first onto his bed, still in jeans and a T-shirt. His room was too quiet after the night they'd had—the engine of the car, the music, and Neil's laugh echoing down Granny Smith Pike. Without it, the silence pressed in like static.

He rolled onto his back and stared at the ceiling. His shirt still smelled faintly like Cal's house, but underneath that... Neil. Cade couldn't have said what exactly—

laundry soap, skin, something warm—but it clung to him, and it made his chest ache in the best way.

He grabbed his phone off the nightstand, thumb hovering. He'd already sent the first text—*still thinking about that kiss. You're in so much trouble, but you're still my good boy*—and Neil's reply had lit him up like a stadium.

Goodnight, boyfriend.

Cade grinned into the dark, cheeks actually sore. Boyfriend. He'd tossed the word out casually in Italy, like it was a joke, but the truth was—it wasn't casual. He'd wanted to say it, needed to. And hearing it come back from Neil? It made him feel steadier than he had in years.

He scrolled through his photos without really seeing them, his mind replaying the night in flashes: Neil leaning across the console to kiss him, Neil's hand finding his, Neil laughing so hard he almost cried, all took precedent. Under it all, the steady disbelief that someone like Neil—quiet, solid, better than Cade probably deserved—actually wanted him too.

His parents hadn't picked up when he called earlier. Not surprising. They rarely did. But Neil's family had left the porch light on. Neil's mom had probably been peeking through the curtains. And instead of it feeling suffocating, Cade felt... jealous, almost. Hungry for it.

For once, he hadn't minded being under someone's roof, in someone's care.

He pressed Neil's text to his chest like it could soak into him. *Goodnight, boyfriend.*

Cade Riley, golden boy and life-of-the-party, wasn't sure about a lot of things. But he was sure of this: he'd never wanted to be someone's anything so badly in his life.

The next morning, the kitchen at Cade's house smelled faintly of the usual fresh coffee and lemon cleaner. Tilda always made sure things felt lived-in, even when his parents were on the other side of the world. She moved easily around the kitchen, hair tied back, sleeves rolled up, flipping pancakes on the griddle like she had a hundred times before.

Cade sat at the counter in one of his dad's abandoned barstools, still in a T-shirt and sweats, staring at the stack of pancakes growing on the plate between them. He was grinning, but only halfway—the kind of grin that looked borrowed.

"Okay," Tilda said, without looking at him. "Out with it. You've been sitting there like a balloon about to pop."

Cade dragged a hand through his hair. "You always know."

"Of course I do. I changed your diaper, Caden. You're

not that mysterious."

He laughed, but the sound cracked. He stared at the pancakes, voice low. "Do you think... do you think my parents would take it well? If I told them. About me. About Neil."

Tilda set down the spatula and finally met his eyes. Her face softened, the way it always had when he was little and scared of thunderstorms.

"Your mom," she said carefully, "will probably find it fashionable. She'll turn it into a cocktail-party line—'my son is gay, isn't that marvelous, darling?'—and she'll dine out on it for a year. She likes anything that makes her seem ahead of the curve."

Cade snorted, rolling his eyes. "That sounds about right, and I'm bi."

"Your mother will never say you are bi. Saying 'gay son' would be much more progressive. Your dad..." Tilda sighed, honestly. "I'm not sure. He's harder to read. He may not understand at first. But here's the thing, Cade—" She leaned on the counter, voice firmer now. "Their approval is not the sun you orbit around. You've built yourself without them a thousand times over. You've always had people who see you. Me. Your brother. And now Neil."

Cade swallowed, blinking fast. "Yeah, but my

brother's practically moved into his girlfriend's house, and you... I mean, you've been here forever, but sometimes I feel like you're the only one who really knows me."

"Maybe I am," Tilda said with a little smile. "But that's not a bad thing. It just means I get front-row seats while you figure yourself out, and I'll be here whether your parents come around or not. That's not negotiable."

The knot in Cade's chest loosened. He pushed his plate away and leaned forward, pressing his forehead briefly against her shoulder like he used to when he was six. "Thanks, T. I don't say that enough."

"You don't," she teased, brushing his hair back like she had when he was a boy. "But I don't need thanks. I just need you to know you're not alone."

Cade pulled back, managing a crooked grin. "So basically, I get fashion points with my mom, a question mark with my dad, and full-time backup from you?"

"Exactly." She slid another pancake onto his plate. "And personally? I think that's enough to keep you standing tall until the rest catches up."

Cade picked up his fork, the grin settling deeper now, more real. "You always know what to say."

"That's always been my job," Tilda said, ruffling his hair before turning back to the stove. "Still is."

Chapter Thirty-Six.

The next night, Nashville shimmered around them like a city lit just for the two of them. The car traveled through the dark stretch of I-65, headlights painting twin tunnels through the night as one Eli Lieb song gave way to another—something moody, pulsing, made for cruising with the windows cracked.

Neil leaned his head back against the seat, watching the skyline grow closer. The AT&T "Batman" Building's twin spires jutted into the night like some neon crown, while Broadway's chaos spilled out in flashes of neon—honky-tonk bars, cowboy boots in window displays, and music pouring from every doorway.

Cade downshifted, guiding them off the highway and into the glow. He drummed his fingers on the single-spoke steering wheel, perfectly in time with the beat. "This is my favorite part," he said, nodding toward the street where tourists stumbled and pedal taverns rolled by. "It's like Nashville showing off, and you get to pick which version you believe."

Neil smiled, stealing a look at him. "And which one do you believe?"

Cade thought for a second, eyes flicking over the lights, then back to the road. "Honestly? This one. The messy, loud, too-much version. It's alive."

Neil pressed closer to the window, watching cowboy hats bob past the glass and hearing guitar riffs spilling from an open bar. "I've lived here my whole life," he said softly, "but I've never seen it like this."

"Maybe," Cade said, glancing at him again, "you've just never seen it with me."

"Maybe you'll be a part of this someday," Neil said.

"Maybe," Cade affirmed.

They cut across the river, and the water below caught the city lights in ripples. Cade rolled down his window, letting the Tennessee night rush in. "Feels like flying, doesn't it?" he asked.

Neil nodded, closing his eyes for a moment, the wind in his hair, the music swelling. And it did—it felt exactly like flying.

They cruised past Broadway, past the clamor of neon and cowboy boots and bachelorette parties spilling into the street. Cade kept driving, letting the music fade into something softer, until the city lights fell away behind them.

Neil glanced over. "Where are we going?"

"You'll see," Cade said, a half-smile tugging at his mouth.

A few minutes later, Cade turned onto a narrow road that curved up a ridge. The city reappeared behind them, glittering now, the skyline stretched wide like a photograph. At the top, Cade eased the Citroën into a small overlook and killed the engine. Suddenly, the world was still—just the muffled cicadas in the trees.

Neil looked out at Nashville glowing below them. "Wow," he whispered. "It's... beautiful."

"Yeah," Cade said, but his eyes weren't on the skyline. They were on Neil, appreciating that he could see him when he missed four days of such a beautiful vision.

Neil shifted under the weight of it. He didn't quite know what to do with Cade's gaze, that full attention. "You've got a thing for dramatic reveals, don't you?" he teased lightly.

Cade leaned back in his seat, grinning. "Maybe I'll provide the view if you'll provide the narration." He looked at Neil as if he were studying him, then raised both hands and made a clicking sound to simulate taking his photo in the moment.

The silence stretched, but it wasn't empty—it pulsed with something Neil wasn't sure he was ready to name. He fiddled with the seam of the seat, his voice quieter now. "So, uh... about the other night."

"The party?" Cade asked.

Neil nodded. "Yeah. The kiss. The... everything. That was—brave." He swallowed. "But also a little reckless. I mean, I'm not... I'm not used to being the center of attention like that."

Cade reached across the console, his hand covering Neil's. Warm. Steady. Now leaning on the center armrest, he said, "I know. I could see it freaked you out." His thumb brushed over Neil's knuckles. "But it wasn't about showing off. It was about you. About us. I don't want to hide this, Neil. Not from my friends, not from anyone. You matter so much to me."

Neil's breath paused, the words settling into him like heat. He stared out at the city lights again, his pulse racing. He'd dreamed of being wanted like this, but dreams didn't usually sit in a car beside you, holding your hand and waiting for your answer.

Neil slumped down to the center armrest to meet Cade's eyes.

"I have never met anyone like you." He squeezed Cade's hand back, almost shyly. "I guess I just need to catch up."

Cade smiled, slow and relieved, and for a long moment they sat there together, the city glowing beneath them, Nashville theirs alone. He kissed Neil.

"You're caught," Cade said.

And then—*whap!*—something buzzed against Neil's ear. A cicada launched itself in through the open window, rattling its wings like a jackhammer.

"Holy—get it out!" Neil yelped, swatting at the air.

Cade flailed in perfect, unhelpful panic, half-laughing, half-screaming, until Neil shoved the door open and shooed the bug into the night.

They both froze, breathing hard, staring at each other in the aftermath. Neil's hair was mussed, Cade's shirt was half-untucked, and for some reason, the ridiculousness of it all cracked something wide open between them.

Cade let out a shaky laugh. "We are never telling anyone about that."

Neil grinned, breathless. "Deal. Way to kill a moment, Cicada."

Before the moment could dissolve into more laughter, they leaned across the console, caught in the same impulse. Their lips met—quick and a little clumsy at first, then deeper, steadying. A kiss born not out of perfect timing, but out of chaos, relief, and everything they'd been holding back.

Outside, the cicadas were still noisy in the trees, but inside the car, it was just the two of them, with Theo Tams playing on the Bluetooth; the steaminess was all theirs after that.

"No, Cicadas! This one is all mine," Cade said before kissing Neil again and smiling against Neil's lips.

Chapter Thirty-Seven.

The first Monday back at Penderton Academy felt less like school and more like a press conference with a twangy tone. Neil had spent his life so far in Nashville, but after ten days in Europe, the middle Tennessee accent had suddenly felt like it had been dialed up to eleven.

Neil had barely stepped onto campus before he felt the shift—heads turning, whispers, a ripple effect that followed him from the parking lot to the front steps.

It wasn't his grades this time. Or the Governor's Award. It was *them*: his relationship with Cade.

Apparently, the rumor mill had been grinding

nonstop since the Europe trip ended, fueled by Instagram posts, screenshots, and a grainy-but-obvious photo of their Eiffel Tower kiss. By now, everyone knew: Cade Riley, Penderton's golden boy, and Neil Erickson, resident overachiever, had come back from Europe as... a thing.

"Smile," Cade muttered beside him, slinging an arm around Neil's shoulders with a practiced ease that made Neil's stomach swoop. "If we act like it's no big deal, it won't be."

"Yeah, easy for you to say," Neil whispered back. "You've been in the spotlight since middle school. I've been in the library."

Cade grinned at him, sharp and unbothered, though Neil could see the flicker of nerves under it. "Then welcome to the other side, book boy. We have snacks."

"Apparently, we *are* the snacks," Neil said.

As they pushed through the double doors, it was impossible to miss the clusters of students pretending not to stare at them. Some smiled, some smirked, and some just gawked openly. A couple of Cade's old friends raised their brows in a mix of curiosity and respect.

Neil kept his chin up, trying to channel some of Cade's ease. But inside, he was beaming—half pride, half panic. This wasn't Europe, where anonymity and adventure gave them cover. This was Penderton Academy, where reputations had roots, sometimes for generations.

Still, when Cade's hand brushed his—deliberately, publicly—Neil let himself squeeze back. Just for a second. Just enough to make it clear.

Penderton might not have asked for it, but they were going to get it anyway: Cade and Neil, front and center.

The hallway was louder than usual, like the volume of Penderton had been cranked up just for their arrival. Neil noticed it immediately: whispers in pockets, the quick dart of eyes, and a couple of double takes so exaggerated they could've been out of a sitcom.

"Feels like the paparazzi forgot their cameras," Neil muttered.

Cade, of course, looked delighted. He walked taller, his easy grin turned up just enough to disarm anyone who dared stare too long. When a sophomore basketball player gave him a thumbs-up from across the hall, Cade returned it like he was running for class president.

"You realize you're terrifying me, right?" Neil said under his breath.

"Nah," Cade replied. "You're crushing it. Just don't run into a locker and we're golden."

Neil didn't say anything, mostly because he'd just

swerved to avoid an open locker door.

By the time the bell rang and he slid into AP English, Neil thought maybe—maybe—the attention would fade. Except for the second he sat down, Mia Hollingsworth turned in her seat, grinning conspiratorially.

"So, Neil," she stage-whispered, loud enough for the three people around her to perk up. "Do you, like... feel different now?"

Neil blinked. "Different how?"

"You know." She leaned in, her blonde ponytail swishing. "Now that you're... you know... with Cade. Is it true what they say about—" she lowered her voice dramatically—"kissing athletes?"

Neil's ears went nuclear. He opened his mouth, closed it, then muttered, "I uh—I don't think there's a rulebook about it."

The guys in the next row snickered. Mia, oblivious, pressed on. "No, but seriously! I think it's amazing. Like, finally, Penderton has its own power couple. Totally rooting for you. Do your parents, like, know? Are they cool with it? Because if not, I can recommend my aunt's therapist—she specializes in—"

"Mia." Neil tried not to sound like he was begging. "We're about to start Hamlet. Can we not?"

"Oh! Totally, totally," she said, sitting back with a

knowing smile. "But for real, if you guys ever need a double date buddy—"

Thankfully, the teacher's voice cut through, saving Neil from further interrogation. He hunched over his book, cheeks still hot, shooting Cade a mental *help me* across the hallway, where he could see him in his class through the open doors. Cade smiled bigger than usual because he somehow heard all of it.

"Sonic hearing," Cade mouthed, pointing at his ear.

Chapter Thirty-Eight.

"Oh, my God, we are about to start Thanksgiving break, and we haven't even talked about prom," Neil muttered at his locker the next morning, forehead pressed against the cool metal. "Prom is earlier than usual this year. What are we going to do?"

Cade leaned lazily against the locker next to his, as if this were any other Tuesday. "We?" he echoed, one brow raised.

"Yes, we, right?" Neil hissed, waving a hand between them. "Prom is basically the social Super Bowl of Penderton Academy. And you—" he jabbed Cade's chest—"are usually the MVP. Meanwhile, I'm, at best, a water boy, and I mean the movie version."

Cade grinned, unbothered. "I really don't like it when you undercut your importance around this school. Plus, water boys play a crucial role in the sports ecosystem. Everyone gets dehydrated without them."

Neil groaned. He could already imagine it: the stares, the whispers, the speculation about whether Cade Riley was really going to show up with him. "I just... I don't want it to be some spectacle."

"Or maybe you do. Newsflash, book boy," Cade said, lowering his voice so only Neil could hear. "It's going to be a spectacle no matter what. People still aren't over us holding hands in Europe. Prom? They'll lose their minds."

"Exactly!" Neil said. "So what do we do? Go ironically? Pretend to be too cool? Skip it entirely? I mean, you haven't exactly asked me to go to prom with you, so there's also that."

Cade tilted his head, studying him. "I mean, we could go together. As in, actually together. Tuxes, dancing, bad punch, the whole thing. Let 'em look."

Neil's stomach swooped. The thought of walking into prom side by side with Cade—Penderton's golden boy— was equal parts thrilling and terrifying. He rubbed the back of his neck. "You make it sound so simple."

Cade shrugged, leaning closer; his voice was now softer. "Because it is. You're the only person I want to go with. Also, has it ever occurred to you that we are opposite sides of the same coin?"

"What?"

"I'm at the top of my game on the athletic side. You are at the top of your game on the academic side. Athlete and mathlete. The respect is the same."

Neil had never... *never* thought of it like that before.

Neil's heart did a backflip. Of course, Cade could say something like that in a crowded hallway and make it feel like they were the only two people in the world.

"Okay," Neil mumbled, trying to collect himself. "So, I don't even know what I'd wear. My mom's already hinting she wants me in something traditional. It's a picture thing for her."

Cade's grin turned mischievous. "Good. Then you can match my tux. Because, newsflash, Neil—you're not escaping prom with me."

Neil sighed, half-dreading it, half-excited. "God help us."

Cade leaned in just enough that Neil caught the spark in his eyes. "Correction: God help everyone else."

"Fair," said Neil, shutting his locker.

They wove through the crowded hallway, dodging

backpacks and earbuds, the word prom hanging between them as if it was spelled out in neon lights.

"So," Neil said, lowering his voice, "do we really want to wear matching tuxes? That feels a little... I don't know... *bridal registry at Macy's.*"

Cade smirked, tilting his head like he was picturing it. "What's wrong with that? Black tuxes, maybe navy or bright blue, and a sharp bow tie. Coordinated, but not corny."

"Coordinated is cringe," Neil shot back. "Next thing you'll suggest is we enter with 'Tale As Old As Time' playing."

Cade grinned, unbothered. "Not a bad idea. We'd own the place. Besides, why wouldn't we match? We'd look unstoppable."

Neil gave him a side-eye, hugging his books to his chest. "We'd look like the world's most committed groomsmen."

Cade leaned closer, voice softer. "Or like a couple who know exactly what they want."

That made Neil stumble a step, heat rushing to his ears. Cade caught his elbow before anyone else noticed, steadying him with that effortless touch that constantly rattled Neil more than it should.

"You're impossible," Neil muttered.

"And yet, you keep walking with me," Cade teased. "Matching or not, I just want to show up with you. That's all that matters to me."

The Penderton Champawat Tiger moved slowly behind them, ready for a sneak-pounce.

Students parted like a flock of birds sensing a predator. Orange-and-black fur rippled under the fluorescent hallway lights. One oversized black boot stepped in front of the other, impossibly light for something that looked like it ate freshmen for breakfast.

Neil caught the movement first.

"Oh no," he murmured.

Sophie followed his line of sight. "Is... is that tiger creeping?"

Jenna whispered, "That is *absolutely* a creep-walk."

Mads silently grabbed a bell she mysteriously had in her bag and rang it.

Kip went from the tiger back to himself.

"Thank you, Miss M," he said. Then he turned his attention to Neil and Cade. "Did I hear—you two are gonna match tuxes?" It was Kip Wendell, balancing his messenger bag on his hip. "That's... actually kinda NOT legendary."

"Big bet. Legendary," said Mads, sliding up on their

other side. "It's also adorable. Power couple vibes."

"NOT... legendary," Kip said, maintaining his stare at Mads.

Kip maintained his position behind as the others moved forward.

Neil's stomach dropped. "We weren't—"

"Oh my God, can you *please* do white jackets?" Mads pressed, clasping her hands. "Like Old Hollywood red carpet? That would slap."

Cade was grinning like he'd just won Prom King already. "See? Told you."

Neil groaned. "This is why I said it's corny."

"You say corny, we say *not* iconic," Kip shot back. "Half the class is already betting on whether you guys show up as a pair. Just go big."

Then another voice—Sophie—chimed in: "Honestly? If you two win Prom Kings together, it'd be exactly the progress this school needs."

Neil blinked. Cade raised his brows, impressed.

Mads started texting a friend like she had an idea.

Kip continued to air claw.

"Prom Kings, huh?" Cade drawled, already filing it away like a challenge.

Neil stood there, cheeks hot. "Why do I feel like the entire hallway is in on our conversation?"

Cade slung an arm around Neil's shoulders like it was no big deal.

"Seems to me like they settled it. Matching tuxes, as voted in by committee."

"Cade," Said Neil.

"Neil," Said Cade.

"No matching tux."

Kip moved forward in his Champawat Tiger walk, took Neil by the arm, and said, "Walk."

"You all will talk about it when you ask him properly," Kip said to Cade as they continued to walk. "Despite his English last name, he is Italian, and he doesn't work off of suggestions. That's reserved for red lights. Be bold. Be fierce. Be a man."

Neil left Cade standing in the hallway, smiling widely, as he slowly walked with Kip.

"Neil, I just spent fifteen minutes telling you that you're the only person I want to go to the prom with. What do you want? A big production?" Cade shouted down the hall to Neil.

"That's not the same thing as asking me, soccer lad. And no, you know I never need a spotlight like that. Just ask me. Do better," Neil teased with a smile as he walked away.

"Well done, future Prom king," Kip said.

Cade loved it when Neil was demanding and assertive. He also loved it when he told him exactly what he wanted.

"Bottom energy," Cade said in a low tone.

"We HEARD that!" Kip said from further down the hallway. "And it's still not the right words coming out of your face."

"Y'all are good together," Sophie said, tucking a strand of hair behind her ear. "I admire your... joint bravery, I guess."

Cade glanced at her, a softness in his expression that made her stomach dip. "You know," he said carefully, "you could give it a shot too."

Sophie stiffened. "Give *what* a shot?"

Cade's smile was small and knowing but never unkind. "I think you know." He paused, letting the quiet settle between them. "Just... be brave, Soph. Don't discount what is possible. It worked for me, and it just might work for you, too."

Her cheeks warmed. She managed a shy, crooked smile as Cade walked away, leaving her with a truth she wasn't sure she was ready to say aloud—but could no longer pretend she didn't feel.

Neil didn't turn back to Cade, mostly because he was

trying to hide his smirk, and when he turned the corner, he laughed as quietly as he could.

"Do you really think Prom Kings is possible?" Neil asked Kip.

"I think anything is possible if you're vibrating at the right frequency."

Then, Kip's eyes scanned back to see AJ at the bend in the hall that they had just passed. He couldn't tell who he was looking at, but he was definitely focused on someone, and it wasn't him. It would never be him.

Out of Kip's sight, Sophie stood there, focused down the hall where AJ was standing, talking to friends.

AJ eventually caught her glance and looked in her direction.

Sophie paused, looking back momentarily. She smiled and then turned and walked to her next class.

AJ's face changed from a half smile to slight encouragement. He went back to talking to his friends.

Chapter Thirty-Nine.

Thanksgiving, Erickson-style, required the smell of garlic, and it hit Cade before he even reached the front steps. By the time Neil opened the door, the scent of roasted turkey, tomato sauce, and something sweet with cinnamon had already wrapped itself around him like a bear hug.

"Welcome to chaos," Neil muttered, ushering him inside.

'Chaos' was putting it lightly. The hallway was gridlocked with cousins wrestling, uncles shouting football commentary from the TV in the next room, and an aunt hollering in Italian from the kitchen. Cade blinked, stunned.

"This... is one family?"

Neil smirked. "This is only half. My favorite cousin, Everett, couldn't make it this year."

Within thirty seconds, Cade was kissed on both cheeks by Neil's Nonna, swatted toward the dining room, and handed a plate that looked like a competitive eater had piled it: turkey, lasagna, stuffing, meatballs, and marshmallow-topped sweet potatoes.

"Eat, eat!" Nonna commanded, glaring at his plate like it might disappear if he didn't devour it immediately. "You're too skinny. Neil, he doesn't eat?"

Cade shot Neil a desperate look. Neil just grinned, already shoveling food like a professional.

By the time everyone squeezed around the table—twenty-two people elbow to elbow—Cade had learned three things: (1) Neil's family's volume only went up, (2) "No, thank you," was not a valid response to second helpings, and (3) dessert required a second stomach. Cannoli, pumpkin pie, pistachio fluff, and biscotti—laid out like they were back in France and a *boulangerie*[1] exploded.

Hours later, dazed and sugar-high, Cade collapsed with Neil on the couch, watching kids run laps around

[1] *Boulangerie:* a french bakery

the living room. "This is war," he whispered. "A delicious, slow death by carbs."

Neil smirked, bumping his shoulder. "Welcome to the family fodder."

If Thanksgiving was a little league game, Christmas was the World Series, starting with the fish.

Cade was unsure why he had expected something quieter. A tree, some lights, a little gift exchange. He had not expected Santa's workshop to spill over into the living room. The tree groaned under the weight of ornaments and garlands. Stockings sagged off the mantel like overstuffed luggage. Piles of wrapped boxes stretched halfway across the rug.

"Everyone looks exhausted," Cade said. "Everything okay?"

"Yes and no. It's the wind-down from the fish yesterday."

"What?"

"The feast of the seven fishes. It's a thing we do on Christmas Eve. We spend so much time preparing it that we are almost too exhausted to eat it."

Cade glanced down at the one slim package in his hands—his carefully wrapped gift for Neil, a leather journal with his initials embossed—and felt like he'd brought a water balloon to a hose fight.

"Don't panic," Neil whispered, reading his face. "Just smile. They'll love you."

The gift exchange was less of a Hallmark montage and more of a football draft. Wrapping paper flew. Kids shrieked. Adults shouted commentary.

"Who got me socks again?!" someone yelled.

"They're cashmere!" another voice said defensively.

Neil unwrapped Cade's gift carefully, which already set him apart from his family's tornado tactics. When he slid the journal free, his grin softened. "Cade... It's perfect." His voice dropped low enough for only Cade to hear. "Thank you."

Cade's chest went warm, and then Neil's mom appeared with a package almost as big as his head. "This one's for you!"

Cade blinked. "For... me?"

"Of course!" she said, beaming. "You're family now, as far as I'm concerned."

Inside the oversized box: top-of-the-line noise-canceling headphones— something Cade had only mentioned once, back in September, when the lawn crew had woken him too early. He stared at the box, throat tightening. He wasn't used to being noticed this way by a mother. Cade's parents told him that he had $500 to spend on the family credit card.

Cade slipped away from the noise of the Ericksons' Christmas gathering and settled onto the piano bench. No announcement, no preamble—just a quiet breath as his fingers found the keys. He began playing a soft, unhurried version of "Have Yourself a Merry Little Christmas."

One by one, conversations tapered off. The room's laughter dimmed into a warm hush. Neil appeared in the archway, arms folded, smiling like he'd been caught off guard in the best possible way. The last notes drifted through the living room, settling over the family like falling snow.

When Cade finally looked up, everyone was watching him—beaming—and then the applause came, gentle but full.

"That was beautiful," Neil said, stepping forward. "You are just full of surprises, aren't you?"

He wrapped his arms around Cade from behind, chin brushing Cade's hair. Cade reached up with his left hand and squeezed Neil's forearm, cheeks pink.

"I've got to keep surprising you," he murmured.

Nonna Giordano, wrapped in her shawl, smiled from her armchair. "You're definitely part of the family now, *tesoro*."

Cade blinked, moved in a way words didn't quite cover. He turned back to the piano, fingers drifting into a quiet, easy melody—soft background music for the rest of their holiday evening.

And just like that, surrounded by warmth and twinkling lights, he felt it. He truly belonged.

Later, after the living room looked like a recycling plant had detonated, Cade and Neil curled up on the floor by the tree, bagging wrapping paper. The lights blinked softly, casting their faces in alternating red and green.

"Your family," Cade murmured, "they're... overwhelmingly gracious."

Neil tilted his head onto his shoulder. "Definitely the good kind."

Cade thought of the quiet, echoing halls of his own house—his parents' gift boxes wrapped by staff, Christmas Eve conducted like a business meeting. He looked at Neil's family mess: the paper snowdrifts, the laughter still carrying from the kitchen, and Neil's hand threaded through his.

"The best," Cade said lovingly as if he wanted to say "You're the best."

Neil smiled, and Cade knew—holidays would never be the same again.

After card games, the family gathered their coats.

"Coming with us?" Neil asked.

"To Midnight Mass? It's not like I don't know what to do."

"What?" asked Neil.

"You taught me most of it in Naples."

His Nonna woke up from the lounge chair. "What time is it?"

"It's ten-thirty, Nonna."

Neil walked into the other room to find his mom and haul off a trash bag of wrapping paper.

Cade stayed in the living room with Neil's grandmother.

"You're what we call *buono come il pane*," she said to Cade. "Good as bread."

"What gave it away?" Cade asked.

"The way you look at people, especially Neil. I worried you might be a caker."

"I'm sorry. I... I don't know what that is, ma'am."

"Don't pay me any attention; ask Neil what a cake eater is. It's not important what I think."

"Okay," Cade said cautiously, but with a smile.

Neil's sister, Isabella, walked up to her Nonna and wrapped her small arms around her waist.

"Are you okay, *tesoro*?" Nonna asked, brushing a

hand over her hair.

"I don't feel very good," Isabella murmured. "Do you think... maybe I could stay home just this once?"

Nonna shook her head gently. "You go to church, and you feel better. Always works."

Isabella glanced over Nonna's shoulder at Cade with an expression that clearly translated to please save me.

Cade offered an apologetic wince—I got nothing, kid—because challenging Nonna Erickson on Christmas Eve felt like trying to fistfight a thunderstorm.

Still, he wasn't going to leave Isabella stranded. He spotted a couple of leftover candy canes on the table from the morning's unwrapped gifts and held one up.

"My mom used to give me peppermint whenever I felt sick," Cade said, crouching to her level. "You want to try it?"

Isabella nodded, big-eyed and grateful. "Thank you, Cade."

He handed her the candy cane, squeezing her shoulder with a tiny conspiratorial smile and a wink.

Nonna eyed him but said nothing—mostly because Isabella was already perking up, clutching her peppermint like a lifeline.

Sometimes, miracles come in the form of candy canes and a boy doing his best to survive Catholicism by association.

During the liturgy of the sacrament, Neil and Cade stepped back to let family and others in their row pass—just as they had in Naples. Neil's Nonna brushed by first, placing a warm hand on Cade's shoulder before kissing Neil on the cheek. Others followed, heads bowed, shoes whispering across marble.

Once everyone to their right returned and knelt again, Neil lowered himself to the kneeler.

The young cantor lifted his voice, announcing the next hymn.

"Be Thou My Vision."

Neil bowed his head, expecting another familiar quiet moment. But then—a shift of air, a subtle dip on the kneeler beside him—

Cade slid into place next to him in one fluid, unhesitating motion.

As if drawn there, not deciding.

Neil turned his head.

Cade didn't look back.

He stayed facing forward, spine straight, shoulders relaxed in a way Neil seldom saw—except in unguarded, private moments. The sanctuary's candlelight softened the angles of his face.

For a heartbeat, Neil just watched him.

Cade wasn't hearing a hymn of doctrine or tradition.

Neil knew that immediately—instinctively.

Cade was hearing it through a different lens.

Through a different heart, through him.

Even without the lyrics, the title alone carried a gravity Cade couldn't hide:

Be Thou My Vision.

Something longing. Something reverent.

Something like prayer—

but not to God.

Neil's breath caught.

Cade inhaled slowly, steadying himself. Their elbows brushed—barely a graze—yet in the quiet of the sanctuary, it was seismic.

The pastor rose. The congregation followed.

The moment broke, soft as glass.

They sat again, and Cade kept his gaze forward, almost afraid to risk a glance. But under the narrow wooden kneeler they'd shared, his foot shifted. Just an inch. Then another.

Until it touched Neil's.

A gentle nudge.

A subtle offering.

A confession without words.

Neil didn't move away.

A single tear slipped down his cheek before he could stop it.

He felt it too.

Faith—not in doctrine, not in ritual—

but in each other.

Later, Cade wouldn't try to explain what happened.

Some moments are best lived in silence.

He didn't know whether it was irreverent or strange or sacred to hear that hymn and think of Neil instead of anything theological.

He only knew one thing:

That moment—kneeling side by side, the world hushed around them—would stay with him for a very, very long time.

Chapter Forty.

On **New Year's Eve**, Cade had insisted Neil come with him to the Percy Priest Lake party.

"I want you there," Cade said—too earnestly for Neil to resist.

"A lake party, in December. This doesn't sound like your smartest friends."

When they arrived, the lake shimmered in fading sunset, and half of Penderton was already in party mode—music blasting, people stumbling loudly, someone grilling something questionable on a portable stove. The air moved with summer energy.

Cade fit right in, stepping into the noise like it welcomed him personally.

And Neil—well, Neil was there because Cade wanted him there.

It only took Cade fifteen minutes to succumb to his friends' encouragement to do shots and chasers. Thirty minutes for him to go from relaxed to sloppy.

But honestly? It wasn't shocking to anyone but Neil. Cade had a reputation for these nights—everyone had seen him get messy before. They'd laughed, filmed, and cheered him on like he was a spectacle.

What was shocking was that Cade didn't hide it from Neil this time.

He didn't try to hold himself together. He didn't mask. He didn't put effort into staying composed or charming. He let himself unravel, right in front of the person he cared about most.

By his fourth drink, Cade leaned sideways into Neil like gravity had suddenly become mandatory.

"You're very... steady," he murmured. "Like a human anchor."

"I don't feel like that's a compliment," Neil said, cheeks warm.

Cade grinned lazily. "It is to me."

Behind them, Cade's teammates stared with gleeful

anticipation.

"Ohhh, look who's folded!" Trevor yelled.

"Man's running on half a brain cell," Brady added.

A group nearby snickered, and someone said loud enough for the circle to hear, "Classic Riley. Dude's a tank until he isn't."

Like always—like every time Cade got too soft, too human—people saw an opening.

"Yo, Cade, want me to get you a stroller?" someone hollered.

"Make it two!" another laughed. "He's gonna need a nap-nap!"

Cade winced. He tried to sit up, failed, and sagged further into Neil.

There it was—the part Neil had never seen but somehow always felt:

Cade didn't get support when he fell.

He got mocked.

He got dogpiled.

He got turned into a joke because it was more entertaining than helping him.

Neil saw Cade's shoulders curl inward, like he wanted to disappear.

Something flared hot in Neil's chest.

"Hey!" Neil snapped, louder than he'd ever spoken

around these people.

The laughter tapered.

Neil stepped forward, shielding Cade without even thinking. "Enough. He's drunk—not performing for your entertainment."

The group blinked. *Neil*—quiet, careful, never confrontational—was standing there like he'd been waiting years to mouth off.

Brady cleared his throat. "Dude, relax—"

"No," Neil said. "You relax. Maybe try acting like his friends instead of scavengers."

Cade's head lifted a little at that.

Trevor held up his hands. "Alright, alright. Chill."

But Neil wasn't finished. "He's allowed to have an off night. He's allowed to be human. And he's still better to all of you on his worst day than you are to him on your best."

"It's not that serious," Brady said.

Silence blanketed the group.

Cade blinked at Neil, eyes wide and glassy, shocked even through the haze.

No one had defended him like that.

Not once.

Not ever.

Neil knelt beside him. "Come on," he said softly.

"Let's get you out of here."

Cade blinked hard. "Neil... don't leave the party for me."

"The party isn't important," Neil said. "I'm taking you home."

Cade mumbled soft apologies the whole way back.

"You shouldn't... have to babysit me."

"I wanted to be with you tonight," Neil said.

"I didn't mean to... be like this."

Neil just kept one hand on the wheel, one on Cade's arm.

"Cade," he finally said, "you don't have to be perfect with me."

Cade went quiet, breath catching.

Because no one had ever told him that.

The next morning, Cade woke with sunlight in his eyes and a headache pounding like a drumline.

This wasn't his bed.

This room smelled like cedar and detergent and... Neil.

He sat up too fast. "Oh no."

On the floor beside the bed, Neil lay curled under a thin blanket, one hand resting palm-up beside Cade like he'd fallen asleep reaching toward him.

Cade stared at him—at the softness of him, the steadiness of him.

Neil stirred awake. "You're up," he said gently.

"You... brought me here?"

"Yeah. Your house was empty. I didn't want you alone. Do you remember anything?"

Cade swallowed hard. "I remembered you protected and defended me."

Neil pushed himself upright, rubbing his neck awkwardly. "Yeah. Someone needed to, and you've stood up *many* times for me, especially in Europe."

"No one's ever done that for me before."

"I know," Neil said softly. "It was past due, and honestly, it felt good."

Cade paused, taking in Neil's words. "Neil?"
"Yeah?"

Cade's voice cracked. "Thank you."

Neil gave a small smile. "I would do it again, if I needed to."

Cade looked at him—really looked—and vulnerability suddenly didn't feel dangerous.

It felt like trust.

It felt like them.

"Hey, Neil? What's a cake eater?"

"Oh my God, why?"

"Just a term I heard on Christmas Eve. Your Nonna said I wasn't one, but the most important thing was that you didn't think I was one." He paused. "What is it... and do you?"

"Oh. It means a spoiled rich kid," Neil said. "And no. You're not. Maybe you were, but I don't see you like that anymore."

"Good," said Cade.

Chapter Forty-One.

January never really ended in Tennessee. It just stretched—gray mornings, cold turf, and the constant rattle of wind against the bleachers. By the third week of conditioning, Cade Riley's body had adjusted to the ache, but his brain hadn't. Soccer took up much of his spring, and he found it difficult since he had spent late summer and the whole winter with Neil. It was now back to the grind.

Practice started before sunrise and ended long after his breath stopped showing in the air. Coach Lennox didn't believe in "off-season." He believed in running laps until your lungs begged for mercy.

"Riley! Keep your knees up—it's soccer, not speed-walking!"

Cade grinned through the burn. The new first-years groaned behind him, but this was familiar pain, the kind that reminded him he still had something solid—something that didn't depend on words or reputation.

When the world got too noisy, soccer was the one place he could still think clearly.

The afternoon practices gave him at least a good view. Neil was always in the lower section of the bleachers with his books. Often with his computer open, he would do his homework, and sometimes Cade's.

"Hey," Cade muttered as he toweled the sweat from the back and the top of his head. "You hungry?"

"Hello, *you*. Ma's not cooking tonight, so we're free for whatever."

"Cool. Just you and me then, or do you want others?"

Neil shrugged. "I'll see who's around."

"Alright then, I'll hit the shower and see you in fifteen?"

"Yeah." Neil smiled at Cade and watched him as he ran off to the locker room.

When he returned, Neil had gathered Jenna and Mads. Cade brought two of his teammates: Justin, AJ, and Savannah.

"Perfect. I like prime numbers. Well done, us," Neil said.

"I don't know what that means, but I'm happy that you're happy."

At Emerald Squared in Green Hills, the seven of them split three pizzas—or tried to. The teammates inhaled the squares like a halftime snack, and Neil and the girls, fully expecting it, ordered a backup kimchi-topped pizza before the crumbs even settled.

"Hey! We ordered this one for us," Neil laughed. "I didn't think you would eat kimchi."

"We will eat anything after that first practice," said Justin.

"No kidding. I'm a little worried about the sophomores. They looked cooked," Cade said, raising his hand for the waiter. "Could we order another kimchi pizza and a round of sodas, please? Thanks."

"I'm going to take this break to go pee," said Neil.

Cade had developed the habit of putting his arm around Neil when he got off a barstool, as if to assist him. Neil wasn't sure what that was about, but he had learned to like it.

"Okay, babe."

Inside the women's bathroom, Mads stepped out of a

stall to find Savannah at the sink, blinking hard as she tried to wrangle a contact lens into place.

"Hey," Mads said, turning on the faucet.

"Hey," Savannah replied, keeping one eye pried open like it might flee.

Mads couldn't help smiling. "You have pretty eyes."

Savannah froze for half a second, then looked up at Mads in the mirror before turning to face her directly. "Thanks. You, too. Are those contacts or...?"

"Natural," Mads said, shrugging as she dried her hands. "My friend Kip says Elizabeth Taylor had the same color eyes and called them violet. Says it's super rare. What do you think?"

Savannah considered her for a moment—really looked. "I saw her once," she said, "when my grandparents were watching *Cleopatra*. I don't know anything about rare eye colors, but..." She hesitated, the corner of her mouth lifting. "You're pretty."

"Thanks," said Mads in a soft way.

They both went still, caught somewhere between surprise and something softer neither of them had language for yet.

For a breath, they just stood there—two girls, two half-finished sentences, and one moment neither knew how to step out of.

Neil exited the other bathroom, drying his hands and tossing a paper towel in the garbage as he glanced down the back hallway toward their table. Before he could take a step, arms wrapped around his waist and yanked him backward into the dark of a storage closet.

"What the—" His protest was muffled as a hand covered his mouth. He was spun around, heart slamming in his chest—until he saw who it was.

"Cade!?" Neil breathed out, half-laughing, half-panicked in relief. "What are you doing?"

Cade didn't bother answering right away. He crowded Neil against the inside of the door, breath warm, eyes blazing in that way that always made Neil's knees a little unreliable.

"I wanted a moment alone with you," Cade murmured, voice low and urgent.

"Yeah?" Neil whispered back, smiling now.

"Yeah. Plus, someone is wearing a fragrance that smells like dirt."

"Dirt has a smell?" Neil asked.

"It has since we have been home from Europe."

"Your doctor in Doncaster said that might—"

Cade kissed him—fierce, unhurried, and entirely reckless for a storage closet in a crowded restaurant.

Outside, a couple of diners glanced toward the

hallway at the thump against the door, then decided their appetizers were more important than investigating. Their friends at the table figured it out instantly and dissolved into muffled laughter—because of course Cade couldn't wait until they got back to the car.

But they also understood. They all wanted that kind of connection—whatever wild, magnetic thing Cade and Neil shared—so they let it happen.

When a server started down the hallway toward the bathrooms, Justin intercepted with a sudden, overly enthusiastic question about dessert specials. Mads and Savannah, coming out of their own bathroom moment, slid into place like a well-rehearsed secret service unit, blocking the line of sight entirely. Mads casually knocked on the closet door, whispering urgently, "Staff coming! Wrap it up!"

They had Neil and Cade's backs.

Inside the closet, Cade pulled away only slightly, forehead pressed to Neil's.

"We should probably go," Neil whispered, breathless.

"Yeah," Cade said, kissing him again anyway. "In a minute."

Because for that moment—warm light leaking under the door, friends guarding the hallway, laughter drifting from the dining room—they had carved out a tiny pocket of the world just for themselves.

And neither of them was in a hurry to let it go.

After the goodbyes, Neil and Cade walked casually back to Cade's Citroën.

"You and Justin seem to be in sync," Neil said.

"Oh, my God. *Please* be a little jealous."

"Ha-ha. I'm just making an observation. That's all. So maybe later with the jealousy."

"Would it help if I told you that he and I... kinda..." Cade made some crude gestures. "...we maybe kinda pulled for a minute?"

Neil smiled. "Did you?"

Cade was in a teasing mood. "Maybe." He grinned like he wanted Neil to get a little crabby. "Not everyone wants me the way you do, and it wouldn't matter anyway. I'm not giving up now. For Justin? No. Joe Locke, maybe."

Cade reached out for Neil's hand, and they stopped in front of the passenger door. Cade kissed him and then opened the door for him.

Neil followed Cade in the side mirror as he came around to get into the driver's seat.

Cade looked at him like he was saying, 'What?' and

used his left hand on the top of the steering column to start the car. The Citroën began to rise.

"I'm sorry."

"Neil. Get mad if you want to. I kinda like it. There's still nothing there with Justin, but let's role-play that."

"Okay." Neil was still a little embarrassed, but he honestly loved it when Cade was playful.

"Why do you like Justin? Is he hotter than me?" Neil jokingly barked at Cade.

"*That's* what I want," Cade laughed. "As long as it's playful, it's fun."

Chapter Forty-Two.

Soccer was the more popular sport at Penderton. That's saying a lot for a Southern school. Football is almost always king, but somehow the engagement at Penderton was in Soccer. Many attributed it to Cade's outgoing and entertaining personality on the field.

The first home game of the season was against the Brentwood Bruins: Cal Cronwell's school team. Brentwood was Penderton's biggest rival when it came to sports. Their soccer booster was well-funded and well-organized. They would be a formidable foe for the Penderton Gryphons. Cade seemed very confident and ready for the match.

Neil drove Cade's car to the game, parked, and found a spot in the visitors' section among the players' girlfriends. It wasn't his usual crowd, but tonight, it felt right. He was the captain's boyfriend—whether he liked the attention or not.

"Neil!" the girls shouted when they spotted him, waving him over.

He climbed the bleachers, grinning.

"This must be so different for you," said Ava Addison, sliding down a seat to make room.

He laughed softly. "Am I that obvious a newbie?"

"Kinda," she said, smiling and scrunching her nose.

"Not gonna lie," Neil said, eyes drifting toward the field, "this is actually kinda fun. Especially watching Cade out there."

"You two are so cute," Ava said. "Like—total blueprint."

"Aw, thanks," Neil said, trying not to blush.

Savannah Holt plopped down beside her. "Agreed."

"Hey, Sav," Ava said. "You know, Neil?"

"We had Econ last year," Savannah said brightly. "He cooks. Hey, Neil. Glad you joined the *girl* group."

Neil blinked. "Well, I—"

"Savannah," Ava warned, laughing. "Full disclosure, Sav sometimes puts the thought bubble on voice mode, Neil."

"Sorry! I didn't mean it like—you know—uh..." Savannah muttered.

Neil grinned. "Try this: 'Hey, Neil. I'm awesome, all my friends are awesome, and I'm delighted you're being awesome with us.'"

The whole row broke into laughter.

"See what I mean?" Ava said, nudging Savannah. "Told you—he's got the brains and the vibe. No wonder Cade went for him."

"Aww, we really are an awesome bunch of—" Ava paused dramatically.

"Birlfriends?" Neil offered.

"**BIRLFRIENDS!**" they shouted together, the word echoing through the bleachers.

The commotion caught Cade's attention down on the field. He looked up toward the stands, squinting into the lights.

Neil and the girls waved, laughing.

Cade grinned, lifting a hand in return—his smile wide and unguarded. Seeing Neil fitting in so easily made his chest feel lighter than any win ever could.

"Have you ever played any sports, Neil?" Ava asked.

"*The Neighbourhood is deprived of the romance of me being athletic. Such romance as I have is that of the*

Inglese Italianato.[1] Neil thought.

"No, not really," he responded.

Savannah cheered for AJ, who sent a cross into the box. Cade rose for the header, flicking it toward Ava's boyfriend, Micah, whose volley ricocheted off a defender. AJ mildly had time to say a command to Cade under his breath, and Cade lunged for the rebound goal.

Cade was shocked when he heard AJ from a distance. His hearing was top-notch now.

Neil didn't think. He shot to his feet, arms up, shouting before the ref's whistle confirmed it. The stands erupted; the "birlfriends" jumped and screamed around him.

"It's over?" Neil gasped once the final buzzer sounded.

"Over and *won!*" Ava laughed.

Relieved, Neil mentally rehearsed something clever to say before Cade found him—something that didn't sound like he'd only learned what an offside trap was yesterday.

"How long have you and AJ been a thing?" Neil asked Savannah.

"It's not really that serious. I haven't really thought about getting serious with anyone since Cade," Savannah

[1] *A Room with a View*, E.M. Forster (Cecil Vyse)

said, then realized she may have messed up again.

Neil looked at Ava, who seemed really disappointed.

"What?" Savannah said to Ava. "If he's going to be in the group, he can't be in the dark about it."

"Sounds like it was pretty serious before," Neil said.

"I mean, we had a pretty good run, but he's gay now," Savannah tried to recover.

"He's actually bi," Neil pushed back. "Are we cool?"

"Big yes. I was about to ask the same thing."

"Okay, great."

When Cade finally appeared—hair still damp from the shower, duffel slung over one shoulder, and his trademark cowboy hat dangling from his fingers—Neil abandoned his rehearsed line and his resolve to say something cool and soccer-centric.

"Hey!" Cade said, pulling him into a one-armed hug before settling the hat on Neil's head.

"I thought the tradition was that you wore this after a win," Neil said, adjusting the brim.

Cade grinned. "New season, new rule—I get to put it on my boyfriend now."

"Damn," Neil said, tipping the hat lower with a smirk. "Add that line to your wins for the day."

They started toward the parking lot, weaving through a tide of cheers and high-fives. Fans called

Cade's name—and more than a few waved at Neil, too. He wasn't used to that kind of attention; a few months ago, he would've ducked and run.

But standing next to Cade, with the night air cool and the stadium lights fading behind them, the noise didn't feel like pressure anymore. It felt like belonging.

Like it or not, being with Cade meant being seen. And maybe—for once—he didn't mind at all.

The parking lot was almost empty by the time they reached Cade's car. The air smelled faintly of wet turf and rain, headlights washing across puddles as Cade tossed his duffel into the backseat.

Neil climbed into the passenger seat, still wearing Cade's cowboy hat.

Cade slid behind the wheel, glancing over with a grin. "You look better in that thing than I ever did."

Neil raised an eyebrow. "Please. I look like I'm about to start line dancing at a Waffle House."

"Hot," Cade said, dead serious. "Now I want it scattered, smothered, and covered."

Neil laughed, shaking his head. "And hot!"

The laughter faded into a comfortable silence as Cade pulled onto the main road. The radio played softly—something low and twangy, half-love song, half-victory anthem. Streetlights slipped over Cade's face in gold flashes. He looked both exhausted and content, the way athletes do when the adrenaline's finally gone but the win is still sinking in.

Neil stole a glance. "So. Two goals and a hero moment. You planning to make that a weekly thing?"

Cade shrugged modestly. "Depends. You planning to show up every week?"

Neil smiled. "Guess I don't have a choice now. Your fan club kind of adopted me."

"The birlfriends," Cade said, grinning. "I heard about that. You made quite the impression."

"Yeah, well. They're a good bunch. Loud, though. Also, nicer than I expected."

"Loud's not bad," Cade said. "Means people care, like in your family." He hesitated, fingers tapping the steering wheel. "I like it when you're there, you know. Makes the whole thing feel... fresh."

Neil turned toward him, his voice quiet. "It would be fresh anyway, Cade. You'd still play your heart out even if no one was watching."

Cade gave a half-smile, eyes on the road. "Maybe. But it's better when you're watching."

The words hung between them, unpolished and honest.

Neil reached over, brushing his fingers against

Cade's wrist. "Well, good news then. I'll be there."

Cade's grip tightened around Neil's hand just long enough for Neil to feel the pulse of it before he let go, both of them smiling into the soft cadence of the road ahead.

Outside, the night blurred by—quiet, endless, and full of promise.

They turned down Neil's street, the sound of tires on wet pavement filling the space between songs. Most of the houses were dark now—porch lights flickering, sprinklers ticking somewhere down the block.

Cade parked at the curb and let the engine idle. Neither of them moved right away.

Neil broke the silence first. "You tired?"

Cade chuckled. "Exhausted. My legs hate me. My soul's fine, though."

"Yeah, well, tell your soul 'good game'."

Cade laughed softly. "You always know what to say."

He leaned over, his hair still damp, and kissed Neil— just a light press of lips that tasted faintly of Gatorade and spring air.

"Text me when you get home," Neil murmured.

"I will," Cade said, resting his forehead against Neil's for a beat longer before pulling back. "You want to hang out Saturday night? Crew's thinking pizza and bad movies."

"Only if you promise to let me pick one of the bad

movies."

"Deal."

Neil smiled, fingers lingering on the brim of Cade's hat, still perched on his head. "Goodnight, Captain."

Cade grinned. "Goodnight, Birlfriend."

Neil rolled his eyes but couldn't hide his laugh. He put the hat on Cade's head.

Cade waited until Neil was safely inside before he drove off, headlights sweeping across the dark lawns. Neil watched from the window as the car disappeared down the street, phone buzzing a few minutes later with a text.

Cade
Home. Still smiling. See you Saturday.

Neil
Sleep well, handsome.

Neil set the phone on his nightstand and smiled into the quiet room.

He thought more about what Savannah said. Everything felt manageable, but a little more complicated.

Neil pulled out his phone and texted his friends.

Neil
Hey I'm not going to be able to make it Saturday night. Cade's friends invited me to bad movie night.

Mads
We get it, Cade is more important than us
(dies in sarcasm) but really? Last-minute cancellation?

Kip
All of these girls to myself? Did I mention I
am the only straight male in our friend group??

Sophie
Many times, Kip. Somehow we all still
friend-zone you. Neil, have a great time.
We will miss you this weekend.

Jenna
If we keep giving Neil a hard time, we
won't get invited to the wedding. We love you, Neil!

> **Neil**
> haha. I love y'all.

By Friday evening, the week had finally exhaled. Cade's text came through just as Neil was closing his laptop:

Cade
Hope you're ready to embarrass yourself at trivia again.

> **Neil**
> I'll let you win. It's a confidence thing.

Cade
Bring that confidence. And snacks.

Neil smiled, grabbed a bag of chips and a hoodie, and headed out.

AJ's basement was already alive when he got there.

AJ and Savannah were sprawled across the beanbag chairs; Ava and Micah were fighting over the remote; someone had lit the fake fireplace app on the TV for "ambience," ignoring the actual gas logs illuminating the real fireplace.

Cade opened the door before Neil could knock.

"Hey, Birlfriend," he teased, pulling him into a quick hug that smelled like detergent and pizza.

"Hey, Captain." Neil held up the chips. "Tribute."

"Accepted." Cade tossed them onto the snack pile and waved a hand toward the chaos. "Crew's in full form tonight."

Savannah perked up. "Neil! Get in here, Birlfriend. We're deciding who dies first in a zombie apocalypse!"

"Obviously, Micah," Ava said. "He'd stop to film it for TikTok."

"Hey!" Micah protested. "Someone has to document our bravery!"

"That makes me think we are watching *Blair Witch* tonight," Neil said as he cued up to do the nose-drip scene, grabbing a flashlight from his keychain and holding it at his chin. "

Everyone seemed a little creeped out.

"*The Blair Witch Project*. None of y'all have seen this? I think it's from the 90s."

"No, but it looks creepy," said Micah.

"It's really just dumb. Maybe let's put it on the list for another night," Neil said.

Neil slid onto the couch next to Cade, the two of them instantly syncing into easy laughter with the group. It struck him, not for the first time, how normal this all felt—how good it was to laugh without a single what-if hanging overhead.

Cade draped his arm along the back of the couch, fingertips brushing Neil's shoulder. "You realize they'll turn on us first, right?"

"Us?" Neil asked.

"Couples always get taken out early. Too distracted by their feelings."

Neil snorted. "Please. You'd just charm the zombies into joining your fan club."

"That's actually a great plan," Cade said with a grin.

An hour later, pizza boxes were stacked high, and a terrible 90s action movie flickered across the screen. AJ and Savannah provided color commentary; Ava kept score of imaginary plot holes; and Cade leaned quietly into Neil's side, both of them content to let the noise fill the room.

Between explosions onscreen, Cade whispered, "You good?"

Neil nodded, eyes still on the movie. "Yeah."

Cade smiled softly. "I'm glad you're here."

Neil turned toward him. "Well, I'm glad you're here. It would be weird without you."

Cade laughed as his thumb brushed Neil's hand, subtle enough that no one else noticed. The warmth of it lingered through the next bad joke, the next burst of laughter, the next slice of quiet between them.

Neil's phone chimed.

"Everything okay?" Cade asked.

"Yeah. I think Jenna is annoyed at me but isn't saying it directly."

"For what?" Cade asked.

"Because I keep cancelling on them." Neil didn't want to say it directly because he was spending so much time with Cade.

"Well, tell them that you're with someone important," Cade smirked.

"And that person's friends. Maybe you could hang out with my friends every once in a while," Neil suggested.

"Ugh. Sure," said Cade in a very plain way.

Outside, rain started to fall again—the soft, steady kind that made the world feel smaller and safer.

Neil didn't feel like he was escaping anything. He was exactly where he wanted to be.

By the time the credits rolled, the crew was half-asleep in a sprawl of blankets and crumbs.

Savannah yawned, stretching like a cat. "Okay, I love you all, but if I don't leave now, I'm becoming part of the furniture."

"Too late," AJ said, tossing her car keys.

She caught them mid-air, laughing.

Ava and Micah were next, gathering leftovers and arguing over who had to carry the pizza boxes to the recycling bin. Within fifteen minutes, the basement had cleared out, leaving only the TV noise and the low drizzle tapping the windows.

Neil helped Cade stack plates on the counter. "These friends seem really nice."

Cade smiled. "Yeah. They're kind of my chosen chaos."

He rinsed his hands, flicked water at Neil. "You fit in pretty fast, you know."

Neil shrugged. "I had good coaching."

Cade leaned back against the counter, studying him with a faint smile. "You were different tonight."

"Different how?" Neil scrunched his eyebrows.

"Relaxed. Like you weren't trying so hard to read the room."

Neil smirked. "You're saying I wasn't awkward?"

"I mean, you were still Neil-level awkward," Cade teased, "but in a cute way."

Neil rolled his eyes, but felt his face warm. "You should stop before that sounds like a compliment."

"Too late."

They stood there for a beat, quiet except for the rain and the sound of the ice maker in the fridge.

Cade's voice dropped. "You heading home soon?"

"Yeah. My mom's got early-morning appointments, and I have her car. I should beat the curfew she pretends I still have."

Cade nodded, walking him to the door. Outside, the motor court shimmered with rainlight.

"Cade?" Neil wanted to ask him about Savannah and how many others there were before him, but he couldn't justify making a big deal out of what happened before.

"Yeah, babe?"

Neil paused. "I had a really good time."

"Me too. Drive safe," Cade said. "And text when you get home. I rarely get to say that."

"I always mean it."

Neil smiled, leaning in. Their kiss was unhurried, familiar, the kind of quiet punctuation that came from two people who no longer needed to prove anything.

When they pulled apart, Cade brushed his thumb

along Neil's jaw. "Hey—crew's hitting the diner next Friday. You in?"

"Only if they promise to argue about something truly meaningless."

"Oh, guaranteed," Cade said, laughing.

Neil stepped back toward his car, still smiling. "Night, Captain. You're not leaving just yet?"

"Night. I'm going to help AJ clean up, and then I'll head home... birlfriend."

Neil groaned and laughed at the same time. "You're never dropping that, are you?"

"Not a chance."

Cade watched until Neil's taillights disappeared down the wet road, then slipped his hands into his jacket pockets and smiled to himself.

Inside the car, Neil's phone buzzed before he even reached the end of the tree-lined driveway.

Cade
You forgot your hat again.

Neil
Maybe I just wanted an excuse to see you tomorrow.

Cade
That's my favorite play of the season so far.

Neil laughed under his breath and turned up the radio. Outside, the rain fell harder, steady as a heartbeat.

Everything in his life felt exactly in sync.

Neil pulled up the school paper on his laptop at breakfast and found the game on the front page:

🦅 Penderton Gryphons Edge Out Brentwood Bruins in 2-1 Thriller

Brentwood, TN—Friday Night Lights, March 14

The Penderton Gryphons delivered a statement win on Friday night, defeating the Brentwood Bruins 2-1 in a hard-fought district match that came down to the final minutes.

After a scoreless first half dominated by defensive stands, senior captain Cade Riley anchored the Gryphons' back line with multiple key stops against Brentwood striker Josh Kane, keeping the Bruins' offense contained and momentum on Penderton's side.

Penderton broke through in the 63rd minute when midfielder AJ Collins slipped a perfect pass through traffic to forward Micah Bennett, whose initial shot deflected into chaos inside the box. Riley followed up with a clean finish off the rebound, putting the Gryphons ahead 1-0.

Brentwood answered just seven minutes later, converting a curling free kick to tie the game at 1-1. Both teams battled through heavy rain and rising tension as the clock wound down.

With under two minutes remaining, Penderton earned a late corner. Collins sent a pinpoint cross into the box, where Riley rose above two defenders to flick the ball toward Bennett. Bennett volleyed the shot into the upper corner for the go-ahead goal, sending the visiting bench and Penderton crowd into celebration.

Final score: Penderton 2, Brentwood 1.

The victory moves the Gryphons to 3-1-0 on the season and marks their first win over Brentwood in three years. Coach Ramirez praised the team's grit, calling it "a full-squad effort built on trust and persistence."

Next up: The Gryphons host the Franklin Admirals at home next Tuesday at 6:00 p.m.

Chapter Forty-Three.

It was Friday at Penderton—Assembly Day, or Pep Rally, depending on whether there was a game that night. Neil assumed he'd sit with Cade, but when he didn't see him anywhere on the gym floor, he slid into the bleachers next to Jenna.

"Look who finally remembered the little people," she teased, unwrapping gum.

"I was ditched. Don't get used to it," Neil smirked as he hugged his friend.

"We are happy to see you," Sophie said. "Right?" as she looked at Jenna.

"Right."

The principal droned. The school song limped through the students' voices just after the soccer team marched in. AJ caught a glimpse of Sophie and waved. She waved back and smiled. Neil and Jenna were distracted by a conversation as they caught up.

Neil was just zoning out of the assembly when the PA system crackled:

"Penderton Academy's own Jack Herndon!"

Jack was like Penderton's student version of a cruise director. He was the most talented student and really knew how to entertain and rally students into whatever he had dreamed up. He was a singer, a dancer, and a piano player—a true man of talent.

The gym erupted. Jack launched into a crowd-pleaser, then pivoted with a grin as the band dropped a sharp pop beat—Sabrina Carpenter.

The dance team stormed the floor in coffee-cup costumes. Students screamed, phones shot into the air—then one guy in a blond wig strutted forward, pure Sabrina Carpenter. The crowd lost it. A second dancer entered in a slick black wig, circling the blond like a Broadway villain but slightly oblivious to everything.

Neil laughed—until the realization hit.

The lyrics. The choreography. Blond Wig Guy, desperate and breathless. Black Wig Guy, smug and untouchable... *Espresso*. The photo Cade took of Neil.

"Oh my God," Jenna hissed. "Neil."

His stomach dropped. This wasn't random. This was pointed. This was a parody of them: he and Cade. What was the drama department up to?

Then came the paper roll. Unfurling down the stage, the blond wig dancer acted like they got hit with it and fumbled off stage behind the paper. When it was fully unrolled, it had bold black paint blaring:

"I have two tickets to prom. Neil, please be my plus one."

The gym exploded.

Cymbals crashed, the banner ripped apart, and Cade busted through like a rock star, arms raised—Cardboard Leaning Tower of Pisa, Eiffel Tower, gondola—bedazzled props everywhere. The crowd went feral.

Neil nearly collapsed. *This is for... me?*

Cade lifted a glittery cutout of two tickets, shouting into Jack's mic: "Neil Erickson! Will you be my date to prom?"

The entire gym swiveled toward him. Jenna shoved him to his feet, shrieking, "Oh my God. Why are you still here? GO!"

Neil bolted down the bleachers, sneakers slapping, adrenaline electric. An AV kid shoved a mic into his hand. He was certain he would trip on his unreliable feet and legs.

Neil's voice cracked, and he stopped suddenly as he reached Cade. "Yes!"

The gym detonated. Cade grabbed him by the waist and kissed him under the lights, the crowd's roar shaking the rafters—air horns, chants, confetti—phones capturing it from every angle.

Neil kissed him back, dizzy, fireworks behind his ribs. For once, he wasn't hiding in the background. He was center stage—seen, celebrated, loved.

The chaos was volcanic. Chants of "Prom Kings!" and "*La coppia!*" Theater kids mobbing them, teammates clapping Cade on the back. Jenna yelling, "TRENDING, babe!" and shoving a phone in Neil's face with his kiss already looped online.

Cade soaked it up, bowing, fist-bumping, and pulling Neil in close every chance he got.

Neil, flushed and overwhelmed, hissed, "Are you loving this?"

Cade kissed his temple, grinning. "This is actually insane, and yes," Cade responded.

By the time they hit the hallway, the school was a mob. Chants, selfies, TikTok requests—*Espresso* echoing from half a dozen phones. Neil had never been more exposed in his life. And yet—with Cade's arm around him—he'd never felt so untouchable and protected.

Then came Mrs. Donnelly, cutting through like a blade. "Boys. A word."

Minutes later, they were in Principal Winters' office. She smiled, warm but exasperated. "Well. That was... unforgettable."

"Thank you, ma'am," Cade replied.

Winters chuckled. "Congratulations are in order. That was brave. But you've also turned Penderton upside down. I think—for today—your presence is too combustible. Take the afternoon off. Let the school breathe."

Cade raised a brow. "You're benching us."

Winters smirked. "Let's call it load management."

Neil gaped. "I've never been sent home before. Are we in trouble?"

"No, Neil. However, we need to get the school back in order," Principal Winters said.

Cade stretched, utterly smug. "Day off with my boyfriend? Works for me."

As they stepped into the sunlight, Neil groaned, covering his face. "I can't believe this happened."

Cade slung an arm around his shoulders, steering him toward the lot. "Believe it. Nashville's ours for the day." He grinned, leaning close. "And you owe me a milkshake."

Neil laughed despite himself, heart racing. After everything that just happened, it felt like the beginning of something promising and maybe a little crazy.

Chapter Forty-Four.

Cade's car purred out of the school lot like nothing dramatic had just gone down, as if half the student body wasn't still excited about the kiss and the paper sign and Jack Herndon on stage. Neil slumped in the passenger seat, forehead pressed to the glass.

"An entire gym of people cheering for me," he muttered. "Definitely didn't have that on my high school bucket list."

Cade smirked, one hand easy on the wheel. "Yeah? What'd you have on your bucket list?"

"I don't know," Neil said. "Maybe 'finally figure out what's in Jimmy's cracked corn.' Turns out I don't care.

Not after today."

Cade laughed, pulling onto West End Avenue, passing Vanderbilt University on one side and the Parthenon on the other. "You're funny."

"I'm serious," Neil said, twisting in his seat. "They must think I'm some transfer student. No one knew who I was before, like, four weeks ago. And now—" He gestured vaguely. "—now people are posting fan edits of me and you with Italian pop songs?"

Cade shot him a look, all warmth. "That's not true."

"Yes, it is," Neil insisted. "I was invisible."

Cade shook his head, pulling into the lot of his favorite Italian spot—a low-key trattoria with red awnings. He shifted into park, then turned to Neil, eyes steady. "Listen. I knew who you were. Everyone knows who you are. You just like to think you're invisible, like you move mysteriously under a wizard cloak, and don't you dare think people didn't notice you before. I did."

Neil snorted. "Alright."

"Neil," Cade said firmly, leaning in like he wanted to make sure the words landed. "You're going to be valedictorian."

Neil blinked. "What?"

"Okay, fine," Cade amended, grinning. "Probably salutatorian. But still. People know you. They respect you. Again, you're like... me, but on the academic side of the school. The smart side."

Neil froze, the words tumbling into place in his chest in a way he hadn't expected. Him? The *Cade* of academics?

"I..." He rubbed the back of his neck. "That still might be the most terrifying compliment anyone's ever given me."

Cade grinned, nudging his arm as they got out of the car. "Get used to it. You're not invisible, Neil. You never were."

Inside, the waiter greeted Cade by name, already leading them to his favorite table. Neil sat across from him, trying to decide if he was more overwhelmed by the day or by Cade saying things like "you matter" so casually, as if it was the simplest truth in the world.

The menus were barely in their hands before Neil leaned forward, eyes glinting with mischief. "Okay, but what if I try something?" he said, and when the waiter came back, Neil squared his shoulders and asked— haltingly but confidently—in Italian if he could place the order in Italian.

The waiter blinked at him, then broke into a laugh. "I don't speak Italian, but I appreciate the effort."

Neil flushed, fumbling to close the menu. "Oh. Uh.

Okay, I'll have the—"

The waiter took the rest of their order in English and wandered off, still chuckling.

"Oh, and two espressos with foam on the side. I like to make my own art," Neil said.

Cade waited a beat, then leaned back in his chair and lifted both hands like a magician showing off a trick. "See? Exhibit A."

Neil frowned. "What?"

"You're the smartest person I know," Cade said simply, like it was as obvious as the sky being blue. "Who else even tries that? I've been coming here for years and never thought to order in Italian."

Neil shook his head, smirking, still pink. "Yeah, and it bombed. Also, you don't speak Italian."

"No," Cade said, pointing at him with his fork. "But it impressed me, and you impressed him, even if he didn't speak the language. You just... always try. You always go for it."

Neil tried to roll his eyes, but Cade caught the tiny smile breaking through and grinned wider, victory stamped all over his face.

Cade twirled his fork, then glanced at Neil with that mischievous look that meant he'd been building up to something. "Remember that train ride?"

Neil raised a brow. "You're gonna have to narrow it down. We've been on, like, twenty."

"The first one," Cade said. "When my eyes were patched. You were the one describing everything to me—the river, the rooftops, the first glimpse of Paris. You helped me see things I couldn't."

Neil smiled a little, remembering the way Cade leaned into him back then, soaking up every word. "Yeah. I remember. I also remember making art on your espresso, even though you couldn't see it at the time, and I'm going to do it again right now."

"Well..." Cade set his fork down and pulled out his phone. "Maybe it's my turn to show you what you're not seeing."

He slid the phone across the table. On the screen was one of at least four Instagram posts from the assembly—the dancers, the banner, the kiss, and Neil's stunned face as the gym exploded into cheers.

Cade didn't say another word. He didn't have to.

Neil groaned, dragging a hand down his face. "Okay, okay, enough of all that." But his eyes still lingered on the post. And then, curiosity getting the better of him, he tapped into the stats.

#promkings was trending.

Neil shoved the phone back like it had electrocuted

him, cheeks heating. The waiter appeared right on cue with their salads.

Neil stabbed a piece of lettuce and muttered, "Fantastic. I'm trending on the internet and eating arugula with my amazing boyfriend at the same time. Dreams really do come true."

Cade burst out laughing, bright and unrestrained, and Neil uncomfortably smiled back.

Chapter Forty-Five.

Days later, back at Neil's house, his mom asked if they were hungry.

"Sadly, no, but thank you, Mrs. Erickson," Cade said.

"Neil, there's mail for you," she said.

Neil pulled a letter from the kitchen mail holder.

"It's from the National Aristeia Society!"

"What's that?" Cade asked.

"It's an honors society..." Neil paused as he read briefly. "Oh, my God."

Cade looked at him, waiting for more details.

"Well?" Mrs. Erickson asked.

"I got in. They accepted my essay and qualifications."

"Got what?" Cade asked.

"We wish to congratulate you on your placement into the Aristeia National Honors Program. Your benefits package is included..." He checked the second page. "There's a scholarship program!"

"Oh wow. That's great!" Cade picked him up in a tight hug.

"I still have to do a statewide debate."

"You're famous from the last one. Everyone seems to know about your success last year."

"Yeah, but Cade. That was one time, and this one is so much bigger. This will be really tough to win." Neil responded with a stressed smile.

"I'm not worried," said his mom.

"I'm not worried, either," said Cade.

"Okay," Neil responded, almost as if he were catching his breath. "I'm going to do it. You'll both be there?"

His mom and Cade happily agreed.

Neil went upstairs to his room with Cade and plugged his phone in to charge while he played music through his Bluetooth speakers.

"So that's exciting. I get to see you debate, finally," Cade said.

"Weird, right?"

"Neil?" Cade stepped toward Neil in concern. He didn't seem thrilled about something. "Is everything okay?"

Neil sat down on his bed.

Cade sat down beside him.

"I guess I'm starting to feel like I don't see my friends as much as yours, and I'm adapting to what your friends do and talk about. Real talk here: They are great, and I like hanging out with them, but I guess I'm just struggling a little with my own authenticity. Does that make any sense?"

Cade looked concerned. "Did something happen?"

Neil didn't want to make Savannah's *since dating Cade* comment an issue, so he struggled to say anything about it. After a moderate pause, "I guess I hadn't thought about you going out with someone before me. We never discussed that, unlike my breakup with Kyle. I don't want to be weird about any of that stuff. You know?"

"100%," Cade said. "It hasn't occurred to me that you would even care about who I dated before. I'm an open book, Neil. You know I'll tell you anything you want to know."

"I guess maybe that's part of it. I feel like you maybe should have brought it up already before sitting me with your ex-girlfriend in the bleachers. Right?"

"Are you talking about Ava?" Cade asked.

"OMG, Cade. How many of your friends have you dated?"

"Ugh, I kind of feel like there's not going to be a win for me in this, so I don't know what to do to make you feel better about any of it," Cade said cautiously. "You know I low-key like it when you are jealous, but this one is kind of scaring me."

Neil started to raise his voice, then realized his mother was downstairs, and his younger siblings were in earshot. "This isn't about jealousy, Cade. This is about communication, not putting me in weird situations. It's difficult enough for me to have your spotlight following me around all day; add to that the feeling of being ambushed because I don't know the backstory of anything between you and the people around you. Plus, you never want to do anything with my friends."

"No offense, but your friends are kind of sentient beige," Cade said under his breath.

"Why? Because they don't get drunk and make fun of people?"

"Things like that are going to happen, though," Cade said.

After a beat, Neil spoke softly. "Well, maybe I don't

want my friends to be a joke or find myself trapped with people who know more about you than I do."

Cade looked really hurt. It never occurred to him to have said something earlier about people who were now circling Neil that he had a romantic history with.

"Neil—"

"Plus, you have never respected my privacy. You shout to the rooftops that you're with me, but you never consider how that affects me." Neil paused. "I'm just not sure there are two people in the relationship sometimes. It seems like you get to decide things for both of us."

"Neil, please—"

"I think I just need some time to work some stuff out and maybe spend some time with my friends, for once. I have cancelled on them a lot lately."

"Okay, but Prom is coming up and—"

"Cade ...space."

"Okay," Cade reluctantly said.

Cade left the house, got into his car, and drove away, both unsure where they stood.

He made it to the end of the block before bursting into tears.

Neil felt bone dry—emotionally flatlined in a way that surprised even him. He kept waiting for panic or heartbreak or some cinematic rush of feelings... but nothing came. Just a quiet, stubborn relief under his ribs.

That bothered him most of all.

He didn't *want* to feel relieved about putting distance between himself and Cade. He didn't want any part of him to find comfort in the calm. But Neil had to be honest: his nature was a quiet one. Low-profile. Low-stress. Predictable. Contained. And since Cade Riley barreled into his life—golden, chaotic, impossible—Neil had felt like he'd been living inside a blender.

Maybe space was the only way to hear himself think.

Later that night, half out of habit and half out of dread, Neil opened Instagram.

And instantly wished he hadn't.

Cade's name flooded his feed—tagged in post after post. A bonfire. The lake. Red cups. Black hoodies. Someone blasting music loud enough to distort the audio. And surrounding Cade were those guys. The ones Neil couldn't stand. The ones who'd made fun of him for years, sometimes subtly, sometimes not. The ones who treated him like human garbage.

And Cade—*his* Cade—had chosen them to spend the night with after their disagreement.

Neil's stomach didn't drop so much as twist, slow and tight.

He'd told himself he needed space.

He hadn't expected Cade to fill it so easily.

Three days later, a text message came in from Cade.

Neil didn't answer. Neil wasn't sure he wanted to see Cade before, during, or at all, yet.

Neil's cousin, Everett, was super cool and very good-looking at 6'4" with a linebacker build, resembling Clay Matthews of the Green Bay Packers. Neil asked him to accompany Jenna, so he could walk into the prom with them.

"Yeah, of course. Do you want to make him jealous or what? " Everett asked.

"I just don't want to walk in there stag," Neil explained.

"It'll be fun, plus the girls at your school are hot."

Cade walked into the Garden Hills Coffee Shop hoping—praying—to run into Neil. Neil basically lived off this place's cold brew, and Cade had timed his arrival down to the minute. He picked a table near the pickup counter, opened *That's Debatable* by Jen Doll, and positioned it strategically for maximum Neil-comment potential.

"That looks like a fun book," an unfamiliar voice said.

Cade glanced up. A guy his age stood beside the table—dark hair pulled back, easy smile, giving the book a lingering, curious look.

"Yeah," Cade said. "Someone special to me is in a debate scholarship competition. Thought this might be a fun way to help."

"That's actually really sweet," the guy said. "Are you visiting? I haven't seen you in here before."

"I live in West Meade," Cade replied. "I don't come here that often."

They kept talking—books, art, random Nashville things—Cade politely, cluelessly unaware of the incoming doom.

Outside, Neil biked into the parking lot. He pulled off his helmet, tugged open the door—then froze.

Inside, he saw Kyle.

Kyle.

Neil's ex. The human red flag factory.

Kyle was talking to... someone sitting down facing him. Someone he couldn't quite see.

Good, Neil thought bitterly. *Maybe he's finally*

obsessed with someone else.

Then the guy stood to shake Kyle's hand.

Neil's heart stopped.

Cade.

"Cade??" Neil whispered to himself. "No... no, no. Do they know each other? Am I really this big of an idiot?"

A car pulled into the space beside him. Neil barely noticed the driver ducking down to grab something—he was too busy drowning. The passenger door swung open.

Mads hopped out.

"Neil? What's wrong?"

"I just—I can't—you'll see. Inside. I gotta go."

"Neil!"

But he was already back on his bike, speeding away, tears slipping hot down his cheeks. Mads watched him go, stomach dropping. Neil never cried. Not like that.

Inside, Kyle and Cade were still deep in conversation—books, art, sounding entirely too comfortable.

"Oh, shit no," Mads said.

Mads stormed in.

"Hey," she said sharply to Cade, making sure not to say his name. The last thing they needed was Kyle connecting dots and detonating. "Hi, Kyle."

"Mads!" Kyle lit up. "Long time."

"Yeah," she said tightly. "So—" Mads turned to Cade. "Can I talk to you outside?"

"Sure?" Cade said, confused. He grabbed his book on the way out. "Great meeting you... what was your name again?"

"Kyle," he supplied, grinning.

Mads grabbed his arm and hurried him away.

"Right. Okay. Bye."

Before Kyle could reply, the barista sarcastically called out:

"Kyle! Venti iced Americano—five shots decaf with almond milk, extra ice, eight honey, seven matcha, double blended, double cupped!"

Cade's eyes went *huge.*

Mads hissed, "Keep... walking."

Outside, Cade stopped dead on the sidewalk.

"That was Kyle?" he asked, horrified. "As in Neil's psycho ex, Kyle? I just spent ten minutes talking to *that* Kyle?"

"Oh, honey," Mads said. "It's so much worse. Neil was here. He saw you two talking."

"FUCK!" Cade scrubbed both hands through his hair. "What do I do? What do I do? I don't know what to do."

From the car beside them, someone sat up. The passenger window rolled down.

"Hi," Savannah said, sounding like this was the world's worst stage cue.

Cade paused and stared. "You've GOT to be kidding me. Did Neil see you, too?"

"I don't think so," Savannah said carefully.

"Great," Cade muttered. "Perfect. Neil already thinks I've hooked up with half of Nashville. Now he sees me talking to Kyle? **KYLE**?! I can't do this. I'm done. I'm tapping out."

"Cade." Savannah stepped out and around the car, voice firm. "We're going to fix this: Mads and I. We don't know how yet, but we will. You two belong together."

"How?" Cade demanded. "Everything I do looks so bad. I keep screwing up."

"Cade." Savannah looked him straight in the eyes. "Go home. Do nothing. Don't spiral. Don't go out. And do *not* get shit faced. Mads and I have this. No promises, but we're your best shot."

Cade exhaled shakily. "Okay. Okay... what the hell just happened? Also, Mads, thank you." He paused, looking at Savannah and Mads. "Wait. Why are **you two** together?" He paused again. "You know what? Never mind. I don't want to know."

He got into his car and drove off.

Mads crossed her arms, watching him go. "I think I

know a way to fix this," she said. "But it's going to take planning. And a lot of luck."

Savannah smirked. "I'm in, Brains. Whatever it is—I'm in."

Several days later, Jenna showed up at Neil's front door with a garment bag slung over her shoulder.

"Your tuxedo," she said gently, lifting it. "I grabbed it so you didn't have to."

Neil exhaled, not meeting her eyes. "Thanks. I just... I can't run into him right now."

"Yeah, for sure, babes." Jenna stepped inside and closed the door behind her. "You wanna talk about anything?"

Neil brushed a thumb under his eye. "Only that you were right back in France. If this doesn't work out, it's not like I'm going to see him after June anyway."

Jenna didn't comment on that—she knew Neil too well. The tightness in his voice, the way he held his shoulders like they were carrying something heavy... he was still hurting. Badly.

"So," Jenna said softly, shifting gears, "what's the plan for prom?"

Neil let out a wet, humorless laugh. "I don't know yet."

His voice cracked on the last word.

Jenna stepped forward and pulled him into a hug. "Okay," she murmured against his shoulder. "Let's map out prom first. And then after that, we'll map out everything else. One thing at a time."

She kissed his cheek. "You always do better with a plan."

Neil swallowed hard. "Thing is, Jen..." He paused, struggling to pull the words together. "I think for the first time—maybe ever—I don't think there is a plan for this."

Jenna stayed quiet, letting him finish.

"Maybe I was too hard on him," Neil went on. "But if I don't set boundaries, I'll never see any of you again. I'll just... disappear into his world because it's easier."

"Were his friends really that bad?" Jenna asked gently.

"No," Neil said immediately. "But that's not the point." He sank onto the edge of his bed. "It can't just be his friends or my friends. There has to be give and take. Otherwise, I end up losing myself—and eventually all of you."

Jenna sat next to him. "You're setting a really good foundation for all of us, honestly. When the rest of us meet our person someday, I hope we remember what you're doing now."

Neil stared at his hands for a long moment. Finally, he said, "This is going to sound weird."

"What?"

"Right now..." His voice trembled. "...I can only afford to think about me."

Jenna blinked, then sat back slightly. "Whoa. That's fresh."

Neil huffed out a laugh that was half sob. "I know."

"But? It's also healthy," Jenna said, cupping his face. "You're finally choosing yourself. And I'm proud of you for it."

Neil leaned into her touch, exhausted but steadier than before.

The night before the prom.

Cade
Hey, can I pick you up for the prom?

Neil
I have an SUV with the girls.

Chapter Forty-Six.
Prom Night

"Could I pick you up? I really don't want to show up alone at the prom," Cade asked.

"That's probably a bad idea. I'll meet you right inside, and I'll get there early. OK? You don't want to show up with anyone. Be ready to take Neil home. Now go home and get ready."

Cade knew Savannah was right. Once dressed for the prom, he played "Lost" by Blake Rose on his radio and headed toward downtown. He couldn't get Neil out of his mind. Tonight would probably be his last chance to fix things with him, and his chances felt slim.

The Bridge Building shimmered against the

Nashville skyline, glass walls glowing over the Cumberland River.

Inside, Cade spotted Savannah and AJ near the edge of the dance floor. The theme of the evening was Last Night at Versailles.

"Promise me you'll talk to him tonight," Savannah said. "Prom is the perfect setting to make your point."

The DJ slid into Fly By Midnight's *No Choice*.

"We'll see. I don't have any options but to respect his boundaries."

"You'll work it out. I know you," Savannah replied. "You're always all in or all out."

Cade stared at the door, baffled about what to do when Neil walked in, which had to be soon. It still felt wrong that he wasn't on the prom committee, wasn't here early, wasn't in control of any of this. He knew it was because he was spending all his time with him and had abandoned many of the responsibilities he would normally be in charge of.

From the valet line, Neil could feel it—the low thrumming bass rolling out of the ballroom, the pop-electronic pulse of Pale's *Not In Love* echoed down the street. Cars lined up, headlights cutting through the mist as students in sharp tuxes and pastel dresses stepped out, their laughter rising over the beat.

Neil climbed from the black SUV with Jenna, Everett, Mads, Kip, and Sophie. Jenna adjusted her silver heels; Mads checked her lip gloss in the reflection of the glass; Sophie twirled her mom's bangle like a nervous tic.

"Okay," Jenna said, linking her arm through Neil's. "We are entering with confidence. No weirdness. No crying. And if you see Cade, you are *not* allowed to run into the river."

"Noted," Neil muttered, his stomach already falling. "I'm sorry Wyatt couldn't be here tonight for you."

"Meh. College boys. It worked out. You were available. Sort of." Jenna looked at Everett.

"Hold my arm," Everett said. "I'll look like a bisexual stud walking in with you two on each arm."

"Hottest throuple, ever," Neil said. "Even if it's with your cousin."

"Challenge accepted," Mads said, walking past the valet.

"Wait. What? Is she competing for hottest throuple?" Jenna asked.

"None of us has any idea, I fear," Neil said. "Hold on, Everett. 'You have to go cold into a battle that needs warmth, out into the muddle that you have made yourself,'"[1] Neil said under his breath.

"Correct," Jenna responded, to Neil's surprise. "Neil is quoting his favorite book again."

"Well, it sounds like fun," Everett exclaimed.

Inside, the ballroom was alive—walls washed in violet light, an LED-backed DJ booth flickering, and the crowd jumping to a Drake/Billie Eilish remix. The floor seemed to breathe.

Neil had barely taken ten steps before he saw him.

Cade Riley.

Across the room.

Charcoal tux, no tie. One hand in his pocket, the other holding a Sprite that somehow looked like champagne. Savannah laughed beside him at something that sounded fake.

Cade noticed Neil almost at the same time—on Everett's arm, jacket shimmering navy under the lights, bow tie perfectly tied. For half a heartbeat, the room dissolved into neon and river shimmer between them.

The music distorted, then Cade looked away, honoring the boundary Neil had set a week ago after the argument. *"I just need space,"* Neil had said, and Cade had listened.

Then Neil looked away.

[1] *A Room with a View*; E.M. Forster Pt2, Ch19 (Mr. Emerson)

The air between them crackled. Everyone else felt it too—heads tilting back and forth like a well-dressed tennis match. Whispers slipped through the crowd. They'd all heard the rumors, and the fact that Cade and Neil arrived separately only confirmed the speculation.

Mads leaned in, eyes wide. "So are we pretending there isn't any tension? Because it's screaming. Cade genuinely seemed clueless at the coffee shop."

"Please don't," Neil said quickly, his voice thinner than he wanted. "We're just... fine."

"Sure," Jenna said. "Don't get it twisted, though—you both look like Spotify breakup playlists incarnate, and nobody wants to hit play."

Neil let out one small laugh and tried not to look again.

He looked again.

Near the main entry of the event space, Neil and Mads discussed the situation:

"I shouldn't have come," Neil said.

"Okay, Mopey. Let's dance this shit out," Mads said.

Meanwhile, to the front left, Cade and Savannah were having a similar conversation.

"I shouldn't be here tonight," said Cade to Savannah.

"Let's dance. Work it out through something

physical," Savannah said.

Cade wasn't laughing anymore. *Who was this guy Neil was with?* He'd moved toward the dance floor with his group, body loose but eyes too focused. Neil joined his own friends instead, letting Mads drag him into a chaotic circle of prom poses and TikTok choreography. Two circles. Two people pretending not to orbit each other. Almost everyone else was dancing while straining their necks, waiting for someone to serve the ball.

Every time the lights flared, Neil caught flashes of Cade—the tilt of his head, the gleam of his grin, and the small muscle that jumped in his jaw when Neil spun too close.

When the tempo slowed to a mash-up of various songs, the crowd thinned, and Neil felt the shift. The songs softened; the air seemed to wait.

Across the floor, Cade looked up.

For a second, neither moved.

The bridge lights glittered beyond the glass, casting ripples over the dance floor. In the blur of color and sound, Neil realized the space between them wasn't distance anymore—it was gravity, until it wasn't.

Neither of them crossed the dance floor. After a pause, Neil walked away first, leaving Cade visibly disappointed. He had hoped that would be their moment.

For the rest of the night, it was like some invisible force kept them apart—Cade on one side with Savannah and the soccer crowd, and Neil on the other with Jenna, Everett, Mads, Kip, and Sophie. Between them, lights spun like starlight, and bass rolled through the floor like distant thunder.

They didn't speak. They didn't wave, but they noticed everything.

Cade noticed the way Neil's jacket shimmered under the LEDs and that tiny twitch of nervous laughter when Everett cracked a joke. Neil laughed for him like that, not this guy.

Neil noticed the way Cade's shoulders relaxed when he smiled—just enough to make it hurt.

Every few songs, their eyes met.

A flicker. A catch. A look that said everything they'd spent a week not saying.

Then one of them would look away, pretending it hadn't happened.

Around them, the night unfolded—flashes of phones, glitter on the floor, and bursts of laughter. But for Neil, it was all background noise to the intensity of Cade's presence.

"Are you okay?" Mads asked softly during a slow

song.

Neil nodded too quickly. "Yeah. I'm fine. Thanks." He forced a polite smile.

She gave him that look—the kind that saw through every layer. "You don't have to be."

He smiled anyway. "I know."

"Okay, if you're fine, I caught a dub with a cute boy, so... yeah," Mads said.

"I'm fine. Seriously, go get it," Neil smiled, happy for her. Neil was now alone in his thoughts, with blaring music in every direction.

Across the room, Cade was grinning at something Savannah said, his hand jammed in his pocket, his grandfather's ring catching the light.

The song changed again, louder now—something trending on TikTok—a remix of Halsey's *Graveyard*, a lot of bass and flash. People shouted the lyrics like an anthem, lights bouncing off the river outside the windows.

Neil joined in, laughing, losing himself for a minute in the noise. When he finally turned back toward Cade's side of the room, the spot was empty.

His chest tightened before he realized—Cade hadn't left. He was standing near the balcony doors now, eyes on the Cumberland River, back to the crowd.

For a moment, Neil thought about going.

Just walking across the floor, saying something—anything.

But he didn't. AJ beat him to it.

So Neil stayed with his friends. Cade stayed by the river with AJ.

Under the glow of the bridge, in the soft pulse of Nashville's skyline, they let the night hold what they couldn't say.

The music cut out mid-beat, replaced by the principal's voice echoing through the mic: **"Alright, everyone, it's time for what you've been waiting for—your Prom King and Queen!"**

A drumroll from the band. Whistles. Someone in the back shouted, "About time!"

Cade met with some of his soccer teammates on the balcony.

"And your prom king is..." the announcer drew it out, "...Neil Erickson!"

The gym exploded in cheers. Neil froze for half a second, then Jenna gave him a gentle nudge toward the stage. Neil went red to his ears but smiled as the crown was placed on his head. He scanned the crowd, dazed, then found Cade's eyes—Cade clapped the loudest of anyone. This moment would have been better with him.

He didn't want this attention without Cade. None of it meant anything to him without Cade.

"And your prom queen is..." Another pause, "...Savannah Holt!"

Applause, though less explosive than before. The students appeared to hold Savannah at fault for the tension between Cade and Neil.

Neil wasn't surprised it was Savannah. He had expected it to be her and Cade.

Savannah, tall in her glittering gown, didn't head straight for the stage. Instead, she went to the table for the panel responsible for the election. Mads, as committee chair, met her there and handed her the tiara. That's when a ripple moved through the crowd. Students started chanting, first a handful, then dozens: "Prom Kings! Prom Kings! Prom Kings!"

Neil stood there on stage, confused, freaked out, wearing a crown, in the spotlight that he never wanted. *What is happening? What are they talking about? What is there to discuss?*

The Bridge Building sparkled—lights, velvet ropes, glossy photo backdrops, the works. But at the edge of the ballroom, Mads stood squared off with two members of the faculty prom committee, hands on her hips, curls vibrating with the righteous fury of Medusa.

"So let me get this straight," Mads said, voice sharp enough to slice the centerpiece hydrangeas. "You're refusing to announce two prom kings because... why exactly?"

Mr. Landers cleared his throat. "Tradition dictates—"

"Nope. Try again," Mads snapped. "Because 'tradition' isn't a policy. It's a dusty excuse people use when they don't want to update their thinking."

Mrs. Kirkpatrick folded her arms. "We have never had two boys win before."

"And whose fault is that?" Mads shot back. "The student body voted. Overwhelmingly. So, unless you want to go out there and tell a hundred teenagers you're overturning a democratic vote, you're going to announce both kings."

Savannah, standing a few feet away, tried—and failed—not to grin. She whispered, "Oh my God," delighted, under her breath.

Mr. Landers bristled. "Madison, this isn't your decision."

Mads stepped closer. "You're right. It's not. It's the students', and they elected me to certify this vote. If the school denies them a legit outcome because of one faculty member being scared of optics, imagine the optics when this gets out." She raised her brows meaningfully. "Because it will get out. You'll violate the bylaws and charter, become the new face of our school's reputation for promoting autocracy, and that is leaving out denying Caden Walker Riley, the son of the school's biggest donor, the spotlight and crown."

Mad's eyes appeared to go black.

Mrs. Kirkpatrick's face paled.

Savannah leaned into the conversation, voice low and deceptively sweet. "She's right. Would be… incredibly embarrassing, wouldn't it? You installed me as prom queen for whose benefit? How about the headline: 'Let Them Eat Cake?'"

Mr. Landers looked between the two girls—Mads the firestorm, Savannah the calm confirmation—and realized he was outmatched.

He sighed. "Fine. Two prom kings."

"Excellent choice," Mads said, brushing invisible dust off her dress like a queen adjusting her cape. "I'll go let the photographers know."

As the faculty retreated to lick their wounds, Savannah stepped up beside her, grabbed a microphone, eyes bright, each of them on their way to announce the verdict.

"Mads," she murmured, "that was iconic."

Mads shrugged, smirking. "Someone had to say it." She headed to the photographers.

"Yeah," Savannah said softly, admiringly. "But only you could say it like that."

Savannah smiled—then strode over to Cade. After a quick nod, she turned to Cade with a microphone and a grin.

"We have the first-ever co-kings! " she announced, taking his hand. "You both deserve this."

Neil's eyes started to water. He wasn't sure how to manage this moment. It felt like a lifetime under the spotlight of something trying to make the point that Cade was his one and only. He felt similar to back in Italy when Cade kissed him in the rain.

The room erupted. Laughter, whistles, stomping. Cade ducked his head, laughing, as Savannah gently set the smaller tiara on his head. He kissed her on the cheek, with a sincere "thank you," before making his way across the stage to stand beside Neil. "This is your moment. Go get your king," Savannah said sweetly to Cade.

The DJ, quick on the cue, spun a sweet song for the couple: *Die With A Smile*, by Bruno Mars and Lady Gaga.

Cade looked in Neil's direction, and for a moment, he saw him at a church altar. He began to walk in his direction to the stage in that southern swagger Cade was known for.

Neil's heart hammered. The sight of Cade—broad-shouldered soccer star, tiara slightly crooked, hand reaching for his. It was almost too much to process.

Cade pulled Neil into the center of the dance floor, tiara glinting under the sparkling lights. He thought of that manifestation from the Royal Mile close and said with his own unique mix of humility and confidence, "Do you trust me? "

Neil smiled, his heart felt warm in the best way, and slipped his arms around Cade.

Cade was visibly relieved that the tension between them was breaking.

The crowd clapped and swayed around them, some still chanting, "Prom Kings! " as they danced slowly, wearing their crowns. For once, Neil didn't feel like he was borrowing someone else's spotlight. He was exactly where he was supposed to be—right beside Cade, chosen by his classmates.

The crowd parted for them, applause still echoing as the last verse poured through the speakers. Cade tugged Neil close, their hands sliding into place like they'd been practicing all their lives.

Neil swallowed, looking up at him. "So, Prom Queen, huh? " His grin tugged sideways, teasing.

Cade smirked, adjusting the tiara like it was the most natural thing in the world. "Hey, I wear it well. Don't pretend you're not into it."

Neil snorted, nearly tripping over Cade's foot. "I won't deny it, but that's a me problem."

They both laughed softly, but their laughter was lost in the swell of music. Around them, classmates swayed and whispered, some with phones still recording, but Cade's attention stayed fixed on Neil.

"You realize," Neil whispered, "the entire school is watching us right now..."

Cade leaned down, his breath warm against Neil's ear. "Good. Then they know who I belong to, and they chose you, just like I did."

Cade flinched to secure his tiara from falling.

Neil's grip tightened on Cade's shoulder. "You can't just say things like that in front of a thousand people," he muttered, voice shaky.

"Why not? " Cade smiled, eyes searching his. "It's true. Besides..." He gave a smooth, tiny spin that pulled Neil flush against him again. "...maybe I like saying things you'll remember." Cade paused, looking deeply into Neil's eyes. "Please tell me I didn't mess this up."

"We're going to be fine. We just need to communicate better."

"I'll do anything you say, boss. I never want to lose you, especially to that guy."

"Everett? He's just my cousin, trying to get me through a rough evening," Neil said.

"So not someone I have to fight, then?"

"No," Neil laughed, almost through a tear.

"It's Tennessee. I mean, there could still be something there. I'd still fight for you."

Neil shook his head, though his lips curved despite himself. "You're the best."

"And you're perfect," Cade said it casually, but it landed like a weight and a promise all at once.

Neil buried his face in Cade's shoulder for a second, overwhelmed. The music soared. His crown tilted dangerously, Cade's tiara glittered crookedly, and still— they moved as one.

The music changed to Zee Machine *Everybody Wants It.*

Neil leaned back just enough to look at him. "Did you ever think this would be how you spend prom?"

Cade's smile softened, almost reverent. "Nope, especially the last few days."

The lyrics wrapped around them, and for that moment, the venue, the school, and the whole world faded. Just two boys, dancing close, holding tight, not caring who saw.

Neil whispered, almost like a secret, "Okay. Then I guess I don't mind all the talk anymore. I admit it, we're better together."

Cade kissed his temple lightly, right beneath the edge of his crown. "I suppose we shall have to live now."

Neil looked at him puzzled, recognizing the quote from E.M. Forster's *A Room with a View*.

The crowd roared again as if they somehow knew this was the exact moment that sealed their devotion. This was a couple that the whole school wanted to support.

The applause didn't stop—it shifted and multiplied as classmates began flooding the dance floor. Couples, groups of friends, and even the prom committee, with their electronic tablets set aside. Within seconds, Neil and Cade were surrounded.

But even as the crowd closed in, they didn't break. They stayed chest to chest, swaying slowly while the beat kicked up, lights pulsing in rhythm. Everyone else was bouncing, laughing, and spinning in twos and threes, but Neil and Cade kept their orbit steady, like nothing could push or pull them apart.

It was ridiculous, slow dancing in the middle of a pop track. Somehow, that made it even better. Their own secret tempo. Their own rules.

AJ approached Sophie near the edge of the dance floor, straightening his tie like he needed the confidence boost.

"Hi," he said softly. "You look amazing."

Sophie flushed. "Thanks. You, too."

He held out a hand. "Dance with me?"

She nodded—nervous, excited, and unsure all at once. "You're not dancing with Savannah?"

"You *noticed*," AJ said, with a little glee.

"I did."

"She and I aren't... like that," he explained. "She just likes the appearance of a boyfriend sometimes. Makes guys back off. She's dealing with some heavy stuff, but it's not really my story to tell."

"Oh," Sophie said, absorbing that. "Okay. I can respect that."

"Sophie..." AJ started, then paused to swallow his nerves.

"Yeah?" She waited, gentle as ever.

"Would you maybe want to go out sometime?" He winced. "With me? I mean... just us."

Sophie's face flickered—joy mixed with sudden dread. She felt her heart leap and sink at the same time. She liked him. But she also knew she had to tell him about herself before any of this went further.

AJ, misreading her expression, rushed on. "I know I'm not the smartest guy you've ever met, but I just thought... maybe... you know?"

Sophie shook her head, touched. "Please don't put yourself down."

He stepped closer, voice softer. "You're so beautiful and smart."

Sophie paused before she spoke, steadying herself. "I'd love to. Really. But... we should talk first."

AJ nodded quickly—eager, nervous, and hopeful. "Okay. Yeah. Whatever you need."

The music swelled, and he took her hand, waiting for her to lead the next moment—however it needed to go.

"Isn't AJ going out with Savannah?" Kip asked Jenna, sounding puzzled.

"I thought so, yeah," Jenna answered.

Mads swooped in from nowhere.

"They aren't together. It was a ruse." Mads said with authority. "Please don't ask how I know this, but I definitely *have not* been making out with Savannah."

Jenna and Kip looked at her, even more puzzled, but Mads wouldn't look them in the eye.

"Whoo! Is it hot in here?" Mads said, fanning herself.

"You are Savannah's side piece?" Kip asked.

"Bish, if anything, Savannah's *my* sidepiece," she said with mock superiority. "As if."

Back on the dance floor, Neil tipped his head up, his crown glinting under the strobes. "I have something to tell you later," he said quietly, almost lost in the thrum of the bass.

Cade's lips curved, one eye watered, and the tiara tilted mischievously as he leaned close enough for only Neil to hear. "Good. I instinctively feel like my response will be 'me too'."

Neil's breath caught, his smile breaking wide despite himself. They held tighter, spun once—awkward in a circle of cheering classmates—but never let go.

For all the noise and all the flashing lights, it felt like the room had shrunk to just the two of them again. Neil was thinking deeply about what he felt for Cade.

Neil's throat was tight, but the words pressed out anyway, too heavy to keep. "Well, in that case..." He swallowed, eyes locking with Cade's. "I love you, Cade. I can't imagine loving you more than I do right this minute, but I know in my heart that it's growing."

Cade's breath hitched like he hadn't expected to hear it here, of all places—crowded dance floor, music surging, classmates cheering. But then his face broke open in the kind of smile Neil had only dreamed of. He took the loose tiara off and held it to his side.

Cade pulled Neil in tightly, full of emotion, and then, after regaining his composure, he released him so that he could see Neil's face again.

"Me too. I mean, I love you, too." His voice cracked a little on the "too," like the truth of it punched him, and before Neil could say anything more, Cade pulled him closer and kissed him. He said, "My Italian boyfriend with a British name." Cade picked up Neil in a hug.

The room around them roared—not for them, but it may as well have been their applause, laughter, and a few playful shouts—but all Neil felt was Cade, steady and sure, grounding him in the middle of the chaos.

"Well," Neil said, "actually, half Italian. It's my mother's family—"

Cade leaned in, voice low and warm against Neil's cheek, and interrupted him.

"Hey," he murmured. "You want to get out of here, Your Majesty?"

Neil laughed, breathless, and nodded. "Yeah. I would like that a lot."

Jenna and Kip watched from across the room and squealed a little together. Mads looked up from her snog with Everett in the corner, smiled, gave Savannah a thumbs up from across the room, and went back to her snog.

The valet brought the car around, and it looked like it was on its toes; the car's body was at the top of all the tires. The valet driver got out and hopped down from the vehicle, an unusual height. Neil just laughed like it was a joke.

"I'm not sure what I did wrong, but it just rose when I took the handbrake off," he said, looking embarrassed.

"It's not a handbrake; it's a riser," Cade explained as he put the floor lever back down to the proper height, and the car lowered like a camel. "Happens all the time."

"Cool car."

"Thanks. It's French. Have a good night."

Cade drove while playing with Neil's hair with his right hand, his arm resting on the top of the seat between the headrests. They planned to spend the rest of the evening into the early morning at Cade's house, a place he hadn't taken Neil to yet.

"So, I finally get to see my queen's castle."

"Yup. Great night for it. No one is home."

"Oh no... that's just terrible," Neil cried sarcastically, and smiled.

Outside, Sophie and AJ sat on a bench by the main entrance near the valet.

AJ held Sophie's hand.

Sophie was silent for a moment, removed her hand from his, and then said,

"Before we can go out, there's something about me that you need to know," she said.

"I can handle it. I promise."

She looked at him as if assessing his comfort level.

"I'm trans, AJ. Is that something you can deal with?"

AJ took a moment, looking like he was processing the information. Then he took her hand again, and tenderly said, "Sophie, ..."

"Yeah?"

"You're going to be the prettiest man I have ever seen," he said earnestly.

Sophie laughed loudly with a short burst.

"I'm a trans *girl*, AJ. I'm not going back," she said through laughter. "Your heart is in the right place, though."

"Oh! Well, in that case—" AJ very politely leaned in to Sophie, she met him for her first kiss.

Jenna opened the SUV door just as Sophie walked up for the ride home. She could hear someone inside. She looked at Sophie and opened the door to find Mads, Everett, and Savannah. Everett and Savannah were going at it making out. Mads was watching and looked at the door when Jenna opened it with Sophie over her shoulder, both with gaping mouths.

"We are going to... we will take a ride share home," Jenna said as she slowly closed the door, going back for one last peek like she didn't believe what she was seeing.

Sophie tapped the SUV, giving the all clear.

"I know who can take us home," Sophie said with a smirk.

"Who?" asked Jenna, with a puzzled look.

Sophie grabbed her phone.

Sophie
Our SUV was commandeered by a bunch
of love-sick hippies. Any chance you
might drive me and Jenna home?

AJ
BIG yes! Meet you at the valet.

"What??" Jenna said to Sophie. "What the fuck happened tonight?" Jenna laughed. "Either I've missed a lot tonight, or we have quantum jumped."

Chapter Forty-Seven.

Cade's Citroën rolled up the long, winding drive and stopped in front of a mansion so sprawling Neil had to blink twice to be sure it was real. White columns rose like they'd been stolen from some antebellum fever dream, and endless windows glowed with the soft light of spotlights set to pretend somebody was home.

Neil stepped out of the car, and his mouth immediately gaped.

"You live *here*?" he asked, his voice cracking halfway through.

Cade rubbed the back of his neck, suddenly looking way less confident than usual. "Yeah."

Neil let out a stunned laugh, eyes sweeping the façade. "This isn't a house. This is a museum. If I drop my backpack, the floor's gonna call its lawyer."

Cade snorted. "You're not wrong. I can barely find the kitchen, and when I do, I'm not allowed to touch anything."

"I bet the girls you brought home totally lost their minds."

"Well... plot twist. I've never brought anyone here." Cade shrugged. "Not like this."

"Wait. Ever?"

"Neil—" Cade's smile softened. "I've been on dates. I've kissed girls... and guys. But I've never brought someone *home*."

Neil blinked, his heart doing a weird somersault. "Why not?"

"Because I've never been in love before." Cade's voice was steady now. "Until you."

"Can I kiss you again?" Cade asked.

Cade's expression had changed. He looked like someone who'd just figured out the meaning of life and wasn't sure what to do with it. He straightened up, wiping a tear from his face, and kissed Neil sweetly.

"Okay," Cade said, voice shaking just enough for Neil to hear it. "You asked for full transparency, so... I'm going to lay it all out."

He took a breath, steadying himself.

"I've loved you since the first day you walked into Penderton in the eighth grade." Cade's eyes flicked away, then back. "It was a thirteen-year-old's crush, sure, but it was real. You were real, and I was instantly a goner."

Neil stared at him, heart pounding.

Holy crap. He's perfect.

Cade kept going, words tumbling out like he'd been holding them back for years.

"I didn't understand it at the time—not fully—but by the end of tenth grade, right after you came out, it finally clicked. And then you started dating Josh, and I was just..." Cade huffed out a breath, frustrated at his own past self. "A mess trying to figure myself out. Trying to figure out how to even talk to you."

He scrubbed a hand over his face, then continued.

"By the time I grew a pair and was actually ready to say something, you were locked in with Kyle." Cade let out a humorless laugh. "For the record, I didn't even recognize him in that coffee shop until they called out his complicated order. I remembered it from when you found his Instagram on the train. Mads saved me from the world's most awkward situation. I deadass thought I'd fumbled the ball completely."

Neil reached out and placed a hand on Cade's waist. A small gesture—but grounding, anchoring, a message of *I'm here* pressed into skin.

Cade's shoulders dropped in relief, but he wasn't done.

"I know now that I spoke for both of us too many times. Even back in Italy." He shook his head, eyes soft. "I was, and am, so proud to be your boyfriend, Neil. Proud of you. Proud of us. I thought showing that pride was the right thing, but... I didn't consider what you wanted. Even worse, what you needed, and I'm really sorry. Also, I don't know why I called your friends 'sentient beige.' I don't feel like that at all."

This is what he wanted from Cade for so long: emotional availability, openness, and to understand him better.

Cade swallowed, stepping a little closer.

"So standing here tonight, with you, after prom, in front of my... ridiculous house..." He let out a disbelieving laugh, brushing a tear from the corner of his eye. "Neil, we are literally the first ever Penderton prom kings." Cade shook his head, smiling through the emotion cracking his voice. "I'm so deep in my feels right now, it's actually really embarrassing."

Neil laughed—partly because Cade really did look

like a golden retriever trying not to cry in a tux, and partly because he had never felt so lucky in his entire life.

Cade wasn't the obnoxious jock in Scotland anymore. He had grown into someone real, tender, and self-aware. Neil loved watching that transformation as it unfolded in front of him.

Neil loved *him*.

"Arghhh! Cade, you drive me crazy, but, as you say, 'and yet, here I am.'" Neil paused. "I guess it's my turn to be honest. I saw the photo you took of me. When I uploaded the coffee photo, I saw it next to it in your Photos app."

Cade blinked. "Oh. Yeah, I figured you might. No secret revealed there. I kind of wanted you to find it. Also, it was espresso." He laughed. "That's why I asked you to AirDrop me that pic. My lazy way of sending the world's most subtle message—like, *'Hey, I've been looking at you.'*"

Neil smiled. "Espresso, right."

Cade laughed. "Right. That's literally what I said."

Neil rolled his eyes, but he was grinning now.

"You were just... so cute, looking out that window," Cade said, softer this time. "I had to take the shot. Total creeper move, but I couldn't let that pass."

"I love that photo, though," Neil admitted. "It's my favorite one of me. That sounds so narcissistic."

Cade's smile turned shy again. "Yeah. Mine too."

"The doctor told me that losing your vision could cause delusions. I think I wrote off your first few flirts as that. I think I made you work harder than you needed to to convince me this was real," Neil confessed.

"Well, I *tried* to talk to you in Edinburgh. Twice. I blew it both times."

"In Edinburgh? When?" Neil asked.

"It was so dumb," Cade groaned. "I did that stupid formal bow thing on the Royal Mile, and my friends started laughing, so it looked like I was making fun of you—total fail. I made so much noise, thinking for a while that it would get your attention. Then I was in that little pass-through thing, and you walked by with Jenna, and I fumbled again."

"You mean when you were standing in the close? The alley?"

"Yeah."

"That was about *me*? Cade, I almost turned around to check on you because I saw you kick a step."

Cade winced. "Yeah... that was me beating myself up. I'd just reorganized my entire speech in my head, and then boom—game gone. But then I got another chance."

"Well, you got hurt."

"Worth it. After waiting so long to tell you how I felt,

maybe getting hit in the head was what I needed to finally shoot my shot. Or," Cade paused to think, "...maybe it was Mads who woke me up because after I kicked that step, she passed by and handed me a tissue. It's actually kind of funny now."

"I sometimes feel like Mads always knew."

"I don't think she liked me back then, but she definitely knew I wanted you," Cade said.

"Mads is incredibly observant."

"You seemed so relaxed since got back to Nashville."

"That's all you. I guess it felt good to let someone take the reins instead of always being responsible for everything. You let me be a goofy kid sometimes, and that feels really good," Neil explained.

Cade grinned and wiped at his eyes. "Let's go inside." He put his arm around Neil's neck.

Neil was now wearing sneakers with his tuxedo, which echoed against the high ceilings when they squeaked on the marble floor. Every room they passed looked like it had been staged for a magazine photo shoot—gleaming surfaces, carefully placed art, and not a single sign of actual life.

"See what I mean?" Cade said softly, watching Neil's expression. "It's big. Impressive. But cozy? Warm?... It's not."

Neil's eyes flicked to him, and Cade's voice grew gentle. "That's why I like your house better."

Neil blinked, caught off guard. "My house? Cade, it's—"

"Home," Cade interrupted, with a little shrug. "Yours feels like home. This? This feels like a museum, like you said."

Neil suddenly realized how much Cade wanted to belong somewhere with warmth—and how much he wanted to offer him that.

"I know you said you wanted to be alone with me tonight," Neil said as his sneakers squeaked again in the grand foyer on the pristine marble floor, "but I think I may have a better idea."

Cade tilted his head, curious. "What's that?"

"You'll see."

They returned to Cade's Citroën, and the car rushed down the drive to the entry gate.

Tilda caught them driving away through an upstairs window facing the gate drive, and she was happy for Cade because she knew he was safe with Neil, and Neil made him feel like he was always home.

The Strike's *Miles Ahead* played on the car radio.

Neil texted his mom quickly on the way:

Which was code for *engage super-parents mode.*

By the time they pulled into the driveway, the porch light was already on. Neil's parents opened the door before they could even knock.

"Cade!" Neil's mom said, sweeping him into the kind of hug that left no room for escape. "Look at you, still handsome even after a full night of dancing."

Mr. Erickson clapped him on the back. "Prom kings! And you didn't even break a sweat. Come inside; the food's still warm. Did you work up an appetite?"

Cade laughed, almost bashful, as if he hadn't been raised on marble floors and dinner parties. He followed them into the kitchen, where the table was already casually set again, with *pastina* reheated on the stove and lasagna slid out of the oven, as if it had been waiting just for him and Neil, but primarily for him.

Neil slid into his chair, watching Cade settle in as if he'd done it a hundred times. His mother kept piling food onto Cade's plate, beaming when he ate, as if it were the best thing in the world. His dad teased him about looking sharp in his tux, while Neil's little brother popped in just to gawk at "the actual prom kings."

And Cade—this boy who came from a house too big to echo with love—looked more at home here than Neil had ever seen him anywhere else.

Neil couldn't stop studying him. Not the unbuttoned tux. Not the smile. But the way he softened under the weight of ordinary familial affection. Ordinary, maybe, to Neil, but to Cade, it was extraordinary.

Love was in the lasagna. Love was in the way Cade's laugh blended with Neil's dad's. Love was in Neil's mom, nudging a second helping onto Cade's plate no matter what he said.

This—this was the gift Neil could give him. Not a classic car or mansion. A family who adored him without question, the way he adored Neil.

Cade grabbed Neil's hand, kissed it, and pulled him into the room with the baby grand piano. He sat Neil next to him on the bench and played a little warm-up and then softly, almost quietly, played a very soft version of *In Case You Didn't Know* based on Brett Young's version. He played and sang softly, mostly for Neil to feel it personally, but also for Neil's family.

His voice was so strong for the softness of the words. He had difficulty calibrating the obnoxious, loud guy; Cade was back in Edinburgh with the caring, sweet man, singing to him now.

Don and Gianna, in the adjacent room, reached for each other.

"I think someone loves him," Gianna said softly to Don.

"But that family, G," Don said.

"Remember what my dad said when he found out we were going out?" Gianna burrowed into Don's chest. "I don't want to be like that for our kids. I definitely don't want Neil to have to make his case the way we did. I don't want to make being in love harder."

Back at the piano, Cade finished the song and put his arms around Neil, sitting next to him still, and then rested his head on Neil's shoulder.

Isabella fell asleep to the song upstairs in her room, the glow of her Nintendo Switch illuminating her face. Maxx was still on the sofa, snoring adorably.

"I guess I just feel like being sentimental tonight," Cade said.

"I love it when you're sentimental," Neil replied. "And it's a perfect night for it."

Cade's smile softened. "Good." He paused. "I picked up something for you."

He reached into his bag and pulled out a small parcel wrapped in navy paper, tied with a cream ribbon. A pink wax seal stamped with the Penderton crest.

Neil turned it over in his hands, studying it like it might be fragile—or dangerous.

"What is it?" he asked.

Cade lifted one shoulder. "Open it."

Neil slipped the ribbon loose, peeled back the paper, and froze.

"*A Room with a View*," he breathed, staring at the cover like it had just materialized.

Cade nodded, almost proud of himself. "First edition. I still can't believe I found it."

Neil looked up, eyes bright. "What made you think of this?"

Cade's voice went quieter. "Because it's your favorite book. You told me on the train in Europe... when I was bandaged up and half useless."

Neil smiled, then found the cardstock inside, handwritten in blue ink, "*You once told me that this is your favorite book. Now I understand why. -C.*"

Cade added, "I read it while we were apart last week." He hesitated, then admitted, "I get it now. I think I understand you better after reading it."

Neil's mouth quirked. "I'm Lucy, aren't I?"

Cade laughed softly. "Yeah. You kind of are."

"And you're George."

"I think there are similarities," Cade said.

Neil pulled him into a tight hug, pressing his face against Cade's shoulder like he didn't want to let him back out into the world.

"Thank you," Neil whispered.

"For?" Cade asked.

Then, still holding him, he murmured against Cade's ear, "For loving me. Much like George Emerson,[1] you are simply unavoidable."

Cade's grin widened, warm and triumphant.

"Good," he said. "That was the plan all along."

Cade went out the back door for some fresh air.

"Mom, Dad? Neil asked"

"Yeah?"

"Can Cade maybe sleep over?"

Don and Gianna looked at each other. They knew what was up.

"You would rather stay here than the Riley mansion in West Meade?" his father asked.

"I'd rather him wake up to family that he doesn't have at his house, if that's okay with you both."

Gianna kissed her son on the cheek. "Don't forget to lock your door. You have two young siblings in the

[1] *A Room with a View*, E.M. Forster

house."

Don winked at him and squeezed his shoulder.

"Thank you. I love you both!" Neil said as they walked upstairs, waking Maxx on the way.

Neil met Cade outside, the night air was cool, carrying the faint smell of basil and rosemary from his mom's little garden. Fireflies blinked lazily across the yard. Neil sat on the steps, tugging at his tie, and Cade eased down beside him, still quiet from dinner.

For a long moment, Cade just stared out into the yard. He looked softer now, stripped down from the spotlight of prom, almost vulnerable.

"This was..." Cade's voice caught, and he rubbed Neil's shoulder. "God, Neil. This was the best night of my life, and I'm not even talking about just the prom anymore."

Neil tilted his head. "The lasagna beat prom? Honestly, that's not a tough competition."

"I'm serious," Cade said, turning toward him. His voice was low, almost unsteady. "The way your parents hugged me like I've been here all along. The way your mom kept trying to feed me was like it was her job. The way your dad actually wanted to know about me, or your little brother..." He swallowed, eyes bright in the porch light. "That doesn't happen at my house, Neil. It never has. It never will."

Neil's throat lumped because he knew Cade wasn't exaggerating. "Then come here whenever you need it," he said softly. "Because they love you already. And me? I—" His throat tightened. "I love watching you happy like that. Plus, you already know that I love you."

"Say it in Italian," Cade prompted.

"*Ti amo*," Neil looked at him with glassy eyes. He rested his hand on Cade's and whispered, "*Nel caso non lo sapessi*"[2] just before laying his head on Cade's shoulder. "In case you didn't know."

Cade reached for his hand, threading their fingers together as if it were second nature now. "It felt like... like family," he admitted. "Like what it's supposed to be. I didn't even know how much I needed that until tonight... and I love you too."

Neil squeezed back, steady. "Then you have it. You have us. Your last name might be Riley, but you're an honorary Erickson now."

For a long moment, they sat in silence, the night wrapping around them. Fireflies flickered, cicadas sang, and Neil's heart beat steadily against Cade's shoulder.

Finally, Cade let out a quiet laugh.

[2] *Nel caso non lo sapessi*: In case you didn't know.

They leaned into each other, the porch light glowing softly above them, the night stretching easily and endlessly.

Neil shook his head, still laughing, and leaned into Cade's shoulder again. Cade didn't move; he just let him rest there like it was precisely where Neil belonged. The quiet wrapped around them again, not heavy, but warm—like the whole night had been leading to this.

Cade turned slightly, brushing his thumb over Neil's hand where it rested between them. "You know what else I realized tonight?"

Neil tilted his face up. "What's that?"

"That I'm not scared anymore." Cade's voice was quiet but sure.

"Since when have you ever been scared?"

"Not about us. I've never cared about people knowing about you and me. I'm just not scared of telling my parents anymore. When I was sitting at your dinner table, watching your family love you the way they do... I thought, 'Yeah.' This is worth it. You're worth it. We are worth it, Neil. Bringing me here tonight when most people our age would have chosen the privacy of my house." Cade paused, nearly choked up. "You're just so fucking smart."

Neil felt the words settle deep, all the way down to

his bones. His chest ached with it—in the good way. He shifted, lifting his hand to Cade's jaw, fingers tracing the line of his cheek like he still couldn't believe this was real.

They kissed. Soft and steady, not a fireworks-and-cheering kind of kiss like at prom, but the quiet, certain kind. The type that promised more tomorrows.

Cade leaned in fully, cupping Neil's face in both hands, deepening it just a little before pulling back with his forehead resting against Neil's. His breath was warm, his smile impossibly close.

"Best night ever," Cade murmured.

"Yeah," Neil agreed, his grin matching his own. "So far."

Meanwhile, a conversation was happening behind the scenes.

"Well played tonight," said Mads.

"Only because you were on prom committee. Total luck on my part," Savannah answered.

"And Neil winning on his own? Chef's kiss."

"Do we know where they disappeared to after prom?"

"Cade's house," Mads said.

"Stop. He NEVER takes people there."

"Really? Well, that's wild. Sooo... what do you think they're doing all night?" Mads asked with a smirk.

"Please. We both know. How long have *you* known about Cade being into Neil?" Savannah asked.

Mad replied, "Since Edinburgh. Cade messed up twice, spiraled, then confessed after I sarcastically offered him a tissue. Felt bad for the dude. Jock's got depth, but had no rizz with Neil."

"You're freakishly observant. Glad we're on the same side." Savannah proclaimed.

"Obviously. Nerds plus prom queens equal elite covert alliance."

"Technically, Cade is the Prom Queen."

"YAAAS, Kween," Mads yelled.

Everett moaned. "Whuuut?"

"I think we wore him out," Savannah said.

"I could go again," Everett said.

Then he started snoring softly, ...again.

Chapter Forty-Eight.

The house was finally quiet. After the noise of prom and the laughter outside under the porch light, Neil pushed open his bedroom door, heart galloping like he was sneaking someone in. He was already anticipating what would likely come next.

Cade followed, jacket slung over his shoulder. The faint glow of street lamps spilled through the blinds, striping the room in shadows.

Neil shut the door behind them and locked it only for the third time in his existence. For a moment, they just stood there, mildly out of breath and anxious.

"Stay with me tonight," Neil said softly.

"Your parents..." Cade whispered, a grin tugging at his mouth. "Wouldn't it be less awkward at my house, where we don't have to think about them in the next room?"

"They're asleep... probably," Neil said, though his voice came out softer than he meant. "Anyway, we're good. I told them that you are staying the night."

Cade leaned in. Neil met him halfway.

The kiss started slow—careful, testing—but months of jokes, sidelong glances, and almost-touches crashed through them like a wave. Cade's hands framed Neil's face, sliding into his hair, pulling him closer as if even that tiny distance between them was unbearable.

Neil pulled back just enough that Cade felt the shift.

"What's wrong?" Cade asked, breath still unsteady.

Neil hesitated. "My body. It's okay, but... I don't have abs like you. Or arms like yours. Your body is just—" he exhaled, defeated, "—intimidating to look at, or touch."

"I've seen your body, Neil. Many times."

"This is different," Neil said.

Cade blinked, then gently turned Neil toward the mirror near the door. He stepped behind him, his hands resting lightly on Neil's waist—steady, grounding, nothing more. Their reflection stared back: two boys lit in stripes of shadow and soft gold. Cade wanted Neil to see his body for what it really was: a trim waist, an outline of abs without cuts, and a naturally defined body with a proper upper chest. To Cade, he couldn't be more perfect. He was 100% his magnificent Italian boyfriend.

"I want you to see what I see," Cade said quietly as he unbuttoned Neil's shirt.

Neil swallowed. "Cade—" He wanted to say, 'You don't have to do this.'

"No." Cade's voice was gentle but sure. "Look."

Neil's eyes flicked up reluctantly. Cade's hands didn't roam; they just held him, firm enough to keep him present, respectful enough to let him move away at any moment.

"This," Cade said, meeting Neil's gaze in the glass, "is the guy I fell for. The one who overthinks everything. The one who tries to hide how kind he is. The one who walks into a room and makes it easier for me to breathe."

Neil relaxed his body, which enhanced his chest and abs that he hadn't seen before.

"You think I'm intimidating?" Cade asked softly. "Neil, you're the one who blows me away. You're the one I'd do anything for, and you have no idea how good you look when you're brave enough to let someone see you." Cade paused and took a deep breath. "The only person who does not see you is you."

Neil's throat bobbed as he tried to swallow the emotion rising there. He knew Cade was right. It all made sense to him now. All of the times he stood down, and the times he let Kyle talk down to him, he had only escaped valuing himself.

"And from now on," Cade added, "you don't have to try to be perfect for me. You just have to be you. You're already perfect. Whatever we do next, whatever we don't do—it's your call. You're in charge. I'm right here." Cade kissed Neil behind his ear, taking in the scent of his hair.

Neil let out a shaky breath. "Okay."

Cade smiled—the soft, relieved kind—and rested his forehead against the top of Neil's head. Not pushing for more. Not asking for anything. Just staying.

Neil looked at their reflection again. He didn't look away.

For once, he let himself see what Cade saw: someone wanted. Someone enough.

His breath hitched—not from fear this time, but from the warmth building low at his back, radiating from Cade.

He turned back toward Cade, and Cade met him with a grin that was half laugh, half disbelief at the miracle in front of him.

When they kissed again, it wasn't hungry or frantic.

It was certain.

They were choosing each other all over again, only deeper.

The music magically swelled, now playing New Constellations' *Hot Blooded*, which sounded like a heartbeat, carrying them deeper into a new world together. The tip of Cade's thumb rested at the edge of Neil's chin, anchoring him with his fingers passionately wrapped at his throat. His other hand firmly wrapped Neil's lower back as he eased him down to the bed. He pressed his weight over Neil's body, not heavy but grounding, every inch saying, "You're safe with me." Neil's right hand found Cade's chest, feeling the steady thrum beneath bone and muscle, and a fierce certainty bloomed: no harm could ever reach him here. Not like this. Not with Cade.

"I'm not sure I'm ready for, you know... everything, but I want to... eventually," Neil said cautiously.

Cade acknowledged the boundary with a nod.

"It's okay," Cade said. "I love you so much, Neil.' Cade said just before kissing Neil's neck softly.

The rest was beautifully slow, because it was their first time together.

Neil remained silent, as if in a trance, wanting to savor every micro-minute.

Cade held him tightly, breathing into Neil's ear.

Still embracing, Neil spoke first. "Did that go as well as I think it did?"

"Yeah." Cade kissed him. "You're... a champ." Exhausted, Cade rested on Neil's right side. He fell asleep in the sweetest way, holding Neil.

Tangled together in the half-dark, Neil could still feel Cade's breath against his collarbone, steady and sure while *O mio babbino caro* played, soft as a whisper. Neil reached over to lower the volume, then pressed a kiss to Cade's temple on his return. He thought of the moment when he discarded Kyle's photo to make room for Cade. He was secure that this was real. Cade was finally serious enough to be trusted with his heart.

When Cade woke again twenty minutes later, Neil was asleep in his arms, curls shadowing his face.

Gratitude hit Cade so suddenly that it stole his breath. This beautiful person had stayed with him on the train, had taken care of him before Cade even knew how to ask for it. Neil had stood between him and the world when comfort and safety mattered most.

Cade adjusted his grip, drawing Neil closer—not out of fear, but certainty.

He had spent years learning how to survive. Now, finally, he understood what it meant to stay. To protect. To choose someone without conditions.

Neil loved him.

At last, Cade understood the mystery of Neil's quiet comment on the Ponte Vecchio in Florence — why he hadn't explained it then. "It was personal," Neil had said.

Cade understood.

Neil hadn't wanted to lead him there. Hadn't wanted to explain it into existence or risk cheapening it with too many words. He wanted something chosen freely—their own life with a view.

End of Book One

Book Two Preview

Breakfast the night after prom

By the time they wandered into the kitchen—Cade barefoot, Neil's borrowed T-shirt slouched across his shoulders—the whole thing felt so absurdly domestic that Cade actually stopped short in the doorway.

"Wait," he whispered, leaning toward Neil like they were about to pull a heist. "You're telling me this—" he gestured down at himself in Neil's clothes—"is this okay? At the family table?"

"So... is Cade coming on vacation with us this summer?" asked Maxx.

His sister, Isabella, looked over the top of her phone.

The room froze for a half second. Even the fork paused halfway to Neil's mom's mouth.

Neil's head whipped toward Cade, pulse hammering.

Cade looked startled, too, but only for a moment. Then he smiled—small and certain, like the answer was obvious. "Yeah," he said softly. "Maybe, *if* I get invited."

The Debate

Neil was paired with George Santorini, a senior from Elmsworth Academy, a rival school in middle Tennessee.

Cade sat with Neil's family and couldn't stop smiling.

Neil looks sooo good up there in his navy school blazer with that beautiful dark wavy hair. He looks like a successful politician, Cade thought.

"Okay, we are going to get this started," the host said. He introduced Neil and George, who shook hands. "Neil Erickson is the vice president of the Gay-Straight Alliance at Penderton Academy. George Santorini is the president of the Young Republicans at Elmsworth, with a platform opposing the expansion of minority rights. Each will take their respective positions in their organizations. Mr. Santorini, an earlier coin toss determined that we will start with the opposition. The floor is yours."

Sophie's first date

Sophie kicked off her shoes by the door and leaned back against it, exhaling like she'd been holding her breath since before the bell rang.

"Good night?" her mother asked from the kitchen, already knowing the answer mattered.

Sophie smiled, small but real. "Yeah. It was."

Her father looked up from the table, folding the newspaper he hadn't actually been reading. "You hungry?"

"No," Sophie said. "Just... tired. In a good way."

"Well?" she asked gently. "How did it go?"

Sophie hesitated—not because she didn't know, but because she wanted to say it right.

"It was awkward," she said honestly. "And sweet. Maybe a little scary. Not in a bad way—just... new."

Her father nodded. "That sounds normal."

Her parents exchanged a quick glance—nothing dramatic, just shared history.

Sophie smiled faintly. "He didn't pretend to understand everything. But he didn't minimize it either. He said he wanted to learn. That he knew he'd get things wrong."

Her mother nodded slowly. "That's honest."

She shrugged, suddenly shy. "I really like him."

Her father cleared his throat. "Did you feel safe?"

"Yes," Sophie said immediately. No pause. No qualification.

That seemed to settle something deep in both of them.

Her mother reached out and squeezed Sophie's hand. "Thank you for telling us."

She yawned then, the day finally catching up to her.

"I'm going to bed."

"Good night, sweetheart," her mother said.

Sophie headed down the hall, pausing once to glance back at them—two steady points in the same place they'd always been.

"I'm okay," she said, just to be sure.

When she was behind the door, her dad made one simple statement.

"I hope this doesn't change her college plans."

About the Author

Zan Hough lives in Atlanta, Georgia, with his husband of twenty-three years, and together they have two grown sons.

Zan wrote *Blindsighted* as a heartfelt guide for queer youth navigating the often confusing world of dating and relationships. He hopes to offer readers a foundation—a way to approach love with confidence, recognize healthy dynamics, and avoid harmful or toxic situations. By telling stories that reflect real challenges and real possibilities, Zan aims to ease anxiety around relationships and help young people see the opportunities that await them when they're open, informed, and ready.

Follow for More

www.ZanHough.com

♪ @ZanHoughBooks

⧉ @ZanHough

▶ @ZanHough